Praise for R. Cameron Cooke's novels

"A GREAT SUBMARINE STORY."
—Nelson DeMille

"ACTION PACKED."
—W.E.B. Griffin

"RIVETING SUSPENSE."
—Thomas Fleming

"MARVELOUS."
—Bernard Cornwell

"ONE HELL OF A READ."
—David Hagberg

"THE BEST I'VE READ IN YEARS."
—Stephen Coonts

continued . . .

"*Pride Runs Deep* carves its own territory. The time is one year after the Japanese attack on Pearl Harbor, and Cooke has nailed the details with the finesse of a concert maestro. So far as I'm concerned there's only one problem with Cameron's novel . . . I've already finished reading it and now I have to wait for his next novel. One hell of a read!"

—David Hagberg

"R. Cameron Cooke is a lieutenant commander in the Naval Reserve who brings his extensive knowledge of submarines and those who man them to bear in this gripping novel of naval combat during World War II. Cooke highlights the emotions of ordinary men engaged in war, describing acts both brave and stupid with a clarity that springs from personal experience . . . Cooke knows the Navy, knows the history of WWII combat in the Pacific, and knows how to combine the two to present a top-notch tale of men at war. For those who love history, this book puts a human face to WWII submarine conflict."

—ReviewingtheEvidence.com

"A fast-paced story . . . Come aboard the crew of the *Mackerel* and become part of some of the bravest men in the fleet."

—wkrc.com

Praise for

RISE TO VICTORY

"A sensational seaborne thriller." —W.E.B. Griffin

"Will hold your interest from the moment you pick it up . . . The battle scenes between the two submarines are excellent and very stirring . . . This is one of the best naval thrillers I have read in quite a while. It is very reminiscent of the books by Douglas Reeman and Edward Beach, two of the most outstanding naval fiction writers. This author will join their rank. Put this on your list of 'to-be-read.'" —MyShelf.com

"Makes the reader feel they are part of the action."

—*Roundtable Reviews*

SINK THE SHIGURE

R. CAMERON COOKE

JOVE BOOKS, NEW YORK

THE BERKLEY PUBLISHING GROUP
Published by the Penguin Group
Penguin Group (USA) Inc.
375 Hudson Street, New York, New York 10014, USA
Penguin Group (Canada), 90 Eglinton Avenue East, Suite 700, Toronto, Ontario M4P 2Y3, Canada
(a division of Pearson Penguin Canada Inc.)
Penguin Books Ltd., 80 Strand, London WC2R 0RL, England
Penguin Group Ireland, 25 St. Stephen's Green, Dublin 2, Ireland (a division of Penguin Books Ltd.)
Penguin Group (Australia), 250 Camberwell Road, Camberwell, Victoria 3124, Australia
(a division of Pearson Australia Group Pty. Ltd.)
Penguin Books India Pvt. Ltd., 11 Community Centre, Panchsheel Park, New Delhi—110 017, India
Penguin Group (NZ), 67 Apollo Drive, Rosedale, North Shore 0745, Auckland, New Zealand
(a division of Pearson New Zealand Ltd.)
Penguin Books (South Africa) (Pty.) Ltd., 24 Sturdee Avenue, Rosebank, Johannesburg 2196,
South Africa

Penguin Books Ltd., Registered Offices: 80 Strand, London WC2R 0RL, England

SINK THE *SHIGURE*

A Jove Book / published by arrangement with the author

PRINTING HISTORY
Jove mass-market edition / August 2007

ISBN: 978-0-515-14334-8

JOVE®
Jove Books are published by The Berkley Publishing Group,
a division of Penguin Group (USA) Inc.,
375 Hudson Street, New York, New York 10014.
JOVE is a registered trademark of Penguin Group (USA) Inc.
The "J" design is a trademark belonging to Penguin Group (USA) Inc.

PRINTED IN THE UNITED STATES OF AMERICA

10 9 8 7 6 5 4 3 2 1

In memory of Dan Crisp (USS *Aludra* from 1942 until her sinking in June of 1943, and USS *American Legion* from 1943 to the end of the war) and Richard Hudson (USS *Sperry* from 1952 to 1955), two former sailors who helped shape my life.

Acknowledgments

As with each of my novels, I could not have written this one without the assistance of some very fine people. Thanks to my two guardian angels at Berkley Books, Natalee Rosenstein and Michelle Vega, for their guidance and patience. Thanks to Rick Willett for his invaluable contribution. Thanks to Bernard Cornwell, for helping me to set my sails. Thanks to my agent and mentor, Ed Breslin, for his tireless devotion to my cause. Thanks to Mom and Dad for being the best of parents and for believing in me from day one. And, last but not least, thanks to my beautiful wife, my soul mate and best friend, Eva, and our sweet kids, Cami and Ethan, for living with a writer.

Independent Bank

RECEIPT   Drawer: 17009   02/18/20
            Trans#:   38   11:35:35
DDA Deposit   ************7949

$150.00

Visit us at www.ibtx.com

Independent Bank

RECEIPT   Drawer: 17004   02/18/20

           Trans#:   31   11:37:02

DDA Deposit   ************9768

$458.00

Visit us at www.ibtx.com

Prologue

USS Seatrout, *Philippine Sea,*
two hundred sixteen miles southeast of Formosa
January 1943

"**FIRING** point in thirty seconds, Captain."

Lieutenant Commander Geoffrey Rickerby removed his perspiring face from the periscope lens to cast an acknowledging glance at the young lieutenant standing by the torpedo data computer in the aft port corner of the conning tower. The lieutenant's face also dripped with sweat, running in long streaks through day-old stubble. His white T-shirt was soaked to the skin, but the miserable heat and humidity appeared to have little effect on his concentration. The young officer's eyes remained focused on the myriad of wheels and dials spinning before his face.

A quick glance around the room assured Rickerby that the other men in the cramped compartment were also holding steady in the stuffy air and stifling heat. The shirtless helmsman, the outline of his spine and back muscles glistening with sweat, clasped his hands tightly on the shiny metal wheel, which was also coated with beads of condensation. The headset-laden sonar operator—lost in another world, it sometimes seemed to his shipmates—turned the dial on his panel to steer the submarine's hydrophones toward the enemy ships. The periscope assistant, crouching low like a linebacker, anticipated his captain's next move, right or left. The executive officer, leaning over the small chart desk, hastily plotted and updated the tactical picture on an oversized piece of chart paper already covered with countless lines and scribbles.

They were all perspiring—even the bulkheads were perspiring—and each man had shed articles of clothing to deal with the extreme humidity brought on by the eight-hour submerged approach on the Japanese convoy. But despite their apparent discomfort, they appeared to be absorbed in their jobs, and somehow Rickerby knew that the seventy-four other members of the *Seatrout*'s crew were dutifully manning their battle stations in the various compartments below. All were busy at their jobs, going through the same routines that had become so familiar through countless months at sea, countless war patrols, and countless attacks. The thought left Rickerby feeling somewhat out of place. Even though he was the most senior officer aboard, holding the rank of lieutenant commander, and had himself completed four war patrols on other boats, he still felt somewhat like an unseasoned tenderfoot around these men. For this was only his second month as their new captain. Every man aboard the *Seatrout* knew full well that this was his first time commanding a submarine on war patrol—and that this was also his first time taking one into battle.

Perhaps they were not worried about him after all—at least not visibly—though they certainly had a right to be. It was only natural for any crew to have doubts about an untried captain, especially when that new captain's predecessor—*his* predecessor—had been so popular among the crew. But so far on this patrol, the crew of the *Seatrout* had shown Rickerby nothing but respect and confidence in his capability to lead them, and he appreciated that. Of course, they had shown no shortage of confidence in their own capabilities, as well, and rightfully so. The war was hardly a year old, and they had already earned a reputation as the best boat in the SoWesPac sector, and from Rickerby's observations they certainly knew it.

"No indication of any escorts, Captain," reported the sonar operator.

Rickerby nodded and placed his face to the eyepiece again, waiting for the remnants of a low wave to wash clear of the lens before he could focus on the enemy ships above. It was a small convoy: three coal-burning freighters, traveling in column, each displacing little more than a thousand tons. Their general course indicated they were heading somewhere to the north, probably to Okinawa, or perhaps to the Japanese mainland, and even though they cruised along at the creeping speed of five knots, the crystal clear weather had forced the *Seatrout* to spend most of the day submerged as she worked into a favorable firing position. Rickerby had been foiled more than once by an unfavorable zig, but after many frustrating hours of slow, methodical maneuvering— hours spent with the submarine's air-conditioning plant, among other things, secured to conserve power—Rickerby had finally gained the position he wanted, just off the convoy's port beam. The freighters were now less than fifteen hundred yards away and passing from right to left in his field of view, their broad rust-streaked hulls directly ahead of the *Seatrout*'s bank of six forward torpedo tubes lurking silently beneath the surface with outer doors wide open.

"We're at the firing point, Captain," the lieutenant at the torpedo data computer announced.

"Very well. Final bearing and shoot, middle freighter!"

"Ready!" replied the lieutenant, after preparing his panel for the final observation.

Rickerby turned the periscope handles minutely, steadying the reticle on the forward midships mast of the middle freighter.

"Mark!"

"Zero-five-one!" announced the periscope assistant.

"Matches!" announced the lieutenant.

"Fire one!"

Rickerby did not have to take his face from the eyepiece to know that the man at the firing panel had hit the torpedo firing plunger. He heard a loud *whoosh!* and the deck rumbled beneath his feet as the three-thousand-pound weapon was launched into the sea. Then he felt the expected pressure on his ears as the impulse air used to eject the giant weapon from its tube was vented inboard.

"Number one torpedo fired electrically," announced the sailor who had hit the firing plunger.

"Fire two!"

Again the *whoosh,* the rumble, and the pressure change.

Through the periscope, Rickerby could see the bubbly wakes of the two torpedoes as they sped away toward the enemy vessel.

"Shift to the leading freighter!" Rickerby said quickly. There was no time to waste. With the clear visibility above, there was no telling when the Japanese lookouts might sight the submerged weapons streaking toward them.

"Set!" announced the lieutenant.

"Fire three . . . Fire four!"

Rickerby watched the two new wakes appear on the surface, taking sharp turns to the left, according to their gyroscope settings, before speeding off in the direction of the lead ship.

Rickerby had decided to let the third freighter go for now, saving his remaining torpedoes in tubes five and six in the event that one of the others missed. Now he had to wait through an excruciating interval of uncertainty and self-doubt as the torpedoes ran their course and the lieutenant's low voice counted off the seconds to impact.

But the range was close, and he did not have to wait for very long. As he watched, an enormous column of water and debris suddenly engulfed the middle freighter, followed almost immediately by a loud *whack!* clearly audible through the hull. The first torpedo had struck home. Moments later, the second torpedo hit just below the freighter's chugging smokestack, the ensuing explosion ripping open the hull on the port side and starting fires all along the freighter's superstructure and main deck. Rickerby noticed a giant plume of steam entrained with the thickening columns of black smoke, and concluded that one of the ship's boilers must have ruptured in the explosion. The enemy freighter was crippled now, and by the time the hundreds of bits of debris had rained back down to splash into the sea, it was already down by the bow and sinking rapidly. As the freighter's squat stern rose out of the water, so did her two giant screws, still spinning, high and dry above the surface, until they simultaneously came to a screeching halt, perhaps seizing from a loss of lubrication oil, or damaged reduction gears.

Seeing the fate of their sister, the other two freighters began to turn away in an effort to evade, but the maneuver came too late for the leading ship. The torpedo from tube three struck her stern on the port side, sending a wavy ripple through her structure and masts, followed immediately by a massive secondary explosion large enough to shake the *Seatrout* at over a half mile away. Rickerby waited patiently for another explosion, but apparently the last torpedo had missed—or more likely had malfunctioned, as American-made torpedoes were prone to do. But when the smoke finally cleared from the first detonation, Rickerby saw that another torpedo would not be necessary. The leading freighter was finished. Half of the ship, from the pilothouse to the stern, was gone. It had completely disappeared, evidently obliterated by the massive explosion. Only the forward section remained, standing upright on its end and resembling a giant black pyramid against the blue horizon. A dozen small figures climbed desperately to reach the peak of the barnacle-covered bow as the mangled and now useless structure began to slide slowly beneath the waves.

Rickerby stared mesmerized for several seconds at the destruction his own hand had created, but eventually he found the will to put it out of his mind and turn the periscope toward the final freighter. Men in the conning tower and the control room below were cheering and shaking hands at the success of the attack, and Rickerby found himself almost salivating as he suddenly realized that he had attained the goal of every submarine officer that wore the gold dolphins. He had put two enemy ships on the bottom on his first patrol as commander of his own boat. The patrol would go down in the books as a complete success, and he and his crew would be decorated with the coveted combat pin. Suddenly, visions of future glory and honors overtook him, and he saw himself someday becoming one of the famed tonnage leaders—the submarine aces—whose exploits were taught at sub school and at the Naval Academy.

The one remaining freighter steadied on its new course, chugging out a pall of black smoke as it poured on emergency speed to get away from the American submarine, and Rickerby pulled his own thoughts back into the present in order to devise a plan to sink her. The Japanese captain was no fool, and certainly knew the general location of the *Seatrout,* simply by tracing back the clearly visible torpedo wakes left on the surface.

Rickerby took his face away from the periscope and cast a lively glance at his executive officer.

"What do you think, Exec? End around run to get ahead of him? Or should we try for a long shot up the shitter?"

"New contact, Captain!" the sonar operator announced agitatedly, before the shrugging executive officer had a chance to respond. "High-speed screws, bearing zero-four-zero!"

Rickerby plastered his face to the eyepiece in an instant. He steadied the lens on the reported bearing, and felt his face go white and his hands turn ice cold as the charging bow of a destroyer came into view. The swift enemy warship maneuvered like a race car, effortlessly skirting the aft end of the burning freighter before steadying up on a direct course for the *Seatrout*'s periscope. The destroyer's markings were like none he had ever seen before, with jet black paint covering every square inch of the bow section along with the forward dual-gun turret. The upper tips of the two slanted smokestacks were also ringed in black paint. The sharp contrast with the pure white spray thrown up by the knifing black bow made the deadly warship even more menacing—almost angry, it seemed. Now less than a thousand yards away and coming on at full speed, nearly thirty knots, it would be directly above them in less than a minute.

Slapping up the periscope handles, Rickerby cursed his foolishness for keeping the periscope up for so long.

"Down scope! Helm, all ahead full! Diving officer, take her down fast! Full dive! Flood negative!"

As the deck tilted downward, he saw the previously smiling faces in the compartment around him turn suddenly grim. Undoubtedly, they could tell by his own somewhat pale complexion that their victory was short-lived, and that they were now in extreme danger.

"Rig for depth charge!"

The word went out to all compartments, and the sound of hatches clanging shut in the compartments below resounded throughout the conning tower. There was no sense in being quiet, since the enemy destroyer was traveling at a speed certainly too fast to use its own listening hydrophones. The important thing was to get the ship ready for the barrage that was sure to come.

As the deck took on an extreme angle, Rickerby grabbed the nearby railing for support, his eyes making contact with those of the fidgeting sonar operator at the same time.

"I don't know how he could've gotten so damn close, Captain!" the sonar man uttered in apparent frustration. "I'm sorry, sir."

"That tin can was being masked by the freighter all this time," Rickerby offered to the room in general, almost as an explanation to the men he had just placed in such jeopardy. "She must have joined up with the convoy sometime in the last hour. Probably came up on their starboard side sometime after their last zig. I never even caught a glimpse of him."

Ohwee-ohweee! . . . Ohwee-ohweee!

The first pulses emitted from the destroyer's active sonar bounced off the *Seatrout*'s hull. The destroyer knew exactly where they were. Only depth could save them now. It was a guessing game, with the destroyer captain having to guess the submarine's depth, setting his charges to go off accordingly. Rickerby would also have to guess on the best evasion depth.

As the *Seatrout* drifted farther into the deep, propelled by the negative buoyancy of her flooded tanks and the downward thrust of her diving planes, the needle on the depth gage drifted past the one-hundred-fifty-foot mark at an agonizingly slow pace. Before it hit one hundred sixty feet, the destroyer's churning screws suddenly became audible through the hull.

"Destroyer's directly on top of us now, sir!" called the sonarman. "She's shifting to attack frequency! Passing bow to stern!"

The punishment had to be only seconds away. The nerve-wracking screw noise grew louder and louder until the giant whirling propellers, only two hundred feet above them, drowned out the voice of the diving officer down in the control room. The destroyer would be dropping its deadly ordnance at any moment, and Rickerby gritted his teeth in anticipation of the sonar operator's inevitable report that depth charges were on the way down.

But seconds passed by, and the report never came.

Instead, the unexpected. The screw noise began to fade.

"I don't believe it!" the sonarman whispered in disbelief, holding only one earphone to his ear. "She's gone by, Captain, and she didn't drop a thing!"

Rickerby exchanged a confused glance with his executive officer while the other men in the compartment wore smiles of relief, taking a moment to breathe easier and to wipe the beading sweat from their brows.

"What the hell's he doing," Rickerby muttered to himself. "That bastard was pinging the hell out of us. He had us dead nuts on target."

"Maybe he had a problem with his racks, Captain," the executive officer offered unconvincingly. "Or maybe he's out of depth charges."

Just then, a raspy grating sound filled the room, like the sound of metal scraping upon metal. It seemed to come from everywhere at once, and left everyone staring at the curved pressure hull surrounding them.

"It's coming from outside," the sonarman said. "Something's scraping along the hull. It sounds like we're caught up in a cable or a chain or something."

"It couldn't be a mine cable," Rickerby said, staring up at the overhead. "Not out here. So what the devil is that bastard up to? He's streaming something behind him. Maybe he's trying to foul our screws."

A dozen different possibilities entered Rickerby's head before the scraping noise came to a sudden halt, ending with a loud *clunk!* that sent a sharp vibration throughout the submarine. Just as suddenly, the sound of the destroyer's screws faded completely, and the conning tower was left again in an eerie silence.

Rickerby shot a glance at the sonarman.

"I don't know what that noise was, Captain," the sonarman reported, as he followed the enemy warship with his hydrophone. "But that tin can's just reduced his speed considerably. I'm getting a low turn count out of him, probably no more than five knots. I think he might have lost us, sir."

"Passing two one zero feet, sir." The diving officer's voice floated up through the open hatch. "We're passing the thermal layer."

Rickerby noticed the veteran sailors around him breathe a sigh of relief at the report, echoing his own feelings. The blessed thermal layer, the layer of cold water that had already saved dozens of American submarines time and time again during this war, was now above them. Rickerby knew from his previous experience as a navigator in these waters that the layer was especially strong here, reflecting active sonar pulses like a great sound barrier. Assuming the enemy destroyer had lost contact on the *Seatrout*, it would be hard-pressed to find her again now that she was below the layer.

"Helm, all ahead one-third. Diving officer, level off at three hundred feet. Pass the word, rig for silent running."

Orders were acknowledged and quietly relayed throughout the ship. Rickerby moved over to the chart desk to take a look at the tactical picture hastily drawn there by the executive officer's lightning-fast pencil and parallel ruler. The position markings on the sweat-stained chart paper were pure speculation, based on dead reckoning navigation and sporadic sound bearings. But they were at least something to start with, if he was to slip away from this pesky Japanese destroyer, whose captain seemed to border on the verge of incompetence. Still somewhat baffled by the absence of any depth charges on what appeared to have been a perfect attack run, by the senselessness of dragging a cable or a chain, or whatever it was across the *Seatrout*'s hull, and now by the seemingly flaccid pursuit, Rickerby decided to put all speculation out of his mind until later, when it came time to write the patrol report. For now, he could safely assume the destroyer had lost all contact on the *Seatrout*, and was trolling along at a low speed, listening for its elusive prey. The order of the day now was to escape, slowly and silently beneath the protection of the dense thermal layer.

"We'll run south for a while, XO. We'll head in the opposite direction of those freighters' last base course. With any luck this tin can will lose interest and go running back to his convoy."

"Or what's left of it, Captain," the executive officer added with a weary grin. "Congratulations on your first attack, Skipper. It looks like the *Seatrout*'s got another ace at her helm."

"Thanks, XO." Rickerby gave an appreciative smile before ordering, "Helm, right full rudder. Steady course south."

"Right full rudder, steady course south, aye-aye, sir," the helmsman replied cheerfully.

"Sonar, keep me informed about that destroyer. Let me know if anything changes."

"I think Tojo's confused right now, Captain. He's not even echo-ranging anymore. As far as I can tell, he's making large circles in the ocean right now, probably wondering where the hell we went."

"And where the hell those two freighters went," added the periscope assistant with a toothy grin.

Several of the men chuckled at the remark. They had all just faced a close brush with death, and the emotions always came out much more freely in the aftermath of such an event.

The *Seatrout* eased onto a southerly course and began to creep away at three knots, riding silently beneath the layer of cold water. The smoking lamp was lit, battle stations secured. Off-watch hands climbed wearily into their damp racks for a few moments' sleep. There was little else to do. No maintenance could be performed under silent running conditions. At three knots, it would take hours to clear away from the area.

Rickerby lit up a cigarette of his own, cursing at having to strike his match five or six times in the oxygen-deprived atmosphere. Despite the abhorrent air, the dismal heat, and the slimy humidity, he was beaming inside. The attack had gone smoothly—much more so than he had expected. Every man on board had done his job, and had done it well. These men—his crew—were experts, and not even the sudden appearance of the enemy destroyer had fazed them. They were among the best in the fleet. They had been trained exceptionally well. But Rickerby knew that was none of his own doing. He had his predecessor to thank for that.

Rickerby had hardly gotten to know the man during their brief week together. It had been all business that week, going through a mountain of ship's records and turning over an enormous weight of responsibilities. Of course, he had known

of Lieutenant Commander Jack Tremain long before he ever
met him. Jack Tremain had made an enviable name for himself prior to the war when, as a junior officer, he saved a crippled submarine from disaster by some quick and imaginative
thinking. The incident had made him something of a celebrity
in the submarine community, not to mention the envy of every
junior officer in the fleet, Rickerby included. When he finally
met Tremain to take over the reins of the *Seatrout*, Tremain
proved to be everything he had expected him to be: quiet, yet
commanding in presence; friendly, yet unapproachable in
many ways; extremely intelligent, yet just as inspiring as your
favorite high school football coach. He was a relatively young
man—probably in his mid-thirties—but more seasoned than
most admirals Rickerby had met in his career. He was eager—
showing a tireless devotion to his men—but extremely war-
weary at the same time, having personally observed the long
retreat from the Philippines, to Java, to Darwin, and finally to
Fremantle. Rickerby clearly remembered the rebellious hair,
slightly longer in front than regulations allowed, having to be
combed to one side to keep from covering his face. He could
still see Tremain's smile that accented the creases in the corners of his eyes, the eyes that seemed to perpetually exude
both merriment and sorrow at the same time.

During the change-of-command ceremony, Rickerby remembered staring with silent envy at the Navy Cross dangling
from the left side of Tremain's white choker jacket. But the
one thing that stuck out in his mind the most, the thing that
left the most lasting impression on Rickerby, was how eager
Tremain was to see his wife again. He had hardly spoken of
anything else during the entire week of turnover. She was
back in the States, and apparently he had not seen her for
more than two years—long before the war began. Rickerby
closed his eyes, picturing Tremain's face as he had seen it on
that last day, the day the *Seatrout* left Fremantle harbor, more
than a month ago. As the submarine pulled away from the
wharf, a casual sweep of his binoculars had found a solitary
Tremain standing at the edge of the pier, looking gloomy, almost misty-eyed as he waved good-bye to his former ship and
crew. It was the first time since the beginning of the war that
the *Seatrout* had put to sea without him, and even from the

long distance Rickerby could tell that the emotion of the moment was tearing Tremain apart.

Rickerby suddenly wondered where Tremain was at this very moment. He wondered if Tremain would ever read of this attack. Perhaps someday, while curiously leafing through patrol reports looking for news of his old ship, Tremain would happen upon it and feel a small sense of satisfaction that he had left his old boat in good hands. Rickerby certainly hoped so. He knew that if he ever ran into Tremain again, he would certainly buy him a drink and thank him for putting together such a superb crew.

"XO, take the conn." Rickerby put out his cigarette in an ashtray hanging from a nearby pipe bracket. "It's been a long chase, and I haven't slept since God knows when. Continue south and let me know if that destroyer shows any signs of reacquiring us. I'll be in my stateroom."

"Aye, aye, sir."

Rickerby moved toward the hatch, patting a few of his men on the back as he shuffled past them. He was about to descend the ladder when the sonar operator suddenly went rigid, his hands pressing the headphones firmly against his ears.

"What is it?" Rickerby prompted.

"Destroyer's stopped circling, Captain. She's picking up speed fast!" The sonarman turned the dial to adjust the direction of his hydrophone. "I see no bearing rate, sir! He's on a steady bearing! He's heading right for us!"

"How the hell did he find us?" a sailor exclaimed incredulously.

"He's got to be bluffing," Rickerby said in a calming tone. "It's an old trick. Speed up and pretend that he's got us to try to get us to do something stupid and give away our position. But we're not going to fall for it, gentlemen. We're going to stay right here, on present course and speed. We should be okay under the layer, men. Believe in the layer!"

But the destroyer kept on coming, closing the distance with amazing speed, until once again the warship's racing screws were audible through the pressure hull.

Ohwee-ohweee! . . . Ohwee-ohweee!

The ominous probing sonar once again resounded through the deep, hitting the *Seatrout*'s three-hundred-foot-long hull.

There was no way to tell if the return echo had enough energy, after passing through the thermal layer, to show up as a spike on the Japanese sonarman's display. But the destroyer continued to make minor course corrections, remaining on a steady bearing, indicating that it knew exactly where the *Seatrout* was.

"He's almost on top of us, sir!" the sonarman reported, obviously taking great pains to temper the apprehension in his voice.

"I think we're in trouble, Captain," the executive officer whispered in Rickerby's ear. "Recommend going deeper, sir."

"Yes, XO," Rickerby said in a tone of malaise, staring at the overhead, baffled almost to the point of speechlessness at the enemy destroyer's detection capability. Was his sonar able to penetrate the thermal layer? Did the Japanese have some new means of submarine detection? If so, he'd never been briefed on it at PCO school. "I think you're right. Diving Officer, make your depth—"

"Splashes, Captain! Depth charges in the water!"

"Go deep! Dive! Get us down fast! Go to four hundred fifty feet!"

They had only one hope now. The Japanese captain might have set his depth charges too shallow to do any major damage. It was a fairly favorable hope, too, since as far as Rickerby knew there was no way for a lone destroyer on a single attack run to accurately detect a submarine's depth. It was a guessing game. With any luck, the charges would go off too shallow, and he would have a chance to turn the *Seatrout* onto a new course before the destroyer started another attack run. Rickerby grimaced as he watched the needle on the depth gage pass the red line at the four-hundred-foot mark—the *Seatrout*'s test depth.

The seconds passed by without any shallow explosions. Each man looked despairingly at his shipmates, some cursing their bad luck, some cursing the Japanese, as the realization set in that the enemy depth charges were set to go off deep. They were still falling, hurtling downward through the blackness, approaching the *Seatrout*'s depth at the rate of ten feet per second. If the enemy destroyer had been lucky enough to drop them in the right spot . . .

Click-click . . . Wham! . . . Click-click . . . Wham! . . .
Click-click . . . Wham!

Three depth charges, three arming triggers, three devastating explosions. The first two detonated no more than fifty feet away, but the last . . . the last detonated directly alongside the aft starboard quarter, perhaps only an arm's length from the curving hull. Well aimed—perhaps lucky—but lethal all the same.

The *Seatrout* buckled from stem to stern, rolling heavily to one side, shaking the men inside her like the rattles in a baby toy. Every lightbulb in the conning tower shattered, and the room turned pitch black. Men were thrown bodily into bulkheads, valve stems, electrical panels. Limbs dislocated, necks snapped, skulls cracked on blunt steel.

Rickerby came to his senses under the pressing weight of two or three unmoving men. Reaching out with a hand, he could feel the familiar knobs and dials of the torpedo data computer and suddenly realized that the deck was tilted sharply upward. He was lying beneath a pile of bodies at the extreme aft end of the conning tower. He could not move his legs, and his face was covered in a warm liquid, which he knew to be blood. No one around him moved a muscle, and he was somewhat thankful for the darkness, for he had no desire to see the faces of his dead men. An ear-splitting whistle emanated from the control room hatch, and he immediately concluded that a high-pressure air line must have ruptured. Someone down in the control room eventually isolated it, because the sound abruptly ceased, replaced by the horrific groans and screams of men in immense pain. Then he heard voices—shouting voices.

"Pressure hull ruptured in the aft torpedo room! Three compartments flooded!"

"We're slipping backward! Full rise on the stern planes! Get control of your bubble! Take the angle off her!"

"I've got no fucking control!"

"Shit! We're passing six hundred feet!"

Rapidly, the angle grew steeper and steeper, until Rickerby was lying flat on the aft bulkhead. The *Seatrout* had to be nearly vertical, with her bow tubes pointing at the glistening

surface, and her heavy aft end, with multiple flooded compartments, dragging her down into the dark abyss.

The sporadic flash of a battle lantern bathed the lip of the
control room hatch in yellow light, and soon after, a shadowy
head poked through the opening to peer inside the conning
tower. The light probed around the room for one complete
sweep, and then the head disappeared—whoever it was evidently concluding that all in the conning tower were dead.
Rickerby tried to call out, but he could not take in enough air
to speak above the gut-wrenching whine of the overstressed
steel, and he suspected he had a collapsed lung.

A muffled explosion came from back aft, as another compartment, probably the forward engine room, succumbed to
the enormous pressure. The extra tons of water introduced by
the flooded compartment threw the buoyancy equation decid-
edly in the sea's favor, and the *Seatrout* began to accelerate
downward even faster.

It was like riding an elevator headed to the ground floor,
only the ground floor was a few thousand fathoms down, and
the elevator would never make it there in one piece. The cylindrical pressure hull was already buckling as it fought against
the pressing sea. The hungry beast outside was clawing, desperately wanting to get in.

Screams of despair and some sobbing came from the control room, as all came to the realization that their fates were
sealed. No damage control effort, no amount of high-pressure
air—not if they had enough air to blow every tank bone dry—
would stop the *Seatrout*'s rapid descent. This would be her last
dive.

Rickerby lay there in the darkness, resting his head against
the cold, straining pressure hull, thinking of his wife's eyes,
of taking his little boy to his first Dodgers game, of Sunday
afternoons in autumn. He said a short prayer to God, asking
forgiveness for the things he had done wrong, for his short-
comings as a husband and a father, and for leading his men to
their deaths. Strangely, he thought of Jack Tremain, too, and
how he would never know what happened to his old ship and
crew. He prayed that death would be brief and painless for
them all, and he heard others in the control room praying,

too. One recited the Lord's Prayer in a clear and steady tone, as if he were sitting in the pew on Sunday morning.

"... deliver us from evil. For Thine is the kingdom, and the power, and the glory forever ... Amen."

An instant later, the pressure hull cracked, the compartment imploded, the sparse air ignited for a brief moment and then extinguished in a rush of three-hundred-pounds-per-square-inch water that ripped apart pipe bundles made of steel, hardened electrical panels, and flimsy human bodies.

Within a matter of seconds, the rest of the submarine's compartments imploded in quick succession, and the lifeless hulk of the *Seatrout*—once the pride of the submarine fleet—fell broken into blackness, never to rise again.

PART I

PART I

Chapter 1

USS Chevalier, *Western Solomon Islands, Pacific Ocean*
October 1943

LIEUTENANT Commander Jack Tremain emerged through the wardroom's heavy steel door and stepped onto the main deck of the destroyer USS *Chevalier*. The patch of ocean which the destroyer now plied and the deck on which he stood no longer felt the rays of the blazing sun, but the lingering heat and humidity gave testimony to the sweltering day it had been. After spending the past three hours basking in the refrigerated air of the destroyer's wardroom, he could now feel a sticky layer of perspiration growing beneath his uniform button-down khaki shirt. He took in a deep breath of the salty air and then let his gaze fall to the dimming horizon. The towering columns of a distant thunderstorm jutted above the northern horizon, the bubbling western edges of the cumulus still bathed in the light of the setting sun. Periodically, a flash of purplish lightning streaked across the darker sides, revealing the clouds' immense proportions relative to the flat sea below.

A spattering of sailors milled about the deck around him— some stowing gear, some performing maintenance, some merely enjoying a smoke after the evening meal. Tremain knew that every eye was on him, either inconspicuously or otherwise, but he pretended not to notice, gaining a brief moment of inward levity as he strode to the amidships lifeline.

He was, after all, an oddity—a submarine officer on a surface ship. Over the past two days, he'd gotten used to the stares and jeers, a fair indication that the rivalry between those who lived above the surface and those who cruised unseen beneath the waves was still alive and well. Tremain had witnessed the rivalry on more than one occasion during his fifteen-year career. Normally, it was nothing more than a harmless pastime, giving the men something else to think about besides the misery of their lives at sea. But like all pastimes, it could be taken too far, as he had experienced two days ago, the day he came aboard the *Chevalier*, when he had a startling encounter with one of the destroyer's sailors, a second-class electrician's mate, whom he later learned was named Fabriano.

Fabriano had taken the liberty to exhibit his own expression of the so-called harmless rivalry by directing a raised middle finger squarely in Tremain's direction. The offense had happened in clear view of a dozen other sailors and quickly drew a reprimand from an observant division chief strolling by, but beyond that, Fabriano had gotten away with the insolent behavior scot-free. Tremain quickly gathered that young Petty Officer Fabriano was one of those sailors who found himself standing before his captain fifty-two Sundays a year, and that this infraction probably paled in comparison to some of his other stunts. That would explain the division chief's mild reproof.

Still, insulting an officer was a serious offense. "Prejudice to good order and discipline" was how the Uniform Code of Military Justice put it. Tremain had little desire to get involved with the *Chevalier*'s disciplinary routine. After all, that was her own captain's business. He was only a rider—a mere passenger. The only thing that mattered to him was how fast the *Chevalier*'s big dual screws could get him to his new command. In a few days, he would disembark, and Fabriano's little insult would be forgotten. Still, he might have pressed the issue, might have even demanded Fabriano's head on a platter, if it weren't for one mitigating circumstance which had come to his attention over dinner on the evening of the event in question.

While dining with the *Chevalier*'s officers, he had learned the true source of the young Fabriano's emotional display. The sailor's rudimentary insult could be traced back to a dark day in the Pacific Fleet's history just over a year ago—a single day in September of 1942—when a lone Japanese submarine unleashed its destructive power with brutal efficiency on an American carrier formation in the Coral Sea.

Tremain knew the story well. Who didn't? He'd even taught the incident to his wide-eyed students at submarine school. It had been a textbook submarine attack.

On that sunny day in September of 1942, a lone submerged Japanese submarine sneaked into an American task group and proceeded to level the playing field between Japanese and American carrier strength in the Pacific. Torpedoes came from the deep, striking without warning the carrier *Wasp*, the battleship *North Carolina*, and the destroyer *O'Brien*, all within the span of a few minutes. All three ships were severely damaged, but the *Wasp* was by far the least fortunate. While in the midst of arming and refueling aircraft, she absorbed three torpedoes and quickly became a floating hell on earth. From the decks of the other American ships present, thousands of sailors looked on with horror as the majestic carrier at the center of their formation transformed into a blazing inferno right before their eyes. Fires raged on the *Wasp* all day and her casualties mounted by the hour. As the fires crept aft, they reached and ignited her fuel reservoirs and magazines, blasting to oblivion the valiant crewmen trying to save their ship. The thundering explosions gutted the carrier, sending bodies, aircraft, debris, and smoke high into the air, high enough to be seen by ships well beyond the horizon. When all was said and done, the *Wasp* was abandoned, and her shattered hulk scuttled. *North Carolina* and *O'Brien* fared slightly better, but they had suffered sufficient damage to give them both appointments with the shipyard for the next several months. The *Wasp*'s casualties measured in the hundreds. And while the loss of ships and men was always a tragedy, the strategic loss to the Pacific Fleet overshadowed everything else.

The *Wasp* was gone, and with her went the American carrier advantage. For well more than a month after the sinking, Admiral Nimitz's staff in Pearl Harbor bit their nails over the gnawing reality that the USS *Hornet* was the only operational aircraft carrier left on this side of the world. It was a dark day indeed for the U.S. Navy.

Apparently, young Fabriano and his brother, also a sailor, were crewmembers aboard the *Wasp* at the time. While Fabriano managed to make it off the ship relatively unharmed, his brother was not so lucky. A massive secondary explosion ruptured a gas line and sent a torrent of burning aviation fuel into the air and onto the flight deck just as his brother was preparing to abandon ship. Fabriano, who had jumped mere moments before, bobbed helplessly on the water's surface below as he watched the flaming fuel cover his brother from head to foot. His brother screamed, evidently blinded and disoriented, as he ran this way and that in a desperate attempt to find the edge of the flight deck to leap into the quenching sea. But the flames rapidly consumed him. His screams grew weaker, and with each passing moment he seemed less and less coherent, less and less responsive to the sailors in the water below trying to coach him toward the side. He never found the edge of the flight deck. Eventually, his screams subsided. From the water below, Fabriano watched as the imperceptible form of flaming mass that had once been his brother crumpled to the deck. He had witnessed it all, every agonizing second, and he would undoubtedly carry the image with him to his grave.

As he stared out at the night sky, Tremain concluded that young Fabriano, like many surface sailors, probably considered submariners a wicked, demented bunch. Tremain even knew some admirals that still believed submarine warfare to be a gutless, below-the-belt method of naval combat. At an officers' ball in Manila—a hundred years ago, it seemed sometimes—Tremain had even heard one surface admiral dub submariners the "cowards of the sea."

Of course, Tremain knew differently. He could still see the faces of ninety such "cowards" he had once commanded on the *Seatrout*. They lived now only in his dreams, ever since that painful day long ago when he had received word that they were "missing and presumed sunk."

As he stared out at the darkening waters of the South Pacific, Tremain took in another deep breath of the gentle sea breeze. He could hear the faint whine of *Chevalier*'s probing sonar echoing off the sandy ocean floor, one hundred fathoms below. The evening was sublime, and he could not deny how good it felt to be in the war zone again. Like a powerful herb, every nautical mile closer to enemy waters seemed to revive his spirit. He had been away for so long, and now, for the first time in a very long time, he felt alive again, invigorated. He was suddenly able to think much more clearly about his future, and his painful past. Never, during the months of convalescence leave, or during the mind-numbing months teaching young ensigns at the submarine school in New London, had he felt as clearheaded as he did at this moment. Never, not one day—not one moment—since the last time he saw her green eyes and perfect lips smiling up at him on that precious, sacred, and awful day. The last day they would ever spend together on this earth.

The day she died in his arms.

Judy Tremain, beautiful Judy, had been a casualty of the war on the home front. Unbeknownst to him, all those years that he was away, she had been working in a factory, making fire-retardant clothing out of asbestos, supporting the war effort in her own way. It was just like her not to tell him about it, and he did not find out until he finally made it home to New London in mid-1943, to rest and recuperate from his wounds sustained on the *Kurita* mission. At that point, her health had already started to deteriorate. Her lungs were rapidly failing her, constantly filling with fluid. On the same day that he was discharged from the hospital, she was admitted, and within a month she was gone.

He remembered sitting beside her bed on one of those tough nights, listening to her faint, short breaths and the incessant drip of her intravenous fluid injection.

"I have faith," she had said in a weak, wheezy voice. "The Good Lord will take me to Heaven on the Day of Judgment. My soul will leave my body and go with Him. That day may be a thousand years away, but it will seem like the blink of an eye to me. You know, Jack, that time is a constraint only for this world, but not for Him. I'll go to sleep and wake up in His kingdom, and you'll be there to meet me, Jack, smiling like you are now, along with Papa and Mama, and Buddy, and all the others." Her face had lit up briefly as if she could see it all in her mind's eye.

"Yes, my dear," he had said softly, trying his best to sound as certain as she was. "That will be wonderful."

"I'm not afraid of death, Jack." She was staring deeply into his eyes now. Her body may have been as limp as a dish towel, but her gaze still carried that same strength that could some- how always force him to look at her. "For me, Heaven isn't far away. I won't have to wait long. But you, my love, you will. You'll have to wait. You'll have to live out the rest of your life, spending years—maybe decades—without me. I won't be here anymore to keep you from spilling mustard on your dress whites." She smiled as playfully as her condition would allow.

"Honey, don't say such things. You're going to get better."

"It frightens me, Jack," she said, ignoring him. "The thought of you brooding alone for the rest of your life; it frightens me more than death itself. I think about it a lot these days." Then she had grabbed his hand in both of hers, looking into his eyes with a sudden fervor. "Oh, Jack, you were born to be at sea. You were born to command a submarine. You're not supposed to be penned up in New London, in some classroom, teaching tactics to twenty-year-old ensigns. Promise me you won't give up. Do whatever it takes. Find another ship. Live and love again. Do everything we never got to do. But above all, Jack, promise me that you won't give up, and I'll promise you that I'm not afraid."

He had embraced her, holding her frail body as close as her hospital bed would allow.

"I promise, Judy-love," he forced himself to say, trying his best to sound resolute. It was all he could say, but deep down inside, he wasn't sure that he meant it, and he surmised that she probably sensed it. She knew him all too well.

She died two days later, just a week shy of her thirty-fourth birthday. It seemed so unfair. He'd learned to deal with death during the first years of the war, but this was different. This was his beautiful Judy. This was his devoted and loving wife— so young, so full of life, the one thing he had been fighting for. She wasn't supposed to die. Thousands of nineteen-year-old kids died every day in this war, but she wasn't supposed to die. Why Judy? Why had he spent so many years away at sea and not in her arms?

Tremain gripped the *Chevalier*'s steel lifeline cable and felt its coolness bring him back to the present. He had allowed himself a somber moment to think of Judy—just as his doctor had instructed him to do in moments like these. Now he needed to move on with life once again.

He suddenly noticed a figure standing all alone on the *Chevalier*'s forecastle, gazing out at the sea in a similar fashion. He was surprised when he realized that it was Fabriano, the sailor who had flipped him off. The young man's stout frame was unmistakable. Beneath the Dixie cup hat, pushed down low over his brow, a dwindling cigarette, glowing reddish orange in the failing light, hung loosely from his pursed lips. His sunken, expressionless eyes stared back at Tremain just as they had done two days ago.

Tremain suddenly got the idea to do the unexpected. He would meet this hostile young sailor head-on, and see where it got him. Besides, he had nothing to lose. Chances were he would never run into Fabriano ever again in his career, and maybe some good would come of it. Some sailors just needed a little nudge to bring them back to the fold, to set them on the right path.

With forced nonchalance, Tremain strolled over toward the staring Fabriano. The grimacing sailor immediately took notice and stood up straight to face him squarely. Then, when Tremain was only a few feet away, the *Chevalier* suddenly took a rogue wave on the opposite beam, leaning the deck hard over to port. After so many months on dry land, Tremain's unaccustomed legs lost their balance, very nearly sending him headlong into the starboard lifeline before he regained his footing. It would have been an embarrassing moment for anyone, let alone a lieutenant commander, and the spectacle seemed to amuse several sailors lounging nearby. With a red face, Tremain stood up straight and smiled. What else could he do but acknowledge that he had slipped? Out of the corner of his eye, he saw a khaki uniform staring down at him from the starboard bridge wing high above his head. It was the *Chevalier*'s captain, undoubtedly shaking his head in disgust.

The rugged destroyer captain was probably wondering why he ever agreed to give this rubber-legged submariner a ride to Australia.

Of course, what these surface sailors did not understand— Tremain concluded, to make himself feel better—was that a little staggering was understandable in a submariner, since the cramped bridge of a submarine never allowed a man to walk thirty paces in a straight line.

"He's laughing at you, sir," Fabriano said suddenly, boldly, almost like a challenge.

Tremain glanced over his shoulder at the starboard bridge wing. The *Chevalier*'s captain had already disappeared into the pilothouse, obviously with a thousand more important things to do than gape at a lubberly submariner.

"I think I'll let him," answered Tremain with a casual smile. "Another smoke, sailor?"

Tremain took a pack of cigarettes from his shirt pocket and motioned for Fabriano to take one.

Fabriano stared at the extended pack of cigarettes, obviously not expecting such geniality from a senior officer, especially one he had insulted two days before. Tremain mused inwardly at the befuddled expression.

"I swore I'd never salute a submariner as long as I live," Fabriano finally muttered. "I don't reckon I'll accept any smokes from one neither."

"Suit yourself." Tremain shrugged, taking a cigarette for himself and returning the pack to his shirt pocket. "How about a light, sailor?"

Fabriano contorted his face in annoyed confusion, but eventually produced a matchbox from his pocket and half-heartedly handed it to Tremain. The gesture seemed to give him great physical discomfort.

"Relax, sailor," Tremain finally said, chuckling. "Listen, we're on the same team here. Tremain's my name. What's yours?"

"My name?" he stammered, not meeting Tremain's eyes. "My name's Fabriano, sir. If you'll excuse me, sir, I've got some work to do."

With that, Fabriano instantly began to walk away, obviously

frustrated and fighting to hold back the painful memories that fueled the ill-temper within him.

"Thanks for the light, Fabriano," Tremain called after him trivially.

Fabriano stopped in his tracks, but did not turn around to face him.

"That was my brother's name, too, sir," he said lowly, then briskly marched away.

Tremain stared after him for a moment, taking long drags on his cigarette, contemplating the significance of the sailor's last statement. Could Fabriano possibly hold him, and all other submariners, in some way responsible for his brother's death? What kind of end around reasoning could come to such a conclusion?

At that moment, the tall, dark form of Lieutenant Wally McCandles emerged from the shadows of the forward deckhouse, shaking his head, apparently in amused bewilderment at the retreating young sailor. He had obviously witnessed the entire event.

"Don't mind him, Jack," McCandles said with a warm smile, joining Tremain by the lifeline. "He hates everybody."

"It's not going to keep me up tonight, Wally, if that's what you're thinking."

"I'll talk to him."

"Don't bother. It's no skin off my back if he doesn't salute me. We'll be in Brisbane in four days, and then I'm shoving off. Let him have his enemy, if it means that much to him."

"Actually, Jack," McCandles grinned slyly, "we may be a little late dropping you off in Brisbane. I just came out here to tell you . . ."

"Tell me what?"

Tremain glanced aft and noticed that *Chevalier*'s frothing white wake had begun curving to the right. She was turning to the west, definitely not the way to Australia.

"We've just received new tasking. We're going into combat. Orders are still coming through from the task group commander." McCandles pointed at the two dark shapes across the water, one ahead and one astern of the *Chevalier*. They were the *Selfridge* and the *O'Bannon*, two more destroyers making up the balance of *Chevalier*'s small flotilla. Blinking signal lamps flashed from their superstructures as signalmen on the darkened bridges translated and relayed messages back and forth between ships.

"The situation seems pretty cut-and-dry," McCandles continued. "The Japanese are going to try to pull their troops off Vella LaVella tonight. I guess they're finally going to give up that little scrap of an island. They're all set to abandon it, but you know what that means, don't you, Jack? It means they'll leave Vella LaVella tonight and tomorrow we'll find them burrowed in on the next island up the Slot. Then our army pukes'll have to start all over again. Another landing, another month of snipers and leeches, another slug-fest in some nameless jungle—more casualties."

McCandles and Tremain gazed out at the darkening western sky as the *Chevalier* and her consorts steadied on their new course. Occasionally flashes of lightning marked the distant squalls, almost as if they were a symbol of the bloody battles that had taken place in these waters over the past year—waters which had a tendency to change hands almost weekly. While the Allies had conquered a substantial portion of the Solomon Island chain, the western Solomons still remained very much in contention. The tiny island of Vella LaVella, lying just beyond the dull horizon, somewhere beneath those distant squalls, was the latest front line in the island-hopping campaign. For weeks, New Zealand Army troops had been herding the Japanese defenders into a small pocket against the potato-shaped island's northern shore. Now the Japanese defenders were faced with two choices—escape to fight another day or *banzai!*

"But the bastards aren't going to get away tonight," McCandles said with sudden determination in his voice. "Tonight, we're going to stop them, damn it!"

"Like the time you stopped that UW tackle from breaking through the line at the Rose Bowl?" Tremain grinned at his old friend. "The one that damn near cleaned Ira McKee's clock!"

McCandles laughed. "Shit, toss me a line, would ya? I was just a plebe at the time! One's gonna get through every now and then. Besides, it's good for a quarterback to have to scramble once in a while. Keeps 'em honest—and appreciative!"

"Too bad we tied that game, Wally."

"Yeah," McCandles said distantly, as if he were reliving the memorable day in his mind. "Those were good days, eh, Jack? Look how far we've come since then. We're a long way from Dahlgren Hall, now."

Tremain winced imperceptibly at the mention of the building at the Naval Academy where they both had graduated and received their commissions. But to Tremain, Dahlgren Hall carried an even greater significance. It was where he had met Judy for the first time, at one of the many balls thrown there during his senior year. The memory was almost too painful for him to bear. After spending the last few months putting the past behind him, trying to get on with his life, begging for medical clearance, pleading for a submarine to command, anything to get him back to sea again, he'd finally begun to see the traces of the man he had been before. Now the wound had been torn open again.

"We're never very far, Wally."

Chapter 2

THE three camouflaged destroyers, their hulls painted from fore to aft with exotic emerald bands and inconsistent jagged designs, steamed with urgency across the black sea. The knife-like bows sliced the waters before them, dipping and rising but pointing steadily to the northwest. The column of swift warships left behind them a single collective wake, a green luminous trail in the black sea, clearly marking every minute change of course along its five-mile length. The ships were arranged as they had been before, with the Porter class destroyer *Selfridge* parting the night ahead of the small formation, and the two Fletcher class destroyers, *Chevalier* and *O'Bannon*, following at even intervals closely behind. The smokestacks of all three ships chugged out rising columns of semitransparent exhaust, merging into one long, dark cloud high above the little fleet.

Holding the middle position in the small fleet, the *Chevalier,* like her two sisters, had prepared for action. All obstructions had been long since cleared away, all potential obstacles to damage control parties stowed away, all watertight and flood control doors fastened shut. Her three-hundred-odd sailors—some bedecked in bulky salt-stained life vests, some in cumbersome steel gray helmets, some shirtless—assembled at their various battle stations inside and out of the destroyer's 376-foot hull, waiting anxiously for the inevitable encounter with the as yet unseen enemy.

Like her two cohorts, the *Chevalier* was made for war, with nearly every piece of equipment above her waterline devoted to that end. Two Mark 12 five-inch, thirty-eight-caliber gun turrets sat one behind the other on her forecastle, the rearmost gun situated atop a single-story deckhouse slightly higher than its companion. Farther aft she carried three more such guns, one amidships and two on her stern, making up the balance of her main armament. They were controlled by a gun director turret high above the main bridge, the five long muzzles swinging in elegant unison from port to starboard, as if they belonged to a giant sea creature directing its venomous stingers at a circling predator. The five-inch guns were impressive by any standard of modern naval warfare, but they were by no means all that the *Chevalier* could deliver against an enemy. Along her length she carried a sprinkling of twenty-millimeter Oerlikon guns that could stave off approaching enemy aircraft, while on her stern she carried an array of K guns and angled racks holding dozens of drumlike depth charges to deal with any enemy submarines that might appear. But perhaps the most lethal weapons carried by the *Chevalier* were her ten Mark 15 torpedoes, and these were much more along Tremain's line of work.

The torpedoes were encased in two quintuple mounts located amidships, just above the single-story deckhouses, one forward and one aft of the number two smokestack. Each torpedo mount consisted of five torpedo tubes, all bundled together and resembling a horizontal row of large cylinders, each cylinder containing a torpedo. The mount itself was affixed on top of a giant swivel that could be trained to either side of the ship to aim the tubes at an enemy vessel on the beam. Turning the mount meant turning the entire bundle of tubes, all together. Each torpedo mount was manned by three men and controlled from a small panel with two seats mounted directly on top of the tube bundle itself.

It was here, at the forward torpedo mount, atop the amidships deckhouse, that Tremain had chosen to make his battle station. As a mere passenger on board with no assigned battle station, he had kept with navy tradition, first offering his services to *Chevalier*'s captain in any capacity he deemed appropriate. But the *Chevalier*'s captain had told him to go wherever he liked, as long as he stayed out of the way when things finally got hot. Tremain could have chosen to stand on the bridge, but decided against it out of courtesy to his counterpart. No captain ever wanted another captain standing on his bridge, especially during the heat of battle. So Tremain had chosen the forward torpedo mount. It was far from the bridge, but still afforded an elevated spot from which to view the coming engagement. More importantly, it was out of the way, and he wished to remain out of the way since the sum total of his experience on destroyers amounted to a brief sea tour on a World War One era four-piper during his first year as an ensign. Back in those days, all officers had to serve mandatory time in surface ships before they branched off to other professions, like aviation or submarines. Although the tour on the four-piper technically counted as a sea tour, Tremain never considered it as such. The old rust bucket spent most of its time high and dry in a Virginia shipyard, seldom ever venturing out into Chesapeake Bay. It was certainly a far cry from the state-of-the-art Fletcher class, like the *Chevalier*.

"There goes another one!" said a torpedoman standing beside Tremain, and wearing a phone headset.

Tremain followed the torpedoman's gaze up into the night sky and saw a brilliant speck of light, brighter than any of the stars peeking out from behind the scattered clouds. The flickering light illuminated the ocean all around the little task group in a most disturbing fashion, prompting the men manning the Oerlikon guns on the main deck to train their long barrels skyward, undoubtedly out of aggravation. But there was nothing they could do about it. The revealing light seemed to hang in the air for an eternity, but after a long minute or two it finally fell into the sea, extinguishing itself in a dazzling blur of white smoke astern of the *O'Bannon*.

"Another fucking flare!" the fidgety sailor cursed. "That Zero's been on our ass all night. I wish the bastard would get close enough to let our twenty mike-mikes get a piece of him."

"That ain't no Zero, dumbshit," said a first-class petty officer sitting on the bench seat at the mount's control station. He was in charge of the quintuple mount. "They don't use Zeros for night recon. It's a float plane, or something else, but it ain't no Zero." Then to Tremain, "Don't mind him, sir. Smitty here's a newbie."

"That makes two of us," Tremain replied, with a smile in young Smitty's direction.

The mount captain laughed heartily beneath his steel helmet, elbowing the sailor sitting next to him, then said in a deep voice, "You ain't no newbie, sir. Don't let Mr. Tremain fool you here, boys. I hear he's got himself two Navy Crosses, that's what I hear."

"Maybe. But I sure didn't get them on a destroyer."

"Say no more, sir." The mount captain raised an open palm. "I know all about it. You submariners can't talk about nothing. You've probably sunk more ships than Smitty here's ever set eyes on, but you can't tell us a lick about it. I know, I know, the silent service and all that hoo-hah! Well, don't you worry none, Commander. As soon as the old man gives the word, me, Smitty, and Hegemeyer here are gonna show you how tin-can sailors shoot torpedoes." Another hearty belly laugh exuded from the good-natured torpedo captain, and again he elbowed the nervous-looking Hegemeyer in the ribs.

While the cheerful petty officer seemed completely at ease about the coming action, his two compatriots—Smitty and Hegemeyer—did not. Both appeared anxious, and both scanned the sky with uncertainty. Whatever kind of plane had dropped the flare—the third to be dropped over the task force in the last hour—the plane was certainly Japanese.

Looking aft, Tremain saw the *Chevalier*'s wake curve to port, following the lead of the *Selfridge*, which had already steadied on a new southwesterly course. The maneuver was obviously an attempt to slip away from the harassing aircraft, but the unseen Japanese plane seemed to have little difficulty keeping on top of the American destroyers. Its effect on the sailors was apparent. They no doubt had put two and two together. The enemy plane would be radioing his findings to all Japanese ships in the area, eliminating any hope of surprise. The enemy ships, thought to be somewhere in the darkness beyond the *Selfridge*'s bows, would certainly know they were coming and be ready for them. Obviously, this did little to dissuade the task group commander from proceeding with his mission, since the destroyer column continued its advance westward at high speed.

Tremain took heart from the three men with him on top of the torpedo mount. The buoyant mount captain certainly had the situation well in hand. The mount trainer and gyro setter—Smitty and Hegemeyer—though anxious, appeared to be knowledgeable and very familiar with the torpedo mount control station. They knew their jobs and could obviously perform them blindfolded.

Squinting at the southwestern horizon, Tremain thought he could just make out a low black mass. No doubt, it was Vella LaVella. Somewhere over there, on that dark, untamed island, weary New Zealanders crouched in muddy foxholes beneath the steamy jungle canopy. Tomorrow, they faced another day of hacking through dense underbrush, uncovering deadly snipers and unearthing sinister booby traps; another day of fighting yard by yard to wrest the island from the hands of the Japanese defenders. If the intelligence reports were correct, and the Japanese were indeed evacuating the island tonight, perhaps the New Zealanders would not have to fight tomorrow. Perhaps tonight, in one of Vella LaVella's isolated coves, hundreds of Japanese troops were piling aboard barges and transports to make their escape. If that were the case, then it was a certainty that enemy warships would be covering the retreat. Now that the enemy search plane had spotted the three American destroyers, the Japanese admiral would conclude that they were on their way to interfere with his plans.

As *Chevalier* steadied on the new course—and *O'Bannon*, in her turn, did the same—the men remained quiet at their stations. Visibility was reasonably good, up to ten or twelve thousand yards, with spotty clouds and an intermittent moon that bathed the ships in a pale blue light, casting long shadows upon the glistening water to starboard. Visibility was so good, in fact, that Tremain might have thought twice about approaching an enemy convoy, had he been on the bridge of a submarine at this moment.

Wally McCandles came aft along the portside main deck,

stopping briefly to converse with the men at the twenty-millimeter mounts, before climbing up the deckhouse ladder to join Tremain on top of the torpedo mount. As *Chevalier*'s torpedo officer, McCandles's battle station was at the Mark 27 torpedo directors up on the bridge, but like any good division officer he was probably taking this one final opportunity to check on his men before things got hot.

McCandles stood with his hands on his hips, his face in a wild expression as he regarded the three sailors beside Tremain. Tremain remembered seeing the same expression many times prior to their college football games.

"You boys ready?" McCandles asked assertively.

He received a unanimous acknowledgment from the three torpedomen, the petty officer in charge giving an enthusiastic thumbs-up

"This is it, Jack." McCandles was animated as he turned to Tremain. "We've got them on radar now, dead ahead at thirty thousand yards. Seven ships in all. We're going to sink the whole damn lot of them."

Tremain nodded uncertainly at his friend's confidence. He'd had a chance to take a look at the intelligence reports for himself before the task group went to general quarters. The reports indicated that several Japanese destroyers were unaccounted for and might be cruising in these waters tonight. There was no way to tell if those seven radar contacts were lightly armed transports or heavily armed warships.

"You're sure they're transports, Wally?" Tremain whispered low enough so that the three sailors could not hear.

McCandles shrugged. "Whether they are or not, the task group commander has decided to go in." Then he seemed to sense Tremain's skepticism and added, "Anyway, we have no choice now. They know we're coming. Every Japanese transport with a spinning propeller or a paddle's going to be running for the horizon as fast as they can. If they're loaded with troops, Jack, we can't let them escape. Besides, Larson's task group is coming up behind us, fast as they can. They'll be here in forty-five minutes."

All the more reason to wait, Tremain felt like saying, but instead he held his tongue. The second task group coming up consisted of the destroyers *Talbot*, *Lavallette*, and *Taylor*, under the overall command of Captain Harold Larson. They were not yet visible in the darkness astern. They had received the same tasking as *Chevalier*'s task group but had been farther away when their orders reached them. In Tremain's mind, it made sense to wait for Larson's group before proceeding into battle against an enemy potentially comprised of seven warships. But the task group commander in the *Selfridge* was calling the shots, and Tremain resigned himself to the fact that—standing atop the forward torpedo mount—he knew a lot less about the situation than did the task group commander, who undoubtedly had a virtual torrent of data coming into him in the *Selfridge*'s combat information center.

In the moonlight, Tremain could make out the stern of the *Selfridge* up ahead. She was turning back to the right again, steadying on a westerly course. Moments later, *Chevalier* did the same, steadying on the same course five hundred yards directly behind the group leader. The sudden turn caused a small wave to break over the splash shield protecting the portside twenty-millimeter gun down on the main deck, dousing the men there from head to foot and drawing several muttered curses.

McCandles turned to Tremain and held out his hand. "I'd better get back up there, Jack. Good luck with these guys. They'll take care of you." McCandles nodded to his torpedomen and then slapped one hand on Tremain's back. "Now you'll see how the real navy fights, Tremain!"

McCandles jumped down the ladder and trotted forward, headed to his battle station on the bridge. It wasn't long after that the phones buzzed with what all had been anticipating.

"Bridge reports enemy column in sight!" Smitty reported, holding a hand over one earphone. "Enemy destroyers heading southeast, six thousand yards ahead."

The American task group was heading southwest, on a course of two four zero, directly perpendicular to the enemy's course. Tremain didn't have to be a surface warfare officer to know what that meant. The enemy column was in the advantageous position of crossing the "T" on the American column, the textbook maneuver in a surface engagement that brought all guns in the crossing column to bear on the lead ship in the disadvantaged column. Tremain climbed out to the edge of the torpedo mount platform to try to gain a glimpse of the enemy ships, but the stacks and superstructures of both the *Chevalier* and the *Selfridge* obstructed his line of vision ahead.

At any moment, he expected to see a dozen water spouts erupting in the ocean all around the *Selfridge*, but remarkably the Japanese ships held their fire. He could only surmise that they were beyond their effective gun range. The task group commander in the *Selfridge* must have realized the unfavorable position his destroyers were in, because he suddenly ordered a column turn, bringing the *Selfridge* forty degrees to the right, essentially pointed west, before steadying on the new course. In proper sequence, the *Chevalier* and the *O'Bannon* followed suit, maintaining the column's integrity throughout the turn.

With the maneuver complete, Tremain could now clearly see the small, dark shapes of the Japanese column, just off the port bow and traveling on a parallel but opposite course to that of the American destroyers. He made out four squat silhouettes, no more than forty-five hundred yards away. They were unmistakably enemy destroyers, unmistakably traveling at high speeds, judging from the white froth being kicked up at the waterline beneath their sharp bows. They looked ghoulish in the moonlight, growing larger before his eyes as the range closed rapidly.

Tremain had seen his share of enemy destroyers before, but never quite like this. This was traditional point-blank naval combat in column formation, and he could hardly believe that no ship on either side had yet opened fire. For a brief moment, it appeared that the opposing columns might render honors to each other rather than unleash a fury of weaponry, but then the orders came over Smitty's headset.

"From the bridge." Smitty relayed what he heard in his headset. "Stand by for torpedo action, port side, bridge control."

With hurried courtesy, the mount captain ushered Tremain aside and directed Smitty to take up position on the bench next to Hegemeyer in front of the tube-training mechanism. With his helmet pushed back on top of his head, Smitty peered through the boresight and began spinning the associated hand crank, while Hegemeyer fingered the gyro control panel. Both men worked calmly but speedily under the watchful eye of the mount captain.

Tremain felt disoriented momentarily as the entire quintuple tube bundle began to move beneath his feet, rotating to port. As Smitty continued to crank on the training handles, the torpedo mount slowly swiveled to the left, until the tube muzzles hung directly over the port side main deck, directly above the heads of the men manning the twenty-millimeter guns there. After a few fine adjustments, the tubes were pointing slightly forward of the port beam.

"To the bridge," the torpedo captain said in a fatherly tone, patting Smitty on the shoulder. "Number one torpedo mount is standing by for torpedo action, port side, bridge control."

Smitty pressed the microphone button on his phone set and relayed the report to the bridge.

Glancing aft, Tremain saw that the number two torpedo mount was also trained to port, its own five tube muzzles poking out from behind the aft smokestack. Then, looking far up forward to *Chevalier*'s port bridge wing, he could just make out a dark figure dressed in khaki, obviously an officer, peering into the boresight on the bulky torpedo director, a man-sized piece of equipment that served the same functions of a target bearing transmitter and torpedo data computer on a submarine. The officer was undoubtedly McCandles, setting up a solution on the enemy column, trying to obtain the exact firing angle necessary for the *Chevalier*'s ten torpedoes to rendezvous with the enemy column. Tremain could see another figure standing next to McCandles, wearing a bulky headset like Smitty's. No doubt this was the individual talking to Smitty on the other end of his phone circuit.

The enemy shapes continued to grow larger across the dark expanse of water. Then, suddenly, something didn't feel right. There was something non-uniform about the enemy column. Tremain had set up solutions on hundreds of targets in his years aboard submarines, and perhaps it was that experience alone that allowed him to detect the trickery that aspect and distance could play on the eye at night. The Japanese destroyers were not in a column formation at all, but were rather in a staggered echelon formation, with the trailing ship farthest to the left of the formation and therefore closest to the American column. It explained perfectly why the Japanese ships had not yet opened fire. Only one of their ships was inside effective gun range. It seemed that the enemy ships had been caught with their pants down. Remarkable, considering the prior warning they must have received from the reconnaissance aircraft. Now they were quickly trying to correct their blunder, closing formation in an attempt to bring all guns into range of the American destroyers. The American task group commander had been handed a stroke of luck and now needed only to exploit it. Tremain couldn't imagine why the column hadn't opened fire yet on the closest enemy destroyer.

"From the bridge," Smitty announced. "Match pointers."

With silent efficiency Smitty and Hegemeyer spun their knobs and hand cranks, closely watching the torpedo tube course and gyro indicators until they lined up perfectly with the settings transmitted electrically from the torpedo director on the bridge. The mount captain leaned between the heads of his crewmen to double-check the settings before patting Smitty on the helmet to indicate that everything was indeed ready.

"Bridge, number one torpedo mount," Smitty said into the microphone. "Pointers matched!"

Looking out over the twenty-one-inch barrels, Tremain could see they were aiming for a patch of ocean just ahead of the closest Japanese destroyer, a mere thirty-five hundred yards away now and presenting its port beam to the American column. The darkened enemy destroyer seemed menacing at this range, her gun turrets clearly turned to port and aimed at the American column. Tremain had to coolly remind himself that he'd shot torpedoes from much closer ranges before.

The wait seemed like an eternity, but the order finally came.

"From the bridge," Smitty announced in a disappointed tone. "Prepare to shoot one-half salvo from *number two* torpedo mount, high speed, one-and-a-half-degree spread, depth setting twelve feet."

"Motherfuckers! Them assholes always get to shoot first!" muttered the mount captain, as he stuck his lip out and glanced aft at the number two torpedo mount. "Favoritism! That's what it is, boys. Mr. McCandles's got a hard-on for the number two mount—begging your pardon, Commander Tremain, sir—that's the way I see it. But stand ready, boys. Our turn's bound to come."

Moments later Smitty reported, "The bridge is passing the word to the number two mount to fire torpedoes."

A loud pop sounded from behind the aft smokestack. Tremain and the others looked aft just in time to see the first two-ton, twenty-four-foot, Mark 15 torpedo leap from its tube, soar over the crouching gunners on the main deck, and belly flop into the sea. In rapid succession, four more percussion caps popped as one by one all torpedoes in the number two mount were fired and sped away into the black sea, leaving a mixture of green phosphorescent bubbles on the surface to mark their paths.

Tremain wondered if the *Selfridge* and the *O'Bannon* had fired their torpedoes, but he assumed that they had. Surface ships were used to fighting in formations and took pride in the disciplined uniformity of their maneuvers. Assuming the *Selfridge* and the *O'Bannon* had each put five torpedoes in the water to add to *Chevalier*'s five, the Japanese ships now had a small armada of fifteen torpedoes speeding in their direction.

Tremain had hardly had time to digest the thought when a deafening salvo blasted the night apart. The *Chevalier*'s main gun battery had engaged. The deck shook from the simultaneous reports, until Tremain thought the whole ship might shake apart. The sea along the port side glowed orangish yellow as each long five-inch barrel spewed out a storm of fire and metal. Seconds later, as Tremain fumbled for the small pieces of foam he'd forgotten to put in his ears, more booming percussions echoed across the water from ahead and astern as the *Selfridge* and the *O'Bannon* opened up with their own main batteries.

When he finally grew accustomed to the incessant fusillade of crashing guns all around him, and could finally see straight, Tremain could follow the frenzied storm of luminous five-inch tracer rounds floating across the night sky in long arcs and landing in the vicinity of the nearest Japanese destroyer. Small flashes rippled up and down the length of the Japanese ship. At first he thought they might be hits, but then he realized that the enemy destroyer was returning fire. He waited with gritted teeth for the resulting shell splashes, but none could be seen landing anywhere around the *Chevalier* or the *O'Bannon*. He could only conclude that the *Selfridge*—now masked from view by the smoke of her own guns—was the one on the receiving end of the enemy arsenal.

"Whooeee!" the mount captain cheered, his sweaty face glistening eerily yellow with each flash of *Chevalier*'s five-inch guns. "That's a hit!"

A towering column of white water shot up and through the Japanese destroyer, driving skyward as it streaked globs of burning fuel oil and debris. At least one of the American torpedoes had found its mark, and Tremain's practiced eyes could already tell that the hit was a serious one. The enemy warship began to slow visibly, with bright fires blazing uncontrollably on her bridge and superstructure, illuminating the sea all around her. Burning equipment—or perhaps burning Japanese sailors—could be seen rolling off her decks in droves.

"*Selfridge* is coming right!" a man down on the main deck shouted, pointing at the flagship up ahead.

"He's coming right to make sure we don't meet the same fate as those Japanese bastards," the mount captain commented, nodding toward the crippled ship.

Tremain mentally kicked himself for his submariner state of mind. The thought had never occurred to him that the Japanese ships had undoubtedly unleashed a torpedo salvo of their own. Of course enemy torpedoes would be in the water by now, and wisely, the task group commander in the *Selfridge* was turning away to present the smallest possible underwater profile to the unseen weapons.

Following suit, the *Chevalier* leaned over to port as she also began an evasive turn to the right. The maneuver gave Tremain a small sensation of relief—but he soon learned the relief was misplaced, when two of the loudest explosions he had ever heard ripped apart the night, dwarfing the reports of the five-inch guns.

Whack! Kaboom!

For an instant the deck jolted beneath his feet, and then

everything went black. He felt an immense pressure wave hit his face, ears, and chest. He felt his feet leave the torpedo mount, and then he was spinning in midair—spinning and falling for what seemed like minutes.

Then his body hit something very flat, and very solid—and he lost all consciousness.

Chapter 3

ELECTRICIAN'S Mate Second Class Michael Fabriano picked himself up from the deck of the *Chevalier*'s second-level passage, favoring an aching hip and shoulder. Moments before, he had been rushing to the bridge to repair the gyro compass repeater that had started acting up again—like it always did whenever the big guns started firing. The intense vibrations always wreaked havoc on the *Chevalier*'s power grid. It was probably another short circuit in a place he'd never checked before. He'd fixed the bridge gyro compass twelve times in the last month. This time would have made a baker's dozen.

But then something exploded within the ship, and he found his ears ringing and his six-foot-two, two-hundred-thirty-pound frame flying through the air, crashing through the door to the CO's stateroom. Ferociously, the deck bounced up and down, and then up again, as if some great leviathan had grabbed hold of the *Chevalier*'s bow and was using her to swat flies on the ocean's surface. The sound of overstressed, groaning metal filled the compartment, and then a succession of loud *pops* split the air, the sound of giant steel girders being ripped in two. Just as suddenly as it had begun, the shaking subsided, and Fabriano regained his footing with the deck now tilted forward at a very noticeable angle.

In the dim red lights, he could see a figure stumbling down the ladder from the bridge. The man was disoriented, walking directly into the bulkhead at the base of the ladder, rebounding into the center of the passageway, and then stumbling bodily into Fabriano.

"Hey, watch where you're going!" Fabriano said, as he pulled the sailor up straight.

Only then, holding on to the sailor's slippery arms, did he realize that the man was covered in blood from head to foot. He had no face. It had been smashed into an unrecognizable form, a horrific bloody mess, with no eyes, ears, lips or nose. Only the remaining teeth in a loosely hanging lower jaw bore any resemblance to something human. The sailor stood silently for what seemed like minutes, staring back hollowly through dark cavities, before finally collapsing to the passage floor, unquestionably dead.

With trepidation, Fabriano stared at the ladder which the bloody sailor had descended. The bridge was a crowded place during battle stations. He concluded that it must have taken a direct hit. Whatever hellish carnage existed at the top of that ladder, Fabriano had no desire to see it. The gyro compass would certainly be wrecked, along with everything else. There was no point in continuing with his previous orders. Now he needed to concentrate on saving himself.

With one arm on the bulkhead to maintain his footing, Fabriano headed down the angled passage in the opposite direction. The ship tilted more and more with each passing second, spurring him to move faster.

As he passed the ship's office, he instinctively popped his head in to see if anyone was there. The room was a complete wreck of dislodged drawers, scattered papers, and overturned typewriters, but no one was inside. That was good. At least he wouldn't have to worry about carrying anybody down the ladder to the main deck.

He was just about to continue on his way, when something in the far corner of the small office caught his eye, something peeking out from behind the yeoman's overturned desk. It was the safe, where the ship's disbursing officer kept all of the

Chevalier's ready cash. The big iron box had been dislodged from its fixture and now lay at an angle, leaning against the bulkhead, with its massive door hanging wide open.

Fabriano's legs must have moved on their own, because the next moment, he found himself kneeling in front of the teetering safe, peering inside, cursing the dull illumination afforded by surviving lightbulbs. The door to the hardened safe was much too robust to have been jarred open by the blast, and he surmised that the disbursing officer must have been finishing up some last-minute accounting when the ship went to general quarters, and had forgotten to spin the tumbler before he left. That was the only explanation Fabriano could come up with as his hand moved entirely on its own, reaching inside the safe and taking out the rectangular aluminum box—the same one he had seen the disbursing officer use many times before—the same one that held all of the ship's cash.

The next moment, the box lay open on the cluttered deck, and Fabriano's eyes gleamed in the red light as if they beheld the lost treasure of Atlantis. Before him lay a small fortune of neatly stacked bills, all bound in rubber bands, all separated into their appropriate trays from right to left, largest denomination to smallest, with proportionally more of the larger denominations. No doubt, this was the money to be used when the *Chevalier* reached Brisbane—some to procure stores, some to disburse to the crew for liberty, some to pay for ship-sponsored parties and balls.

Somehow, a few of these stacks ended up inside Fabriano's shirt before he knew it, and then a gleeful grin appeared on his face as he reached out for more.

After all, who would miss a few stacks of hundred-dollar bills? The disbursing officer? The captain? Both were probably dead. The ship was most likely sinking, anyway. All of this money would end up in Davy Jones's locker if he didn't take it now. Besides, the navy owed it to him, and to his brother's poor widow, now left to raise her son alone with little hope of the two ever living above the poverty level. He'd take only a few stacks, just a few, and consider it payment in full for his poor sister-in-law's misery. Just enough to get her back on her feet again, and then maybe a little more to get the kid some new clothes. Okay, maybe he'd take a little for himself, too—just a little—to compensate for the years he'd given the navy—the hard years spent on countless ships from one side of the globe to the other, kissing officers' shoes every fucking day, only to be kicked like a proverbial dog in return. What else did he have to show for a career spent toiling on the lower decks? A dead brother, two measly chevrons on his sleeve, and a lousy seventy-eight dollars a month.

As he stuffed the fourth stack of bills into his shirt, a deterring thought suddenly came to mind. What if the ship wasn't sinking, after all? Someone would later discover that the money was missing. There would be an investigation. Some overzealous junior officer would finger him as the culprit and bring him up on charges. It would be the end of his naval career, and a ticket to the federal penitentiary—or worse, the navy brig. His sister-in-law and nephew would be alone in the world, with no one to take care of them.

As he knelt there trying to make up his mind, Fabriano heard voices down the passageway. Men were shouting. Someone was coming this way. His decision was academic now. In a matter of seconds, he removed every stack of bills from his shirt, crammed them all into the aluminum box, and shoved the box back into the safe.

It was just a sailor's fantasy, he thought, as he left the ship's office and headed down the passageway toward the voices at the far end. Undoubtedly, repair parties were being formed at this very minute, and undoubtedly his chief already had work for him to do, and was probably cursing up a maelstrom at his absence. He would head to his division spaces, join the effort to save the ship, purge any thoughts of that small fortune from his mind, and become a good and faithful sailor once again.

Reaching the men at the end of the passage, he recognized the ship's executive officer in the dim red lighting issuing orders to a small gaggle of wide-eyed apprentice seaman looking for guidance. The XO suddenly made eye contact with him, and Fabriano instinctively looked away, as if the ship's second highest officer could have somehow known what he had been contemplating only moments before.

"Fabriano!" The XO moved out of the cluster of sailors and approached him. "Have you been up to the bridge? Is anyone alive up there?"

Fabriano shrugged, feigning shell shock. "I don't know, sir."

"I'm going up there to check on the captain. Listen, you're more senior than these guys, and I need you to do something." The XO shoved several large canvas bags into Fabriano's hands. "We took a torpedo hit on the port side forward. It's bad—real bad—and she may be lost. Take those bags and get to the radio room. Tell the radiomen to gather up their codebooks, encryption equipment, and anything else that's sensitive and make sure it all makes it to the bottom. If the radiomen are all dead, then you'll have to do it. Understand? Weight those sacks with anything you can find, but make sure they sink. Got it?"

"Aye, aye, sir."

Without another word, the XO slapped Fabriano on the shoulder, and then he and his troop of sailors brushed past, heading up the ladder to the bridge. Fabriano was left alone in the passageway, holding the canvas bags. The ship lurched again; the red lights flickered overhead, and the deck beneath Fabriano's feet took on an even larger angle. Stressed steel groaned all around him as it took on the new strain. It seemed that the *Chevalier* was sinking, after all, coming apart at the seams. But who knew how long it would take? It could take hours. It could take minutes. Either way, there was no time for him to delay. The radio room was just down the passage. Like the good sailor he was, he began to make his way carefully along the tilted deck to carry out his orders.

He couldn't help it if the ship's office was on the way.

TREMAIN'S skin felt warm and then cool—sticky and then slippery. He couldn't breathe for what seemed like minutes, and then all of a sudden he could, taking in deep breaths of a strangely putrid yet sweet smelling mixture of air and petroleum vapor.

The old wound throbbed on the side of his head, along with several new ones. His whole body ached, but he was familiar with the side effects of a concussive shock wave, and after a few moments he had the wherewithal to force himself to breathe evenly.

Certain of nothing, except that he was still alive, Tremain eventually regained his vision and discovered that he was lying flat on the *Chevalier*'s starboard side main deck, staring up at the breech end of the pivoted forward torpedo mount several feet above him. He had obviously been blown off the mount by the explosion. The deck around him, his face, his hair, his clothes were all covered in thick black oil, fresh from *Chevalier*'s fuel tanks. Mere feet away lay the twisted and broken body of a young sailor, the lifeless eyes staring hollowly in his direction. Dark blood trickled from the sailor's mouth to mingle with the shiny crude.

After staring at the motionless body for several minutes and collecting his senses, Tremain finally concluded that it was not one of the men who had been with him on the torpedo mount. Rolling over onto his side, he felt a sensation that the ship was rapidly slowing. One glance forward through the drifting clouds of smoke told him why. The *Chevalier*'s starboard breakwater shield was missing, allowing Tremain an uninhibited view up forward. And his eyes could scarcely believe what they saw. The *Chevalier*'s bow had been severed, completely blown off. *Chevalier*'s elevated bow, her two forward five-inch gun mounts, and a good portion of the forward deckhouse—essentially everything forward of the bridge—had simply disappeared. Obviously she had suffered a hit from a Japanese torpedo. Only a torpedo striking below the waterline could have caused such massive destruction. Tremain was amazed that she was still afloat. Not fifty feet from where he lay, the sea was lapping over the starboard-side main deck and undoubtedly flooding into the compartments below. *Chevalier*'s starboard turn was still on, but she had slowed substantially due to the loss of her hydrodynamic bow.

With his body aching and his head throbbing, Tremain managed to get up onto his knees. Almost instantly he heard agitated voices calling from back aft. Men were shouting warnings. Were they shouting at him?

Suddenly, one voice yelled loudly and distinctly above the others, *"Look out!"*

Instinctively Tremain turned around and looked over the lifeline rail just in time to see the towering bow of the destroyer *O'Bannon* emerging from the smoky mist, no more than fifty yards away. It was headed straight for *Chevalier*'s starboard side at full speed. Obviously still adhering to the rigid column formation and blinded by the smoke of its own forward guns, the *O'Bannon* had not seen *Chevalier* take the torpedo hit, and therefore had no idea that she had slowed to nearly a complete stop.

Tremain had mere seconds to act before being smashed between the two hulls. Leaping for the amidships deckhouse, he found that all of the doors were shut, but he managed to grope his way aft, scrambling along the slippery deck until he eventually found a small nook in which to take shelter. An instant later, the bow of the two-thousand-ton *O'Bannon* knifed into *Chevalier*'s starboard side with a bloodcurdling crash. Nestled behind the thin deckhouse bulkhead, Tremain felt the hull shake deep beneath his feet, and then heard the spine-tingling grind of metal upon metal. Stanchions and rails snapped; wires and cables parted; depth charge racks were either shorn off or else smashed between the two giant hulls. The deck rolled several degrees to starboard and remained there for a moment, and Tremain's oil-soaked hands struggled to hold on to the bulkhead. Letting go meant sliding across the angled deck and over the side. Allowing a quick glance around the corner of the deckhouse, he saw the menacing bow of the *O'Bannon*, like the upper jaw of a giant shark, locked in a pincer hold on the sagging stern of the *Chevalier.* The force of the collision had been so great that the *O'Bannon*'s prow now extended far inboard, far enough to scrape along the starboard side of the deckhouse. The *O'Bannon*'s huge, grinding hull was only a few feet away from him, and her algae-ridden starboard anchor swung loosely from its hawser just above his head. He could clearly see that the lower half of *O'Bannon*'s bow had been peeled back like a tin can, all the way back to her hull numbers, while the upper half remained completely intact. He surmised that the *O'Bannon* must have been making close to thirty knots when she rammed into the *Chevalier*, bending the high-strength steel back as if it were paper. The two ships remained steadfastly together for what seemed like minutes, and Tremain began to wonder if they might go to the bottom locked in their deadly embrace, but moments later, the *O'Bannon* finally put on an astern bell and backed away from her stricken sister. As the two hulls came apart, *Chevalier*'s stern popped up out of the water, bringing the deck just level enough for Tremain to regain his footing and let go of the bulkhead.

He tried to catch his breath there for a moment, but another unsettling crash rang out from up forward. The *Chevalier*'s pilothouse and bridge, with no supporting structure beneath them, had collapsed. The ship was literally falling apart around him.

Men began to emerge on deck from every hatch and door, some passing damage control equipment, some tending to the wounded, some moving the dead, some grabbing tools and heading below to try to salvage the *Chevalier*'s rapidly flooding engine rooms. The ship was listing heavily to starboard, and Tremain suspected the collision with the *O'Bannon* had ripped her hull away below the waterline. He recognized the ship's executive officer gathering men on deck in an attempt to jettison any loose equipment from the starboard side to give up some weight in an effort to keep her from capsizing.

In a matter of minutes, the deck all around him transformed into a makeshift morgue and hospital, with ever lengthening rows of horizontal bodies, both dead and wounded. A group of sailors brought a headless, armless body aft and set it gently in line with the other lifeless bodies. The headless corpse's tattered shirt was red with blood and black with oil and was quite indistinguishable. The trousers, however, seemed oddly clean. As the *O'Bannon* resumed firing her main batteries at the enemy warships, the light of the muzzle flashes reflected off a customized brass belt buckle Tremain had seen before. The dismembered corpse was Wally McCandles.

One of the sailors bearing the litter noticed Tremain's blank stare and must have felt obligated to provide some explanation.

"He was up on the port bridge wing looking through the torpedo director when that torpedo hit us, sir. He was right above the impact point. We found him hanging from the port whaler davits—or what was left of him, anyway."

Tremain gave an appreciative nod to the sailor, but said nothing. He decided that he didn't need to see the body up close. He felt no need to add this to the dozens of indelible images this war had already lodged in his brain. He was fine remembering Wally McCandles as he had last seen him—alive, and lining up Japanese destroyers in his sights.

"Commander Tremain . . . ," a voice called weakly.

Tremain looked left and right, unable to discern who was calling his name. Men were rushing past him in all directions, men were lying on the deck wounded and bleeding, men were desperately hacking away at heavy equipment and throwing it over the side, but all seemed completely engrossed in their duties, all completely oblivious to his presence.

"Commander . . . ," the voice called again.

This time Tremain had the notion to look up, and saw Seaman Smitty's very pale face, several feet above and staring down at him, peering over the edge of the torpedo mount. He appeared to be badly wounded.

Tremain quickly banished the thought of McCandles's mutilated body from his mind and dashed up the ladder as fast as his wobbly legs would take him, reaching the top of the torpedo mount in seconds. There, he found no sign of the cheerful torpedo mount captain. He had probably been blasted over the side when the enemy torpedo hit. The sailor Hegemeyer still sat upright on the control bench clutching the gyro handle as Tremain had seen him do just prior to the explosion, but he was quite dead now. Some fragment had sliced open his stomach and his entrails now lay in a bloody mess around his boots. Seaman Smitty was still moving, but looked only slightly better. His legs lay loosely inside his trousers, pointing in odd directions and not moving with his body. They were either broken or severed, Tremain could not tell which. There was blood all over the torpedo mount, but he wasn't sure whose it was.

Tremain quickly knelt down and cradled the wounded seaman's head in his oil-covered hands. Smitty's helmet was nowhere in sight, but remarkably he still wore the set of headphones.

"I'm afraid it's too late for Hegemeyer, son," Tremain said consolingly, "but don't you worry. I'm going to get you out of here."

Smitty reached up and grabbed Tremain's wrist with a cold, bony hand. The young sailor was having difficulty talking.

"Not until we shoot our fish, sir!" he finally managed to utter, coughing up blood as he shook his head violently from side to side. "We've got . . . orders . . . from the bridge . . . to shoot our fish!"

Tremain had almost forgotten they were still engaged in a battle, a battle in which two of the three American destroyers now sat crippled and dead in the water. Several thousand yards ahead of the *Chevalier* and the *O'Bannon*, the *Selfridge* continued to fire round after round at the distant enemy ships. The *O'Bannon* was doing her best to provide support, but her smashed bow was making her extremely unwieldy and she had to struggle to keep her guns aimed at the enemy.

Tremain could make out the distinct shapes of the Japanese destroyers, still off the port beam. From what he could tell, only the burning Japanese destroyer had taken any damage— the one that had absorbed the task group's torpedo salvo. It was still the nearest of the enemy ships, now three thousand yards away and slightly abaft *Chevalier*'s beam. From this close range, Tremain could clearly see that she was dead in the water. Fires raged along her length, reaching high into the night sky, exuding a pall of dense black smoke which the stiff trade winds swiftly carried off to the west.

"We've got orders, sir . . . to shoot our load at that burning ship," Smitty mumbled, wincing from pain. "The bridge says she's still shooting her main guns . . . We've got orders to take her out . . ."

Tremain found it implausible that anyone was left on the *Chevalier*'s bridge to issue such orders over the phone set. The disoriented youth was probably hearing voices in his head. But whatever the source of the orders, Tremain knew that the young sailor was determined to carry them out. It was the determination of the doomed that Tremain had seen so many times before, and he knew that he would never get the young man off the mount without first acceding to his wishes.

Tremain sat down next to the dead Hegemeyer and attempted to operate the torpedo mount's training handles, but a few turns on the handles yielded no movement at all. The mount wouldn't budge an inch.

"The mount's jammed, sir," Smitty mumbled. "You'll have to shoot using the gyro setting."

Great, Tremain thought. *I'll have to eyeball it. I haven't done this since PCO school.*

The torpedo tubes were already trained out to the port side, so at least that was a good thing. But they were aiming at a point forward of *Chevalier*'s beam, and the Japanese destroyer, at this moment, was abaft the beam. In order to compensate, he would have to set the gyroscopes on the torpedoes to turn hard left once the weapons hit the water. Since he had no way of measuring the precise angle needed to hit the enemy ship—a value normally calculated on the bridge by the torpedo officer, Wally McCandles, now lying dismembered on the main deck below—he would have to make an educated guess.

"That dial over there . . . ," Smitty groaned, pointing to the control panel smeared with Hegemeyer's blood. "That controls the gyro setting."

Tremain reached beneath Hegemeyer's outstretched arms, prying the dead man's fingers off the gyro setting dial and drawing uncomfortably close to the sailor's open-eyed face in order to read the angle indication. As Tremain peered over the control panel at the burning Japanese destroyer, the drifting smoke from *O'Bannon*'s gun battery sporadically obstructed his line of view, providing many chances for error. He finally decided to go with an angle of twenty-six degrees to the left, and dialed it into the control panel.

"All right! The gyro angle's set! What's next, Smitty?" Tremain looked around for the firing controls. "How do you fire this—"

A loud whack shook the tube bundle beneath his feet and a cloud of smoke enveloped the mount as the first torpedo blasted from its tube, just clearing the port main-deck railing as it plunged into the sea.

Half-startled, Tremain turned on the bench seat to see Smitty struggling to raise a small hammer over the percussion cap of the next torpedo in the line. Smitty had mustered the strength to manually fire the first one, but he couldn't manage to shoot the rest. He could barely lift the hammer above his head, and Tremain quickly removed it from the sailor's shaking hand before the young torpedoman did more injury to himself.

"Are they all primed and ready to go?" Tremain asked, motioning to the percussion caps for the unfired torpedo tubes.

Smitty nodded.

Balancing the hammer in his right hand, Tremain moved down the row of tubes, bringing the hammer down on the firing pins of each percussion cap, one after another until all four were fired.

A noisy *Pop! Rumble! Splash! . . . Pop! Rumble! Splash! . . .* resounded as each cap fired true and launched its two-ton weapon into the sea. *Chevalier's* last five torpedoes were now heading for the enemy at forty-five knots.

Tremain stared after them as each luminescent green wake stretched away from the *Chevalier*, turned sharply to the left, and then streaked away in the direction of the fiery Japanese destroyer. Tremain crossed his fingers as he calculated in his head the time to impact.

Let's see, three thousand yards at forty-five knots or fifteen hundred yards per minute. It'll take them about two minutes to get there.

As he waited anxiously, Tremain noticed the dark silhouettes of now five enemy destroyers, traveling in a tight column formation several thousand yards beyond their crippled sister. The enemy column must have performed a complete 180-degree turn sometime in the last few minutes, because they now appeared to be heading on a northwesterly course, running parallel to the defiant *Selfridge*.

The *Selfridge* was all by herself now, far out ahead of the crippled *Chevalier* and *O'Bannon*. Arcing shells from all five Japanese ships rained down, turning the sea around her alive with geysers. With the muzzles of her own guns swung out to port, the *Selfridge* gallantly engaged the enemy, returning every enemy salvo with one of her own. But things did not look good for the *Selfridge*. She was outnumbered five to one, and it was only a matter of time before one of the Japanese gunners found the range and pummeled her without mercy.

Then Tremain saw a flash out of the corner of his eye. He looked back at the burning Japanese destroyer to see a towering column of water shoot skyward and then come crashing back down onto her decks, temporarily extinguishing some of the flames there. One of the *Chevalier*'s torpedoes had found its mark. For a moment, the enemy destroyer's main deck seemed to lift visibly in the water and then sag, like a lid on a percolating kettle. Then, a massive secondary explosion tore open the night sky, flashing searchlight bright, illuminating the clouds above, and sending a resounding roar across the water. When the flaming explosion finally subsided, Tremain could no longer make out the form of the Japanese destroyer. It had been replaced by a red-hot mass of flattened, twisted metal. A moment later, the molten hulk cracked open at its middle, releasing a torrential blast of steam that sent vibrations through *Chevalier*'s deck, over a mile away. The enemy destroyer, if it could be called that anymore, quickly broke into two distinct pieces, each sinking within seconds of the other. Only a ghastly mixture of burning oil and flotsam remained on the surface, along with a few clusters of bobbing heads.

This brief moment of victory brought cheers from several of *Chevalier*'s sailors down on the main deck. But the levity did not last long.

Another bright flash appeared in the night. A column of white water shot up from the *Selfridge*'s waterline. She had taken a massive hit on the port side. Another highly accurate, Japanese Long Lance torpedo had run true. Tremain felt his heart sink as he watched the flagship of the task group shudder from the explosion, buckling from her waterline to the top of her mainmast. The gallant *Selfridge*'s guns fell silent and she rapidly lost speed, eventually slowing to a crawl. Soon thereafter, flames peeked out above her port-side forecastle, burning perilously close to her forward ammunition-handling rooms.

"Sons of bitches!" a sailor on the deck below shouted.

"We're dead dogs now!" exclaimed another.

Dead dogs! Tremain thought that summed it up quite appropriately. All three ships of the American task group had been knocked out of action. The *Chevalier* was finished and likely sinking; the *O'Bannon* was undoubtedly fighting massive flooding in her shattered bow compartments and trying hard to stay afloat, while the *Selfridge* was frantically fighting back fires to avert a main magazine detonation and her instant destruction. The American task group was now virtually defenseless against the five unscathed Japanese destroyers. The Japanese admiral now held all the cards.

Tremain watched perilously as the enemy destroyers, now less than five thousand yards away, made a group turn, transforming their thin silhouettes into mere slivers. They were heading directly toward the crippled American destroyers, holding their fire as they closed the range. Undoubtedly, the Japanese admiral had decided to wait until his guns could not possibly miss, before resuming the battery. Who could blame him? Why should he waste valuable ammunition at long range when he could close in and pound the American wrecks point-blank? Nothing could stop him now.

As frustrated as he was by the feeling of helplessness, Tremain knew that he would have done the same thing had he been in the Japanese admiral's shoes. The nightmarish barrage could be only minutes away. To make matters worse, the putter of the niggling enemy aircraft once again resounded overhead. Half a dozen flares appeared above each American warship, turning the night to day, clearly illuminating the green gray American hulls for the Japanese gunners. Several of the *Chevalier*'s twenty-millimeter guns blared out, their tracer rounds streaking up into the clouds in a vain attempt to bring down the enemy aircraft.

The flares shed some of their light on the closing Japanese destroyers', too, and for the first time Tremain got a clear look at the enemy. Their hulls were camouflaged, much like the American destroyers', except with a fresher paint job. The short Japanese masts swayed right to left above the squat superstructures as their bows plunged in and out of the flickering waves. Tremain instantly recognized them as two of the Kagero class, two of the Shiratsuyu class, and one of the Yagumo class.

"The *Shigure*!" Tremain heard a man cry out down on the main deck, and several other sailors repeated the name, adding a few expletives. Tremain had heard the name before, with many other less vulgar, but more infamous denotations attached to it: "The Scourge of the Solomons," "The Phantom of the Slot," "The Cruiser Killer," "The Unsinkable Tin Can." Tremain had read the name in at least a dozen reports since the outbreak of the war. She had been sighted at nearly every naval engagement, large and small, and had apparently emerged from them all unscathed. Many times, American skippers had returned to port claiming to have sunk the *Shigure*, only to find themselves looking down her five-inch barrels at the next engagement. She alone could take credit for sinking at least two American heavy cruisers and a handful of destroyers and escorts, not to mention the havoc she had wreaked on the submarine force, with three kills to her credit. This was all information Tremain was privy to because he had a high-level security clearance, but the *Shigure* seemed to have plenty of notoriety among the common sailors, as well, since most on the deck below had stopped what they were doing to gape at the infamous warship.

The *Shigure* was on the right flank of the enemy formation, and this was the first time Tremain had ever set eyes on her. Her unique markings seemed to lend credence to the scanty intelligence reports he had pored over during his instructor tour in New London. The destroyer had the oddest camouflage Tremain had ever seen. It was very identifiable, even in the flickering light of an illumination flare. A sharply rising bow was painted jet black all the way past a single dual-gun five-inch gun turret forward—which was also painted jet black—then a streak of almost white gray paint ran aft until it met another band of black paint on her stern. From this vantage point, Tremain could only assume her entire fantail along with her aft gun turrets were covered in the same black paint. To top things off, she had two black bands painted around the tops of her two smoke stacks. As odd as it might appear, Tremain could clearly see how effective the camouflage was at night. Even in the light of the fading flares, the strange paint job made the *Shigure* appear to be only half of her actual size. And the deception certainly had a practical use in battle, since misestimating the length or height of a ship could throw off a torpedo firing solution or even a gunner's optical range finder just enough to make that crucial difference.

"What's . . . going on, sir?" Smitty groaned, breathing

heavily as he struggled for words. From his prostrate position on top of the tube bundle, he had not witnessed any of the events of the last few minutes.

"Nothing, Seaman," Tremain answered with forced confidence. "Our fish hit the target, that's all. You can chalk up one Japanese destroyer for the number one torpedo mount."

Smitty grinned weakly, showing a set of bloodstained teeth in the flickering light. "I knew we'd get 'em, sir. Oh, God, I'm thirsty! Do you see my canteen, sir?"

Tremain looked around the mount for a canteen or a bottle of water, but if any had been there, it must have been blasted over the side with the mount captain. He didn't know how he could comfort the suffering young sailor, and saw little point in it, since it would be over for all of them in just a few minutes. If the boy was lucky, he'd die instantly in one of the first salvos.

As their fates rapidly approached, some of the men on the main deck cursed fervently at the enemy ships, now only four thousand yards off the port beam. Some touted how the Japanese could never stand up to them in a fair fight. Others simply stared at the approaching doom with silent resignation.

The range closed to three thousand yards, almost close enough for the *Chevalier*'s twenty-millimeter guns to engage. But the Japanese admiral was no fool. In perfect unison, the Japanese destroyers simultaneously turned northwest, on a course parallel to that of the spread-out American column. Now the enemy ships were presenting their full broadsides and had an unobstructed line of fire.

Tremain expected them to open up at any moment, grimacing at the thought of what was to come. The Japanese ships continued steaming to the northwest with white froth appearing at their bows and sterns, indicating they had increased speed. When they finally reached their new speed, Tremain's seasoned eye judged them to be traveling near thirty knots.

What the hell were they doing? Tremain thought curiously. The range was opening quickly now, and if they didn't start firing at the American ships soon, they would nullify their entire range-closing maneuver.

But the major barrage never came. Instead, a few guns here and there flashed out along the enemy battle line, their projectiles falling well short of the burning *Selfridge*. The barrage was sporadic, halfhearted, and obviously intended to be little more than harassing fire to cover their retreat. Amazingly, the enemy column steamed away into the darkness, opening the range farther and farther, until the five silhouettes blended in with the dark sea and sky to the northwest, disappearing from view entirely.

They were gone.

As Tremain stood there wondering why the Japanese admiral would beat a hasty retreat in the face of such an overwhelming victory, the answer suddenly came into view. Off to the southeast, in the fading light of the lingering illumination flares, the charging bow of an American destroyer appeared. It was followed by another, then finally a third. It was Captain Larson's task group, arriving on the scene just in the nick of time. The three destroyers must have spent the better part of the last half hour running at flank speed with all boilers on-line to get into the fight, but now the fight was over. They had probably observed the engagement from afar but, being forty-five minutes behind, had been unable to help. Undoubtedly, it was the appearance of the new American destroyers that had prompted the Japanese admiral to retreat. His primary mission had been to protect the transports taking troops off Vella LaVella, and Tremain could only assume that that mission had been accomplished. The Japanese transports were probably halfway across the Solomon Sea by now, scattered and packed to the gills with the thankful defenders of Vella LaVella. By morning, they would reach New Guinea, and live to fight another day. The battle had been a complete victory for the Japanese.

Tremain did not have long to ponder the defeat. The deck beneath his feet suddenly lurched to starboard, coupled with a great vibration which emanated from deep within the bowels of the ship. Belowdecks, one of *Chevalier*'s watertight compartments had probably given way, instantly flooding one side of the ship, placing the ship in danger of capsizing. The battered destroyer could not take much more.

"Abandon ship!" someone on deck yelled. "Abandon ship!"

The mass of men around the amidships deckhouse began filing aft toward the fantail. Two motor whaleboats, presumably from the *O'Bannon*, circled in the waters astern of the *Chevalier*, preparing to come alongside and take the men off. *Chevalier* was settling rapidly now, tilting heavily to starboard until her decks were awash. Girders creaked and groaned in protest of the awkward strain, which weakened even further the already overstressed steel. Sailors hurled life vests, life rafts, wooden crates—anything that would float—into the water, mindful that the two whaleboats did not have enough space to take off the entire crew in one trip, and a second trip might be too late.

"Come on, Smitty," Tremain said as he gently but quickly hefted the young sailor across his shoulders in a fireman carry. Smitty did not protest. In fact, he appeared unconscious, and Tremain immediately feared the worst for the young man. He tried not to concentrate on Smitty's condition for the moment, only on how to get him off the ship.

Until he took the boy's full weight onto his back, Tremain did not realize how weakened his own legs were, probably a side effect from the adrenaline rush and muscle contraction brought on by the concussion of the torpedo blast. His legs and arms shook visibly as he climbed down the starboard ladder to the main deck with Smitty on his back. It was all he could do just to hang on.

As he stepped off the ladder onto the main deck, his shoe plunged into six inches of water. The deck had angled much more than he had realized. The main deck was already submerged on this side of the ship. He had two choices—let go of the ladder and slide into the sea, or let go of Smitty and climb back up to the torpedo mount and skirt over to the port-side ladder, where the main deck was still dry and he might make it to one of the waiting whaleboats. Smitty had not moved once in the last few minutes, but the choice was obvious.

He would stick with Smitty.

Kicking off his shoes, Tremain placed an arm across Smitty's chest, planted his hip firmly into the sailor's back, and stepped off into the cool water. The angled deck quickly fell away beneath his feet as he lugged Smitty away from the ship. He tried not to think about the ocean bottom hundreds of feet below, or about any of the dorsal-finned creatures that might be lurking just beneath the dark waves, or about the layer of putrid fuel oil that now covered his face and freely flowed into his eyes and mouth. He simply swam away as fast as his weary arms and legs could take the combined weight of two men. He had always prided himself on being a good swimmer, hardened by a dozen different beaches at a dozen different homeports throughout his career, but tonight the water seemed to suck the very life out of him. He began to feel disoriented.

There were a hundred reasons you didn't want to be next to a destroyer when it went down. It could capsize and land on top of you. A compartment could implode, creating a swirling eddy that could drag you under. A boiler might explode, exposing your fragile body to a torrent of five-hundred-degree steam bubbles. A depth charge might go off, crushing your body with the resulting pressure wave. There were many grisly deaths to be had floating in the water near a sinking ship, and Tremain swam as fast as he could in an effort to avoid them all. It was a double-edged sword, really. For swimming away from the ship also meant swimming away from the concentration of floating sailors that would eventually beacon the rescuing whaleboats.

Between wave troughs, Tremain caught sight of a few bobbing heads within a few dozen yards of his position. He assumed they were other sailors. He could not be certain in the sporadic moonlight. His low height of eye prevented him from seeing if there were any floatation devices in the water around them. Once or twice, he tried to swim closer to one of the dark bobbing heads, but he never seemed to make any headway. His body was reaching the point of exhaustion, and he began to wonder if he was hallucinating. It was all he could do to keep Smitty's lolling head above the water, and he was certain that he could only manage it for a few more minutes. Soon, he would have to let Smitty go or risk being pulled under himself.

The thought had hardly had time to rankle in his brain, when an oily hand and muscular arm suddenly appeared before his face. The hand grabbed the collar of Smitty's shirt and yanked the unconscious sailor out of Tremain's grasp and out of the water. Before Tremain's exhausted mind could realize what was going on, the same hand and arm lifted him out of the water.

Moments later he found himself on his back, his legs and one arm dangling into the lapping water, as he lay across the flat wooden frame and web netting of a life raft. A humid breeze wafted across his wet skin and sent a chill running through his sore body. As he regained his breath and his senses, he was surprised to see Fabriano's grim face hovering over Smitty's prostrate form, lying next to him. Fabriano nodded briefly to Tremain before turning his attention back to the unmoving Smitty. The young torpedoman's eyes stared emptily up at the dark clouds through half-open eyelids.

"He's gone," Fabriano finally said soberly.

Tremain sat upright and coughed up a few mouthfuls of oily saltwater. All of his efforts to keep the boy from sinking had been in vain. For all he knew, the boy was dead before they had abandoned ship.

When he had sufficiently regained his breath, Tremain got the chance to sit up and look around. The *Chevalier*'s dark hulk lay a hundred yards away, and the battle's devastation was all too clear. The broken tatters of her superstructure hung loosely over the spot where her bow had been ripped away. A giant hole gaped in her forward stack, where some large piece of equipment—possibly the port-side torpedo director along with Wally McCandles's head and arms—had gone clean through on its way skyward. She sat much lower in the water, but her starboard list had subsided a little, most likely due to the countereffect of bulkheads breaking and compartments flooding up forward. Puttering whaleboats sifted through the bobbing heads all around her stern, pulling up survivors and busily ferrying them back to the nearby *O'Bannon*. Eventually, the boats would make it over this way and rescue them as well.

Farther off in the distance, the *Selfridge* appeared to have contained her fires, although her damage appeared extensive. Like the *O'Bannon*, she would need a prolonged period in the shipyard, but she would survive this night.

"Why'd you bother to rescue me?" Tremain asked Fabriano, who was still leaning over the dead Smitty.

Fabriano shrugged. "Call it a moment of sympathy, sir."

Tremain smiled wearily, and then noticed something on

the raft next to him. It was a small, tightly wrapped canvas bag, and Tremain guessed that it contained some of Fabriano's personal belongings. Fabriano appeared to notice Tremain's interest and quickly moved the bag to his other side and out of sight.

"I still hate all you submariners . . . *sir!*" Fabriano sneered, appearing slightly uncomfortable, or annoyed that Tremain had been eyeing the bag.

Fabriano had obviously meant the remark in defiance, and, at a time like this, it should have invoked all of the rage brewing inside Tremain, but it didn't. Instead, it had the exact opposite effect. He found himself laughing from deep within himself, laughter with tears, uncontrollable laughter that echoed across the water and turned the heads of several dozen floating sailors. The laughter was completely inappropriate in the presence of the dead Smitty, completely out of place in light of the dismal battle, and half the men that heard it must have thought he was crazy, but it felt so good. It felt so good to laugh again, after so long.

"What will you do now, Fabriano?" Tremain asked curiously, ignoring the petty officer's impertinence. "You've had two ships shot out from under you now. That's a surefire ticket back to the States. You can kick your feet up at some shore job for the rest of the war, if you want."

"I'll find another ship, sir," Fabriano said succinctly.

"Another destroyer perhaps? Then you can go on hating submariners."

At this, Fabriano looked at Tremain quizzically, but only for a brief moment. His gaze then shifted past Tremain's shoulder to the meandering whaleboats beyond.

"I think they're coming for us now, sir."

Tremain could hear the puttering whaleboat getting closer but did not turn to look at it. Instead, he kept his eyes fixed solidly on Fabriano.

"I have a proposition for you," Tremain said slyly. "Call it a challenge, from an old submariner who thinks you've still got a lot to learn. I'm curious to know if a man who despises submariners so much could ever last a single day in their shoes."

Fabriano looked more defiant than ever, but Tremain's challenge must have piqued his curiosity, because he took his attention off the approaching whaleboat and focused squarely on Tremain.

"Go on, sir," he said skeptically. "I'm listening."

PART II

PART II

Chapter 4

Fremantle, Australia
November 1943

IT was one of those balmy days in Fremantle, Australia—one of those days when the low, puffy clouds floated over the town and changed shape before drifting out to sea. From his position in the backseat of the drab green staff car, Tremain rolled down the windows and took in deep breaths of the splendid coastal air, clearing his head after the long hours spent cooped up in the C47 "Gooney Bird." It had been a long, buffeting flight from Brisbane, wedged in with the rest of the passengers between two big crates of who knows what—obviously something more important than any of the rest of them—but the plane had made it here in one piece, and he was thankful for that.

A WAVE lieutenant in the driver's seat skillfully navigated the staff car through the Fremantle traffic, her subtle perfume wafting into the backseat and out the open window, driving Tremain's senses wild. He thought it odd that she would have such an effect on him. She was a lieutenant, perhaps thirty years old, and somewhat attractive—pretty, in a sort of no-nonsense way. There was nothing really special about her, except perhaps her smile when she met him at the airfield. Her smile carried with it that delightful blend of amusement and mischief that somehow woke the animal within him, and he found himself staring wistfully at the back of her head. Her long, dark brown hair was done up in regulation style, and he began to wonder how it might look draped across her pale, naked back. He began to wonder where she was from, whether or not she was married, and how she felt about submarine commanders. Of course, these feelings left him with a sense of guilt, especially so soon after losing Judy, but he had them nonetheless.

Suddenly, he noticed that the WAVE was looking at him in the rearview mirror. He instinctively directed his eyes elsewhere, and felt his face turn beet red in an instant. He had not been prepared for that, and could only imagine how he had appeared to her. For all he knew, he had been drooling, with his mouth hanging open. But a muffled giggle from the front seat told him that she was probably more entertained than offended.

They made a right turn onto Queen Victoria Street and entered downtown Fremantle. It had been almost a year since Tremain had commanded the *Seatrout* out of this homeport, and now he relished immersing himself in all of the familiar sights and sounds once again. While many things looked the same in Fremantle, many things had certainly changed, most notably the vast horde of soldiers and sailors from a half-dozen Allied countries lounging, walking to and fro, and lining Fremantle's narrow sidewalks, turning the onetime quiet coastal town into a bustling hodgepodge of multicolored uniforms. Like a swarm, they filled the local establishments and restaurants, giving the owners more business than they could ever have hoped, or wished, for in a lifetime. Everywhere, young faces of all colors smiled, laughed, and jeered in the sun, as if this were merely a huge Boy Scout rendezvous and not the remote forward outpost of a horrific world war.

Who could blame them? thought Tremain. Who knew what the future could bring? Live life to the full while you can, young lads. In a month's time, you may be dead.

As the car drove on, Tremain thought he recognized some

of the smiling faces whizzing by, but he knew it was merely a trick of the mind. His men on the *Seatrout* were long since gone, lying quietly in a dark, watery tomb beneath some distant sea. But their expressions, their quirks, their faces sporadically materialized in these young men passing by.

Eventually, the crowds lining the streets diminished as the car left the downtown area and made a sharp left turn onto Stirling Highway, heading north onto Stirling Bridge. As the car reached the bridge, which crossed the Swan River at the eastern edge of the Fremantle harbor, Tremain got his first glimpse of the waterfront. On this sunny Sunday afternoon, several dozen merchant ships and tankers of various allied flags rode gently on the harbor swells, their sides pushed up against nearly every available foot of pier space around the rectangular harbor. Along the North Wharf, a small fleet of warships also rode at their moorings. Among them sat two or three squadrons of submarines nested in long rows which extended out into the harbor from two immense tender ships.

"In case you were wondering, that's your boat over there, Commander. The *Whitefin*."

Two smiling eyes in the rearview mirror stared back at him. She had obviously noticed him curiously gazing at the harbor.

He hesitated for a moment, somewhat disturbed that she had read his thoughts exactly. But then finally he asked, "Which one is she?"

"She's the third one in," she said, pointing her hand out the open window. "There, on the starboard side of the old *Pelias*."

From his first glance at the harbor, Tremain had noticed the familiar bulky shape of the submarine tender *Pelias*. The unwieldy, awkward ship with its wide beam and jumble of cranes was a floating repair and supply ship for submarines, equipped with everything from machine shops to spare torpedoes. He'd moored alongside her in the *Seatrout* countless times, and right now several submarines were doing the same. The *Pelias* had her port side up against the wharf, a clutter of lines, cables, and hoses drooping from her high bulwarks down to the decks of the submarines. Even from this distance, Tremain could clearly make out the slim shapes of the five fleet boats nested on her starboard side. The mammoth tender completely dwarfed the little boats, all moored side by side and completely indistinguishable from one another except for a few minute variations above the waterline. But as similar as all the submarines were, Tremain's eyes focused on only one, his boat, the third boat in the line—the *Whitefin*. The gradual sloping deck, the businesslike conning tower, the soaring masts and periscopes all looked identical to any other submarine on the waterfront, but this was *his* boat, and that made her special. He began to feel that familiar surge of pride he had felt only twice before in his career. It was a feeling that never waned, no matter how many times Tremain experienced it, and he found himself looking over his shoulder out the car's back window, completely spellbound by the handsome submarine until the car reached the end of the bridge and a mass of trees and buildings obstructed his view. He had a sudden urge to go aboard her. He couldn't wait to get acquainted with his new ship, just to feel the cold steel of her bridge railing under his fingers, just to let her oily diesel fumes fill his nostrils. He was so preoccupied with the notion that he almost missed the main gate to the North Quay as it zipped by.

The WAVE giggled, apparently quite amused at his daydreaming.

"You've got the longing stare of a little boy looking in the window of a candy store, Commander."

Tremain glanced at her eyes in the rearview mirror, wondering exactly which longing stare she was referring to.

"You seem to have an odd interest in submarines yourself, Lieutenant. And, by the way, didn't we just miss our turn?"

"Actually, they're all the same to me, sir. And, no, we didn't miss our turn, because we're not going to the wharf. Today's Sunday, and the admiral spends his Sundays in the country. We're going to his getaway house, just outside Perth. Don't you worry, it won't take us long to get there." She added with playful eyes, "There should be plenty of things for you to look at along the way."

"So, how long have you been driving for the admiral?" he asked, trying to steer the conversation toward something he could control.

"I'm not his driver," she said, for the first time sounding slightly offended. "I'm his personal secretary. The usual marine driver is on liberty today. I like getting out of the office and going for a spin every now and then, so I volunteered to pick you up."

"I'm sorry."

"About what, Commander?"

"I'm sorry I didn't catch your first name."

She paused for a moment, and then smiled again with a mock salute. "It's Melinda. Lieutenant Melinda Lawhead, reporting for duty, sir."

"My name's Jack."

She eyed him suspiciously in the mirror for a long moment, and he could have kicked himself for being such an idiot. Could he have been any more forward?

They drove on in uncomfortable silence. She turned onto another road that headed inland, and the car quickly sped away from Fremantle and the bustle of activity around the harbor. Soon they had passed through the larger and even livelier town of Perth and were heading into the Australian countryside with rolling hills in all directions, dotted by clumps of wild trees. Despite the surrounding beauty, both inside the car and out, Tremain could not get his mind off the *Whitefin*. His month-long journey from New London had almost come to an end. He'd had but a mere glimpse of his final destination. Once aboard her, he would truly be home again—the only home he had now. Whatever the admiral had to say to him, he hoped it would be brief.

A few miles outside of Perth, Melinda suddenly pulled off the road onto a hidden drive which Tremain would not have seen had she sped past it. The drive led between two clumps of trees, through a thick patch of brush, and then suddenly came to a small gatehouse that obviously served as the entry point to an immense property surrounded by a ten-foot block wall topped with barbed wire. Melinda stopped the car, and two helmeted but otherwise resplendent marines in olive drab, bearing M1 carbine rifles, instantly appeared at the windows on both sides. She flashed her identification to the closest marine as casually as if she were ordering him to check the tires. Without being prompted, Tremain did the same, and after a brief check, both marines snapped to attention and waved them through.

The menacing fence around the property was obviously something constructed for the war's benefit, because once through the gates, Tremain found that they had entered one of the most cultivated and polished landscapes he had ever seen in western Australia. The bush had been beaten back from these grounds for several generations, and they were now immaculate green with a perfectly maintained grass lawn surrounding a large two-story mansion situated on a sloping hill at the end of the winding drive. The house matched the grounds with its splendor and had most likely been built during the colonial era, with the English influence still quite apparent. Surrounded by the exquisite lawn and shaded by the great canopy of half a dozen century-old eucalyptus trees, it had that cozy feeling of the various noble estates Tremain had visited with Judy during their many trips to London before the war. It was cozy, except for the maze of very modern communications antennas protruding from the roof.

As they pulled into the drive, Tremain started to utter some kind of thank-you to Melinda, but before he had the chance, a marine in white gloves appeared and opened the door, ushering him out of the car, up the stairs, and through the open double doors of the house, where he was met by a well-groomed naval lieutenant junior grade, flawlessly bedecked in dress khaki uniform jacket and trousers, topped off by a perfectly centered black tie. A gold-braided epaulette hung neatly from one shoulder, denoting him as the flag lieutenant. Tremain was so distracted by the glimmering epaulette that he missed the young man's face entirely, not to mention the fact that the young officer had been grinning from ear to ear from the moment he entered the house.

Tremain's eyes came to rest on the dingy pair of gold dolphins worn over the young officer's left breast pocket. It was the only thing unsatisfactory about the lieutenant's otherwise perfectly manicured uniform, and he could tell that the lieutenant had spent many long nights applying coat after coat of polish to try to improve the appearance of the ancient set of "fish."

The gold dolphins had been new once, long ago, when two

young and naked newlyweds drank champagne to their cele-
brated significance in front of a roaring fireplace on a snowy
New London night. But the dolphins were old now and beyond
saving. They had seen far too many watches on the bridges of
windswept submarines over the past sixteen years.

Tremain knew this, because this particular set of gold dolphins had once been his.

"Lieutenant Commander Tremain, sir!" a familiar voice
said energetically.

"Ryan!" Tremain said, extending his hand to this now very
recognizable young officer. "Ryan Wright, what a surprise to
see you Down Under!"

Lieutenant Ryan Wright had been an officer in Tremain's
last command, the *Mackerel*. Only six months had passed
since they had last seen each other in Pearl Harbor, but it
seemed like ages. The *Mackerel* had been an interim command for Tremain, a short diversion on his way back to New
London after giving up the reins of the *Seatrout*. But during
those brief months as *Mackerel*'s temporary captain, he had
grown quite attached to her officers and crew. He felt a special
regard for Wright, whose efforts had saved the *Mackerel* on
more than one occasion. Through numerous harrowing battles, Wright had proved his worth as an officer and as a submariner time and time again. In fact, he had shown such
potential that Tremain had felt a fatherly impulse to ensure
that the young officer's talents were not wasted. Before leaving the *Mackerel* to report to submarine school in New London, and his long-awaited reunion with Judy, Tremain had
given his original set of gold dolphins to Wright as a parting
gift, and also as a symbol of Wright's new status as a fully
qualified submarine officer. That was six months ago, when
Wright was a mere ensign. Now, as a lieutenant junior grade,
the young officer looked older and different in so many ways.
The wide eyes of a green ensign had been replaced by the ma-
ture, wizened eyes of a submarine veteran.

"I can't tell you how thrilled I was when I heard that you
were coming, sir. I was overjoyed," Wright said, still grinning.
"I never thought I'd see you out here again, sir."

Wright casually patted the gold dolphins on his chest. Obviously, the gift had meant a lot to him, since he now chose to

wear the dilapidated insignia instead of replacing it with a newer set, which any flag lieutenant certainly had ample access to.

"You never thought you'd see me? Hell, Wright, the last time I saw you, you were laid up in the hospital in Pearl."

"If you remember, Captain, you were laid up there yourself."

"And look at you now. A lieutenant junior grade—and a flag lieutenant, at that."

"Yes, sir. I can't imagine who in the world could've recommended me for it," Wright said facetiously.

"Now, don't go blaming me for that gold lasso you're wearing."

"Well, regardless, Captain, I never got the chance to thank you." Wright touched the old set of gold dolphins. "Thanks for everything."

Tremain patted Wright on the shoulder.

"You earned it, Ryan. And it's great seeing you again. Just like old times. Now," Tremain's voice suddenly took on a professional tone as his eyes glanced at the staircase leading up to the second floor, "is he ready for me?"

"The admiral will be with you shortly, sir," Wright said formally, but then said under his breath, "Let me show you to his study. His, er . . . other guest has already arrived and is waiting there."

"Other guest?" Tremain responded uncertainly.

But Wright remained tight-lipped, ushering Tremain up the staircase and down a large hall to another set of double doors. Pushing both doors open, Wright admitted Tremain into an enormous octagonal study ringed with bookcases on every wall, their shelves filled to capacity from floor to ceiling with rich maroon and black leather-bound books of all sizes. Four large windows with their curtains drawn looked out onto the stunning lawn below. The room contained little furniture except for a few large leather chairs the color of burgundy and an eccentrically clean mahogany desk situated in the middle of the room. The room, like the rest of the house, smelled of mildew, revealing its age, and the floorboards creaked under every step of Tremain's shoes. But despite its age, the room seemed suitable for a flag officer of any navy. Tremain found himself wondering how many uses the room had seen in its long history, or if its designers ever conceived that it might be used as a country office for an American admiral in a great world war.

"The admiral will be right with you, Commander," Wright said stiffly, shooting a friendly smile at Tremain before leaving the room and closing the big double doors behind him.

Close to a minute had transpired before Tremain realized that he was not in the room alone. At the opposite end, casually leafing through the pages of a particularly ancient-looking volume, stood a flawlessly groomed officer of the British Army—or at least, that's what Tremain deduced from the loose-fitting khaki trousers and blouse. The man appeared to be Caucasian, but one could scarcely tell since his skin was so tan that he could have belonged to any one of a dozen ethnicities. Tucked into one shoulder epaulette was a folded beige beret displaying the winged sword emblem of the British SAS. The color of the beret matched the man's short, blond hair, which was oiled and neatly combed over to one side. From all appearances he looked to be roughly Tremain's same age. But whether he was older or younger, senior or junior, the British officer made no acknowledgment whatsoever of Tremain's presence, never once even looking up from his book, as if Tremain had never entered the room at all. Only the persistent ticking of an enormous grandfather clock in the far corner disturbed the thick silence between them.

It wasn't long before a bookcase on one side of the room suddenly opened, revealing a hidden door into an adjoining chamber, and Rear Admiral Steven Ireland emerged. He paused for a moment just inside the open door, speaking over his shoulder to an unseen person in the room beyond. That all-too-familiar deep, callous voice stirred a thousand latent memories in Tremain's mind, both good and awful.

". . . and tell him he'd better get those damned fuel trucks moving up to Exmouth Gulf before the week is out or there'll be hell to pay!"

A voice in the other room uttered something like a weak acknowledgment, before Ireland closed the bookshelf door behind him.

"Hello, Jack," he said in a suddenly sociable tone, marching across the room and extending a hand. "So good to see you again."

"Hello, Admiral Ireland."

They greeted each other as would two casual acquaintances, but their relationship was much more complex than it appeared on the surface. Tremain had served under Ireland in various commands, including once as his XO when Ireland commanded a submarine before the war, and more recently as one of his captains when Ireland commanded Submarine Division Seven, the division that the *Mackerel* had belonged to. Over the years, their relationship had vacillated with the tides—sometimes cordial, sometimes fraternal, and sometimes downright icy. Tremain had last seen Ireland six months ago in the hospital at the Pearl Harbor naval base. The admiral had been only a captain back then and had come to visit Tremain, who was recovering from the wounds he had received on the *Kurita* mission. Ireland's visit had been a brief, but friendly one. In one of the warmest tones Tremain ever heard him utter, Ireland had wished him all the best at his new sub school assignment, as well as a happy reunion with Judy. Though somewhat discomforting, it had been a good parting, all in all.

Ireland had seemed so much younger back then. Now he had bags under his eyes, and the close-cut hair appeared almost white. There was something slightly dragging and worn out about his countenance, something only noticeable to one who had known him as long as Tremain had. His regulation black tie, khaki shirt and trousers, perhaps the same uniform Tremain had seen him wearing six months ago in Pearl Harbor, hung loosely on his frame as if he had lost ten or fifteen pounds. But despite these initial observations, Tremain had little doubt that the admiral was still as spry as any twenty-year-old on the waterfront.

"Might I congratulate you on your promotion to admiral, sir?"

Ireland shook his head dismissively.

"Let me start off by expressing my sincerest condolences to you, Jack. I'm so sorry about Judy. She was a splendid woman. Such a loss."

Tremain gave an appreciative nod, though in the back of his mind he felt like Ireland was merely dispensing with the obligatory sympathetic remarks to avoid appearing as the complete cold-blooded ogre he really was.

"Now," Ireland said perfunctorily, as if to say, *Now that that's out of the way.* "I assume the two of you have met?"

"Don't believe I've had the pleasure, old boy." The British officer was suddenly standing next to him, having discarded the book and crossed the room in the blink of an eye, his merry accented voice bearing no indication that he had been rudely ignoring Tremain only moments before.

"Lieutenant Commander Jack Tremain, this is Major Ian Farquhar of His Majesty's Royal Army."

"How do you do," Tremain said, shaking the major's icy but firm hand.

"Major Farquhar is with the Royal Army commandos, on special assignment here," Ireland said, eyeing Tremain coolly. "He flew in just this morning from General MacArthur's headquarters."

Major Farquhar kept the smile plastered to his face, but Tremain could tell that he was inwardly sizing him up.

"The major specializes in guerilla warfare," Ireland continued. "He spent some time in Malaya and . . . other places. He's going with you on this patrol, Jack. You'll be delivering him to a classified location, and then picking him up again three weeks later. But don't worry, everything's specified in your sealed orders."

"Very well, sir."

"You're in good hands, Major. Commander Tremain is one of my best captains, a *real* submariner. He's served under me on numerous occasions."

"If you say so, sir. I can see that he every bit fits the part."

Tremain did not like the way Farquhar spoke about him in the third person. He especially did not like Farquhar's delightful smirk, or his aloof glance at the hem of Tremain's khaki trousers, which rode a full two inches above his ankles. Tremain cursed inwardly but kept up an outwardly warm smile. During the stopover in Brisbane, he had had to buy new uniforms to replace the ones he lost aboard the *Chevalier*. A uniform shop reasonably close to the train station had come recommended, but the damned tailor had botched the job. These trousers were the best he could salvage from the lot.

Ireland chuckled heartily. "Don't you worry, Major. Commander Tremain may look like a lubberly midshipman, but he's the real deal. He'll get you where you need to go."

"Oh, I'm not worried at all, Admiral," Farquhar said airily. "I've worked with enough Americans to know that I shouldn't judge them by their outward appearance."

"So what is my mission, precisely, Admiral?" Tremain asked irritably, now more than a little annoyed.

"It's to get me to my destination as fast as you possibly can," interjected Farquhar in a suddenly forceful tone; then he paused for a moment before continuing in an amiable manner, "Sorry to be such a bore, old boy, but that is all you need to know for now. It's all hush-hush mumbo jumbo you needn't concern yourself with."

"It's all in your sealed orders, Jack," Ireland added, as if sensing that he needed to temper the fury brewing inside Tremain. "Tomorrow evening, when Rottnest Light is far in your wake, you can open them. Understood? You'll be getting under way tomorrow at oh-nine-hundred hours."

"Of course, you never know who's watching the shipping in the harbor these days," Farquhar said with raised eyebrows. "Nor what some bloody shipyard loafer's going to blather over his beer in the pub the next day. You never can be too careful, you know. Don't suppose you'd have an extra set of khakis I could borrow, would you, old boy? You know, just to get me aboard discreetly." Farquhar cast a pitiable glance at Tremain's trouser leg. "Perhaps you'd have a pair a little longer than those?"

Tremain bit his tongue, holding back the impulse to tell the major just where he could put his khaki trousers.

"I'll be going aboard ship before the sun comes up, Major," Tremain finally managed to say with forced courtesy. "You're more than welcome to come aboard with me at oh-four-thirty, if it suits you. It should be dark enough for you to get aboard relatively unnoticed."

"Splendid!" Ireland said quickly, before Farquhar could respond. "It's settled then. Now, Major, if you don't mind, I'd like to have a few private words with Commander Tremain."

"Certainly, sir," Farquhar said indifferently, popping up a quick openhanded salute to the admiral, then nodding casually to Tremain. "Until tomorrow morning then, Commander."

"Until tomorrow, Major."

After Farquhar had left the room, closing the large double doors behind him, Ireland keyed a buzzer on the desk. An instant later, the WAVE lieutenant, Melinda, entered the room carrying a carafe of coffee and two cups on a small tray. She smiled briefly at Tremain as she crossed to the desk, and then poured two cups of the steaming brew, the first of which she handed to the admiral. Tremain noticed the two make eye contact for the briefest of moments, but it was long enough for him to jump to conclusions about their relationship. The awkward hesitation, slight and barely perceptible, spoke volumes. There was something between them that went beyond the role of admiral and secretary. That much was obvious. Somehow, the pretty WAVE with the alluring smile and enticing eyes had gotten involved with the admiral. Just the thought of Old Ireland having an affair with a woman practically young enough to be his daughter—a woman Tremain had come on to so lamely only moments before—made him slightly nauseous. After all, he had never known Ireland to do anything outside the professional boundaries of the submarine service. In the past, he had always seen Ireland as a dispassionate upholder of the faith of their profession—a submariner monk of sorts—sworn to a celibate life of duty beneath the sea. Tremain had never taken Ireland for one to have a fling on the side, but then there were probably a lot of things he did not know about the man, despite the fact that their careers had intertwined on too many occasions to count.

As Melinda handed Tremain the other cup of coffee, he noticed that there was more hiding under the surface than originally had met his eye. She seemed uncomfortable, wearing a smile that appeared somewhat compulsory. And it left Tremain to wonder if her relationship with the admiral were something in the past, not the present. Perhaps their relationship had ended in a bad way, and now Ireland only kept her on his staff to avoid the story getting out.

But it was all purely speculation on his part, Tremain concluded, and the idea certainly did not stop his eyes from following Melinda's rather striking form as she exited the room, leaving the two men alone.

"You have friends in high places, Commander," Ireland said in a businesslike tone, much different from the one he had used when the British major was in the room. Perhaps he had taken notice of Tremain's trancelike gaze.

"I'm not sure I follow you, sir."

"This is something I would never say in front of the major, or anyone else for that matter, Jack, but you should know this. I strongly disapproved of your request for a new command."

"You disapproved?"

"Yes, I did." Ireland nodded evenly. "But what I think doesn't seem to matter much to ComSubPac. I voiced my dissent to Admiral Lockwood in the strongest terms, but he outranks me so here you sit. Evidently he, or one of his staffers, caught wind that you were looking for another command and they pushed your orders through. So, you can thank ComSubPac for giving you a boat, not me. I guess they feel like they owe you something, after the *Kurita* mission you pulled off with the *Mackerel*, putting that Japanese battleship on the bottom within a stone's throw of the Japanese coast. I guess they feel you can be of some use out here."

Tremain felt confused, somewhat betrayed, and immeasurably irritated. To think that Ireland, his mentor and near father figure, had not stood up for him, after all the years of service they had had together, it was a despicable act.

"I'm afraid I don't understand, Admiral." Tremain did his best to temper his tone of voice.

"I'm not sure I understand either, Commander. I'm not sure why a certain submarine captain, who was begging me to put him ashore not six months ago, now suddenly wants back in the war. I'm not sure how a certain submarine captain with a medically disqualifying concussion suddenly and miraculously gets cleared for sea service. You can bet I'll be looking into that, by damn!"

Tremain kept his best poker face. The navy physician whose clearing signature appeared on his medical record was an old family friend—an old family friend who had given in only after many dinners at the best restaurants in New London.

"The original prognosis by the doctor in Pearl Harbor was in error, sir. I'm fully recovered now."

"Do you expect me to believe that?"

"Yes, sir, I do."

"Well, it doesn't matter, anyway. The reason I disapproved of your request had nothing to do with your physical readiness. I don't think you're fit to command anymore, Jack. Hell, I don't even think you're fit to be my valet. It's your motivation for getting back in the war, that's what concerns me. That's why I disapproved your request."

"My motivation, sir?"

"Have you ever done something simply because it was your duty, Commander? That's what I really want to know, because I don't think you ever have. At least, not in my experience with Jack Tremain. I think Jack Tremain has been, and always will be, in it for himself."

"You have the gall to say that to me, *Admiral*, after all the bullshit you've put me through? I've taken damn near every mission you've given me, accomplished every last one of them with flying colors—including that damn mess with the *Kurita*! I've done every last thing you've ever asked me to do, and now you have the balls to lecture me on duty!"

"If you remember correctly, Commander," Ireland interjected, "you begged me to let you go on the *Kurita* mission—once again for your own reasons. There was no sense of duty in it. You wanted to go on that mission because you'd grown attached to the *Mackerel*'s crew and you felt a captain's loyalty toward them. You didn't give a hoot in hell about the mission, and don't try to tell me any differently!"

Frustrated, mostly because there was much truth in what Ireland said, Tremain pointed a menacing finger at the two silver stars on Ireland's collar. "It's *my* blood, and that of *my* men, that won you *those*, damn it! Not to mention Judy's broken heart. You kept me in the Pacific while she was dying back home—yes, dying, you son of a bitch! She was dying while I was off on one of your damn missions! I lost precious months with her, months I'll never get back. So you and your damn duty can just go to hell, Admiral!"

Tremain took a deep breath. He knew that his face was an

angry red, and that he had ventured well beyond any understandable skirting of the customary etiquette due to a flag officer. But Ireland had gotten to him, and now he had gone over the top. From the smug expression affixed on Ireland's face, it was exactly the response that he had been waiting for. Ireland now had what he wanted—a reason to take away his boat. One little tirade like that, one uncontrolled display of emotion, was all Ireland needed to declare him unfit for command.

"Are you quite through, Commander?" Ireland finally said calmly, as if it were a common occurrence for one of his captains to fly off the handle in such a manner.

Trying his utmost to regain his composure, Tremain nodded and slouched down in the leather chair.

"I know these are hard words, and you don't want to hear them," Ireland said with slightly less enmity, "but I've got a lot more at stake here than Jack Tremain's pride. Sure, you're one hell of a submarine skipper, I'll give you that. I've always thought that. You've shown me you can do a bang-up job on any mission—as long as I'm holding a carrot at the end of it."

Tremain started to butt in, but Ireland silenced him with a raised hand.

"And that's the real rub here, Jack. You're a remarkable commander, believe you me, and you've done some incredible things for me—but only when I gave you some personal reason to do them. Whatever it was, whether some promised promotion, or promised shore leave at home with Judy, or promised accolades to the men under you, I always knew how to get Jack Tremain back out to sea."

Ireland paused as a wave of uncharacteristic emotion flashed across his face, as if it actually pained him to say these things. He casually strolled over to look out the nearest window.

"I'm not holding out a carrot this time, Jack," Ireland said distantly, the sunlight shining brightly onto his face, outlining every crack and crevice, as he gazed down at the green lawn below. "There's no pot of gold at the end of this rainbow. I honestly don't know why Jack Tremain wants to come back to sea. So, I can only guess why. And you know what my guess is? My guess is Jack Tremain's come back here to die. He's lost his wife, and with her everything he's ever loved in the world. He sees no more reason to go on, so he's decided to let the Japanese put him out of his misery. That little foray on the *Chevalier* only confirms it in my mind. You've lost your sense of self-preservation, Jack, your very will to live, and that frightens me. It frightens me for you, but even more for the crew of the *Whitefin*. I don't need a sub commander who's going to throw away his own life along with a fleet submarine and her eighty-man crew."

"I can assure you, Admiral, those are not my intentions."

Tremain self-consciously dismissed Ireland's deductions as complete nonsense. He didn't have a death wish. He just wanted to get to sea again, and do his part in the war, that was all. What the hell did Ireland know about real loss, anyway?

"Well, it's out of my hands now, anyway. The *Whitefin* has to sail, and you're her commander for the time being." Ireland paused, and then repeated, "For the time being."

Ireland turned away from the window and walked back over to the leather chair where Tremain sat. He gave him an almost fatherly pat on the shoulder, as if to imply that it was nothing personal, and that they could now move on to other things.

"That action off Vella LaVella was pretty awful, I expect," he said, this time in a much friendlier tone.

"Pretty bad, sir." Tremain nodded, still trying to digest the twisted logic Ireland had presented him with moments before.

"I've read the report. One destroyer sunk, two more knocked out of action, over a hundred men killed or missing. And as far as we can tell the Japs lost only one ship, not to mention they got all their troops off Vella LaVella." Ireland paused, staring into his coffee cup. "I hear the *Shigure* even showed up that night."

"I actually got a look at her, sir, from about three thousand yards."

"Did you really?" Ireland asked in an eager voice. He was talking now as if they were old friends again, as if the whole haranguing about not being fit to be his valet had never happened. "Damn shame those DDs didn't put a couple fish into her. *Damn* shame! I'd give my left nut to have the *Shigure* on the bottom. That blasted Jap bastard's been a bane to us down here, you know. But then of course you would know, wouldn't you, Jack, since your old boat was the first one she racked up."

"What? I'm sorry, Admiral, did you say the *Seatrout* . . . ?" Ireland had said it in such a passive manner, so matter-of-factly, that Tremain almost missed what he said.

"Heavens, Jack, I thought you knew! Of course, we've only just received the report ourselves, so maybe you don't know. Well, the story goes like this. One of our operatives in New Guinea got word that the captain of the *Shigure* was ordered back to Rabaul a couple months ago to receive a medal for sinking four of our submarines. Don't ask me how our intel boys got their hands on it, but they ended up with a copy of the bloody citation. Hell, maybe the Japanese transmitted it back to Combined Fleet HQ and one of our listening posts picked it up. Who knows? But it had everything, Jack—dates, locations, you name it. It clearly stated that the *Shigure*'s first victim was an American submarine caught in the Philippine Sea back in January of this year. That corresponds perfectly with the last position reported by the *Seatrout*. It's all unconfirmed, of course, but we had no other subs in the area at the time, so we can only deduce . . . Well, you know how these things go."

The memory of the sub and crew he had lost was still vivid in Tremain's mind. Almost a year had passed, but he still remembered each man's name, each hometown, even the names of their wives and girlfriends back home. From the evacuation of Manila at the beginning of the war, to Java, and through some of the first submarine patrols against the Imperial Fleet, Tremain had commanded them, and together they had made a good team. The *Seatrout* sank 15,240 tons of Japanese shipping before he received orders to transfer back to the States. He could still see them covering *Seatrout*'s main deck and small conning tower, their faces beaming, their hands waving wildly in a last tribute to their former captain as they pulled away from the pier for the last time. The sight of his ship leaving port without him had left Tremain feeling empty inside, but that emptiness could not compare with the overwhelming sense of guilt that consumed him several weeks later, when he learned that the *Seatrout* had been declared missing and presumed sunk.

"I can see that her loss still bothers you," Ireland said glibly.

Tremain noticed Ireland's eyes suddenly shift to a spot on the wall, as if the normally unflappable admiral had suffered a brief moment of embarrassment at having brought up the painful subject.

What the hell was Ireland up to? The crusty old bastard was the king of manipulation, one reason Tremain never felt at ease around him. Ireland didn't make idle conversation. To Ireland, everything had a purpose, and Tremain was beginning to think that this little piece of intelligence about the *Shigure* had been shared with him selectively. But if Ireland didn't trust him—a fact he had made abundantly clear only minutes ago—why would he bother to bring up this dismal piece of news about the *Shigure*? What possible purpose could it serve? Perhaps Ireland was trying to give him another "carrot," as he had called it, something to live for, like retribution for his lost crew on the *Seatrout*. But the fires of revenge no longer burned within Tremain's heart. He no longer blamed the Japanese for what had happened to his ship and crew. The captain of the *Shigure*, like any captain on either side, was only doing his duty when he sank the *Seatrout*. It was just another tragedy of war.

At least, that's what he believed most of the time.

"Jack, there are still a few things I want to tell you about this patrol," Ireland said, in a completely different tone. "After you drop off the major, your orders will direct you to proceed to a patrol area in the South China Sea, and of course to sink any enemy shipping encountered there. It's nothing you haven't seen before. But what your orders won't tell you is *why*. And you know, Jack, I like to be forthcoming and up front with my captains as much as possible. I like my captains to know *why*."

Tremain thought of the many words he'd applied to the admiral during his career. Never once had he used the terms *up front* or *forthcoming*.

"You see, Jack," Ireland continued, "MacArthur's been pushing the Japanese across the Solomons for the better part of a year now—island hopping, advancing, island hopping, advancing—until now we're at the doorstep of their big naval base at Rabaul. Any fool with half a brain can see that the writing's on the wall. Soon, the Japanese are going to lose

New Guinea, and once that's gone, their supply lines from the East Indies will be in real jeopardy. Hell, the Japanese aren't fools. They know what's happening, and they're trying to suck off every last drop of crude while they can and fetch it back to the Japanese homeland. And to do this, they're sending large convoys of tankers, larger than anything we've ever seen before, ten or fifteen at a pop. We already know of two such convoys that slipped by in the last few weeks. Both made it all the way to Japan virtually unmolested because our subs were off covering other areas. That's partly the fault of our intelligence, and partly my fault. I'm determined to not let that happen again. The next fleet of tankers is going to end up on the bottom or I'm personally going to give up my stars. This time, we've got better intelligence, and we've got enough submarines to use concentration of force. Intel reports indicate that the next tanker fleet is assembling in Kobe harbor with hulls high in the water. Their tanks are bone dry, no doubt, ready to load up all the crude they can carry from Singapore, Jakarta, and Hong Kong. We also know that the escort for this fleet is expected to be relatively light, and that the Japs intend to cover the convoy primarily with land-based aircraft all the way down. They'll probably play it cautious, ducking in and out of ports, drawing big 'Z's' in the ocean, but we're going to have a picket line of subs waiting for them, covering almost every sector. Once you deliver the major to his destination, you'll be taking your boat to the South China Sea to become a part of this picket line. Your boat and the other boats will be strung out for a thousand miles across the tankers' likely route, with each boat patrolling its own sector. So, it's vitally important that you arrive at your patrol sector, and remain there until the tanker fleet arrives. Is that clear, Jack? The planning has already been done for you. All you have to do is find those tankers, and sink them."

TREMAIN left the mansion within the hour through the same set of double doors, immediately shading his eyes from the bright afternoon sun.

He always felt exhausted after a meeting with Ireland, like

he had just testified as the key witness in some high-stakes trial. He was obviously out of practice, since the old bastard had managed to get to him. Still, he had his command, and that was at least something. Ireland might relieve him when this patrol was over, but for now, he would command the *Whitefin*.

The staff car sat idling on the drive at the foot of the stairs, and the sight of it suddenly raised Tremain's spirits. He skipped lively down the stairs, returning the salutes of the marine sentries, eagerly anticipating a delightful drive back to town in Melinda's enjoyable company.

But when he reached the foot of the stairs, he was surprised to see a burly marine stick his shaved head out of the driver's window.

"Ready to go, Commander?" the marine asked eagerly.

Tremain stood there motionless for a moment, his hopes dashed. Even worse, there was someone sitting in the backseat, and that person also stuck his head out the window. It was the British officer.

"It seems this is the only ride going back to town," Major Farquhar said mildly, a cigarette hanging from the side of his mouth. "Well, don't just stand there gawking, old boy. Are you coming or aren't you?"

Tremain heard a female giggling behind him, and turned to see Melinda standing at the top of the stairs with a mischievous look on her face. He could only imagine how foolish and blatant he looked, gaping like some star-crossed schoolboy who had just learned he couldn't walk home from school with his crush.

"Corporal Grady will take you to the Lucknow, Commander," she said with amused eyes that seemed to know him inside out. "Or wherever else you'd like to go, compliments of the admiral."

As Tremain climbed into the backseat next to the major, he wondered if it had indeed been Ireland who called for the marine driver, or had she done it to avoid driving back to Perth with a salivating submariner in the backseat.

She was still standing at the top of the stairs as the car pulled out, and Tremain felt compelled to wave to her. She waved back with a bright smile, her lips mouthing the words "good luck" before she and the mansion faded into a cloud of dust stirred up by the automobile as it accelerated down the drive toward the main gate.

Chapter 5

"FAHHHHBRIANO, huh? I never heard of you!"

The midday sun shone brightly over Fremantle harbor, reflecting brilliantly white off the set of papers comprising Petty Officer Mike Fabriano's official transfer orders. The hitherto spotless documents were now being turned over and over by the grimy hands of a big chief petty officer who had stopped Fabriano at the end of the *Whitefin*'s brow. Blindingly resplendent in his new white jumper uniform, Fabriano had made his way from the big submarine tender *Pelias*, across the brows of two nested submarines, and now stood patiently on the *Whitefin*'s dipping brow, balancing a huge seabag on his shoulder as only a truly seasoned sailor could. He was fully aware that the chief was making a show entirely for the benefit of the sailors working nearby.

Fabriano sneaked a few glances up and down the *Whitefin*'s slanted black hull and wasn't sure what to make of it. As a destroyerman, he had always referred to submarines as sewer pipes, or pigboats, or any of a number of other derogatory terms that described the dismal living conditions inside the odd-shaped craft. The *Whitefin* measured 311 feet in length and 27 feet in breadth. He'd learned that from a spec sheet posted somewhere in one of the squadron offices he'd waited in for hours on board the tender while he was being checked in. But looking at her now, she barely looked half that size. He could hardly imagine how ninety men squeezed inside that narrow hull for weeks on end, and he could scarcely believe that he would soon be one of them.

The chief, scruffily dressed in a dingy blue baseball cap with khaki shirt and trousers, scowled as if Fabriano had intruded on his domain. The chief read the orders aloud as if he had never seen such a document before. Behind him, several sailors walked to and fro on the submarine's wood-planked deck, slowly ferrying a stack of cardboard boxes to an open hatch where periodically a pair of hands would appear to receive them. Several of the sailors wiped the sweat from their brows and momentarily stopped what they were doing to gawk blatantly at the newcomer, as if he were the only member of the crew who had not come straight from the womb to the deck of the *Whitefin*. Fabriano knew the routine well from a half-dozen other ships before this one. It was the same at every ship. All new sailors were treated like outcasts until the next batch of new sailors showed up.

"I don't know nothing about this," the chief said, pushing his hat back on a sweaty brow. "Who the hell are you, anyway?"

Before Fabriano could answer, one of the shirtless sailors on deck spoke up.

"Aw, Chief, look at the size of that fuckin' seabag. He's gotta be a skimmer. The boy sure as shit don't know about subs."

"Did I tell you to stop working, Penn?" the chief retorted scornfully. "And that goes for the rest of you maggots! Get back to work! We ain't got all day! We can't get under way tomorrow without those stores loaded. Now, get moving, all of you!"

The sailors grudgingly resumed their work, but Fabriano noticed the one called Penn casting a longer glance than the rest. His face seemed transfixed with a permanent grin, a grin that Fabriano instantly disliked, a grin that contained more malevolence than levity.

So this was the *Whitefin*'s asshole, he thought. Every ship had one.

"I won't ask you again, asshole." The chief was talking to the daydreaming Fabriano this time. "Who the hell are you?"

"I'm Electrician's Mate Second Class Mike Fabriano, chief, reporting on board as ordered."

"I dunno," the chief said, scratching his head. "I know we're short as shit on electricians, but I'm the duty chief today, and I didn't hear nothing about this."

"Chief McCune!" a voice called. "Is that the new electrician reporting?"

Fabriano looked up to see a lieutenant commander dressed in khaki calling down from the *Whitefin*'s conning tower. He had one foot kicked up on the aft railing, and Fabriano assumed him to be the ship's duty officer.

"That asshole never tells me nothing," the chief mumbled under his breath, low enough so that only Fabriano could hear it. Then in a much louder voice Chief McCune answered, "No one ever told me he was coming, Mr. Monroe, but this guy's an electrician, all right!"

"Squadron just called this morning to tell us he was coming," Monroe replied. "Go ahead and get him checked in and situated."

"As if I didn't have enough to do already," Chief McCune mumbled through gritted teeth as he outwardly smiled and waved to the officer. "Three fucking crates to load and stow, and now I've got to wet-nurse your ass."

"I'm a quick learner, Chief," Fabriano said, solidly. He had been in the navy long enough to know how to make a chief an ally. "Just tell me where I'm bunking and I'll go stow my gear. I'll be back on deck in no time. I sure as hell know how to unload a crate."

"You do, huh?" Chief McCune's eyes squinted under the brim of his cap, and then something of a smile appeared on his weathered face. McCune must have been easy to please, because Fabriano's display of eagerness seemed to have won him over in no time. "Oh, well, I guess I can give you a quick once-around the boat. It won't take too long. The last thing I need is you falling down some hatch, or going someplace you got no business going, and breaking something you got no business breaking."

The chief turned to the gaggle of sailors. "Which one of you maggots wants to take Fabriano's gear to his rack while I give him a tour of our fine ship?"

A rush of blood reached Fabriano's face at the realization of what McCune had just said. *He couldn't let anyone take his seabag.* He could feel the small, round tin can poking through the canvas fabric and into the meaty part of his shoulder. The can was watertight, and it held his toiletries—along with a few girlie magazines he'd picked up in Brisbane—but it also held the money, the $47,780 he'd taken from *Chevalier*'s safe, all of it packed neatly in tight rolls beneath a thin felt panel he'd constructed to give the can a false bottom. He had to think of something, and fast. But before he could come up with a viable excuse to stay with his bag, the overtly cheerful Penn appeared at the chief's side.

"I'd be happy to take our new shipmate's bag, Chief," Penn said, a bit too eagerly, as he reached out with a grimy hand to pull Fabriano's seabag off his shoulder. Fabriano instinctively gripped the bag tighter, not letting go until he noticed a subtle comprehension in Penn's eyes, a comprehension that made Fabriano inwardly curse his own stupidity.

Holy shit, why did I fucking resist? Now that asshole knows something's up.

If Penn had half a brain, he'd know that Fabriano had something in the bag, something he could not easily part with. Whatever Penn did with that knowledge was now completely out of Fabriano's hands. Any move now would surely give up the jig, and Fabriano tried not to watch too hopelessly as Penn hefted the seabag onto his shoulder and disappeared down one of the open hatches in the deck.

Fabriano cursed himself again for his own foolishness, as the chief showed him the four-inch deck gun mounted just forward of the conning tower.

He tried to pay attention as best he could. After all, he needed this submarine, probably more than it needed him. He needed a place far away from the suspecting eyes of the destroyer command in Tulagi. So far, things had worked out perfectly, and all he needed to do was lay low on this boat for a few months until it rotated back to the States for an overhaul. Then he could ask for shore leave and get the money back home where it would be safe, and where the navy would never find it.

That night, floating in the water off Vella LaVella, he'd been sure he'd be found out. There he was floating on the open sea, alone on a raft with a canvas bag full of money. When someone rescued him, they were sure to make inquiries. There would be no way to hide it. He had thought about pitching the money overboard when he saw Commander Tremain float by, struggling to keep Smitty's dead body afloat, and then he suddenly realized what a grand stroke of luck he had been dealt. He fished Tremain out of the water, operating on a hunch that whoever eventually rescued them would pay much more attention to a naval commander than a mere sailor toting a canvas bag. His hunch was right. *Chevalier*'s officers in the motor launch seemed in a frenzy to help Tremain off the raft, paying little notice to Fabriano. That distraction allowed him to slip aboard the overcrowded launch without anyone asking questions about his small cargo. Once aboard, he simply mingled in with the other survivors. They boarded the waiting *O'Bannon* en masse and still no one noticed the bag, or if they did they never said anything about it. Within minutes he had found a nice hiding spot for his loot belowdecks, and then quickly returned to the deck to help the others pull bodies—both Japanese and American—from the drink and line them up in neat rows on *O'Bannon*'s fantail. As the first light of the morning sun appeared in the eastern sky the next day, the wounded *O'Bannon* and *Selfridge* cleared the area, heading back down the Slot at less than ten knots. Fabriano had watched from *O'Bannon*'s fantail as the deserted, broken, and heavily listing *Chevalier* fell farther and farther astern, and eventually over the horizon. He learned later that day that the stubborn ship had stayed afloat most of the morning, refusing to sink until one of the destroyers from the other division scuttled her with a torpedo.

Once the *O'Bannon* made it to Tulagi, *Chevalier*'s surviving crew went ashore, and again he successfully transferred his loot without drawing any attention. A couple of days later, the captain called the crew together and stood before them with a harsh expression on his face. It seemed that *Chevalier*'s disbursing officer had not been killed in the battle after all. He was picked up by another ship the day after the battle and had just arrived in Tulagi. The surviving officer had brought with him troubling news. It seemed that just before abandoning ship he had gone to the ship's office to collect the *Chevalier*'s cash, but when he got there, the money was all gone. Someone had taken it. Fabriano's heart skipped a beat at the announcement, but that was the last he heard of the incident. The next day it was announced that *Chevalier*'s crew would be divided among the fleet. Commander Tremain, true to his word, had filed a request that Fabriano be reassigned to submarine duty and accompany him to Fremantle. The commodore must not have had any objections to Tremain's request, because the next day, Tremain came looking for him, told him to pack his seabag, and within the hour, they both hopped aboard a PBY headed for Brisbane.

And now here he was reporting aboard a new ship thousands of miles away from Tulagi and the suspicious eyes of the *Chevalier*'s disbursing officer. He had come a long way with that loot—too far to let some half-wit like Penn foil his plans.

As Chief McCune continued the tour of the *Whitefin*'s main deck, Fabriano found himself glancing broodingly at the open hatch in the deck. McCune pointed out cleats, shore power connections, sewage connections, potable water connections, periscopes, induction valves, etc., but it all melded into one long, agonizing blur that seemed to take an eternity. Fabriano scarcely comprehended a single word, all the while preoccupied with thoughts of what might be going on belowdecks, wondering where Penn was, what he was doing, and whether or not he had opened his seabag.

TREMAIN had taken the staff car from the admiral's house to the Lucknow, an elaborate mansion in Perth procured by the navy to house submarine officers during their brief lulls in port. There, he ditched the British major, spent about four and a half minutes checking in and dropping off his seabag, before returning to the waiting staff car and bribing the lance corporal to shuttle him back to the navy wharf in Fremantle. It was simple anesthesia to stand at the edge of the pier and stare longingly across the water at the *Whitefin*'s dark silhouette nested among the other submarines, all bathed in the yellowish light of the late afternoon sun. But it wasn't long before a few overbearing seagulls lighted on a wooden stanchion beside him and ruined the moment, prompting him to move along before he became their target. After a long stroll along the quay, passing sailors of every navy, throwing up salutes right and left—and after several much-needed cigarettes—he finally made his way to the "Warehouse."

The old abandoned warehouse beside the crowded navy wharf had been converted into a large officers' club back in 1942, when Fremantle harbor was fast becoming a major naval base for the Allies. Officers from the dozens of warships moored at the wharf often visited the club at the end of the day to unwind and have a few drinks. Of course, the Warehouse was nothing fancy, and it suffered from a severe shortage of single female patrons, but it was amply stocked with a seemingly endless supply of hard liquor and home-grown Swan beer, unlike the local Fremantle pubs, which had nothing to drink at all since alcohol had been rationed in Australia to support the Aussie troops fighting overseas.

The club was mildly crowded this evening, with a small band playing a wistful rendition of "White Christmas" while a few junior officers from various navies danced slowly with their dates beneath a dense blanket of cigarette smoke. Tremain had come here to relax, to mentally prepare himself for the next day, when the weighty responsibilities of command would once again rest on his shoulders. But any hopes of enjoying a quiet drink alone were soon dashed. He had hardly entered the club before three old acquaintances—all lieutenant commanders, all from his squadron, and all submarine captains in their own right—whisked him away to a side table.

"So, you met with old Ireland today, did you, Jack?" said Marty Pancheri, the commander of the *Triggerfish*, who was sitting opposite Tremain. Marty added merrily, "How the hell did that go?"

"The usual." Tremain shrugged. "He's the same old bastard I remember. Very calculating. A real charlatan."

"I don't suppose he told you why we're all getting under way this week."

"Damn it, Marty!" said one of the other officers, who was the commander of the *Hammerhead*. "Keep your mouth shut, will you? Oh, hello, Sophie!"

All four men fell silent as the pretty young Australian waitress who had been waiting on their table stopped by with another round of drinks.

"Hi, boys. Anything else I can get you?"

"No, thanks, doll!" Marty said, winking.

"That's just the kind of thing I'm talking about, Marty," the captain of the *Hammerhead* said, once Sophie was out of earshot again. "One little slip of the tongue to someone like Sophie and the next thing you know all of Fremantle will know the squadron's getting under way this week."

"Well, excuse the hell out of me!" said Marty, who was slightly drunk but still wholly cognitive and still jokingly nudging Tremain across the table. "But who the hell, except for the blind, is not going to notice the sudden absence of six submarines and damn near six hundred men. It doesn't take Sherlock Holmes to figure it out. All someone's got to do is look outside."

"He's got a point there," said the third officer, the commander of the *Stingray*. "Wilson's boat pulled out yesterday, Campbell's today. The rest of us by the end of the week. It doesn't take a trained spy to know something's up." He added snidely, with a quick glance at Tremain, "But I wouldn't worry about Sophie, there. She seemed too preoccupied with my good looks. I think she's in love, fellas."

Suddenly a rancorous clash reverberated across the room. The four commanders all looked up to see a table toppled on the opposite side, and a disheveled officer lying flat on his back beneath it. The man had obviously drunk himself there. Within a few moments two junior officers appeared, hoisted the drunk between them, and began dragging him toward the door. Most of the club's patrons seemed unfazed by the disruption and carried on with their revelry as if it were a common occurrence. The band never missed a single bar of their lazy melody, but Tremain caught the disdainful glances of two

Dutch naval officers standing near the bar, scrutinizing the scene with raised eyebrows.

With a slight smirk on his face, Marty looked across the table at Tremain and motioned in the direction of the officer being carried out of the room.

"What do you think about that, Jack?"

"A pathetic disgrace to the uniform," Tremain answered, downing the shot of whiskey in his hand. "It's not even six o'clock yet. The Aussies and the Dutch will have a good laugh over that one. I hope they throw the bastard in the brig."

Marty exchanged restrained glances with the other two captains before all three broke out in side-splitting laughter.

"What the hell's so funny?" Tremain demanded with feigned brusqueness.

"Oh, Jack," Marty said between hearty belly laughs. "I hate to be the one to have to tell you this, but you've just been introduced to your new XO."

All three broke out in uproarious laughter once again, so much so that they drew attention from some of the nearby tables.

"Shit!" Tremain muttered, motioning to the waitress for another round.

"His name is Chris Monroe," Marty said, after finally restraining himself. "But he's known around here as *The Floater.*"

"The Floater?"

"Jack, do you remember the *R-15* incident?" Marty asked, suddenly serious.

Tremain was very familiar with it. What submariner wasn't? The story had been told and retold in every submarine wardroom prior to the war. The *R-15*, an aging submarine cruising on the surface on a calm day off the Virginia coast suddenly and unexpectedly submerged in deep water and never came up again, leaving the watch officer and three lookouts floating on the surface to be rescued by a nearby fisherman. Tremain had been on the other side of the world when it happened, commanding the *Seatrout* out of Manila, but he distinctly remembered the chill he felt as he perused the incident report a month later. The report had included a message warning the entire submarine fleet about the hazards of overriding torpedo tube interlocks at sea, which a board of inquiry had concluded was the culprit in the disaster. Apparently, the officer of the deck, who remained nameless in the report, had testified that the *R-15* sank in less than fifteen seconds, leading the board to conclude that an open torpedo tube had caused the disaster. The fact that the captain of the *R-15* had given permission to conduct torpedo tube maintenance only ten minutes prior to the sinking served only to confirm the board's finding. The board's official conclusion was that shabby maintenance practices and operator error were to blame for the incident, and the *R-15*'s captain was held posthumously responsible for the catastrophe, which took the lives of forty-six men, including his own.

"What about it?"

"Well, that's him," said Marty, pointing toward the door through which the intoxicated officer had been carried. "That's The Floater, the *R-15*'s only surviving officer—the guy who was on watch on the bridge that day."

"Maybe that explains his current condition," Tremain said, instinctively defending the man who was to be his second in command, despite the fact that he had never met him. "It must be a tough thing to live with, being the only survivor."

Marty exchanged fretful looks with the other two officers. "He wasn't the only survivor, Jack. Though maybe he wishes he was."

"Meaning?"

"Well, don't go quoting me on this, but there's a well-known rumor around the squadron that one of the lookouts on the *R-15* that survived that day submitted a statement to the board. The sailor caught pneumonia and died shortly after the incident, poor bastard, but according to his written statement Monroe was to blame for the accident."

"Seems like I remember reading in the incident report that the surviving watch officer was absolved of any culpability," Tremain said defiantly.

"Yeah, so says the board of inquiry. That's the official story. The lookout had a different story, a story that never made it into the official report. It was thrown out, never even considered as evidence. Apparently, Monroe's got an uncle on Admiral King's staff."

"C'mon, Marty. This is just hearsay. You can't expect me to believe this. I'm surprised at you, falling for this garbage. You and I both know these rumors have a mind of their own. One part truth, and three parts pure fantasy."

"That might be true, Jack, if I'd heard this from a couple of dockyard loafers. But I didn't. I heard it from Ireland's flag lieutenant. That young j.g. What the hell's his name—Wright. I don't think he'd tell me if there weren't some truth to it."

The mention of Wright's name made Tremain stiffen imperceptibly. He had served with Wright. He knew his caliber. What's more, he trusted Wright, implicitly. The straitlaced lieutenant would never make up such a rumor, or propagate it, unless there was some ring of truth to it. Perhaps he had heard it through the unofficial flag lieutenant channels. Oftentimes, flag lieutenants knew more about what was going on at the ship level than their admirals did.

"This is what I heard, Jack. And I'm only telling you this because you're my friend, and I don't want you going into this new command completely blind," Marty said sincerely. "I heard that it was all Monroe's fault. I heard that he leaned against the diving alarm lever by mistake, and started the whole disaster in motion. Apparently the alarm speaker on the bridge had shorted out a few days before, so nobody heard the alarm on the bridge. Monroe had no clue what he'd done. Down in the control room, the men heeded what they believed was a legitimate order to dive the boat. They opened the main ballast tank vents and the *R-15* started down fast. Everybody knows she used to ride a little heavy. Monroe and the lookouts on the bridge were completely oblivious to the fact that she was submerging beneath them, every one of them with binoculars glued to his face. They didn't realize what was happening until seawater started pouring into the bridge scuppers. Before they knew it, the water level had risen above the open bridge hatch, and the next moment, they were floating on the surface. She went down like a rock."

Diving a submarine with the bridge hatch pinned open was

the stuff of nightmares, and the kind of thing that Tremain preferred not to think about. It didn't take much of an imagination to see the torrent of seawater pouring through the thirty-six-inch-diameter hatch, growing in intensity with each passing foot of depth, filling the control room entirely before the sub even reached periscope depth, knocking the men away from their control panels, swirling them around the compartment like bits of driftwood, holding them under until their flailing bodies moved no more. With the control room flooded, there was little hope of saving the submarine. The surviving sailors, locked inside the remaining dry compartments, would have little choice but to sit and wait for the inevitable.

"You know the rest of the story, Jack. About five minutes later, a flurry of giant bubbles and oil appeared on the surface. Shit, I bet that old rust bucket's aged pressure hull never even made it down to three hundred feet, the poor bastards."

Tremain said nothing, but merely looked into his empty shot glass. Perhaps it was true; perhaps not. Either way, it was a rumor that would have made it to the ears of the *Whitefin*'s sailors, probably embellished tenfold. No telling what effect it had on the command situation, and Monroe's effectiveness with them. But he would learn soon enough. He had an XO with a past, and he would have to deal with it.

"I don't mean to make light of the whole thing, Jack," Marty said, somewhat apologetically. "I know it's bad luck to talk about lost boats the night before an under way."

Tremain simply shrugged and smiled unconcernedly as if the thought had not occurred to him. Sitting back in his chair, he turned his attention toward the dozen or so junior officers dancing merrily with their blushing dates. They looked so young, so incredibly young. He thought he recognized several faces that might have passed through his classroom in New London only months ago. Some of those greenhorns could have completed a war patrol by now. Some of them could even be members of the *Whitefin*'s wardroom, and might have to follow their former sub school teacher into battle in the coming weeks. He would be responsible for getting their young, smiling faces back home to Mom and Dad safely.

He shifted in his chair, throwing back another drink as the

long-absent but familiar tension returned to his shoulders—
the weight of command, the burden assumed by all captains.

*Promise me you won't give up. Do whatever it takes. Find
another ship. Live and love again . . .*

Chapter 6

"**CAST** off all lines!"

The officer of the deck pulled the air valve to operate the *Whitefin*'s whistle, and one long blast resonated throughout the harbor, sending flocks of seagulls skyward and prompting workers and sailors all along the tender and quay to cast an indifferent glance at the departing submarine.

The weather was cool and crisp, a perfect day for getting under way, and Tremain had to fight back a grin as he leaned against the rail on the port side of the bridge, gripping the warm steel in his hands as his ship rumbled to life and the space of water expanded between the stirring *Whitefin* and the moored *Triggerfish*. Over on the *Triggerfish*'s deck, several sailors in blue dungarees waved as they yanked in the lengths of wet hemp that had once held the *Whitefin* against the *Triggerfish*'s side.

The national ensign caught the first wisps of the westerly breeze and began to flutter slackly above the heads of the lookouts up in the periscope shears. With the brown harbor water lapping at her upturned bow planes, the *Whitefin* came to starboard in a long, lumbering turn, finally steadying when her bow pointed directly at the South Mole lighthouse near the far western end of the harbor. Gleaming brilliant white in the morning sun, the distant tower stood forebodingly above the north wharf, marking the harbor's unseen exit to the sea.

"Helm, Bridge, all ahead one-third, steady as she goes," Lieutenant Endicott said into the bridge microphone while casting an uncertain glance in Tremain's direction. Endicott was one of the *Whitefin*'s junior officers and was the designated officer of the deck for the maneuvering watch.

Tremain pretended not to notice the young lieutenant's glance, instead turning his attention to a solitary figure waving his hands wildly from the bridge of the *Triggerfish*. It was Marty Pancheri.

"Good hunting, Tremain!" Marty shouted across the water, cupping both hands to his mouth. "Make sure you leave some for me! See you in a couple months!"

Tremain smiled and waved back to him, and found a moment to wonder how Marty was ever going to get his ship ready for sea in time to make his own departure date, only two days hence. While he and Major Farquhar crossed the deck of the *Triggerfish* earlier that morning, Tremain had noticed the dilapidated state of the *Triggerfish*'s topside and could not imagine how she would ever be ready for sea in less than a month. Happily, the *Whitefin* was in sharp contrast. He was amazed from the moment he stepped aboard. She was every bit stowed for sea, with every man aboard by 0500. All stores had been loaded, every system was operational, and every deck shined like the day she came down the slips. Her cleanliness even prompted a comment from the groggy-eyed British major after they both descended the forward torpedo-room ladder and were met by the six glimmering bronze breech doors and racks of shiny Mark 14 torpedoes painted pea green.

"Your crew is sure one for spit and polish, old boy. Perhaps I should remove my shoes."

Outwardly, Tremain had pretended that it was simply the normal order of the service, but inwardly he had to admit that he was quite impressed by what he saw. It left him wondering how the man he observed getting carried out of the club last night could be responsible for such a good turnout. He had met and spoken with his new XO, Lieutenant Commander Chris Monroe, only briefly that morning as men scurried about to stow last-minute items for sea. Monroe had displayed no indication that he had been drunk off his feet only twelve hours before.

Instead, Monroe had been cordial and polite, reporting that all departments were ready to get under way and that he would be happy to help Tremain get acquainted with the ship in any way he could. They had agreed to talk later in the day, since Monroe still had a few last-minute preparations to attend to. Tremain had detected a slight degree of self-doubt in his new executive officer, but that was to be expected, considering Monroe's past.

Now Tremain could hear the observation periscope creaking in its well as it rotated slowly through the azimuth. He could just imagine Monroe, in the control room two decks below, taking visual bearings on the prominent landmarks, passing bearings to the chief quartermaster who was probably poring over the chart table at this moment, switching rapidly between pencils, dividers, and compass as if he were a surgeon. Down on the *Whitefin*'s main deck, Tremain could see that men were already buttoning things up, stowing gear, rigging the ship for submerged operations.

They were good, Tremain thought to himself. This was a well-disciplined crew that knew what they were doing, despite the fact that most of them seemed to disregard any notion of the uniform or grooming regulations. If the ship appeared immaculate and sparkling, then the crew appeared anything but that. They wore every possible shade of faded blue dungarees and button-down working shirts, some with the sleeves rolled up, some with the sleeves rolled down, and some with the sleeves missing entirely. And the assortment of uniforms was almost outdone by the variety of headgear. They wore battered navy blue ball caps in every position, grimy white Dixie cup hats that looked like they'd been used to clean the lube oil strainers, and even a few Australian army "slouch" hats with dangling chin straps and one side of the brim pinned up.

Obviously, they were a crew that took more pride in their ship's appearance than they did in their own, although they all appeared to have a healthy amount of self-confidence.

Tremain had recognized it from the first moment he stepped aboard. They were proud of their record, and they had a right to be. In the four patrols under their previous skipper, they had chalked up fourteen enemy ships for forty-one thousand tons. That number included a Japanese cruiser and two Japanese submarines—quite an impressive record, for any boat. They had an impeccable reputation for getting the job done, and no matter how difficult the mission given them, they had performed with flying colors.

The *Whitefin*'s officers were typical of most Tremain had encountered on other ships in his career. He had met them all that morning, in the submarine's tiny wardroom, and they had paid him the due courtesies of his rank and station, obviously with little more driving their loyalties than the fact that he would be signing their next fitness reports. Promotions and careers compelled the respect of the officers. But the crew—the crew was a different story. It would take much more than his command pin to win their respect. He had to prove that he was worthy to sail with them, to live with them, to lead them. It was a silent challenge issued by every curious yet defiant eye as he toured the ship's nine watertight compartments that morning. From the forward torpedo room to the after torpedo room, he was looked upon as an outsider, as an intruder to the realm. But then, this was not his first command. This kind of treatment was expected, and it did not prevent him from learning the names of his key watchstanders. The other eighty-five names would come soon enough. He'd know their hometowns and marital status before the week was out.

Despite the icy reception from the crew, he did receive at least one warm welcome that morning, from the chief of the boat, Master Chief LaGrange. The Cob had met him with a wide grin when Tremain stopped to poke his head into the chief's quarters—or goat locker, as it was called.

"Make us proud of you, Captain," LaGrange had said as Tremain shook the squatty man's heavily tattooed arm. The chief's seasoned eyes scrutinized him like a hawk from beneath the brim of a deflated blue combination cap. "And if you run into any trouble with the boys, sir, it might be best to take it up with me first, if you know what I mean. You know, until you get your sea legs back again."

Tremain liked LaGrange from the start. The chief had his priorities in the right place. These were his boys, and he was going to look out for them. He was there to protect them from the enemy as well as from any incompetent new captain that might come along, and that suited Tremain just fine.

Just now, as he peered over the railing, he could see La-Grange strolling along the main deck, watching his "boys" as they checked hatches and lockers for tightness and secured the capstan. Unlike so many other Cobs Tremain had known in his career, LaGrange was not a screamer. He used snarls and grunts rather than shouts to voice his displeasure, and it apparently had the desired effect. Every man aboard seemed to follow him without question, if not worship the very wooden planks he walked on.

Again, Tremain noticed Endicott casting a suspicious glance in his direction before turning back to his binoculars. He was looking astern, apparently sizing up the two range markers on the low hills to the northeast. The two navigation markers looked like, and essentially were, two enormous bright red poles rising up from the Australian countryside. They were situated one behind the other and lined up directly with the exact center of channel. Anyone piloting a vessel through Fremantle harbor could tell whether his ship was lined up with the center of the channel simply by checking the spatial alignment of these two distant markers.

Endicott appeared nervous, holding his gaze on the markers for much longer than was necessary.

"Something wrong, Tom?" Tremain asked calmly. In the short time he had had with the officers that morning, he'd made it a point to learn their first names.

"No, Captain," Endicott said, with little resolve in his tone. "It's just . . . I guess I was expecting you to step in and take over at any moment."

"Why's that?"

"That's what our last captain did, sir—Captain Burgess. Every time we got under way. He'd curse up a storm, relieve me, and tell me to go below. He couldn't stand my ship driving. I guess I made him nervous."

"I've navigated this channel more times than I can remember, Tom. Don't worry, if you do anything that makes me nervous, I'll let you know."

Endicott appeared somewhat dumbfounded, if not panicked. Eventually, he muttered an "Aye, aye, sir," and turned his attention back to the channel ahead of the submarine.

As the *Whitefin* drove down the center of the harbor at five knots, Tremain found himself gripping the rail slightly harder than his casual manner would let on. The turn at Victoria Quay was rapidly approaching.

The *Whitefin* had been moving down the long rectangular harbor, running parallel with Victoria Quay, which made up the southern boundary of the harbor and which was crowded with more than a dozen moored tankers and merchants from a half-dozen different countries. Endicott had been keeping a good two hundred yards of separation from the quay, but now the *Whitefin* was reaching the southwestern end of the harbor, where the quay itself curved sharply to the right, along with the channel. Tremain half-wanted to reduce speed a knot or two, since he knew from experience that the turn was a most unforgiving one and that his submarine was coming along at a pace probably swifter than her conning officer could manage. But even at the *Whitefin*'s present speed of five knots, he knew that she could indeed negotiate the turn—if she were handled properly.

"Bridge, XO," Monroe's voice squawked over the speaker. "Range to the turn, fifty yards. Stand by to mark the turn."

"Bridge, aye," Endicott said into the microphone, acknowledging Monroe's warning and now looking more nervous than ever.

Tremain pretended not to notice. He casually rested his arms on the starboard bridge railing, peering down past the forward gun platform at the men on deck, pretending to be more concerned with what they were doing than with the coming turn. Inwardly, he gripped the rail tightly, and silently hoped that young Endicott had absorbed at least some piloting skills from his former captain.

At the extreme end of the quay sat a large Dutch freighter with its big hulk protruding out into the harbor. A Dutch flag rolled lazily back and forth above the freighter's wide fantail.

High above the squatty vessel, a newly painted smokestack glimmered in the morning sun, in stark contrast to a rusty hole a few feet above the waterline, trickling a stream of dirty liquid into the harbor. Several clusters of Dutch sailors lounged on the freighter's main deck, curiously studying the approaching American submarine, apparently oblivious to any danger it might pose. The *Whitefin* was forced to steer directly toward the freighter in order to reach the turning point. It seemed an awfully hazardous thing to do, but Tremain knew it was necessary to properly line up for the turn onto the next leg of the channel.

"Bridge, XO," the speaker squawked. "Turn bearing will be North Mole lighthouse, bearing two-six-five."

Tremain wondered for a moment why Monroe, the ship's executive officer and navigator, had not yet recommended a speed reduction. Perhaps Captain Burgess had always taken the turn at this speed and was in the habit of squelching any recommendations from his second in command.

"Bridge, XO, mark the turn!" the speaker squawked.

"Helm, Bridge, right standard rudder!" Endicott ordered immediately into the microphone.

One deck below, inside the conning tower, the helmsman spun the ship's wheel, and the *Whitefin*'s bow began edging over to the right. The submarine responded quickly to the rudder and swiftly placed the menacing freighter on her port beam, safely averting any collision. But Tremain could already see that the turn had been just a hair too late. With her present speed the *Whitefin*'s stern was slipping rapidly to the left and there was now a real danger that the large leeway would send her into the buoys marking a shallow slipway just up ahead, off the port bow. Endicott didn't see it. How could he see it, untested as he was at piloting a ship through narrow channels? But it was plainly obvious to Tremain, who had conned so many submarines in his life that he could instantly determine the cause and effect of any action. It was finally time for him to act.

"You should stop the starboard screw, Tom, to help get her head around," Tremain commented calmly, as if it were a suggestion and not an order, as if Endicott could take it or leave it.

But Endicott was no fool.

"Maneuvering, Bridge, stop the starboard motor!"

Maneuvering acknowledged the order, and the stopped starboard shaft had an instant effect on the submarine's turn rate. Her bow came to the right much more rapidly now, sweeping past the shallow slipway, and leaving the marker buoys bobbing along her port side less than twenty-five yards away.

When the buoys had passed safely astern, Endicott sighed visibly and ordered, "Helm, Bridge, steady course two-six-five. All ahead one-third."

The rudder came off, both screws pulled together once again, and the *Whitefin* steadied on her new course. She was pointed straight down the new leg of the channel now, and needed only to drive straight ahead to reach the harbor's exit, where a tall, pea green lighthouse stood solitarily on the extreme tip of the rocky South Mole. But now there was a new danger, and Tremain noticed it half a second before one of the lookouts did.

"The damn net tender!" exclaimed the lookout from high in the periscope shears. "We're headed right for him, sir!"

The *Whitefin*'s bumbled turn had put her well to the left side of the channel. Not a problem during peacetime, but definitely a problem today, since the small motor launch tending the defensive nets at the mouth of the harbor was now sitting on the left side of the channel, directly in the submarine's path.

The defensive nets were an inconvenience of war. They were there to prevent enemy midget submarines from sneaking into the harbor and wreaking havoc on the thousands of valuable tons of shipping there. The Japanese had done it before, with some success, at Pearl Harbor, Sydney, and Diego Suarez, among others. Their Italian allies could boast of altering the balance of power in the Mediterranean for a few months when they penetrated the British-held port of Alexandria back in '41, mining and sinking the battleships HMS *Queen Elizabeth* and HMS *Valiant*. Drawn across the harbor's entrance at the narrowest point, the simple nets, along with an array of electronic indicator loops, were Fremantle's insurance against similar attacks.

This morning, the boat tending Fremantle's defensive nets

had been alerted well beforehand of the *Whitefin*'s departure. It had already towed the nets out of the way and now sat on the left side of the channel along with a disorderly clump of marker buoys bunched up beside it. The little net tender was idling there, waiting patiently to draw the nets back again after the *Whitefin* had passed through. As Tremain focused his binoculars on the little open boat, he observed its five-man crew, lounging and smoking and paying little attention to the approaching submarine. But as he continued to watch, he could see the realization set in. One by one, the expressions on their faces grew grave, as they comprehended the danger. The *Whitefin* was on a direct collision course with their frail little craft.

Endicott glanced at Tremain as if seeking advice, but there was little that he could give. Technically, the net tender had the right-of-way since it was severely restricted in its ability to maneuver. There was no question that the *Whitefin* was the "give way" vessel in this situation—but, realistically, there were other factors to be considered. The *Whitefin* was a vessel of war, departing on war patrol. She was valuable to the war effort, much more valuable than the little motor launch, which could be replaced within the hour if necessary. Any course change to the right might place the *Whitefin* in further jeopardy, heading her toward the rocks along the North Mole. The other option, slowing down or stopping, would cause the *Whitefin* to lose steerage way at the narrowest point in the channel, just when she needed her speed the most. There was nothing to do but remain on present course and speed, making it dreadfully clear to the coxswain of the net tender that his little craft must move out of the way or get plowed under.

Endicott sounded five short blasts on the ship's whistle—the danger signal—and then picked up the speaking trumpet to bellow a hail of warnings to the net tender. It wasn't long before the little boat's exhaust pipe belched out a plume of black smoke and a surge of white water appeared at its stern as it glided perilously closer to the rocky mole but safely out of the *Whitefin*'s path, dragging the buoys with it.

As the *Whitefin* drifted past, close enough for Tremain to

look down into the little boat and see the lines of wet hemp coiled between its baseboards, the five civilian sailors watched the submarine go by with loathing. No one could blame them for scowling, and no one could blame them for extending their middle fingers at the amused American sailors on the *Whitefin*'s main deck. But the harbor sailors had little time in which to vent their anger. Soon they became embroiled in the *Whitefin*'s surging wake, and the oldest of the five, a very disgruntled-looking man with a white beard, fought ferociously with the steering wheel to keep his little boat from foundering on the rocks. Despite his dilemma, the old coxswain still found a moment to shoot Tremain one last venomous glance—a glance so hateful that it might have sent the likes of General MacArthur crying for his mother.

Tremain nodded politely, waved, and mouthed a thank-you. But as the little boat fell farther astern, a voice drifted across the water, barely audible above the crashing waves on the seaward side of the mole.

". . . hope the Japs get you . . . bloody yank bastards!"

It was not the most desirable of parting words before a war patrol, but Tremain knew that he would certainly remember them.

As the *Whitefin* finally left the confines of the channel for the vast open sea, all hands on the main deck quickly dropped down into the hull and shut the hatches behind them. Endicott ordered up standard speed and the *Whitefin* began to surge forth, her bow rising sharply to meet the first ocean swell head-on. The first of many rollers crashed against the base of her conning tower, tossing a sheet of foamy spray into the air and drenching everyone on the bridge from head to toe.

As the cold Indian Ocean water streamed and trickled down the bridge scuppers, down the wooden deck planks, down the curved metal skin, Tremain felt a familiar surge of adrenaline rush through his veins. His hair, his shirt, his trousers were all soaking wet, and he felt an icy chill as the brisk wind quickly started to dry them. With the blue ocean stretching out before him, the salty breeze pressing his hair back on his scalp, the cold steel rail shuddering beneath his fingertips, he could not help but grin from ear to ear. He was finally home. He was at sea on a submarine once again. Try as they might, all of the doctors and admirals in the navy could not take this moment away from him.

One journey was over—another had just begun.

Chapter 7

"POSITION report for you, sir," the squatty quartermaster declared as Tremain ducked through the control room hatch and almost ran headfirst into the sailor's bulbous belly. "The XO sends his respects, sir, and reports the two thousand position."

With a toothy grin the sailor held out the small slip of paper. Tremain took it and read the small scribble that contained, among other things, the *Whitefin*'s latitude and longitude as determined by the evening's celestial fix. As he read the report, Tremain fought back the urge to wince from the quartermaster's putrid breath. The sailor had undoubtedly just finished scoffing down his dinner, no doubt a brief diversion before delivering the evening position report, but his breath was so horrid that Tremain seriously considered making it his first standing order that the position report must be delivered by someone who had recently brushed his teeth.

Tremain glanced at the clock. It read precisely 2000 hours. Despite his terrible breath, the stocky quartermaster had delivered the report exactly on time. Tremain made a mental note of it. It said a lot about Monroe, more than it did about the quartermaster. More often than not, an executive officer's demanding duties forced him to rush through the evening fix, performing the calculations on the fly in order to deliver it on time. But the timeliness of this first report revealed that Monroe knew how to juggle his dual role as executive officer and navigator, and that he was proficient at the latter.

"Very well, Owens," Tremain said to the garlic-reeking quartermaster, placing the position report in his pocket. "Thank you. Is the XO still on the bridge?"

"That's where I left him, sir. I haven't seen him come down yet."

"Thank you, Owens. That will be all."

"Aye, aye, sir."

As Tremain crossed the control room heading for the ladder, he realized that he still had a headache from the mind-numbing afternoon he had spent sitting in his stateroom while an endless stream of division chiefs and officers passed a countless number of official reports and forms across his desk. The communications plan, the navigation plan, the engineering maintenance reports, the fuel oil and water reports, the torpedo maintenance schedules—he had reviewed report after report, letter after letter, form after form, until they all ran together in his mind. He had forgotten how agonizingly monotonous the administrative aspects of command could be. He could still feel the matted spot in his hair where the ventilation duct in his stateroom had directed an incessant blast of air for the better part of five hours.

Dinner in the wardroom that evening had done little to alleviate his headache. It was hardly a restful event, since Farquhar had monopolized the entire meal dazzling the junior officers with tales of his exploits against the Japanese in Southeast Asia. The British major had been overbearing, to say the least, and it was certainly outside of tradition for any rider to set the tone of conversation in the wardroom of any ship in any navy. That prerogative was normally reserved for the captain, and Tremain suspected that Farquhar knew it all too well. But Tremain had decided early on to let Farquhar have all the attention he wanted. After all, the Englishman's endless ramblings had allowed him to sit back and learn a little about his own officers simply by noting the kinds of questions they asked, and by observing their reactions to some of the major's more coarse stories. With Farquhar's unwitting help, he had averted that all too awkward first meal between a ship's officers and their new captain, which normally left the captain doing most of the talking while the officers laughed obediently and unconvincingly at his jokes. He needed to learn as much as he could about them and their habits before the ship reached enemy waters. After all, he was coming back to the fleet after a six-month absence, and so many things had changed in the Pacific theater in that small space of time. It could take weeks to learn how to engage with his officers, not to mention the veteran crewmen.

Now, with the first evening meal behind him, Tremain headed up to the bridge determined to finally spend a few moments with his new executive officer. Monroe had been absent from dinner in the wardroom that evening, not too unusual since the ideal time for catching a celestial fix usually coincided with dinnertime. Even if Monroe had been there, Farquhar probably would have kept him from getting in a word edgewise.

As Tremain emerged through the hatch and onto the darkened bridge, he was immediately met by the officer of the deck, Lieutenant Whately.

"Good evening, Captain," Whately said formally, his face glowing ominously red from the dull light emanating from the open bridge hatch, while the stiff westerly breeze threw his hair to one side.

Tremain nodded an acknowledgment and glanced out at the dark sea. The sun had long since sunk into the shimmering Indian Ocean. On the eastern horizon, the Australian coast had diminished and was now merely a black smudge on the sea. Rottnest Lighthouse, with its warm, beckoning stone embrasures, the effective symbol of Fremantle harbor for three generations of mariners and the last landmark he had seen before going below, had long since vanished in *Whitefin*'s phosphorescent wake. The visible sea was barren, except for the *Whitefin* and the small patrol craft escorting her.

"Anything to report, Mr. Whately?"

"Nothing, Captain. We're on schedule, steady on course three-four-two, with an eighty-ninety split on two engines. So far, we've had no con—"

Whately was cut short by the bridge intercom.

"Bridge, Radar. One large, two small contacts, bearing two-eight-five. Range twenty-one thousand yards. Contacts are drawing slowly to the left."

"Radar, Bridge, aye," Whately said into the intercom.

"That'll be the transport *Repose*, along with her escorts," Tremain said, not allowing Whately a chance to consider what action he might take to address these new contacts. "They're heading for Fremantle after a very difficult Indian Ocean crossing. Give them a wide berth, Mr. Whately. I don't want a friendly destroyer dropping depth charges on us on our first night out."

"But we have our own escort, Captain," Whately said doubtfully, pointing to the dark shape a thousand yards off the *Whitefin*'s starboard bow. "Surely, they'll identify us as friendly."

"You hope, Lieutenant. But I can see by your expression you don't fully comprehend the situation. You obviously are unaware that three days ago the *Repose* and her convoy got worked over by an enemy submarine. They lost a freighter and an escort, and never even caught a glimpse of the submarine that sank them." A blank look crossed Whately's face, compelling Tremain to add sardonically, "It was in the routine message traffic this morning, which I'm sure you read up on before coming on watch."

"Yes, sir," Whately muttered, sounding somewhat put out.

"Right now, Mr. Whately, the captains of those two remaining escorts are pissed off and looking to even the score. They're looking for anything that bears a resemblance to an enemy sub, and I'd rather not be the vent for their revenge. We'll go ahead and give them a wide berth. Come to course north until you've lost radar contact, and then return to base course."

"Aye, aye, sir," Whately said, sounding somewhat miffed, before giving the course correction order that turned the *Whitefin*'s bow toward the dark northern horizon.

"Remember, Mr. Whately, always expect the unexpected. Try to stand your watch thinking about the different ways you might be taken off guard. It'll help the time go by faster, and you'll stay more alert."

"Aye, Captain." Whately's tone indicated that he was not overly impressed by his captain's jewel of wisdom. Apparently he considered himself too much of a veteran to receive any guidance from a new skipper, fresh from the lecture halls of sub school.

He'll learn, thought Tremain. *I'll make sure he learns before this patrol is over.*

Glancing aft, Tremain noticed Monroe's dark shape standing on the cigarette deck. He was gazing out to sea with one foot propped on the railing and one hand holding a smoldering cigarette. He appeared to be deep in thought, almost morose, as he stared at the lingering glow on the western horizon. He also seemed oblivious to Tremain's presence; perhaps he was a thousand miles away, or perhaps even in another time.

"What's her name?" Tremain said, after moving over to stand beside him.

Monroe appeared visibly embarrassed and quickly snapped out of his trance.

"Excuse me, Captain?"

"Whenever I see a man stare out at the sunset like that, I think he's got to have a girl on his mind. Am I right?"

Monroe appeared slightly uncomfortable for the briefest of moments, but quickly regained his composure, shooting Tremain a somewhat suspicious glance.

"I sent the quartermaster to you with the position report, Captain," Monroe said, entirely avoiding the question.

"He found me. Thanks." Tremain smiled warmly in an attempt to defuse the business side of this conversation before it got started. Perhaps he had started off on the wrong tack. Monroe obviously had no desire to discuss his love life. He needed to find some other means of engaging him. The ice had to be broken, if the two were to function as a team and effectively lead the *Whitefin* on this patrol.

"We're making good time, it seems," Tremain offered, neutrally.

"Yes, sir. We'll make Exmouth Gulf the day after tomorrow, top off our tanks, and be on our way."

"So what's Exmouth like, besides a refueling stop?" Tremain asked in an effort to make small talk. "It wasn't operational when I was out here last, but I imagine you've stopped there more than once or twice."

Monroe smiled, almost sympathetically. "I keep forgetting

you've been away from this show for so long, Captain. It must be tough on you, trying to adjust."

Tremain wasn't sure he liked the way Monroe had said that.

"Damn it, Chris, I've been on board for twenty-four hours now and I've yet to see an officer or a crewman look me square in the face—except for that damn quartermaster of yours. But that's okay. I can deal with a crew that's not used to me yet. One thing I can't deal with is an XO who doesn't trust me, or who might be worried about my ability to command. Now, we can pull our dicks out right now and see which one's bigger if that's the way you want it, but you're my XO and I need you to have faith in my qualifications. If *you* do, then *they* will."

Monroe looked at him with a slight smile.

"You don't have to worry about me, sir. If there's one man you don't have to worry about, it's me. I know you've got two Navy Crosses. That's more than enough qualifications for me."

"I know things must be difficult for you, XO, with me arriving only yesterday, getting under way for patrol at the drop of a hat, not knowing what I'd expect from you. By the way, I want to commend you for having the ship turned out and ready for sea in such a fine fashion this morning. It looked as good or better than any I've ever seen in my career."

"About that screwup out in the channel this morning, Captain," Monroe said in a tone that indicated he knew better. "I want to apologize, sir. It won't happen again. You have my word."

"I know it won't, XO. Things got off to a rocky start this morning, but I'm chalking that up to the fact that our crew hasn't been to sea for over a month. I expect them to spend the transit time to the patrol area working the bugs out. And that includes our officers, too," Tremain said, casting a glance up forward at the oblivious Whately, whose back was turned to them. "Holy shit, e*specially* our officers."

"He's young, Captain," Monroe said, nodding in Whately's direction. "He was a favorite of our last captain. Got spoiled, no doubt. He's a little disgruntled this evening. He's not used to standing a regular watch. You see, he's our TDC operator, and Commander Burgess always wanted his favorite TDC operator to be fresh in case we went into action unexpectedly. He never let Whately stand watch like the others, so Whately's used to getting a lot of shut-eye. But don't worry, sir, I'm sure he'll warm up to you, given time. Really, he should be pissed off at me. I'm the one that wrote him back onto the watch bill. All you did was approve it, Captain."

"So, I take it that was a policy of Burgess's you didn't approve of."

"No, sir, I didn't. I'd never heard of such a thing before. When you take an officer off the watch bill, the others have to fill in for him. Then they get overworked, and you end up with sleepy officers on the bridge in the middle of a war zone."

Tremain nodded. His thoughts exactly. So far, Monroe and he were in complete agreement professionally.

"Since we're talking about Whately, care to fill me in on the others?"

"Sure, Captain." Monroe paused and appeared to be conjuring up images of the men in his mind. "Let's see. There's Vince Allendale, the engineer and diving officer. He's a mathematician from Yale. He's been on board since the beginning. Took the *Whitefin* off the blocks in Manitowoc, floated her down the Mississippi and through the canal. He's seen three different captains—actually, four now, counting you. I'm sure he'll be putting on lieutenant commander stripes after a couple more patrols. He's got XO written all over him. Good, solid, reliable officer. Then there's Tom Endicott, who took the ship out this morning. He's the assistant engineer and electrical officer. A bit timid, and maybe a little too unsure of himself, but not a bad guy, all in all. There's Robin Tutweiler, the communications officer, not the strongest watch officer, but a good cipher man. Then there's Paul Whately, up there. He's been lucky so far in his career. No screwups. Top of his class in everything. Needless to say, he's a tad full of himself. He's the only guy on board who's been to the torpedo data computer school, and, as much as I hate to admit it, he's damn good at it. Of course, he ought to be after four patrols of doing nothing else but sleep, eat, and shoot torpedoes. And that's pretty much it, sir. Those are the officers you have to work with. Of course, we've also got those two new ensigns, Berkshire and Haaman, but they're untried right now and essentially worthless. I've got them on the watch bill standing JOOD."

"I want them qualified as soon as possible, XO."

Monroe shot him a hesitant glance as if to object, but then finally nodded.

"I'll need your help with all of them, Chris. They need some work. I want them all to learn each other's jobs, and to be ready to take over if they have to. We need to train them to be all-around leaders, not tradesmen or hotshots. It's going to take a lot of effort on your part. I'm the new CO, an outsider in their minds. They don't know me, and right now they're not even sure that I can get them back home safely. Until they build up their confidence in me, they'll be looking to you. Right now, their self-assurance, their optimism to survive this patrol, lies with you."

"I'm not so sure about that, Captain." Monroe looked out to sea with a humorless chuckle. "You obviously don't know who I am."

Tremain feigned a puzzled expression. He had wondered when they would get around to this.

"I was officer of the deck on the *R-15*, sir. You've heard of it, no doubt."

"I'm vaguely familiar with the incident," Tremain lied, trying his best to sound unfazed. "That must have been a difficult thing to live through."

"It's much more difficult to live *with*. To hear the suspicion in the voices of everyone you meet, to see it in the eyes of every sailor on every ship you've ever served on since then. It's in their eyes. I've learned to see it, to recognize it. No offense meant, Captain, but I'm sure you were more than just a little aware of the incident."

"I know you were cleared of any fault in the matter," Tremain said as dismissively as he could. "The case was closed long ago."

"I've never met a submariner who hadn't tried and convicted me in his own mind. This crew knows about it, and they've never trusted me. The admirals, too. But I do my job." Monroe stared out over the bridge rail, then added distantly, "This boat should be mine right now, sir. I'm command rank.

I'm qualified in every respect except for the fact that no command board would ever approve my appointment."

"We've all suffered setbacks in our careers, XO. We've all seen shipmates die. We have ghosts that will haunt us for the rest of our lives. You're no different from anyone else."

"If you say so, Captain. Commander Burgess sure didn't think so."

"That's all in the past now, XO. Let the dead rest. I'm going to judge you based on the here and now. From this moment on, I don't want to hear another word about the *R-15* from you, or from anybody. Is that clear? The only ship that exists right now is the *Whitefin*."

Monroe shot him a sidelong glance, and Tremain suddenly wondered just how much his new XO really knew about him. He could have given himself the same lecture back in the days aboard the *Mackerel* when he himself had brooded over the *Seatrout*'s loss, carrying it around with him everywhere he went.

"We have a war patrol ahead of us, XO, and I'm going to need leadership from you. You are my link to the heart of this ship. You've been aboard her for six patrols. That's six more than I've done with her, so I need you to keep me in tune with the back channels of communication. You'll find that I operate somewhat differently from Commander Burgess. I believe this ship, any ship, performs best when its crew, the whole crew both bad and good, is trained to be a team by good officer leadership. I'm going to rely heavily on your advice, your opinions, and your intuition. In my mind, you're not an XO. You're the future captain of another submarine. And that's just the way I'm going to treat you."

An incredulous look appeared on Monroe's face. He turned his head to face Tremain, apparently speechless for a moment, as if no previous captain had ever approached him in such a trusting manner. Finally, he nodded and stood up straight, flicking the cigarette into the sea, where its orange embers were instantly consumed and swept away in the rolling white froth. There was an awkward pause before he spoke again, this time in a much more enthusiastic tone, as if their entire discussion about the past had never taken place.

"To answer your original question, sir, there's not much at

Exmouth. A couple of fuel barges, a couple of huts that might blow over in the next breeze, and a small Aussie regiment bivouacked on the hillside. That's about it."

Tremain looked at him disbelievingly for a moment, until he realized that Monroe was simply following the orders he had just given him. He was moving on and leaving the *R-15* incident in the past, and he seemed eager to do it, as if he had been waiting for someone to give him the little push he needed for a very long time.

"But it's not all a waste, sir," Monroe added, with the first genuine smile that Tremain had seen on his face. "Sometimes the Aussie officers ask us to row over for a belt. And believe you me, there's no shortage of booze in that camp."

FABRIANO'S bunk in the after torpedo room swung list-lessly as the *Whitefin*'s hull absorbed the dark Indian Ocean's mild eastbound rollers. The ship rolled like a pig on the surface, and Fabriano found himself itching to ask one of the men playing cards nearby when the hell this ship was going to dive—if not to stop the spiraling motion of the hull, to stop the maddening, never-ending throb of the diesel engines, so he could get some sleep. The racket was loud as hell in the after torpedo room, despite the fact that the nearest engine room was two compartments forward. And he'd heard someone say that only two of the four engines were on line at the moment, leaving him to only wonder what kind of clamor all four might produce. He was accustomed to the relatively quiet steam plant on the *Chevalier*, but this diesel noise was something he would have to get used to. He had never considered before that the *Whitefin* would be running on her diesel engines for the majority of the two months they would spend at sea.

From his prostrate position he glanced at the sailors around him, playing cards, shooting the bull about the girls they had scored with in Fremantle, and some talking about their exploits at a submariners rest camp apparently located deep in the Australian outback. They all seemed perfectly at home and oblivious to the blare, and he imagined he would be the same way before the end of the patrol.

After a whirlwind first day at sea, reporting to his division chief and learning the odd jobs that a submarine electrician's responsibilities entailed, and after standing his first watch—under instruction—as the roving electrician, and after scoffing down the surprisingly delicious lasagna dinner in the overly crowded crew's mess, he finally had made it to his rack for a few moments of sleep.

So far, most of the *Whitefin*'s sailors had been fairly cordial to him—cordial relative to the reception he had received on most of his surface ship assignments, but there were certainly a few ready at any moment to give him a ration of shit about being a destroyerman. For the most part they were friendly, if not completely accepting just yet. He found it somewhat comforting to learn that close to a third of the crew were new hands, and most of them had less sea experience than he did.

"Hey, what's the idea, shipmate?"

Fabriano had not noticed that a burly red-haired sailor with blue sleeves rolled up onto his biceps had entered the compartment and was now standing beside his bunk staring down at him.

"What do you mean?" Fabriano said, not moving from where he lay, completely oblivious to what the large sailor could be referring to.

"That's my bunk, shipmate. That's what I mean."

Fabriano sighed heavily as he suddenly realized what was going on. He had seen this kind of thing often enough before to recognize it. Undoubtedly, this was the *Whitefin*'s version of hazing, a special form of treatment reserved for those who were new on board. He noticed that the sailors playing cards had stopped in the middle of a hand, and a noticeable lull had descended on the compartment. Everyone was waiting for his response. Like a new dog inserted into a kennel, this was a test of dominance. He knew that what he did next would determine the way he was to be treated from this day forward.

"Shove off, Mack!" Fabriano said firmly as he placed his hands behind his head and did his best to look relaxed. "The Cob assigned this bunk to me. So, beat it."

The big sailor, who had at least thirty pounds on him, stared at him several moments, apparently incredulous. Fabriano clenched his fists behind his head. He fully expected he would have to fight this man, fully expected a meaty blow to be coming at any moment, fully expected to get his ass kicked from one end of the compartment to the other with his heretofore cordial shipmates transformed into frenzied spectators cheering on their big champion. That's why he was surprised when the hefty sailor's face suddenly broke out into a big toothy grin.

"Oh really?" the sailor said, almost laughing now. "So the Cob assigned you that rack all to your lonesome, eh? I suppose he also showed your majesty that your own private head is located just down the passage there."

Some of the other sailors chuckled at the remark, but most did not look up from their card games, suddenly not so interested anymore. Fabriano knew that he was being made fun of now, but he was still determined not to budge.

"I don't know about the head, but this here rack is mine. You can go talk to the Cob if you got problems with it."

The big sailor's smile began to fade. He sighed heavily and cast an impatient glance at the deck.

"Listen, tin-can man," he said, this time through gritted teeth, "I got no crow to pluck with you. You're new here, and I ain't gonna fault you for that. But you're gonna have to learn that on a boat, everything is share and share alike. Just like you got to share that head with seventy other men, you got to share that rack with me. Hot rackin', we calls it. When I'm on watch, you're sleeping, and vice versa. And I just got off watch, so it's my turn now. So, out with you. I'm only going to say this once."

Fabriano did not know whether he was being taken for a fool or not. The big sailor's reasoning sounded plausible enough, and he certainly did not want to make a big deal out of it, if this was simply the way things were done on a submarine. After a few moments of hesitation, he decided it was time to back down. He grabbed a bracket in the overhead and pulled himself out of the rack, allowing the big man to roll right into it behind him. Within seconds the sailor had adjusted the flannel blanket Fabriano had just been using to cover his legs.

"Damn vent blows right on your feet!" the sailor said as he got comfortable. Meanwhile, Fabriano stood there awkwardly, now not exactly sure where he would take his weary form to alight.

After a few awkward moments, the big horizontal man extended a hand to him.

"Thanks, shipmate," he said smiling. "Name's Clem Shelby. What's yours?"

"Mike . . . Mike Fabriano."

Well, Mikey, it's nice to meet you. Welcome aboard. I hope you have a nice cruise on board USS *Whitefin*. I'd love to jaw with you, but right now I'm petered out, so I'm gonna get some shut-eye. And if you don't mind, I'd rather not have to worry about you hovering over me, so . . ."

Shelby made a simple motion with one hand for Fabriano to move along, rolled over onto his side to face the bulkhead, and was sound asleep before Fabriano could even respond.

Great, thought Fabriano. Now what? He was tired and all he wanted to do was get some sleep, but he was left with few options. He could go to the crew's mess and try to read up on some of the ship's technical manuals as his division chief had advised him to do at every available moment. He could go to the next compartment forward, the maneuvering room, and try to learn something from the electricians on watch there as they operated the controls for the main propulsion motors. Perhaps he might be allowed in the red-lit control room. Maybe they would dive soon, and he'd get to experience that for the first time.

His weary mind was rambling on and on when his eyes suddenly settled on the steel grating covering a ladder well in the deck just beyond the open door to the maneuvering room. The ladder led to the motor room one deck below, where the four electric motors that turned *Whitefin*'s two propeller shafts resided. It was down there, in that seldom inhabited space, during the wee hours of the morning before the *Whitefin* had gotten under way, that Fabriano had hidden the *Chevalier*'s money. Lodged in between two pipe brackets, far into the outboard, hidden behind a flood wall conforming to the curvature of the pressure hull, wrapped in a canvas bag normally used to hold the emergency escape breathing gear—or Momsen Lungs, as he had heard others call them—was the pot of gold at the end of his rainbow, his whole reason for accepting this crazy submarine assignment to begin with. He had had no choice but to hide it away from his locker, especially since he was certain that Penn had gone through his seabag yesterday. Something deep down inside him told him that Penn had found the loot but for some reason had decided not to take it. Fabriano could see his secret revealed in the shifty nature of Penn's eyes during line handling on deck that morning, across the mess room during lunch, and many other times throughout the day when their paths crossed in the narrow passageways. Penn knew about the money, all right, and Fabriano only hoped that the bastard was too much of a coward to do anything about it.

Maybe Penn was afraid of what he might do. Maybe Penn was planning on swiping the money later. Maybe Penn would figure out that it was stolen money and turn him in to the Cob. The thought sent shivers up and down Fabriano's spine. He had come too far to be denied his fortune by some asshole who couldn't keep his nose out of other people's business.

Just then, the hair stood up on the back of Fabriano's neck. He felt like eyes were on him and instinctively turned around to face the aft portion of the compartment. Back by the shiny breech doors of the aft torpedo tubes, a group of sailors were gathered around an upturned bucket, playing a quiet game of cards. A sailor kneeling on the far side of the group glanced up at Fabriano, saw that Fabriano was looking, and then quickly shifted his eyes back to the five cards in front of his face.

It was Penn.

The bastard was watching his every move, thought Fabriano, probably looking for any clues as to where the money was hidden. Now he was certain that Penn intended to take the money whenever he had the chance. Fabriano now knew that he would have to be on guard day and night.

"Hey, all you aft room weenies!" A sailor poked his head through the hatchlike door at the forward end of the compartment. "Captain's authorized a movie tonight. Betty Grable's playing in the crew's mess at twenty-one hundred hours. Better hurry to get good seats."

The men in the room cheered, the card games quickly broke up, and a long file of sailors queued up at the forward door, waiting their turn to pass through the small opening to head to the crew's mess. Penn was among those heading forward, and Fabriano fell in line directly behind him. As the line moved closer and closer to the door, Fabriano could tell that Penn knew he was there. The wiry sailor fidgeted from one foot to the next, but never turned around.

This was it, thought Fabriano. He had to make this son of a bitch scared of him. It was the only way to keep Penn's nose out of his business.

The man in front of Penn ducked through the low hatch, and now came Penn's turn. Penn ducked down to pass through, but was quickly jerked back upright by Fabriano's hand clasped on the back of his shirt collar.

"Let me help you through the hatch there, shipmate!" Fabriano said.

With one hand firmly attached to Penn's collar, Fabriano used his other on the back of Penn's head to forcefully drive the sailor's face directly into the steel knife edge along the upper frame of the door. There was an ugly crunching sound, and a gush of blood that dribbled onto the deck between Penn's feet. Penn let out a howling screech and immediately brought his hands to his shattered nose. Then Fabriano spun the dazed sailor around and shoved him into the outboard. Penn tripped backward over a pipe and crumpled to the deck, blood oozing out between his fingers and running down his arms as he continued clutching his face.

Instantly, Fabriano was seized by the half-dozen men from Penn's card game, snarling and cursing up a swarm of derogatory terms applied to Fabriano and to his destroyer heritage. Two men had his arms braced behind his back, while two more had him by the throat demanding to know why he had done what he did. But all the while Fabriano's face was bulging and turning bright red from the pressure of the squeezing hands, he kept his eyes locked squarely on Penn's. The huddled sailor was staring back at him through tears and bloody fingers, and Fabriano knew that his message had been received loud and clear. It was clear that Penn now knew what he was capable of. Fabriano only hoped it would be enough to make the nosy bastard steer clear of him for the rest of the patrol.

But Fabriano had only a few moments to contemplate it.

Within seconds the other men forced him to the deck and were kicking him, shouting at him, standing on him, pressing in until he thought his lungs would rupture and his ribs would crack. Soon he tasted blood in his mouth, and felt a tooth come loose, but it was at the last moment he felt he could stay conscious without a breath of air that the pressure suddenly let up. The men stopped kicking him, and a deep voice boomed behind him.

"What the hell's all this? I'm trying to fucking sleep!"

"This destroyer asshole shoved Penn's face into the hatch! Broke his damn nose, Shelby!"

"Well, who's to say Penn didn't need his nose busted?" Shelby's voice replied with a snarl.

"Damn it, Shelby, this new asshole just coldcocked one of our own. Aren't you going to do nothing about it?" said another sailor.

Fabriano felt himself being lifted up by two big hands, to stand upright. He looked up to see Shelby's big frame standing between him and the men who had attacked him.

"All right, Mikey, what have you got to say for yourself?" Shelby said calmly.

"The man went through my kit," Fabriano said firmly, wiping away a trail of blood streaming down his chin.

"Now, you see, fellas? A perfectly good explanation. A man don't break another man's nose for no reason." Shelby reached over and with one arm hoisted the hunkering Penn back to his feet. "Penn, did you go through the man's bag? And be honest, because I'll know if you're fucking lying to me."

After hesitating for a moment, Penn finally nodded behind his bloody hands.

"There now," Shelby said compromisingly to the room, "don't we all feel better? I'd say the pot's right, wouldn't you, fellas? Why don't we all just bury the hatchet and forget about the whole thing."

Just then, Master Chief LaGrange's scowling face poked through the door.

"What the hell's going on back here? I heard there was a fight . . ." LaGrange stepped into the room and stood up, his face contorted as he noticed the two bloody men standing on either side of Shelby.

"No, Cob. No fights back here," Shelby said, grinning through crooked teeth. "These boys were just in such a rush to see Betty Grable, they tripped over each other going out the hatch."

LaGrange had been in the navy a long time, far too long to buy such a cockamamie story. But he had also been in the navy long enough to know when he should let certain things go. Shipboard life was so much different from any other life on earth. There was an unwritten law at sea that was almost as important as the Uniform Code of Military Justice, an unwritten law that was just as critical to maintaining good order and discipline in any crew. He knew there had been a fight, but that fight was obviously over, and the two combatants appeared to be suffering from roughly the same degree of injuries. It appeared that whatever quarrel had existed moments before was now settled. Besides, this was only the first day at sea, and they had a long patrol ahead of them.

"You boys better cut along to the corpsman and get patched up," LaGrange finally said, his face slackening. "After that, come and see me. The rest of you go watch your damn movie."

There was a collective sigh of relief in the compartment as the men's faces once again broke out into smiles. Fabriano and Penn left the room favoring their bloody wounds while the rest of the men filed out behind them one at a time on their way to the crew's mess. Soon the room was empty, except for LaGrange and the half dozen or so snoring sailors in the swinging racks.

"We're all getting our sea legs again," LaGrange mumbled to himself. "We've had far too much time ashore."

PART III

Chapter 8

"**STANDBY** to fire the four-inch gun! Shift targets to the next junk!"

Whately shouted the order over the bridge railing, down to the men clustered around the *Whitefin*'s smoking four-inch gun on the main deck. Several gray-helmeted heads turned to glance briefly up at the bridge before returning their attention to the burning junk on the horizon.

The *Whitefin* sat on a glistening ocean, rigged for battle stations surface, driving north at ten knots, with the green mountainous peaks of Bali just poking above the southwestern horizon. Having spent the better part of the previous night working through Lombok Strait, they had now officially left the Indian Ocean and entered the Java Sea.

Tremain felt the blessed sun baking his arms, calves, and ankles. He had decided several days ago to abandon his ill-fitting uniform pants for a pair of infinitely more comfortable khaki shorts and sandals—commonly worn by submariners in these equatorial climates. He could see the evidence of the stress of the previous evening on the faces all around him. It had taken eleven hours to navigate submerged through the closely guarded Lombok Strait, a small water passage separating the islands of Bali and Lombok, along the southern edge of the Pacific's great ring of fire, which also served as the southern boundary of the Japanese Empire. Eleven hours rigged for silent running, which meant eleven hours of hot and humid air with no air-conditioning; eleven hours of waiting, riding the gentle currents from the Indian Ocean to the Pacific, listening for enemy patrols boats, praying that the Japanese had not laid any new minefields in the small waterway. All in all, the passage had been uneventful, which ironically had made it all the more agonizing.

At the first light of dawn, the *Whitefin* had made it through the strait, and surfaced to recharge batteries, giving her crew a much needed break. But within the hour, as the chugging diesel engines attempted to place as much distance as possible between the *Whitefin* and the Japanese-held island of Bali, a small fleet of coastal junks suddenly appeared on the northern horizon, driving west with all sails set. And now the same junks sat three thousand yards off the *Whitefin*'s port beam, three sitting ducks with no chance of escape.

It had not taken very long for the *Whitefin*'s diesels to close the range, and once called, the deck gun crew had sprung to their stations as eager as a pack of hyenas after a lion's cub. After only five shots, they had the range, and had quickly made flotsam of the closest junk, now burning ferociously in the distance, leaving a great black shroud of smoke in the sky. The flames would soon be extinguished, for she was headed down fast.

"Pardon my being nosy, old boy." Farquhar suddenly appeared at Tremain's side. "But would you mind telling me just what the devil we're shooting at."

The British major had spent most of the patrol thus far in the wardroom waiting for the next off-watch officer to play cribbage with, and Tremain had half-expected him to remain there until the *Whitefin* reached his destination.

"Not at all, Major," Tremain answered blankly, pointing in the direction of the smoking junk. "There are three sailboats out there, trying to make it into Java, with war cargo aboard no doubt. We've just sunk one of them, and now we're going to sink the rest."

"Jolly good."

Farquhar withdrew a small pair of field binoculars from a leather case around his neck and brought the lenses to his eyes. He scrunched up his mouth a few times as he watched the fleeing craft.

Wham! The deck gun rang out, shaking the teeth of every man on the bridge.

"Isn't that Bali I see on the horizon?" Farquhar said, going up onto his tiptoes as he followed the arcing tracer shell until it fell into the sea, throwing up a geyser of white spray far to the right of the next farthest junk. "Listen, I hate to be a bore, and I certainly don't want to be one going around citing official orders and all, but didn't yours say to deliver me to Mindanao forthwith, avoiding all contact with the enemy along the way?"

"They did, but I'm using a captain's prerogative here, Major. I don't want to take my ship and crew any farther into enemy waters before we have our first test of combat together. It's essential that we know each other's tendencies before we find ourselves facing a Japanese destroyer."

Wham!

The deck gun rang out again, shaking the deck beneath their feet. Every man watched through his binoculars and saw the shell splash into the sea, this time only a few dozen yards ahead of the second junk.

"Combat?" Farquhar said as the deck gun rang out once more. "More like shooting bloody fish in a barrel, if you ask me."

Tremain said nothing in response, keeping his binoculars squarely leveled on the distant sail craft. At less than a mile and a half away, the ribbed, orange sails of the two remaining junks completely filled his field of view. They were both roughly the same size—more like large yachts—each with the two masts and jib sail he had seen so often in these waters. Their single-decked low hulls were made of dark wood, probably from the teak forests of Indochina, and he judged that each carried no more than an eight-man crew. Both boats were headed southwest as fast as their meager sails could carry them, obviously aware of the fate that awaited them. After crossing the Java Sea from some unknown location, they were on the home stretch of their voyage, no more than a hundred miles from Surabaya, their probable destination. But now they would never reach it. They were in the wrong place at the wrong time and had to be cursing their misfortune to whatever god they prayed to.

Tremain shifted his focus to the closest junk, where several men were rushing about on deck, tossing last-minute supplies into a frail rowboat which they were preparing to lower into the sea. They had obviously come to the conclusion that their chances were slim and had given up.

"I think they're trying to abandon ship, sir," Whately said excitedly. "Shall I have the deck gun shift fire to their lifeboat?"

"No, Mr. Whately, we'll let that one go for the time being. But let's see if we can encourage the men in the other craft to do the same. Pass the word to the deck gun to shift targets to the leading junk and commence firing."

Whately looked slightly confused as he passed the order to the phone talker, who in turn passed the order to the deck gun. From Whately's expression, Tremain guessed that Commander Burgess had been a little more bloodthirsty than he was. The rules of war were easily broken outside the purview of higher authorities, and perhaps Burgess had broken them on occasions such as this one. Who could blame him, when at this very moment armadas of bombers from both sides were turning European cities into rubble, dropping bombs with time-delayed fuses with the sole intention of killing emergency workers as they emerged from their shelters to put out fires and tend to the wounded?

"But . . . but they're civilians, they're sailboats, for God's sake!" The hitherto silent Ensign Berkshire suddenly spoke up from his position on the opposite side of the bridge. This was obviously the first time the young Harvard grad had ever seen the dirty side of war. "How can we do this? They've got no chance at all!"

Never removing the binoculars from his face, Tremain sensed the ensign wince behind him, and could only guess that Whately had planted a stiff elbow in the young officer's ribs.

"Use your head, you idiot!" Whately said. "Those boats are low in the water. They're coming from Makassar, trying to slip across to Java with war materials. Don't you think the Japanese know we've got subs out here? And don't you think they know we're reluctant to sink civilian craft? The bastards have got it all figured out. They can get just as much material across if they send a hundred of these little sailboats, as they can if they send one big freighter. It only takes one torpedo to take out the freighter, whereas these friggin' things have to be hunted down on the surface one by one."

Tremain simmered beneath his binoculars. Whately was an arrogant ass, but he was also right. While most of these craft were owned and operated by civilians—Javanese or Malaysian sailors mostly—they were often used to carry food and supplies that would eventually end up in Japanese hands, since Jakarta and all of Indonesia were now part of the empire. Since the early days in '42, ComSubPac's policy for dealing with these craft had wavered with the winds. But when Tremain commanded the *Seatrout* in these waters, he had made it a point to sink them whenever and wherever he found them. Of course, he took no joy in it. They were civilian craft, and leaving civilians to the mercy of the sea always left him feeling somewhat callous. But, on the other hand, many Indonesians were willing accomplices in the Japanese ambition to control the Pacific. Perhaps they saw it as a golden opportunity to finally win independence from Dutch colonial rule. Regardless of their reasoning—regardless of Japan's consent to their right of self-rule—they were, for all intents and purposes, part of the Japanese Empire, and they would have to be treated as such.

Wham!

The deck gun fired again, the elevated barrel spewing forth a halo of white smoke, the concussion wave turning the green water off the port beam into a shimmering white disturbance. Tremain could hear the spent four-inch cartridge clang to the deck and get pitched over the side as he watched the tracer round through his binoculars. The tiny white dot appeared to drive almost straight out to the horizon and then it came down quickly into the sea halfway between the two junks, throwing up a perfectly vertical water spout less than fifty yards away from each. On the deck of the leading junk, Tremain saw the frantic sailors turn their heads to stare ominously at the column of water left by the *Whitefin*'s shell. But still, they sailed on, never showing any signs of abandoning ship, unlike their comrades from the other junk who had already piled into their own little lifeboat and were now rowing furiously in the opposite direction.

"Why don't you take a closer look at that leading junk, and tell me what you see, Mr. Berkshire," Tremain said, casually.

Wham! The deck gun fired again.

As before, Tremain watched the tiny dot, but this time it came down less than twenty yards from the junk's stern, throwing spray over the panicky crew, who were now waving their hands and shouting something to the men in the second junk's lifeboat, about a hundred yards away.

"Wh-what is it, sir?" the young ensign said inquisitively. "I can't make out anything but a couple of sailboats . . ."

Berkshire was abruptly cut off by Whately.

"Can't you see the damn thirty-foot antenna sticking out for the entire world to see? Peaceful sailing junks, eh? Peaceful junks don't carry long-range comms gear, you fool. What the hell are they teaching you guys at sub school these days, anyway?"

"I . . . I didn't know I was supposed to—"

Wham! The gun fired again.

The projectile seemed to take an eternity to complete its long arc, but it finally struck the ocean only a few yards away from the junk, skipping once before driving straight into the fragile craft's wooded hull. The next moment the junk disappeared in a single bright flash of light, instantly replaced by an expanding white cloud of smoke and splinters. Seconds later, the thundering echo of the detonation rumbled across the water and reached the ears of the men on the *Whitefin*'s bridge.

"Direct hit!" Whately exclaimed in an unfeeling manner. "Just goes to show what good shots our boys are! The bastards never knew what hit them."

When the smoke finally cleared, there was nothing left of the junk but a few bits of smoking wood and cordage. The men in the lifeboat made no effort to row over to look for their comrades among the floating wreckage, since there certainly could have been no survivors. The gun crew was certainly well practiced, but Tremain doubted one four-inch shell by itself could cause such complete destruction. Whether it was fuel or paint or any other number of other volatile substances, the unfortunate vessel's cargo had been its undoing, not the *Whitefin*'s shell.

"Bridge, Radar," the intercom intoned. "Multiple SD contacts, fifteen miles and closing!"

"Bridge, XO." Monroe's voice came over the intercom. He was down in the control room, overseeing the plots and running the day-to-day business of the ship so that Tremain could concentrate on the action. "Those could be enemy aircraft from the airfield at Denpasar. Recommend keeping an eye on the southern sector."

"Watch for aircraft!" Tremain shouted to the men up in the lookout perches. Then to the phone talker: "Pass the word to the deck gun, destroy that last junk ASAP!"

Instinctively, everyone on the bridge looked at the southern sky, squinting to find the invisible aircraft in the white haze. Like duelists sizing up their opponents, the gunners on the forward gun deck and cigarette deck embraced their shoulder stocks and began drawing tight circles in the air with the long, tapered barrels of their twenty-millimeter machine guns.

"Now you know why it's important never to judge a ship by its looks, Mr. Berkshire," Tremain said without looking at the ensign.

"Yes, sir," Berkshire said as he tried to melt into the conning tower's steel skin.

Assuming the aircraft were indeed responding to a distress call by the junks, they would be coming on at full throttle, without any regard for fuel conservation, in an attempt to catch the American submarine on the surface. It would take them less than five minutes to get here.

Tremain was about to shout over the railing for the gun crew to hurry up, when the deck gun erupted again.

Wham!

The wind shifted, catching the white gun smoke and blowing it across the conning tower, obstructing Tremain's view of the target completely. Before the smoke had cleared, he heard a cheer roar down on the main deck. Apparently the shell had

scored a hit on the second craft, a spectacle he and the rest of
the men on the bridge did not get to see. When the painstak-
ingly slow cloud of smoke finally drifted past, Tremain could
see that the four-inch round had smashed into the remaining
junk's bow, turning it to splinters. The damage must have extended below the waterline, too, because he could see the junk's
hull droop visibly as it slowly climbed over each successive
wave. Within seconds, water began breaking over its main deck,
washing gear and crates into the sea. Then the masts finally
gave, snapping off in two consecutive and violent jerks of the
wooden hull. As the broken junk went under, disappearing
completely from view, Tremain could see the men in the distant
rowboat pulling for their lives, obviously fearing that they would
be next since they were now the only craft afloat.

"Bridge, Radar. Aircraft now at ten miles!"

"Two aircraft visible, sir!" bellowed the big red-haired
lookout, Shelby, who Tremain had learned had the best set of
eyes on board. "Bearing one-eight-zero, relative! Fifteen thousand yards!"

"Secure the guns! Clear the decks! Rig for dive!" Tremain
shouted. His comfort zone had been breached. The planes
were too close now.

Instantly, the machine gunners broke down the twenty-
millimeter guns and Browning Automatic Rifles and started
passing them, along with their spare magazines, over the rails
to the waiting hands on the main deck. The guns were quickly
shuttled to the access hatch in the port side of the conning
tower, to be stowed for sea.

"Get a move on!" Tremain heard Whately's shrill voice
yell above the purring diesels. "Get that gun rigged for dive!
Dump that ammo over the side!"

The men on deck responded quickly, the gunner wheeling
the deck gun back around as fast as his arms could turn it, until it pointed directly at the *Whitefin*'s bow. The loaders capped
and locked the gun's barrel and breech and then tossed the
half-dozen or so staged four-inch rounds into the sea. This
was a trade-off. It was more important to get below quickly
than it was to save a few rounds of four-inch ammunition.

Within a minute, the main deck was clear and all hatches
were shut.

"Bridge, Control." Monroe's voice came over the intercom. "We have a green board with the exception of the main induction and the bridge hatch."

"Very well," Tremain said into the microphone, assuming the conn from Whately, "Helm, Bridge, all ahead flank!"

Now that the deck was clear and the hatches secure, he could order up more speed. And the *Whitefin* was going to need all the speed she could manage to assist with the imminent crash dive. He still could not see the enemy planes in the white haze, but the lookout Shelby swore they were there, dots in the sky above the *Whitefin*'s roiling white wake.

"They're nose on and closing fast, sir!" he exclaimed, staring aft from the portside lookout perch.

Tremain felt the other men on the bridge casting doubtful eyes in his direction, Farquhar included. They were obviously wondering why he had not yet given the order to dive. But Tremain knew it was no use simply diving. Undoubtedly the aircraft had already sighted the American submarine and would have no trouble tracing her bubbly wake right to the spot where she went down. Right now, the *Whitefin*'s only salvation was in depth. And in order to get deep, fast, she needed speed. She needed at least nineteen knots to get her down past the surface suction forces in short order. Tremain had been caught up in freak suction on one too many dives during his career. He knew the unpredictable forces could hold up an otherwise negatively buoyant submarine at sixty feet or even shallower for several minutes before releasing it to the deep— and sixty feet would not be deep enough to escape the depth bombs undoubtedly carried by the approaching aircraft.

"Bridge, Radar. Aircraft now ten thousand yards and closing!"

Out of the corner of his eye, Tremain saw Farquhar and the others shoot him disparaging glances. No doubt, they thought this was madness. The aircraft would be overhead within a minute.

"Lookouts below!" Tremain shouted over his shoulder, as he scanned the southern sky for the approaching enemy.

Before he had time to glance up, all three lookouts had slid down from their perches and dropped down the bridge hatch one by one, with Shelby the last to descend.

"They're coming in fast, sir! Seven o'clock low!" Shelby called in parting, his voice echoing as his head disappeared beneath the hatch ring.

Tremain returned to his binoculars, and steadied them on the horizon off the *Whitefin*'s port quarter.

There they were! Two single-engine aircraft coming in low, hugging the waves, apparently in an effort to avoid the submarine's radar. The pair appeared to have bombs slung under their wings.

"Helm, Bridge, mark speed by log!"

"Bridge, Helm," came an agitated voice over the intercom. "Speed by log, eighteen knots!"

It would have to do. Tremain reached over and grabbed the diving alarm handle, pulling it twice.

Aaaooogah! Aaaoooooogaaahhh!

"Crash dive!" he shouted into the speaker, with more fervor than he had intended to.

Then he yanked the diving alarm two more times, and followed the three other officers down the open hatch, almost knocking Farquhar off the ladder as he dropped down right behind him. By the time he reached the bottom of the ladder, and shut the hatch, the deck had already tilted down by five degrees. He heard the familiar sounds of the exhaust flapper shutting, followed by the main induction valve. He felt the pressure on his eardrums increase as the diesel engines gulped in their last breath of air, then came to a crashing stop.

"Green board! Pressure in the boat!" he heard the chief at the ballast control panel announce down in the control room.

"Continue with the dive," the diving officer Allendale's voice said immediately after. "Flood negative!"

With the hatch secure, Tremain climbed down the ladder from the conning tower into the teeming control room, where Monroe and Allendale stood behind the men operating the stern and bow planes. Both planesmen were holding their controls at the full dive position, their eyes fixed to the bubble and plane angle indications. The deck was still angled down, with the bubble indicator showing twenty degrees dive, and Tremain could feel the sense of drag being produced by the ocean as it grabbed more and more of the *Whitefin*'s hull, slowing it rapidly.

"I got a look at those planes through the scope, Captain," Monroe called to him across the crowded room. "They're Zeke bombers. Two bombs each, with twenty-millimeter guns on the wings and 7.7's on the fuselage."

Men were still moving about everywhere, stowing helmets and lifejackets, machine guns and ammunition, and Tremain had to muscle a path through them to stand beside Monroe and Allendale.

"Rig for depth charge."

"Rig for depth charge, aye, sir."

Hatches and ventilation flappers rang shut as the order was broadcast over the 1MC to all compartments.

The depth gauge on the bulkhead read seventy-five feet. The *Whitefin*'s masts were just beneath the surface.

"Negative tank flooded," the chief manning the ballast controls reported to Allendale. "All main ballast tank vents indicate shut."

Allendale calmly pressed two fingers to his lips as he studied the ship's gauges like a lion tamer sizing up his beast for its next trick. In the few days Tremain had known him, the tall, thin lieutenant with an intelligent-looking face had certainly demonstrated his perspicacity as a submariner. He came across as every bit of the intellectual mathematician Monroe had claimed him to be. But he also came across as someone deeply devoted to his ship, almost to the point of obsession. He had a tendency to hold his head such that his short, triangular nose pointed upward slightly, and this had the compounded effect of making him look down his nose most of the time, and at most people. It also had the effect of making his eyes appear to be shut even when he was wide awake. On one occasion earlier in the week, Tremain believed he had caught his engineering and diving officer asleep on watch only to learn with astonishment that the man was wide awake, and alert as ever.

"I know this boat, Captain," Allendale had said with the closest thing to a smile Tremain felt he would ever see on his face. "I don't need to be awake to know that she's all right. I can feel it."

Tremain had not pressed for any further explanation, partly because he didn't wish to get into the mysticism attached to the comment and partly because he remembered Monroe telling him that the odd lieutenant had been with the ship since it was nothing more than a collection of steel hoops sitting on the blocks in Manitowoc. Tremain understood that when a sailor watched a ship grow from its keel laying to its practical application in war, it tended to imbue him with a certain bond that could not easily be explained to those who had not experienced it. He was a *plank owner,* and like any parent who nurtures and cares for a child through its infancy, a plank owner always felt a special affection for "his ship." As the *Whitefin*'s one and only plank owner aboard, Allendale obviously had a special attachment to her.

"We should see the negative tank start to take effect now," Allendale said coolly.

True enough, the deck began to assume a larger down angle. A swoosh from a random wave shoved the hull to one side, but Tremain clearly saw the movement on the depth-gauge dial in the downward direction.

"Eighty feet . . . ," announced Allendale. "Ninety . . . One hundred . . ."

"Make your depth three hundred fifty feet."

"Three hundred fifty feet, aye, sir," Allendale said with barely even the slightest movement of his lips. "Passing one hundred thirty feet . . . one hundred fifty . . . one seventy . . . Ease off on your stern planes. Hold her at twenty-five degrees down bubble."

"All stations report that conditions are normal on the dive, sir," announced a sailor wearing a phone set.

"Very well."

Tremain looked at his watch and counted the seconds. The enemy planes should be reaching the patch of ocean where the *Whitefin* slipped beneath the waves right about now. They probably would not drop on the first pass, he concluded, but would instead climb to an altitude where they could set up for individual bombing runs at steeper angles. Aiming the bombs correctly from such a low altitude would be difficult if not impossible. The Japanese planes would need time to climb to the new altitude, and Tremain planned to use that to his advantage.

"Helm!" he called up the ladder to the conning tower. "Right full rudder!"

"Right full rudder, aye, sir," the unseen helmsman's voice came back.

As the rudder came over, the added drag began to slow the dive slightly, but not by much. The *Whitefin*'s speed through the water had already dropped off quite substantially since submerging, now traveling only eight knots and still slowing. It was her weight now and not her speed that was driving the *Whitefin* so rapidly into the deep, and Tremain forced himself to muster a small measure of confidence that Allendale fully understood that.

"Passing two hundred fifty feet," Allendale announced.

"Passing zero-nine-zero to the right, sir," called the helmsman.

"Helm, steady as you go!"

The *Whitefin*'s head slowed on its starboard turn and steadied out pointing to the southeast. The rudder drag had reduced the speed temporarily, but now with the rudder off, the *Whitefin*'s straining electric motors would bring her back up to her maximum speed of nine and a half knots in less than a minute. It was a speed that depleted her batteries at an appalling rate, and one that Tremain did not want to maintain for very long. He might need a reserve of battery power if an enemy destroyer happened to show up and join in the hunt.

"Passing three hundred feet," Allendale said impassively. The announcement was accentuated by a surging rattle of the hull running from fore to aft as the *Whitefin*'s welded plates adjusted to the increased sea pressure. Every square inch of steel was now being pressed in by the weight of a column of water three hundred feet high.

Still descending, the *Whitefin* rapidly approached the ordered depth, test depth, at a speed that was well outside Tremain's comfort zone. He was about to make a comment, when Allendale calmly began issuing orders.

"Blow negative to the mark. Full rise on the bow planes. Full rise on the stern planes. Zero bubble."

Like a finely tuned instrument, the men at the diving station operated their controls in unison. The chief at the ballast control panel pulled a lever and sent three thousand pounds per square inch of high-pressure air blasting into the negative tank, forcing several thousand pounds of water back into the sea. Removing the weighty water from the negative tank up in the *Whitefin*'s bow had an almost instantaneous effect on the ship's angle. The angle began coming off, assisted by the large surface areas of the bow and stern planes. Within seconds, she had pulled out of the dive. Then gingerly, harmoniously, the bubble in the ship's angle indicator inched up to zero and stopped with the depth gauge needle locked solidly on three hundred and fifty feet.

Allendale certainly knew this boat, Tremain mused.

Just then the sonar operator's head, adorned with a large set of headphones, appeared overhead in the hatch to the conning tower.

"Splashes on the surface, Captain," he reported. "Directly above us."

"How many?"

"I counted two, sir."

"Two bombs from one plane, perhaps," Tremain said to Monroe.

"Then that leaves just two more, assuming we survive these two." Monroe smiled, then turned and motioned to the phoneman standing beside him.

"All compartments," the sailor said into the microphone while keying the handset. "Brace for impact. Depth bombs on the way down."

There was nothing to do now but wait. Tremain had done all he could by going deep and turning ninety degrees off base course. A long whine ran throughout the ship, startling the greener sailors in the room, but it was nothing more than another groan from the *Whitefin*'s stressed steel girders. This was the boat's deepest dive since her initial test dive after getting under way, and the fear was apparent on their unseasoned faces, wondering which they should fear more, the crushing ocean pressing in all around them or the enemy depth bombs hurtling closer and closer.

As he waited for the inevitable, Tremain found it odd that he began thinking about how Fabriano must be faring back at his battle station in the maneuvering room. What had to be going through his mind, after being in surface ships his entire career? The change had been rough, so far. Despite Fabriano's obvious temper problems, Tremain had still been surprised to see the destroyer sailor's name show up on the report list after only two days at sea. Apparently he'd roughed up some poor unsuspecting sailor, probably for some unintended insult. Tremain had let the normal disciplinary routine run its course, since any probing questions or interference on his part would have been inappropriate, even detrimental to Fabriano's chances of fitting in with his new shipmates. The Cob had assigned him extra duties for two weeks, and hopefully that would be an end of it. Perhaps what he was about to be subjected to in the next few seconds would take the sand out of him.

Whack! Swoosh!

The first bomb went off unbelievably close to the *Whitefin*'s starboard side, the massive shock wave rippling along the submarine's length from the center outward. The force of the blast displaced the ship a few inches to port, and Tremain could have sworn that he saw the whole compartment whip lengthwise like a snake. Lightbulbs burst in the overhead. Shattered glass and cork insulation rained down everywhere. Sailors were knocked off their feet, and into protruding valve handles or brackets that bumped heads and left large bruises on arms, backs, and legs.

When the vibration subsided, they were allowed only a fraction of a second of peace before the second bomb detonated on the opposite side of the hull and several feet below, probably set to go off at four hundred feet. The second one did not have quite the sheer horror of the first, but the expanding bubble it created must have encompassed at least some of the submarine's hull as it rose to the surface, because the *Whitefin* suddenly rolled forty-five degrees to port for no apparent reason and then just as suddenly righted herself. Men who weren't ready for it went flying into the port bulkhead and crashed to the deck with winces and moans. Somewhere in the dim light a call echoed for the pharmacist's mate. When Tremain had a moment to collect his own bearings, he noticed Allendale standing behind the diving panel fixed in the same posture as he was before, apparently unfazed by either bomb as he talked lowly to the planesmen to maintain ordered depth. The rest of the men looked more than a little shocked, even the veterans. And Tremain had to admit that the bombs were much closer than he had expected them to be. Those

Japanese pilots up there were either lucky, or damn good! Or perhaps the beleaguered sailors in the lifeboat had somehow vectored the planes to the right location. They were no doubt at this moment watching with amusement as the American submarine received a little of its own medicine.

"Helm," Tremain called up the dimly lit hatch while supporting himself on the ladder rungs. He had to do something, if only to give the men something to think about other than the next two bombs. "Left full rudder. Let's see if we can outsmart these bastards."

"My rudder is left full, sir," the helmsman answered in a strained voice, probably wincing from some contusion he'd received when the first bomb rattled the hull.

"Diving Officer," Tremain said. "Make your depth one hundred fifty feet. They've got their bombs set deep, so let's go shallow."

Allendale acknowledged, muttered a few words to the planesmen, and the *Whitefin*'s bow began nosing up toward the surface.

Bang! A loud noise came from back aft. It sounded different from a depth bomb, but no less disturbing.

Bang! It rang out again, sending vibrations through the deck plates. It sounded like someone was lighting off sticks of dynamite in one of the aft compartments.

Tremain shot a glance at Monroe, who was making scribbles on the status board with a grease pencil as he listened to the phone talker's reports.

"We're just getting damage reports now, sir. That noise is the five-hundred-pound high-pressure air reducer back in the forward engine room. The relief valve keeps lifting. Must've lost its adjustment when those bombs went off. They've got a mechanic working on it right now. We've also got minor leakage in the forward torpedo room, coming from the forward trim manifold. They say they can handle it. Two men up there suffered head contusions. They're being carried to the wardroom for the doc to check them out. No other apparent damage so far."

"Very well, XO."

Tremain considered. It certainly could have been worse, especially as close as that first bomb had been.

"Splashes, Captain," the sonarman called from the conning tower.

"Brace yourselves!" Tremain said to the room in general. "Here we go again."

"Passing two hundred feet," Allendale announced.

Again, the long, agonizing wait. Then suddenly.

Whack! Swoosh! . . . Whack! Swoosh!

Both bombs went off in succession, but the bombs must have gone off much farther beneath them this time. Still, the hull shook and rumbled, but nothing in comparison with the first bomb. Coming shallow had been a gamble, but the gamble had paid off, and now the Japanese were out of bombs, at least for the time being, and could do nothing but circle the area and wait to be relieved by another flight of aircraft. Tremain was tempted to come to periscope depth for a brief look around, but then thought better of it. Perhaps the Japanese would send out a patrol craft next, or even a destroyer. Either way, he did not intend to stick around to find out.

"Dive, make your depth three hundred feet. Those planes may be out of bombs, but I've no doubt they can see us when we're this shallow. The water around here is so clear you can see the bottom in some places."

"Aye, aye, sir," Allendale acknowledged with a shrug, then issued the orders to his planesmen.

"Helm, all ahead one-third," Tremain called up the hatch. "Steer course north."

"All ahead one-third, steer course north, Helm, aye."

Tremain caught the doubtful expressions on the faces of several sailors in the room. Now that the dust had settled, he guessed they were doing the numbers in their heads. Three sailing junks were not a fair exchange for a fleet submarine. Did they think he had been too hasty in taking on the junks this close to a Japanese air base? After all, things had gotten chancy for a few moments. Had that Japanese bomb been a few feet closer, the *Whitefin* might be lying strewn across the bottom right now, in a thousand little pieces, instead of cruising on to her patrol area. But Tremain knew that they needed this baptism by fire, not only the green hands, but all of them. He needed it, too. He needed to remember things that he had learned to shut out over the long months away. In order to be an effective captain, in order to lead his crew in battle, he needed to know the feeling once again of sitting inside a steel tube while the dice rolled and hell rained down from above. This action, as reckless as it might have seemed to some of them, would get them back into their war patrol mind-sets. From here on out, they'd be ready for anything—anything the Japanese, or their captain, might throw at them.

"Let's secure from battle stations, Chris," he said brightly to Monroe. "Return to base course and keep me informed. You have the conn."

Tremain reached for the 1MC microphone on the bulkhead.

"Attention all hands. This is the captain. You can breathe easy for a little while. The smoking lamp is lit for the next quarter hour. I suggest everyone take advantage of it. I want all division chiefs to conduct a thorough inspection of their spaces and report any damage to the control room. So far, it looks like we got off lightly. I want to commend you all on an excellent performance during the gun action. As you are undoubtedly aware, we're in enemy waters from here on out, so be ready for anything the Japanese might have in store for us. We're going to run submerged until nightfall, then surface and continue on to Mindanao in the Philippine Islands to drop off our guest. We should arrive there in three days, weather and enemy permitting. Then it's on to our patrol area, where the real hunting begins. Carry on, gentlemen."

As Tremain hung the microphone back on the bulkhead, he scanned the faces around him. Some were smiling; others were still doubtful. For a few moments they lulled; then they went back to their duties, a few mild conversations breaking the silence as the recirculation fans whirred to life. The big ventilation flappers clunked opened and the air was once again exchanged between compartments. Within minutes the whole room was filled with swirling tobacco smoke.

Tremain headed through the forward door and down the passage to the wardroom, where he poured himself a cup of coffee from the steaming carafe that Miguel, the Filipino wardroom steward, had already prepared and placed on the credenza. Tremain could hear the dependable steward moving about in the pantry, already preparing for the noon meal, as if

the gun action and the close depth bombs had never even occurred.

Suddenly, Tremain realized that Farquhar was also in the
room, sitting quietly in one corner of the booth table, looking
very pale and sweating profusely, his hands shakily holding
a cigarette between his lips which he had already smoked
halfway through.

Tremain poured another cup of coffee and approached him
slowly, placing the steaming cup on the table in front of him.

"Are you all right, Major?" Tremain ventured to say, sliding into his own chair at the end of the table.

"Bloody awful . . . ," Farquhar muttered, and then shot him
a hesitant glance. "That was bloody awful, Tremain."

Obviously, the major had never undergone a depth bombing before, and the experience had left him rather ruffled. It
was all Tremain could do to keep from laughing out loud.

"I believe you were saying earlier, Major, something about
shooting fish in a barrel?"

Chapter 9

IT was a quiet evening aboard the *Whitefin* as the submarine cruised on the surface through Makassar Strait, the broad waterway separating the massive islands of Borneo and Celebes. All traces of the morning's action had been wiped away from the spaces as well as from the faces of her crew, a majority of which sat crowded around the tables in the darkened crew's mess laughing heartily at the Hope and Crosby film *Road to Morocco*. Most of them were seeing it for the twelfth time already on this patrol, but that did not seem to matter much.

Penn was the only one in the mess who was not in stitches over the mindless, slapstick humor. He had other things on his mind at present.

Pretending that he could not get into the jovial mood, he got up from his table and wallowed through the mass of bodies to head aft into the darkened bunk room, and through the watertight door beyond. As he passed through the hot and humid forward engine room, the intense pulsation of the diesels made his throbbing nose hurt even worse. Shouting at the top of his lungs, he cursed Fabriano's name out loud, but his voice was drowned out by the roaring engines and never made it to the ears of the few watchstanders in the room wearing oversized ear muffs. Marching on between the big diesel engines on either side, and then between the matching generator sets, he passed through another watertight door, where he was met by another pair of engines and generators. In this engine room, he saw a few shirtless mechanics, covered in grease and intently working on the only diesel engine on board that was shut down. It reminded him of the dozen maintenance items he had been assigned to do this evening, but he tried not to think about that at the moment. Instead, he focused on the task ahead. After passing through the engine room's aft door and shutting it behind him, he and his aching head welcomed the relative peace and quiet of the maneuvering room.

He heard voices down the passage and around the corner. The men on watch at the maneuvering stand were conversing quietly so as not to disturb the dozen sleeping men in the darkened aft torpedo room beyond. He stopped and leaned against the bulkhead, making sure they were not aware of his presence, for he did not wish to be seen.

With careful hands he lifted the hatch grating on the port side of the room and climbed down the ladder into the motor room, gingerly closing the grating behind him. Since the day Fabriano had broken his nose, he had seen Fabriano come down here more than a dozen times. He knew why. There could be only one reason. That son of a bitch Fabriano had hidden his money down here, and now Penn was going to find where it was.

After rifling through Fabriano's seabag that day, and after discovering the can with the false bottom, and after finding the thousands upon thousands of large bills furled into a tight roll, Penn had set his mind on swiping the hidden fortune at some point during the patrol. He hadn't had time to count it all that day when he found it, but he was sure there had to be at least thirty or forty thousand dollars. Certainly enough to set him up properly after the war was over. There was no way of knowing how Fabriano had come by it, but Penn did not care. He was sure the money was stolen. Why else would Fabriano have taken such pains to hide it? Why else would Fabriano have tried to intimidate him by shoving his face into the hatch ring?

Despite the intimidation, despite his broken nose, despite the urge to forget he had ever seen the money, Penn had determined to swipe Fabriano's loot at the earliest moment of opportunity. And the earliest moment of opportunity had come the day after the *Whitefin* got under way, the day after Fabriano broke his nose. It was one of those rare occasions at sea when the after torpedo room was empty of sailors or officers. It had taken him only a minute to go through Fabriano's locker, from top to bottom, but he could not find the money anywhere.

Then it had occurred to him that Fabriano, although a destroyer man, was no fool. Certainly he had hidden the money somewhere on the ship. No way would he risk hiding it in his personal locker. So Penn had watched and he had waited. He observed Fabriano's moves from afar, looking for any patterns that might suggest the money's location, and it was not long before one particular pattern became very apparent. Every evening, after the meal, and every morning after coming off watch, Fabriano would make a trip down to the motor room. Penn, being a torpedoman by trade, knew little about electrical work, but he knew that no electrician's mate had any reason to visit the motor room that often.

There could be only one explanation, Penn thought as he stood beside the reduction gear box and looked around the room. The money had to be down here, somewhere. Now all he had to do was find it.

Penn had been a pickpocket and a card shark for most of his adolescent and young adult life, and fortunately for him, he knew all about hiding things. He had the mind of a thief and knew exactly the three or four places he would have chosen had he a reason to hide something down here. It took him only about five minutes of casual searching to find the Momsen Lung bag, stuffed behind the flood wall, wedged behind the pipe bracket, far in the outboard. His eyes practically lit up the entire compartment as he opened the bag and pulled out the large roll of newly minted money, turning it over and over in his hands.

He had it, at last!

But before Penn cinched up the bag to spirit his booty away to some more innovative hiding place, a chilling thought suddenly occurred to him. If Fabriano was willing to break his nose and risk going to captain's mast over just the *prospect* of his money getting stolen, what would he do when he found out that his money *had actually been stolen*?

Penn's elation suddenly turned to despair when he realized that he could not possibly swipe the money now and expect to avoid an enraged, vengeance-seeking Fabriano for the rest of the patrol. The destroyer sailor was smart enough to figure it out. He would know exactly who had taken it. There was no telling what he might do. He might break his nose again, or something worse. He might try to shove him overboard, or wait until the ship put in to port and then slit his throat in some dark alley.

Slightly dejected, Penn carefully repacked the money roll, affording it one last longing look before stuffing it back inside the canvas bag and returning it to its hiding place. He would leave the money as he had found it. If he was going to steal it, he was going to have to have a better plan. And he was going to need help, an ally, someone to split the loot with, someone who could keep his mouth shut, but more importantly, someone who could come to his aid if Fabriano ever attempted to get revenge.

"MORE tea, Major?" Miguel Aguinaldo, the wardroom steward, asked in a low, polite voice over Farquhar's shoulder.

Farquhar looked up from his hand of cards while tapping out a few ashes from his smoldering cigarette into the tray on the table.

"Yes, please, Miguel. Thank you. And I must say it's the best tea I've had this side of Calcutta."

Miguel simply smiled and nodded and then proceeded to fill the coffee cups of the three American officers involved in the cribbage game. Tremain peered over the top of his own cards and noticed Farquhar following Miguel with curious eyes, as the steward left through the wardroom's curtained doorway

As Miguel quietly prepared the major's tea in the adjacent pantry, Tom Endicott laid down a hand of cards and rubbed his hands together with delight.

"Fifteen two, fifteen four, fifteen six, fifteen eight, four of a kind for—"

"Enough, Lieutenant, no need to overegg the pudding," Farquhar grumbled, pronouncing the rank "leftenant." "We all know a twenty-nine hand when we see one. Just peg along and try not to rub it in, will you. There's a good chap."

"The thing is, sir, I've never seen a twenty-nine cribbage hand before!" Endicott said excitedly.

"Neither have I," said Berkshire incredulously. He was the other player to complete the foursome and had only learned the game a few days ago.

As Endicott happily moved his peg along the cribbage board, reaching the end of the board and winning the game, Miguel returned with the steaming cup of tea and placed it in front of Farquhar.

"Where are you from, Miguel?" the major asked cheerily, before the steward could leave the room. "I mean, where in the Philippines?"

"I joined the navy in Cavite, sir, but I grew up in Cagayan de Misamis."

"On Mindanao?" Farquhar asked in a suddenly vibrant tone.

"Yes, sir."

"Then I suspect you speak Cebuano like a . . . well, like a native."

"Oo bitaw," Miguel said evenly as he once again disappeared through the curtain.

"First class!" Farquhar stared after him with a wide grin on his face. "I don't suppose you could lend me that chap for a few weeks, Tremain, while I'm gallivanting across the jungle. I promise to bring him back in one piece. He might come in handy."

"Not a chance, Major," Tremain said firmly, and saw an appreciative smile from Miguel through the open pantry window.

Tremain inwardly scoffed at the idea. He would never think of parting with Miguel, whose cheerful attitude and quiet friendliness had been a veritable cornerstone of the junior officer's morale. The value of a good wardroom steward was incalculable, and Tremain would not be surprised if Miguel had helped lift their spirits on more than one occasion during previous patrols. Perhaps he'd left some sandwiches in the refrigerator for the off-going watch officers, perhaps he'd left a fresh batch of cookies on the wardroom table, or perhaps he'd baked a cake on one of their birthdays. It could have been any number of small things, but small things added up. A few acts of kindness here and there, strategically timed, could keep their spirits up for another month at sea, could bring out smiles when the chips were down, could patch them up psychologically and get them ready to stand their next watch, or to take their next depth charging. A good wardroom steward understood that his duties went far beyond just serving the officers' meals. Within moments of meeting him, Tremain had deduced that Miguel was just such a steward, and he wouldn't dream of letting him go away with the major to who knows where.

"Oh, pity, then," Farquhar said, lifting the flap on his left breast pocket and pulling out a silver cigarette case.

As he opened the case for another cigarette, a shiny black object fell out and rolled around on the table's green canvas cover. It appeared to be a metallic capsule no larger than the size of a tooth.

"What's that, Major?" Ensign Berkshire asked somewhat timidly.

"This?" Farquhar picked up the capsule, held it for a moment between his thumb and forefinger, and then placed it gingerly in the ensign's hand. "This, young Berkshire, is my medicine, in case the Japs ever manage to get me."

"Your medicine?"

"It's poison, Ensign," Endicott said casually, while excessively shuffling the cards for the next game.

"Quite right, Lieutenant. Cyanide to be more precise. Inside that capsule is a glass bulb containing enough sodium cyanide to kill every man sitting at this table."

Berkshire instantly dropped the capsule on the table and stared apprehensively at his open palms as if they were now contaminated.

"Oh, don't worry," Farquhar reassured him, snatching up the capsule and placing it back inside the case. "Do you think I'd keep it in here if it weren't safe?"

Berkshire did not look entirely convinced, and quickly excused himself, presumably to go wash his hands. The three other officers now sat staring at one another across the table, waiting for the ensign to return to resume their game.

"So, how'd you ever become a secret agent, Major?" Endicott asked airily while fidgeting with the cards.

Farquhar laughed out loud. "I wouldn't exactly call myself a secret agent."

"Then what would you call yourself, exactly?" Tremain said, somewhat in jest, somewhat serious. After a week at sea, he knew little more about the major now than he had when he met him in Ireland's study.

Farquhar's smile faded, his face taking on a new form entirely, transforming into something slightly gloomy and something slightly harsh all at once. It was as if his jolly nature up to this point had been nothing but a mask, and now the real Farquhar was breaking through for the first time. The major took one long drag on the cigarette and then let out the smoke in a forceful stream aimed at the swinging lightbulbs in the overhead.

After tapping a few more ashes into the tray, Farquhar finally said, "I didn't start out in the commandos. In fact, my official regiment is back in Europe right now, fighting the Nazis. But back in '41, I was just a regular chap—just a captain in the Forty-fifth Indian Infantry Brigade. I commanded a company of foot made up of mostly Sikhs, really. They had a few quirks about them—not one of them ever wanting to touch a piece of meat—but they were a good bunch, all in all."

"So, how did you become a commando?"

"Before the fall of Singapore, when the Japanese were still advancing down the Malay Peninsula—utterly unstoppable— my brigade, along with an Australian infantry division, was thrown into their path to try to stop them. Our orders were to hold them, if possible, at the banks of the Muar River. Well, we held as long as we could with what we had, setting ambushes and blowing up bridges. I remember we blew up one bridge that had a couple hundred Jap troops on it all pedaling bicycles as fast as they could to get across. I'll never forget the sight of all those bicycles falling into the river. We had a few successes, but it was a losing proposition from the get-go. The Japs had tanks, and we didn't. They had air support; we didn't. Eventually, they moved some troops down the coast by boat and hit us in our left flank. Our brigade commander was killed, and the whole brigade began to fall apart. So, we started a fighting retreat, heading back down the peninsula toward Singapore, trying to get back to the island fortress before the Japs overran us. We planned to cross the Simpang Kiri River at a little village called Parit Sulong, but when we got there, we found that the Japs had beaten us to it. Our escape route was cut off, and we were surrounded. For the next two days, we held out, fighting like hell, but the Japs were slowly closing the vise on us. I lost a lot of men, nearly two-thirds of my company. Many of the rest were badly wounded. Eventually, the Australian commander of our force ordered the whole division to disperse. We were ordered to leave the badly wounded behind and to take to the jungle, making for friendly lines as best as each man could manage. You know, every man for himself.

"But that didn't sit right with me. I'd grown attached to my men, and eleven of them were lying helpless in our makeshift field hospital. I just couldn't find it within myself to abandon them to the enemy. So, after leading my company to the river's edge, and seeing to it that they dispersed as ordered, I headed back to the hospital, alone. It was nothing more than a dirty little hut on a rubber plantation, really. But when I got there, I found that the Japs had already overrun the place. I recognized them as troops from the Imperial Guards division. I knew at that point that I could do nothing more for my men, and figured I had better hide my own arse or I'd end up getting captured myself. So, I darted up a rubber tree and hid there. I was so close to the hospital that I could hear the moans of our wounded inside the building. I stayed in that tree for hours and hours, waiting for a chance to escape, but none ever came. There were Japanese troops everywhere. Finally, just before dark, a group of Imperial Guards soldiers began motioning and shouting in broken English for the hundred and fifty or so wounded men in the hospital to come out and muster in a small clearing, assuring them that food and medical treatment awaited. At that point, food sounded pretty dandy to my aching stomach, and I half thought about climbing down and surrendering right then and there. I was starting to really doubt my chances of ever making it back to the lines. Anyway, while I was considering it, the prisoners were shuffling into the clearing, not twenty yards from my tree. I tried to make out the faces of my men, but it was getting dark, and it was no use. They all looked so beaten, so exhausted. I felt bad for them, but then realized that I probably looked just as pitiful. Every one of us had been fighting nonstop for nearly a week. Well, the Japanese guards herded the prisoners into the clearing, and I was thinking about turning myself in. That's when I noticed that the guards were all stepping back several paces, obviously trying to place space between themselves and the prisoners. I knew something was up, and started to shout the alarm, but it was too late.

"Several machine guns appeared in the windows of the huts surrounding the clearing, and they all opened up at once, cutting those men down like dogs. Those machine guns were firing at near point-blank range, each gun pouring out what must have been a thousand rounds into that mass of flailing bodies. Heads exploded. Severed arms and hands flew everywhere. The whole group was shrouded in a dark foggy mist that I knew to be blood. I'm usually not very squeamish, but even I had to turn away from the sight of my men being cut to pieces. I can still hear their screams. I can still hear those damn Jap Type 92s, pecking away like so many woodpeckers. It was all over in a few minutes. Then the Japs started sifting through the bodies looking for survivors. I saw one Jap officer giving orders. He was a colonel in the Kempeitai—the Jap military police—and I knew enough Japanese to understand that he wanted the survivors to be brought to him. They found about a half-dozen men still alive. I recognized one of them as my trusty color sergeant, a remarkable Indian man from Madras, a man who had been indispensable to me in various commands during my service. At the behest of the Japanese colonel, each surviving prisoner was successively tied to a tree and used for bayonet practice. I listened helplessly to the screams and moans of the dazed men as each bayonet thrust penetrated flesh and bone. The bloody Japs were careful not to administer a lethal blow until each soldier had ample time to practice. It took my sergeant over an hour to die. I can still see that bastard colonel as he watched with amusement, sometimes laughing out loud when my sergeant cried out in pain. I'll never forget that shrill laugh."

Farquhar paused and stared distantly at the ashtray in front of him, digging around in the discarded gray ashes with his forefinger, as if he were reliving the terrible moment.

"What happened then, sir?" Endicott asked in a solemn tone. He had stopped shuffling the cards altogether.

"Then? Why then, Lieutenant, the Japs piled the bodies high, drenched them in petrol, and burned them all to ashes. They had to destroy any evidence, of course. They even threw old tires onto the fire to let it burn longer."

"Were you ever captured?"

"No. I eventually made it back to Singapore. And when the garrison there surrendered, I decided not to. I swam back to the peninsula and eventually joined up with a band of Chinese guerillas. The relationship turned out to be mutually beneficial, since they wanted to kill lots of Japanese and needed a trained officer to advise them, and I wanted to live to kill that bloody bastard who massacred my men. After a year or so of fairly successful raids and ambushes—successful enough to get the attention of some of the higher-ups in Whitehall—the Allies made contact with my little group and began to send us regular supplies, anything we needed really."

"So how did you end up here?" Tremain asked.

"Oh, I guess after a while, I got tired of killing Japanese in Malaya, and decided I wanted to go kill Japanese somewhere else. I was given a commission in the Royal Army and reassigned, just like that."

"And now you're working in the Philippines, doing the same kind of thing?"

"Whatever I'm doing now, old boy, is no concern of yours or anyone else's."

Farquhar's smile had returned, and Tremain sensed that the British major had shared all that he was going to. He still felt that the major was somewhat of an aloof ass, that he overstepped his bounds on most occasions, and that the sooner they delivered him to his destination the better—meaning the sooner they got rid of him, the better—but at least now he could have a small measure of sympathy for the man. Perhaps Farquhar was the way he was because it was the only way to keep his sanity after experiencing such things. Perhaps the whole swashbuckling exterior hid a mere shell of a man within.

"Now, where the devil is that ensign of yours, Tremain?" Farquhar said in a much more lively tone, the sullen reflective moment now in the past. "Doesn't he know he's holding up our bloody game?"

Chapter 10

South China Sea, one hundred nautical miles southeast of
the Paracel Islands
Three weeks later

THE *Whitefin*'s thin black and green camouflaged periscope
jutted above the ocean's surface for the forty-seventh time in
this watch, and the weary quartermaster logged the event in his
notebook: *1432, observation, no contacts.* It was the latest in a
series of similar entries that stretched back several pages to the
one marking the day when the *Whitefin* had reached her assigned patrol area in this isolated part of the South China Sea.

Monroe rotated the scope around the azimuth, squinting
one eye and trying his best to stay awake. A thick bank of
snow white clouds hung low above the glassy dark blue sea
and stretched in all directions as far as the periscope's low
height of eye could view. With his surface sweep completed,
he rotated the right handle, which tilted the lens to scan the
clouds above. He was seeing spots after only a few seconds of
staring at the blinding whiteness, and took his eyes away to
blink several times.

"Nothing, sir?" the quartermaster asked tentatively from
the conning tower's small plotting table.

"What do you think?" Monroe said irritably, rubbing his eyes with the fingers of one hand.

"Just filling in the logbook, sir. I suppose our tail is still there?"

Monroe said nothing, but put his face to the lens once again, rotating it around to look directly aft at the swirling water behind the periscope. At the *Whitefin*'s current three knots, the periscope left very little agitation on the surface, beyond a few tiny whirlpools that no airman or destroyer lookout could differentiate from the normal agitation of the sea. But a few yards beyond the periscope, floating on top of the water covering the *Whitefin*'s amidships main deck, Monroe could see the dreaded "tail" the quartermaster was referring to. The thin line of floating petroleum stretched along the *Whitefin*'s track as far as he could see, although the rainbow colors didn't seem to have near the same flashy resilience as he had seen during previous watches on sunnier days.

It hadn't come as too much of a surprise when the *Whitefin* surfaced the day after the gun action with the junks and they discovered that one of the fuel oil ballast tanks, more precisely number 4A below the waterline on the starboard side, had been ruptured by one of the Japanese bombs, most likely the first and closest one. The rupture was small enough that Allendale had not noticed the effects in his nightly compensation, but the telltale line of oil was clearly visible to anyone looking through the periscope or standing on the bridge.

If that Japanese pilot had only known the damage his depth bomb had caused, he probably would have had an extra tot of sake in celebration, for there was almost nothing more detrimental to a submarine's stealth than a leaking fuel tank. It acted like a dye marker on the surface, providing any pursuing destroyer or searching aircraft a clear line to the submarine's exact location.

Monroe remembered hearing Tremain mutter a curse under his breath when he gave him the bad news. After going topside and taking a look for himself, Tremain had appeared outwardly unfazed by the obvious setback, but Monroe suspected that on the inside he was fuming.

"It's okay, XO," Tremain had remarked confidently, after a

brief moment of hesitation. "Barometer's falling anyway. We'll have some cloud cover in a day or two to hide that oil sheen."

Monroe had agreed blandly, as one would agree with a groom left standing at the altar that his bride most likely had a flat tire and would be there at any moment. He didn't voice his true thoughts, that proceeding with the mission was too much of a risk, that they would be clear bait for any patrolling aircraft, that any destroyer would know exactly where to drop his depth charges.

If he didn't speak his mind to his captain now, when all of their lives were at stake, what good was he? Was he that inept as an executive officer? Or perhaps, that was not it at all. Perhaps he'd held his tongue for another reason. Perhaps it was because Tremain had done something for him that no other captain had. Tremain had extended to him the confidence and respect due to an executive officer, and it really had been quite a refreshing change. To feel needed again, to have a valued opinion, to belong —things he had not felt for a very long time. Things he never felt under the egotistical Burgess. Of all the senior officers he had encountered in the years since the *R-15* accident, Tremain was the only one who genuinely appeared not to care about it. And strangely, it spurred an instinct within him to give this man his complete and undivided loyalty, no matter how harebrained his strategies might be. He somehow knew that he would follow Tremain into the very heart of hell, if necessary.

So far, Tremain had been right, and their luck had held. The *Whitefin* had traversed the Celebes Sea, diving only twice for enemy aircraft, reached the north coast of Mindanao, and deposited the British major in a little secluded bay, where they were met by a dozen or more canoes filled with fierce-looking Moro guerillas. Farquhar and the Moros seemed to get along quite well, and Monroe had been impressed when the major went down the ladder over the side and hopped into one of the canoes without a second thought, turning only once to wave good-bye with the same wide grin that had seemed plastered to his face for the entire voyage. It was at that point, as the fleet of canoes disappeared into a cove, that Tremain informed him that the *Whitefin* would be coming back to pick Farquhar up before the patrol was over. Apparently the British commando had purchased a two-way ticket.

That was over two weeks ago. Since then, the *Whitefin* had traversed the breadth of the Sulu Sea to get to her patrol area smack in the middle of the South China Sea, and now was cruising around her patrol area with orders to lay in ambush for the tanker fleet apparently heading this way and set to pass by any day now. So far, the area had been a dud, producing nothing but a single coal-burning freighter about a week back, which Tremain had let go so as not to alert the Japanese that there was a submarine operating in the area. It was a far cry from the action-packed patrols the *Whitefin*'s crew had grown used to under Captain Burgess, and Monroe had already heard grumblings.

"Coffee, XO?"

Monroe took his eyes from the lens to see a dour-looking petty officer with a stocky frame and receding hairline holding out a cup of steaming coffee. His name was Heath, and his simple presence had the effect of sending icicles running through Monroe's veins. Of all the sailors on board who knew about the *R-15* incident, of all the sailors that obeyed his orders with accusing if not insolent glares, Heath was the only one that made him nervous, almost shaking, inside. Heath had a quality that set him apart from the rest. His twin brother had belonged to the crew of the *R-15,* and had gone down with the ship that day. The two looked remarkably alike, and every time Monroe saw Heath's face, it was like a ghost had come back from the deep to haunt him. In fact, Heath was much like a ghost himself. The strange sailor never said much and Monroe often caught him watching him suspiciously whenever the two were in the same compartment together. He often came to the conning tower whenever Monroe was on watch, looking around the room as if to check on things, as if Monroe's incompetence might overlook something and send this ship to the bottom to join the *R-15*. Had it been any other sailor, Monroe would have assigned him extra duties for his impertinence and sent him smartly on his way, but he could not bring himself to do that with Heath. He could hardly bring himself to look into the man's eyes, the same dark eyes that his dead brother had.

"Thanks, Heath." Monroe took the cup and drank a quick sip, trying his best to sound unaffected by the sailor's presence. "That's nice of you. What brings you to the conning tower?"

"Just taking a break from the planes, sir," Heath said, shrugging, staring directly into his face. "One of the youngsters relieved me, so I thought I'd make the rounds."

"Thanks for the coffee." Monroe smiled politely, handing the cup back to Heath and wondering just what rounds he was referring to. With hopes that the morbid petty officer would simply go away, Monroe put his face back to the periscope lens.

"Sure is quiet up here, sir. You'd think the Japanese had surrendered."

Why the hell does he keep talking? Does he really think he can make me feel guilty enough that I'll crack?

"Seems that way, doesn't it," Monroe said awkwardly, never taking his eyes from the scope.

"I don't think I've ever seen a patrol this quiet. Almost as quiet as the grave, sir."

Monroe pretended not to notice the comment, and forced himself to turn the scope slowly as if he were absorbed in the search.

Is he still standing there? What the hell does he want? He wants me to admit that I'm responsible for his brother's death. That's what he's always wanted. Is he still standing there? Do I dare ever put this damn scope down?

Just then, Monroe found something in the periscope lens that would certainly allow him to get out of this encounter with Heath. On the northern horizon, what looked like a line of sticks was poking above the dark blue sea. He counted six of them. They clearly contrasted with the solid overcast sky in the background. Above the sticks he could just make out a slanted column of dirty brown smoke.

"Contact," he said loudly, hoping Heath would disappear. "Masts and smoke sighted to the north. Mark this bearing."

There was a pause and then a voice said, "Three-five-two."

It was the quartermaster's voice. Good. If Heath had still been there, he would have called off the bearing, since he would have been the closest to the periscope. Monroe removed his eyes from the eyepiece to see that his assertions were correct. Heath had gone below to the control room to resume his watch at the bow planes station. Monroe breathed a sigh of relief. He had made it through yet another encounter with Heath.

He watched the swaying masts of the approaching ships. Yes, they were tankers. He could tell by the mast arrangement he'd seen so many times before. And yes, there were at least four ships in view. There was no question that this was their target, the whole reason they had been sent here. Two whole weeks spent patrolling this area with nothing to show for it, and now the tanker fleet they'd been sent to destroy was going to run right over the top of them.

Off to the right of the tankers, he saw a new set of masts appear above the horizon. Smaller, swept masts, adorned with a string of multicolored signal flags. These new masts were moving much faster than the tanker's, and from their arrangement they were traveling on a perpendicular course, probably across the convoy's bows.

A destroyer.

"Captain to the conning tower," he said in a low voice. "Sound general quarters!"

"I can see the hull now of the leading tanker in the port column," Tremain said zestfully, as he peered through the periscope, his back brushing against someone as he spun the scope around on a quick safety sweep before bringing it back to focus on the tanker in question. "Stand by for observation."

"TDC ready," Whately's voice announced from the torpedo data computer at the aft port end of the small room, which had gotten a lot smaller since manning battle stations. It now contained a helmsman at the wheel in the forward end, a sailor acting as the periscope assistant, Whately on the TDC with Berkshire on the antiquated angle solver, Monroe hovering over the plot, the sonarman, Doniphan, on the WCA sound gear, and then himself. Seven men in all. And Tremain knew the other six were watching him with anxious anticipation of the action to come. This was his first time conducting an approach and attack with them, and the jury was still out as to whether they could all function as a team. At this point they

were no longer officers and sailors, they were seven men, each
with a duty to perform, all with a common goal in mind: to
sink the enemy tankers.

In the minute it took Tremain to wake from the cot in his
stateroom and reach the conning tower, the fast-moving tanker
fleet had closed the distance by a quarter of a mile, and he
could now clearly see the leading ship's round, bulbous forecastle as it climbed over the horizon, plowing the seas in its
path. From the myriad of masts decorating the northwestern
horizon, Tremain's mind had sorted them into at least a dozen
ships, formed in two distinct columns of six ships each. He
had yet to see the enemy destroyer that Monroe had sighted
before, and he could only assume that the speedy sentry, like a
sheltie herding its sheep, had dashed to the other side of the
convoy. If the Imperial Navy had only one destroyer dedicated
to protecting this vast armada, Tremain wanted to send them a
letter of personal thanks as soon as he got back to port.

The setup was beautiful. He couldn't have arranged a better approach angle if he had tried. The *Whitefin* was heading
west, less than two miles away from the future path of the
southbound convoy. There was no escort in sight, and he had
all the time in the world to nail down the solution until it was
rock solid. He was certain that he could put at least one fish
into each ship in the port column, then swing the *Whitefin*
around and finish the wrecks off with the stern tubes. This all
assumed, of course, that the convoy did not suddenly zig, and
that all of his torpedoes had normal runs. It looked so damn
easy.

"Bearing to the first ship in the port column," he announced as he switched the lens to high-power magnification
and swept along the tanker's deck. He guessed it to be somewhere around five hundred feet in length, with two distinct
structures, one near the bow, with a long row of windows that
marked it as the pilothouse, and another much farther aft, almost on the stern, from which rose a single large funnel.
There were also two cranes, one forward and one aft, and
Tremain knew from experience that every other part of the
ship below the waterline was devoted to carrying large quanti-
ties of petroleum. This was a big one and could probably carry
sixty or seventy thousand barrels of oil when it was fully

loaded. He decided to use the rusty pilothouse on the bow as his point of reference and lined up the reticle on the small antenna protruding from the structure.

"Mark!"

"Three-four-four." The sailor next to him read off the bearing from the azimuth scale at the top of the periscope ring.

Tremain then flipped the stadimeter switch near his right hand and watched the silhouette of the tanker split into two separate images. Gingerly turning the stadimeter knob with his right hand, he lined up the dual images until they were on top of each other, with the keel of one image just touching the masts of the other. When the images were perfectly aligned, he took his hand off the dial.

"Range, mark. Use a fifty-foot masthead height."

There was a pause in the room, and he didn't have to take his eyes away from the lens to know that the sailor standing opposite him was now scanning the circular stadimeter scale on the back of the periscope housing, searching for the range that lined up with the hash mark for a fifty-foot masthead height.

"Four thousand five hundred yards!" the sailor finally announced, a little later than Tremain would have preferred. Back in the old days, before the stadimeter dial was provided on the periscope, he would have calculated the same range in his head in half the time. But, in today's navy, math skills had been replaced by slide rules and torpedo data computers. It was simple trigonometry really, determining the range to a target by solving for the unknown side of the right triangle formed by the periscope, the target's waterline, and the tip of the target's mast. The angle was obtained by lining up the dual images, while the target's masthead height was either guessed at or known from ship recognition tables. Then all that was left was a simple calculation. Target masthead height *divided by* tangent of the angle *equals* range to target. Of course, doing it quickly that way meant knowing how to calculate tangents in your head, something Tremain had known how to do since his early days as an ensign, but it was probably more than he could ask of this new generation of submariners.

Damn, he felt old sometimes.

"Angle on the bow, port three-five," he said, slapping up the handles. "Down scope!"

As the shiny periscope slid down in front of his face, Tremain waited for Whately to enter the data into the computer. Monroe was hastily walking a set of parallel rulers across the small plot table to determine the solution manually.

Before the periscope had reached the bottom of its well, Whately announced the results. The young officer's speed even impressed Tremain.

"Generated solution on the tanker is course one-seven-five, range four thousand four hundred yards, speed thirteen knots."

"Very well," Tremain nodded. That checked with what he had seen on the surface.

The convoy was coming on fast, and despite his excellent firing position, he would have to move quickly to reach the firing point that he wanted. The tankers were moving a little too fast for his original plan of putting a torpedo into each vessel in the port column.

"All right, XO, here's my plan. We're going to fire two fish at each of the first three ships in the port column. That should put them down, but if it doesn't, it'll at least slow them enough to give us time to bring the stern tubes to bear."

"Aye, Captain." Monroe nodded, looking up from the chart desk.

"Flooding tubes forward!" Tremain peered over the hatch to look at the top of Allendale's head. Allendale looked up at him and nodded, acknowledging the potential impact flooding the tubes might have on the ship's trim. Then Tremain turned to the phone talker standing beside him. "To the forward torpedo room, flood tubes one through six and open outer doors."

The sailor repeated the order word for word before passing it on to the men in the torpedo room through his phone set.

As the orders were relayed, Tremain met the periscope lens at the deck and slapped down the handles before it reached eye level.

He blinked instinctively as a surging wave splashed against the lens, leaving streaks of running water across his field of view. When the water finally cleared, the tanker fleet was there, closer now, with the hulls of the second and third ships now clearly in view following in the wake of the first ship. The long dark hulls rocked gently in the swell, keeping perfect formation, staying in line with their opposite numbers in the starboard column that were barely visible in the background—just misty gray shapes in the distance. The two columns had to be separated by at least a mile or more.

Still no sign of the destroyer. But Tremain knew better than to relax. He was well aware that enemy escorts had a tendency to show up at the most inconvenient moments, popping out from behind one of their consorts just as a firing solution was about to be obtained. And he didn't discount the possibility that there might be aircraft from the distant Paracels snooping around, too, cruising out of sight above the low cumulus, although that particular threat was unlikely since the weather conditions were horrible for searching from the air.

Once again he lined up the reticle on the pilothouse of the leading tanker. He could see dark figures moving about on her open bridge. Men standing watch, completely unaware of the submarine stalking them.

"Bearing . . . mark!"

"Three-three-zero."

"Range . . . mark!"

"Thirty-six hundred yards."

"Angle on the bow, port-five-zero. Down peri— Wait just a damn minute!"

Tremain raised a hand to keep the sailor from lowering the scope while never taking his face away from the eyepiece. Something on the bridge of the leading tanker had caught his attention. He unconsciously twisted the handle for a closer look, although he was already at the maximum magnification setting. There were a dozen or more men on the tanker's bridge, but he focused his attention on one group in particular: a cluster of men standing around a rather large piece of equipment that appeared to be a permanent fixture.

There it was again.

Faint flashing lights. The large piece of equipment was a signal lamp. The tanker was signaling somebody—but whom? Was it signaling the escort? Had the tanker sighted the *Whitefin*'s scope—or its trail of floating fuel oil? For half a moment Tremain thought the lamp might be directed at the *Whitefin*'s own periscope, until he realized that he was looking at the light from the wrong angle. It had to be directed somewhere farther to the south. Assuming the escort was somewhere on the inside of the convoy, the signal could not be meant for her.

Tremain decreased the magnification and rotated the scope slowly to the left, scanning the vacant southwest sector and the equally vacant southern sector. But when he reached the southeast sector, he discovered the intended recipient of the tanker's light signal. A small stick of a mast was poking up just above the southeastern horizon.

"New contact, Captain," Doniphan said from the sonar gear, as if to confirm what he had just seen. "Picking up screw noises to the southeast, sir. Bearing one-five-zero. Slow screws. Merchants."

"Another convoy approaching from the southeast," Tremain announced. "I can see at least two sets of masts. Wait a minute. I see the bridge of the first now. Signals. They're returning the tanker's signal all right. Of course, there's no way to tell who signaled first. Okay, this is a small freighter coming up from the south, along with a transport. I can see their structures now, and there's something else, too. Shit! It's a warship. Probably a cruiser of some sort. Down scope!"

He stared at the bulkhead as the scope slid back down into the well. Suddenly, this patch of ocean had become very crowded.

"All right, everyone. This is nothing more than a chance meeting of two enemy convoys at sea. This doesn't change anything. I saw a good starboard aspect on this new convoy, so it looks like it's heading to the northeast. It's going to pass well clear of us. In fact, it should help us. I doubt if either convoy will zig again until they're well clear of each other. We'll proceed with the attack as planned. Make all bow tubes ready for firing. Set torpedo depth at fifteen feet, high speed."

The orders were relayed to the torpedo room, and he caught Monroe casting an anxious glance at him as he hurriedly erased the last plotted solution and started making new marks to show the southern convoy's contribution to the tactical picture.

"Something on your mind, XO?"

"Just thinking about that destroyer I saw earlier, Captain," he said hesitantly, glancing up between scribbles. "Our fuel tank is leaking like a sieve." He paused. "We could go deep, sir, let them go by, and then surface and do an end around maneuver. We know where they're going, and we know their base course. It'd be a cinch to lie in wait for them down the road a bit at a time and place of our choosing. We could even hit them at night, so our leak won't be an issue."

"They might change base course after nightfall, XO," Tremain said, shaking his head. "We can't take that risk. Besides, the weather is perfect right now. A submarine could make a thousand approaches and never have a setup like this one. We're proceeding with the attack. Stand by for observation. Up scope!"

The scope came up and Tremain pressed his face to the eyepiece.

The tanker convoy was proceeding along nicely. No change in course, and still heading south. The port column of tankers would cross the *Whitefin*'s bows within minutes. It was close enough that the six ships stretched all the way across his field of view in low power magnification. A quick check to the south showed the new convoy heading well to the west of the *Whitefin*'s position, just as he had expected, but those damn lights were still signaling, blinking away. The commodores of these two convoys had a hell of a lot to say to each other, and he wondered briefly why they weren't just using ship-to-ship radios. Surely they didn't think American submarines were so advanced that they could locate the source of radio transmissions.

"Captain, I'm picking up high-speed screws, sir, bearing three-one-five," Doniphan reported. "One of those tankers must've been masking it before. I think it's that destroyer the XO saw earlier."

Quickly, Tremain swung the periscope around to the bearing and shifted to high power. The long port side of the third tanker in the column filled his field of view just as its bulbous bow plunged into a roller, throwing a spray of white mist into the air. And sure enough, as the mist cleared, he could see the knife-like bow of a destroyer protruding just beyond the tanker's bulk. Here was Monroe's destroyer, making its rounds, herding its sheep.

Then Tremain saw something that made his heart skip a

beat. He stared fixedly into the eyepiece, unconsciously uttering a gasp that turned the heads of the other men in the room.

The destroyer had moved out from behind the tanker now. It left a frothing white sea behind it as it picked up speed, moving up the line of ships like a racehorse sprinting for the lead position. The high bow, the black painted five-inch dual gun mounts forward and aft, the stacks of depth charges on its neatly tapered stern were all clearly visible, but they were all things Tremain had seen a hundred times before. He hardly noticed them as he stared awestruck at the bands of shiny black paint covering the destroyer's bow, her stern, and the tips of her stacks. They looked much the same as they did that night off Vella LaVella. Once again he was face to face with the "Scourge of the Solomons," the submarine slayer, and the killer of his beloved *Seatrout*.

It was the *Shigure*.

He watched her, mesmerized, unable to look away, foolishly keeping the scope up as the Japanese destroyer reached its cruising speed and passed the second tanker in the column. She was presenting her perfect beam to the periscope and had obviously not spotted the *Whitefin*'s scope or its trail of fuel oil on the surface.

Then, suddenly, a thought invaded Tremain's dazed mind. It was a crazy thought, but at the same time just sane enough that he knew what his course of action was going to be even before he started rolling it around in his brain. This was indeed the chance of a lifetime, and he'd never be able to live with himself if he passed it up. This was his chance for revenge, a chance to strike one great stroke for all the submariners who had met their fates at the hands of this bloody warship.

But what would he tell his crew? He could sense that the other men in the conning tower were all looking at him, wondering what the delay was.

"Stand by for observation, Mr. Whately," he managed to say with forced coolness, glancing out of the corner of his eyes at Monroe. "Shifting targets!"

He saw Monroe's head look up quizzically.

"Shifting targets, aye, sir," came Whately's cautious reply.

"Bearing, mark!"

"Two-nine-seven."

"Range, mark! Use a ninety-foot masthead height."

"Two thousand yards," the periscope assistant announced after finding the new mast height on the circular dial.

"Angle on the bow, port-seven-five. Down scope!"

As the scope slid down into the well, Tremain shuffled through the crowd of curious onlookers to stand behind Whately at the TDC. The skilled lieutenant was spinning dials and knobs faster than the eye could follow as he entered the new target's information into the computer.

"Speed, sir?" Whately asked over his shoulder.

"Use twenty knots."

At that, the other men in the conning tower exchanged glances. Now they knew what the target was. No tanker in any fleet traveled at twenty knots. Tremain reached over and grabbed the 1MC microphone off the bulkhead, deciding to end their anxiety and stop the rumor mill before it ran rampant over the phone circuits.

"This is the captain," he heard his voice echoing in the other compartments. "I want you all to know that we are about to go into battle against the most famous destroyer in the Imperial Navy—the submarine killer—the *Shigure*. Now, I probably don't have to tell you what this bastard's done, that it's responsible for sinking at least four of our own boats, and that it's been highly decorated for doing so. Some people even think it's a phantom, that it can't be sunk. But that little myth is going to end, right here, today. The illustrious career of the *Shigure* is going to end in Davy Jones's locker on this very day, in this very spot, because we're going to send her there. Now think of the friends you've lost, keep your heads, and do your best. I know you will. This is a standard attack, gentlemen. That is all."

Returning the microphone to the bulkhead, he could sense the anxious stares all around him. They were either thrilled with the idea, or else they thought him mad. Focusing his attention on the torpedo data computer, he tried to avoid making eye contact with any of them, especially Monroe.

Rising from the plot table, Monroe moved closer to him and whispered discreetly, "Begging your pardon, Captain, but this isn't our mission."

"We can't miss this chance, XO. ComSubSoWesPac would want us to go after the *Shigure*."

Monroe started to interject, but Tremain raised a hand to stop him.

"It's settled, XO!" he said in a forceful tone. Then after seeing the disconcerting expression on Monroe's face, he added more soothingly, "Your suggestion to go deep and do an end around attack was an excellent one, and that's just what I intend to do—*after* we've sunk the *Shigure*."

"Once the shooting starts, they may scatter, sir." Monroe was still whispering, as if the other men in the room did not know what they were discussing.

"If they scatter we'll surface and use our radar to track them down one by one. If they stay in formation, we'll run ahead of them tonight and be waiting for them just as you said. Besides, once the *Shigure*'s on the bottom, they won't have any escorts to protect them. That cruiser, with the northbound convoy, appears to be of the Myoko class, so he won't have any ash cans aboard to help the *Shigure* out. His convoy seems to be in a hurry to get to wherever they're going, anyway."

Monroe nodded passively, either satisfied with Tremain's plan or else abandoning all hopes of talking him out of it.

Either way, Whately announced the results from the computer and everyone else was once again attending to his duties.

"Generated solution on the *Shigure*: course one-seven-five, speed twenty knots, range nineteen hundred yards, bearing two-nine-zero," Whately said fervently. "She's moving fast, Captain. We've got to shoot now, if we want to try for a zero gyro angle."

"Understood. I'm confident with that solution, Mr. Whately. Go ahead and enter it. We'll fire a full spread of six torpedoes with one-degree separations to make up for any errors. Final bearing and shoot. Up scope!"

As the scope came up into his hands, he realized that the air was getting humid in the small space. The refrigeration plant must have tripped offline again. No matter, he'd shot torpedoes before with sweat running down the sides of the bulkhead.

Chapter 11

TREMAIN looked through the lens, checking both convoys to make sure neither had changed course, then increased to high power to focus on the *Shigure*. She ran on the same southerly course, paralleling her consorts, now about to overtake the first tanker in the port column. And now her two stacks began churning out a column of dirty gray smoke as she cut in another boiler. A few Japanese sailors strolled on her main deck, while a few indistinguishable heads poked over the railing on the port bridge wing, evidently unaware of the *Whitefin*'s presence. They weren't even echo-ranging.

Had those same men looked triumphantly over the side as the *Seatrout*'s wreckage floated to the surface? Had they laughed at the twisted and bloated bodies of Tremain's men?

This was it, his moment of truth. His moment of retribution.

"Bearing, mark!" he called as the reticle hit the *Shigure*'s forward smokestack.

"Two-seven-seven."

Tremain waited an agonizing five seconds for Whately's report that the bearing agreed with the entered solution.

"Checks!" Whately announced excitedly, followed immediately by "Set!"

The torpedo data computer instantly transmitted the final gyro settings to the spindle mechanisms connected to the torpedoes in their tubes.

"Fire one!" Tremain shouted with zeal, slapping up the scope handles. The periscope assistant took the hint and lowered the scope without waiting for the order to do so.

On the port side of the room, the sailor manning the firing panel pressed his weight against the red plunger on the bulkhead. Instantly the resounding *whack* and *swoosh* of a torpedo being ejected from its tube filled the compartment.

"Number one fired electrically," the phone talker reported.

"Fire two! . . . Fire three! . . . Fire four! . . . Fire five! . . . Fire six!"

The same routine followed as each successive tube launched its lethal cargo to meet its rendezvous with the enemy destroyer a half mile in front of the *Whitefin*'s bows. Each time Tremain felt the pressure on his ears as the tubes were vented inboard. Each time, he sensed the *Whitefin*'s bow dip slightly as the weight of the two-thousand-pound torpedo was replaced by an almost equivalent weight of seawater. And each time, the meticulous Allendale kept the depth steady at sixty feet. Tremain could hear his calm voice wafting up from the control room through the open hatch.

"Half degree down. A little more dive on your bow planes. That's it. Now, zero your bubble."

"All torpedoes running hot, straight, and normal," reported Doniphan as he minutely adjusted the *Whitefin*'s QB sonar hydrophone.

Tremain felt a small wave of satisfaction as the torpedo firing worked like clockwork. It was their first time firing a torpedo on the patrol, but they all performed like it was old hat to them, especially Whately, who seemed to handle the torpedo data computer like it was a further extension of his arms. He saw Ensign Berkshire holding a stopwatch close to his face. It was only a matter of time now before they knew just how good Whately had been at entering and interpreting the data for the solution, and how good his own observations had been. After all, he hadn't done a combat periscope observation since his encounter with the Japanese battleship *Kurita,* over six months ago, when he was in command of the *Mackerel.* Sure, he'd taught plenty of green ensigns how to do observations in the attack trainer at sub school, an almost comical arrangement of miniature models in a large water tank, with a cleverly arranged periscope set up in the room beneath it. But no attack trainer ever fully prepared an officer for the real thing.

"Thirty-five . . . ," Berkshire counted down. "Thirty . . . Twenty-five . . ."

"Up scope!"

He had to watch it. Despite the risks of raising the scope, he had to observe the destruction of the ship that had killed his old crew.

After a quick turn around the azimuth, he steadied the scope on the *Shigure*, its broad port beam now prominently displayed in the lens. It had not changed course or speed and looked incredibly close in high power, so close that he could make out the rusty streaks marring its distinct black paint at every hull opening along its length, and he had to remind himself that the enemy destroyer was still more than a half mile away. After a few seconds he found the six bubbly white streaks left on the surface by the steaming torpedoes' internal combustion engines.

"Fifteen sec—" Berkshire began to announce, but was cut short by a sudden explosion.

Whack!

A towering column of white water filled the periscope's field of view, and Tremain's heart sank instantly. The detonation had been well short of the *Shigure*. A premature. The faulty torpedoes that had plagued the Pacific Fleet since the start of the war had reared their ugly heads once again. As usual, at the most inopportune time.

It seemed the next events happened in slow motion. He watched as the *Shigure*, now alerted by the premature detonation, veered hard to port, a sharp turn, a turn that made it lean so far to one side that he thought it might capsize. It was performed quickly and methodically, and obviously by a very skilled helmsman at the wheel. Within seconds the destroyer had turned ninety degrees and was now heading directly toward the *Whitefin*, effectively combing the paths of the remaining torpedoes. The *Shigure*'s captain certainly knew what he was doing, and Tremain could see that he was steering for the white agitation where the premature torpedo had detonated. It was clever thinking, and obviously an immediate action he'd trained his men in. Assuming the unseen submarine had fired a pattern of torpedoes at him, steering for the exploded torpedo would place him at the hole in the pattern. By now he would have noticed the long, fingerlike wakes of the other torpedoes in the spread, leading right back to the submarine that fired them.

The seconds counted off; Tremain crossed his fingers, but to no avail.

"All torpedoes should have hit by now, Captain!" Whately exclaimed bitterly.

The *Shigure*'s evasive maneuver had worked. The rest of *Whitefin*'s torpedoes would have passed harmlessly down her beams, too far away for the steel destroyer's influence field to set off their magnetic exploders.

For a moment, as if in a daze, he stared at the *Shigure*'s thin form as it rapidly picked up speed, making a slight course adjustment to point directly at the *Whitefin*'s periscope. Great curtains of spray appeared beneath the sharp black bow as it surpassed twenty-five, even thirty knots.

Tremain shook himself out of his trance. The victory against his nemesis had been denied, and now his own apparent doom, and that of the men he had led to it, was swiftly approaching. He had only seconds to act.

"Down scope!" he said angrily, as he slapped up the handles. "Rig for depth charge! All ahead full! Go deep, Allendale, go deep! Get us down fast!"

The helmsman rang up the ordered speed, and the men back in the maneuvering room responded with a short buzz on the telegraph. The ship took an immediate angle forward, and the angle continued to increase as Allendale issued orders to his men down in the control room, his voice finally containing some traces of emotion.

"Full dive on the planes. Thirty degrees down! Flood negative!"

The sound of rushing water filled the conning tower as the ten thousand pounds of seawater rushed into the negative tank, three decks down, and the dual effect of the added weight and the water running over the planes sent the submarine plunging into the deep. The dial on the depth gauge moved alarmingly faster than the second hand on the clock mounted on the bulkhead next to it. As the grumbling noise of the rushing water faded to a sibilance, it was immediately replaced by the portentous sound of the *Shigure*'s twin screws.

Swoosh! Swoosh! Swoosh!

Filling the room as the charging destroyer drew closer, the sound grew in intensity with each passing second until it throbbed in their heads, each man willing the sub deeper as they hollowly stared at the depth gauge.

"One hundred twenty feet . . . One thirty . . . One forty . . ." Allendale's muffled voice counted off.

And the *Shigure* drew closer.

Tremain exchanged glances with Monroe, and saw his executive officer lay a finger on the plot at the last known position of the *Shigure*. When the destroyer had turned to head for the *Whitefin*'s periscope, there had been only a thousand yards of distance between them. The *Shigure* at top speed could make that distance in less than a minute.

"Tin can passing overhead now, Captain," Doniphan announced. The sonarman had already taken off his headset and was now holding only one earpiece to his ear, in anticipation of the coming depth charges.

"Passing two hundred feet!"

Swoosh! Swoosh! Swoosh!

Tremain half thought of changing course in an attempt to throw the destroyer off, but quickly thought against it. Any rudder now would slow the submarine down, and the *Whitefin* needed every knot of speed across its planes to get it as deep as possible.

"Picking up splashes, sir! Depth charges on their way down! Lots of 'em!"

Every man held onto the nearest handhold. The deck was still at a thirty-degree angle in an effort to get deeper, but it was too late. They weren't deep enough to avoid this barrage. The *Whitefin* had not had enough time to evade. The *Shigure*'s captain had them dead nuts.

Click-click Bang! Click-click Bang! Click-click Bang!

The depth charges went off in succession, sending three

distinct shudders throughout the hull. But they were not close. They had gone off at a much shallower depth.

"Shit, is that all he's got?" Ensign Berkshire said, smiling, with apparent relief in his voice. "That was nothing!"

Everyone ignored him, as if it were bad luck to even make eye contact with the inexperienced ensign who had dared call a depth charging "nothing." Only Petty Officer Doniphan allowed the ensign a fatherly grin.

"They dropped a full pattern on us, sir. Those ones were set to go off shallow. The rest are still on their way down."

With his expression gone instantly pale, Berkshire slowly backed into the aft corner of the room, his white-knuckled hands grasping the nearest pipe bracket while his nervous eyes stared helplessly up at the overhead. He did not have to wait for very long.

Click-click Wham! Click-click Wham!

Two depth charges exploded with thunderclap intensity on the starboard side, just outside the *Whitefin*'s hull. The hull reeled from the blows like a great whale pierced with harpoons, lurching rapidly to port. Every man in the conning tower left his feet and was thrown against the port bulkhead. Equipment flew off shelves; cork insulation rained down everywhere. Light-bulbs burst, and the room went black. The sound of grinding metal filled the room, and someone screamed as a massive thud shook the deck plates beneath them.

Click-click Wham! Click-click Wham! Click-click Wham!

Another set of charges detonated almost simultaneously. But this group went off somewhere beneath the hull, shuddering the ship from beneath, as if a great fist had punched it three times rapidly in the gut. The hull seemed to whiplash from the jolt to its midsection. Once again, those men who had regained their footing found themselves flat on the deck when they felt the deck pushing up on their feet, like a downward elevator that had suddenly come to a stop.

Tremain's head ached from the old concussion, and his shoulder felt numb from the knifing impact of a protruding valve stem on the starboard side of the room. Emergency battle lanterns clicked on here and there, their beams outlined in the floating dust from the cork insulation as they swept across clusters of crouched and groaning men. It took him a few moments to regain his bearings, to regain his hearing. He could hear water trickling somewhere nearby, and imagined the sub must have multiple leaks after withstanding such a punishing barrage. The depth charges had been incredibly close, and he guessed that the destroyer captain had set them to go off at one-hundred-foot intervals. Most likely, the *Whitefin* had taken the brunt of her blows from the charges set at two hundred feet.

"Passing three hundred feet," Allendale's voice called through the humid, dusty air.

Light beams swept past the hatch in the deck, and Tremain peered over to look down at his infallible diving officer standing behind the planesmen holding the beam of a battle lantern squarely on the diving gauges.

"Dive, do you have depth control?" Tremain called from his crouched position, trying his best to mask the pain he felt in his shoulder.

There was a pause, and Tremain was about to ask again when Allendale's steady voice answered, "Yes, Captain."

"Then level off at four hundred feet."

"Four hundred feet, aye, sir."

"Helm, all ahead one-third." Tremain winced. "Steady as she goes."

"All ahead one-third," came the ruffled voice of the helmsman. "Steady as she goes, aye, sir."

A hand reached out from the darkness, grabbing his arm and pulling him to his feet in one quick motion.

"Are you all right, Captain?" It was Monroe's voice.

"I'm fine. Check for damage, and have someone get these lights back up."

"I think we've got a few breakers tripped, sir. I'll get on it right away."

As Monroe's shadow disappeared down the hatch to the control room, Tremain held one hand on the bulkhead to steady himself. He waited for the thirty-degree down angle to come off before groping his way toward the periscopes. He had to check them, make sure they weren't leaking. It was one thing he could do while the men around him inspected their gear for damage. Suddenly, his foot came in contact with a large, square metal object, blocking his path. Quickly reaching for a battle lantern, he shined it at his feet to discover the three-hundred-pound SD radar set. The shock from one of those blasts must have dislodged it from its mounting, and now it lay across the deck on its side, its bulky metal housing streaming with rivulets from a small hydraulic fluid leak in the outboard. Tremain quickly concluded that this must have been the source of the grinding metal sound he had heard before. But as he reluctantly shined the light farther along the radar's metal housing, he also discovered the source of the scream. The sailor who had been assisting on the periscope now lay faceup beneath the fallen radar set, his chest completely hidden and apparently crushed by the weight of the three-hundred-pound housing. The young sailor stared blankly at the overhead, his mouth locked in one last desperate gasp as the noxious hydraulic fluid dripped onto his frozen face, forming pools in his unblinking eyes.

"Some of you men bear a hand," Tremain said sullenly.

Two or three sailors helped him to heave the giant radar set off to the aft starboard corner of the room, where it would be somewhat out of the way. Then someone folded down the captain's cot—a small bed that Tremain's predecessor had often used, allowing him to sleep one step away from the periscopes—and the dead sailor's broken body was gently laid there.

Tremain heard the clicking of several breakers, and the surviving lightbulbs in the room came to life again, revealing a conning tower strewn with oily books, plotting instruments, and small patches of blood. One sailor had his head in the outboard as he tightened the flange that was the source of the hydraulic leak, while the others stared blankly at the body of their shipmate lying on the cot. Their expressions weren't exactly sad, but more withdrawn, as if they, too, expected to be dead before long. All of the men in the room had gone through depth charge attacks before—all except Ensign Berkshire, of course, who now appeared to be fighting the urge to cower in the corner—and they all knew what they were in for. That had only been the beginning. The *Shigure* would not give up. She would come again, and again, and again, until one of those charges cracked the hull, and sent them to a watery grave.

"Echo ranging, Captain. Long scale," Doniphan reported. Apparently the sound heads were still functioning. But even without a sonar headset, Tremain could hear the *Shigure*'s active sonar pulses, just above the din of the trickling water coming from the leaks in the control room.

Ohwee-ohweee! . . . Ohwee-ohweee!

The sound waves resounded through the dark depths, searching for the metal skin of the submarine.

"Echo ranging bears, zero-three-zero, sir."

"Very well, Sonar. Helm, right standard rudder. Steady course two-one-zero."

The *Shigure* was echo-ranging to the northeast, so he would turn the *Whitefin* to the southwest, creeping away, all the while presenting the narrowest profile for sonar reflections. Of course, there was little hope of success. The *Shigure* already knew the *Whitefin*'s general location. Regardless of the oil trail on the surface, which had probably been obliterated in the barrage of depth charges, the *Shigure* needed only to conduct a good sonar sweep to pinpoint the sub's exact location. Only a freak layer of cold water could save them now. Tremain cast a hopeful glance at the bathythermograph on the bulkhead, but the trace along the chart paper representing the density of the water relative to depth was virtually a straight line. There was no thermal layer to be found in these waters. No sound barrier to hide under, nothing to escape the probing sonar pulses.

"At four hundred feet, Captain," Allendale called up the hatch. "We're heavy, sir. Recommend more speed."

Apparently, Allendale was realizing the *Whitefin*'s true buoyancy condition now that the speed had fallen off to barely a crawl. At one-third speed, barley three knots, the lift produced by the bow and stern planes was virtually negligible. The *Whitefin* was overall heavy and was dropping out of depth. The choices were to order up more speed and allow the planes to lift her up, or blow some variable ballast overboard and make her lighter. Ringing up more speed, even a few knots, would help greatly and was by far the quieter of the two choices.

"Very well, Dive. Helm, make turns for five knots."

The *Whitefin* slowly crept up to speed and Tremain looked

down the hatch to see Allendale give him a thumbs-up. The
five knots would hold her on depth. Unfortunately, more
speed meant faster depletion of the batteries, and who knew
how long they would need the precious battery power.

"We've got leaks from the seawater cooling in the forward
engine room." Monroe started his report before he reached the
top of the ladder, his khaki shirt and trousers soaking wet and
scarred with grease. "Repair party's on it right now, but there's
a lot of water in the bilge already, which is probably why
we're so heavy."

"I see," Tremain said, fixing his gaze on Monroe to get his
attention and then cutting his eyes at the dead sailor lying on
the cot. Monroe's face registered a moment of confusion, but
then took on a heavy countenance as he caught sight of the
fallen sailor.

"Collingsworth," he muttered, resting one hand on the
dead sailor's cold forehead. He sounded somewhat resigned,
somewhat vague. "He was Commander Burgess's favorite
periscope assistant. Burgess never did an observation without
him. He'd have the poor boy stirred out of the rack sometimes
just to take a bearing on a passing junk. Poor kid. He won't get
racked out anymore."

"About the damage, XO," Tremain said awkwardly, clearing his throat, doing his best not to sound unmoved by the
young man's death, but there was more pressing business at
hand.

"Yes, sir," Monroe said, pausing once more to look at the
dead Collingsworth, as if he needed to see the corpse again to
confirm the sailor's death in his mind. "The impulse air-
charging manifold back in the aft torpedo room ruptured in a
bad place. Took them a while to find it. Air banks two, three,
and four bled down to eighteen hundred pounds before they
could isolate it. Needless to say, we can't fire the aft tubes
until the manifold is repaired and the impulse flasks are
recharged. We've got a pretty good pressure inside the hull
right now, due to that air leak. Up in the forward room, one of
the torpedoes dislodged itself from its rack, but Chief Mc-
Cune is getting it secured with block and tackle as we speak.
It's lodged in a bad way, though, and it'll be a while before
they can reload the forward tubes."

"So, what you're saying is, we don't have any tubes to fire, and we won't for quite some time."

"That's essentially it, Captain."

"Anything else?"

"Minor leaks here and there, sir. A few shorts, a few tripped breakers. E division's dealing with it pretty handily. We've also got water running from the telltale drain for the main induction piping, so we're pretty sure we've got a leak somewhere by the outboard hull valve. But it's sporadic, so the leak is probably minor. Probably just a gland, or maybe one of those explosions unseated the valve for a fraction of a second. We really won't know till we get on the surface and inspect it."

"Any more casualties?" Tremain was almost afraid to ask the question.

Monroe shook his head. "A few concussions in the crew's mess, including one of the cooks, a victim of one of his own pots. Minor injuries elsewhere. Doc's patching them up. Collingsworth is the only fatality."

It wasn't bad considering how close the depth charges had been, but who knew what damage had not yet been detected, like the leaking fuel tank they hadn't discovered until a full day after their encounter with the enemy planes. The *Whitefin* could have some damage somewhere outside the hull that might have already sealed their fates. For all they knew, one or all of the main ballast tanks had been ruptured, in which case the *Whitefin* would never make it to the surface again. Like many things on a submarine, they wouldn't know if it worked until they tried using it.

"Tin can approaching, Captain," Doniphan said. "Screws are picking up speed. He's coming this way. Bearing zero-two-five."

They all looked up at the overhead, and before long the dull thrumming of the *Shigure*'s churning screws was again audible through the hull.

Swoosh! Swoosh! Swoosh!

The noise grew louder and louder until Doniphan's reports became unnecessary. Everyone knew the destroyer was directly overhead.

"Helm, all ahead standard," Tremain said over the din. "Left full rudder."

The *Shigure* would undoubtedly drop a load on them, but maybe he could get some last-minute horizontal separation away from the drop pattern before the destroyer had time to adjust. It was normally a futile effort, since the throwers and rollers on a modified Shiratsuyu class destroyer could create a depth charge pattern large enough to cover a two-hundred-yard area, but he could not just sit there and take the pounding. He had to do something.

"Splashes, sir."

Once again, the deadly ordnance was hurtling toward them, and once again they would have to wait the agonizing seconds for the three-hundred-pound cans of TNT to fall through four hundred feet of water before they knew their fates. Strangely, every man in the room—except for the helmsman, who mercifully had something to do—stood with his eyes transfixed on the dead form of Collingsworth lying on the cot. The body rocked ever so slightly with the gentle roll of the hull, and Tremain could only guess that his men were envying their dead friend at this moment, who was beyond caring, beyond fear, and already beyond the great unknown they were all potentially headed for in the next few moments.

Then it came.

Click-Click Wham!

The hull shuddered as it absorbed the pressure wave from the single depth charge, but it was nowhere near the disastrous barrage they had suffered in the first pattern. Mild vibrations trembled through the deck plates, but nothing to cause any concern. Every man held his breath as if it was too good to be true and the real barrage had to be imminent. Tremain even caught a glimpse of Berkshire opening his hitherto shut eyes in apparent bewilderment. The depth charge had detonated somewhere to starboard, and Tremain could only guess that his last-minute order to steer left had opened the distance enough to make the charge inconsequential.

They waited, and waited, each man breathing heavily, some yawning nervously, all staring at one another, daring to hope that there would be no more.

"I thought I only heard one splash before, but I couldn't be sure," Doniphan whispered softly, returning his headphones to his ears in one motion. "As strange as it sounds, sir, I think that's all of them. And there's something else here, wait a minute. He's not turning around, Captain. It sounds like he's heading away from us."

The echo ranging suddenly stopped, and slowly, but steadily, the swooshing screws of the *Shigure* faded, too, until they were no longer audible through the hull. With silent trepidation every man watched Doniphan until the intent sonar operator finally reported that the destroyer had not turned around and was indeed headed away, back to the convoy. They hardly knew whether to breathe a sigh of relief or be more concerned.

"Is he just playing with us?" Monroe said doubtfully.

"Either that or he's plumb out of depth charges," Tremain said. "An Akizuki class destroyer carries only thirty-six, and for all we know that bastard's used them up already, maybe on one of our brethren covering the northern sectors. We might not be the first sub to jump this convoy. I'll bet that's it—ten to one."

"Captain, there's something strange, sir." Doniphan's face was screwed up as he kept his hydrophone pointed toward the fading *Shigure*. "That destroyer's not going back to the tanker convoy, sir."

"What?"

"He's not going back to the tanker convoy. I can hear the tankers clearly, sir, bearing one-seven-five. They're bearing away to the south now, but that tin can's heading the other direction. He's merging with the screw noise of that northbound convoy we saw earlier. Looks like he might be joining up with them."

"Why the hell would he do that?" Monroe said curiously "He's leaving the tankers unprotected. All the better for us, right, Captain?"

Tremain stared blankly at the bulkhead, trying to put two and two together. It was starting to make sense to him now: the blinking signals to keep radio silence, the early break-off of the *Shigure*'s attack to conserve depth charges, the high speed of the northbound convoy. Undoubtedly in the rash of signals he had witnessed between the two fleets, the commodore aboard the cruiser of the northbound convoy was passing orders to the commodore of the tanker convoy, telling him to relinquish his escort to protect his own convoy. Tremain knew how much of a role rank and status played in the Imperial Navy. Orders from the theater commander could be easily overruled by the senior officer present, even to the extent of causing a tactical blunder. It had happened many times in the past, to the Allies' advantage, sometimes just at the moment it was needed, like now. It was where the Japanese honor system broke down.

"The *Shigure*'s been assigned to the northbound convoy," Tremain said to the gathering of inquisitive faces surrounding him. "It's the only plausible explanation. That explains why she broke off her attack on us, to conserve depth charges. It's a long journey back across the South China Sea, and she's going to need every last charge if she's going to be any use as an escort. That northbound convoy must be carrying something important—something more important than a fleet of fifteen tankers, anyway."

For the rest of the afternoon, the *Whitefin* stayed deep, cruising at one-third speed, listening as the two convoys faded in the distance, one to the north, one to the south. The crew repaired what damage they could, turning out in every compartment to inspect and repair. Deck plates and cabinets were removed to allow easy access to the myriad of leaks, and the *Whitefin*'s cramped compartments were soon transformed into unseemly jumbles of black piping, cylindrical pumps, and odd-shaped valves. Tremain balanced precariously on the wet pipes running fore and aft as he made his way through each compartment, inspecting the damage, speaking quiet words of encouragement to the faces peering back at him from carefully wedged spots behind the masses of equipment. Flailing legs and greasy hands protruded from everywhere, in every room, reaching in from the outboard or up from the bilge to turn wrenches and banding tools with the dexterity and tempo of skilled professionals. He even noticed Fabriano in the motor room, of all places, working on something in the outboard.

"Everything okay, Fabriano?" Tremain called up to him with a heartening smile.

Fabriano looked back at him, apparently a bit startled. He was probably surprised that Tremain would speak to him with such calm after such an intense attack.

"Uh . . . just tightening up a flange back here, sir," Fabriano said with an obviously forced grin. "I'll have it tight in a jiffy."

Tremain could not remember any fluid piping running through that particular area of the engine room, but he decided not to question him any further. The former destroyer-man had endured his first serious depth charging and was probably a little shaken up by the whole experience. He'd soon learn how to deal with the stress of an underwater attack, like all the others.

By the time the submarine ventured to the surface and cracked the hatch to let in the cool sea air, the sun had gone down behind the cumulus blanket covering the sky. As the big diesels coughed to life, the whole crew seemed to breathe easier, as if the running diesels confirmed that they were indeed still alive. The night grew pitch black, and there was a short ceremony on the main deck for Seaman Collingsworth, whose body was wrapped in canvas and dropped into the dark sea with a four-inch shell tied to his feet to ensure that he reached the bottom, twenty-five hundred fathoms below.

After the ceremony, Tremain spent an hour on the bridge, staring out at the dark, rippling sea, deep in thought. Every death now, even that of young Collingsworth, reminded him of Judy's, and left him morbid and brooding. But he was growing more emotionless with each one. He didn't like it one bit, but he could not help it. Strangely, he compared everyone else's pain to his own, and found all others measuring short. He was ashamed to feel this way. Had Ireland been correct? Had he lost all sense of compassion? In the early days of the war, he would have felt a great weight on his shoulders after losing a sailor, racking his brain for many sleepless nights as he tried to come up with the perfect words to put in the letter to the fallen sailor's grieving family.

But now he was already trying to think of ways to succinctly deal with the letter to Collingsworth's parents. Perhaps a short memo would suffice, with the subject line "Welcome to the club of misery." He felt nothing but a detached numbness about the whole thing, and it made him deeply ashamed. It was the same shame he'd felt in the days following the Vella LaVella action, when he consciously avoided penning a note to Wally McCandles's widow. It was a courtesy generally extended by friends of an officer who were present at his death, to help the widow understand the circumstances surrounding her husband's death, beyond the scant information contained in the dreaded Navy Department telegram. In the days he had spent on Tulagi trying to arrange transportation to Australia, he had never gotten around to writing the letter, or, more precisely, he had never made time for it. He should have made time for it. After all, the McCandleses had sent him a letter after Judy's death—or more likely Betty McCandles had sent it, since Wally had been deployed overseas with the *Chevalier* at the time. He remembered turning the envelope over in his hands, the envelope containing the elegant handwriting of a woman, before he tossed it into one of Judy's wicker baskets where he had thrown the other hundred or more unopened sympathy letters.

He had never opened any of them. The pain was too fresh in his mind—and there were *a lot* of them. Judy had been popular among the officers' wives at the various bases where they had been stationed, often corresponding with the wives of his former shipmates for years after he had moved on to another command and had forgotten their names. Mulling through that stack of letters would have been too gut-wrenching, too painful. He could conn a submarine to within a stone's throw of the Japanese homeland and sink a battleship at point-blank range, but he could never bring himself to open those letters. And now he would never open them. He had burned them all in the fireplace of their small New London home the night before he left to return to the war.

The next day, the new owners moved into the home that he and Judy had enjoyed together for such a brief time. The pleasant elderly couple was completely oblivious to the circumstances surrounding the sale. As he showed them around the house in his dress khaki uniform, they seemed very talkative, telling him several times how much they appreciated buying a house from such a nice young man in uniform. But they must have thought him suffering from shell shock when the tour finally reached the garden and he broke down in tears, unable to talk. It had brought to mind the smiling image of Judy on her knees in the rich soil, dwarfed in one of his old button-down shirts, her hair up inside a broad-brimmed hat. It brought to mind how much he cherished the few weekends they had spent together gardening in the summer sun, drinking iced tea in glasses dripping with moisture, playfully wrestling on their small grassy lawn until he finally carried her inside to make love to her within a few steps of the kitchen door.

No doubt Betty McCandles had similar memories with Wally, and maybe she never missed getting a letter from Tremain. Maybe she would have burned it in the fire as he had done. Maybe Collingsworth's parents would do the same. Maybe he didn't need to write a letter at all.

Am I really that remorseless? Tremain suddenly thought.

"We got the air bank patched up, Captain." Monroe appeared at his side. "A two-compressor air charge is in progress. Should have pressure back up in a few hours. Most of the leaks are taken care of, including the gasket on the main induction valve. We're in pretty good shape, considering the walloping we received. We can bring another engine online to start pursuing the tankers anytime you're ready, Captain. Maybe we'll catch up with them tonight. Give them a taste of their own medicine."

With no response from Tremain, Monroe shrugged and gazed out at the *Whitefin*'s green, phosphorescent wake, stubby and short now since the sub was only traveling at one-third speed on one engine to allow for repairs, while the other engine recharged the batteries.

"It's calm up here tonight," Monroe said wearily as a flash of lightning streaked across the northern sky, revealing a boiling bank of clouds on the horizon. "The barometer's still falling. Maybe it's the calm before a storm."

Tremain hesitated. This was the moment of decision, and the moment he would need to be the strongest, the most confident. It was the only way Monroe would buy into and support what he was about to do.

"XO, I want you to put together a contact report on the tanker convoy. Include everything—size, disposition, course, speed . . . everything—and then send it off to headquarters. Make sure you mention that those tankers are traveling unprotected. No sense in letting them get away scot-free."

"Aye, sir." Monroe eyed him suspiciously.

"Then I want you to send another message informing Com-SubSoWesPac that we're heading north in pursuit of a new target and may go well beyond the boundary of our patrol area."

"I take it we're not going after the tankers, sir?"

Tremain did not answer. With forced solidity, he turned his head and called to Endicott, standing near the forward part of the bridge. "Officer of the Deck, bring on another engine, increase speed to full, and set course three-five-zero."

Endicott shot back a curious glance, but eventually acknowledged the orders and soon the *Whitefin*'s bow began to rise and plunge into the black waves rolling from the north. Her wake curved sharply to the right as she increased speed, and then stretched out in a long, green line behind her.

Tremain knew what Monroe was thinking, but the cool executive officer did not give any indication of alarm or objection. Instead he simply asked, "I assume we're going after the *Shigure*, Captain?"

"We're going after the *Shigure*'s *convoy*!" Tremain corrected him, lying. He had to lie. What else could he say? That he was leaving their patrol area, pursuing the *Shigure* to settle a personal vendetta, risking all of their lives and a fleet-class submarine in the bargain. He had to give his XO something to swallow. Something that would allow him to accept this change in the official orders handed down to them by Com-SubSoWesPac.

"That convoy's carrying something important, XO, otherwise, why would it have a heavy cruiser assigned to it? It's headed somewhere in a hurry, and we're not going to let it get away."

"What about the tankers, sir?"

"We've got subs covering the areas to the south. Once they get our contact report, I'm sure one of them will snatch up those tankers. They won't get very far."

"We could snatch them up tonight, sir, if we bring four engines online," Monroe offered vaguely. After a short pause with no response from Tremain, he added, "That northbound convoy's going fast, sir, close to sixteen knots, a lot faster than those tankers. They could be a hundred and fifty miles ahead of us by now. Even at full speed, I doubt we'll catch up with them until late tomorrow night."

"Good," Tremain replied curtly. "That will give you plenty of time to make sure our torpedoes are routined before we use them again. I want you to supervise it personally, understood? I don't want any more premature detonations."

"Understood, Captain," Monroe said in a tone that indicated he was completely aware of Tremain's evasiveness. Tremain had obviously made up his mind to go after the *Shigure*, and no forewarnings of a long sea chase, or the allurement of a juicy tanker fleet in the other direction, would make him change it. As Monroe climbed back down the bridge hatch, he added in a voice so low that his captain could not hear, "I'm sure that'll keep me out of your hair for a while."

Chapter 12

THE *Whitefin*'s bows broke through the crest of the immense green mountain of water, plunging headlong into the trough between the two giant rollers. The deck took on a steep angle, prompting Fabriano to break from the relatively protected portion of the bridge, near the hatch, and make a mad dash for the periscope shears. Normally seas like this wouldn't have given him any trouble; he had handled them often enough aboard destroyers and carriers. But this was his first time experiencing such weather from the meager conning tower of an eighteen-hundred-ton submarine dwarfed by every wave in sight.

He gained the metal rungs of the lookout stand in three or four bounding leaps, his feet slipping at nearly every step. Then he was climbing, as fast as he possibly could, for dear life, while at the same time trying not to lose his grip on the slippery metal rails. He had to reach the port-side lookout perch before the impact of the next wave, now forming just beyond the submarine's knifing bow.

"Come on! Climb, damn it!"

Fabriano looked up to see Shelby's red face streaming with water. The big sailor was extending a dripping hand and motioning encouragingly while he held on to the lookout perch with his other. Fabriano attempted to grab hold of it several times, each time in vain.

The *Whitefin* had glided down the back slope of one wave and was now headed bow-on toward the next one. Out of the corner of his eye, Fabriano could see the fifty-foot wall of churning water rising up ahead of the bow, towering so high that he needed to crane his neck back to see its peak. The surging green monster was poised and ready to strike.

"Get ready!" shouted the officer of the deck, down on the bridge below. His voice was barely audible above the howling wind and crashing seas.

"Here it comes!" Shelby shouted. "Move your ass!"

With a wild lurch, Shelby, with help from Heath on the starboard lookout perch, managed to grab hold of the shoulder strap on Fabriano's harness and with one quick heave yanked him up onto the portside perch, pressing him flat against the periscope housing in one swift motion. An instant later, the *Whitefin*'s bow burrowed heavily into the base of the towering wave, sending a violent shudder throughout the hull that trembled up to the periscope housing. The giant wave enveloped the entire submarine, crashing against the base of the defiant conning tower, throwing up curtains of foamy white seawater that pelted the men on the bridge without mercy. Fabriano held on to the steel rail as the driving water angrily tore at him in an attempt to carry him away, a crushing force that seemed to last for minutes. Eventually, the wave released him from its deadly clutches, its remnants left suddenly harmless and streaming down the conning tower's metal skin in torrents.

Once again, the *Whitefin* had broken free. She had reached the crest of a roller for a brief moment of respite. After fastening his harness lanyard to the rail, Fabriano finally got the chance to take a good look at the mountainous waves all around him, appearing even more ominous when coupled with the angry dark clouds above. At nearly every point on the compass the horizon was filled with shifting mountains of raging water.

"Woo-hoo!" Shelby let out a great howl as he shook his wet mop of red hair out of his face. "Bet you never saw anything like this on that destroyer, Mikey!"

Fabriano simply nodded and then turned his attention back

to the seas, bracing for the next menacing wave. He had to admit that Shelby was right. This entire patrol had been nothing like anything he had ever undertaken before. The idea of being deep behind enemy lines, on your own, with nothing but the ship and its dwindling stores to sustain you, the very idea of being thousands of miles from the nearest friendly ship, was both terrifying and exhilarating at the same time.

Finding his niche among the crew had been a great deal more difficult than he had expected. The first few weeks had been rough, especially after the incident with Penn. For several days after he had broken Penn's nose, most of his new shipmates would have nothing to do with him, and refused to help him complete his qualification card. But Shelby had played a big part in turning that attitude around. Shelby had helped him to qualify on lookout and to complete nearly half of his enlisted submarine qualification in the first month at sea. Whether it was Shelby's likeable nature or his threatening two-hundred-twenty-five-pound frame that had the greater influence, most of the *Whitefin*'s hands seemed to have accepted him by the time they reached the patrol area. Eventually, he started standing watches and pulling his own weight, and that seemed to have a tempering effect on the rest, especially Chief LaGrange.

One evening, after he had recited the names, locations, and capacities of the *Whitefin*'s forty-nine different fuel, oil, ballast, freshwater, and sanitary tanks, LaGrange had given him a surprising compliment, as well as an admonition.

"You're a smart one, Fabriano," the grizzled chief of the boat had said as he signed off on Fabriano's qualification card. "You know your shit, that's for sure. A natural submariner, I'm thinking. But take care that those fists of yours don't put you in the brig."

In hindsight, he could not have agreed with LaGrange more. The attack on Penn had been a stupid and almost disastrous mistake, one that might have turned the inquiring eyes of LaGrange—or worse, Captain Tremain—in his direction. He now realized that his little lapse in judgment might have fouled up his entire plan, had Shelby not covered up for him that night under the inquisitive glare of LaGrange. Since that moment, he had been determined to blend in with the rest of

the crew and remain anonymous for the remainder of the patrol. Of course, being anonymous didn't mean not volunteer-
ing for extra duties. He had to, just to keep himself from
thinking too much about the *Chevalier*'s money—his money
now—hidden down in the motor room.

Shortly after the *Whitefin*'s encounter with the *Shigure*, the
weather had turned foul, incredibly foul, so foul in fact that
he overheard the XO saying something about this being the
southern edge of one of the typhoons that were so common to
these waters. The visibility got worse, and the call had gone
out for more lookouts. Normally, he would have silently
moved to the back of the mass of sailors gathered before
Chief LaGrange's probing eyes, but this time he couldn't help
but volunteer. He'd have given almost anything, even a share
of the *Chevalier*'s cash, to be out in the open air again. He'd
been cooped up belowdecks for the better part of three weeks
with nary a moment on deck, and the claustrophobia was
starting to drive him out of his mind.

Of course, at the time it hadn't sounded so bad. Spend fifteen minutes of every hour on the bridge, in the refreshing
wind and rain, watching for enemy ships. How bad could it
be? But had he known that the fifteen minutes spent on the
lookout perch would be fifteen minutes from hell, fifteen minutes holding on for dear life between the immersing waves,
fifteen minutes freezing his ass off while fighting for every
breath, he would have kept his mouth shut.

The fifteen minutes of pummeling on the lookout perch
was always followed by forty-five minutes belowdecks, thaw-
ing frozen limbs and chugging down hot coffee while the
quartermasters thoroughly inspected his binoculars to make
sure they were not full of water. Then it was back up to the
lookout perch to start the process all over again. In the two
days since he had volunteered for this duty, he had come close
to going overboard more than a dozen times, and going overboard meant certain death. There was no way the *Whitefin*
could turn around to pick up a man in this sea, where the submarine's course was limited by the direction of the powerful
waves.

At this moment, the *Whitefin* was running to the north,

directly into the seas, to prevent it from capsizing. It was the best way for the submarine's unwieldy hull to take on the seas, like a dolphin darting into a wave and out the other side, but it was hard sailing for anyone who happened to be on the bridge.

"Remind me again why the hell we have to have lookouts up here?" Fabriano cupped his hands and shouted over to Shelby on the aft perch. "Why can't we just use the damn scopes?"

"The scopes would never take the beating," Shelby shouted back with a smile. "These waves would bend 'em back like twigs. Either that or the seals would crack, and then we'd have a couple of useless periscopes. They'd be flooded."

"And tell me again why we don't just submerge and go under this shit?" Fabriano said after the next wave had passed and he caught his breath.

"You're such a fucking tin-can sailor, Fabriano!" Shelby shouted above the tumult. "We could go under, but then we'd have to sit around and wait for this weather to blow over. We can't go very far on the batteries, not in currents like these. Eight knots will deplete them within an hour. We need the big diesels if we're going to make any headway against this storm, and to use the diesels we've got to be on the surface."

As if to emphasize that fact, a dirty brown mixture of vaporized seawater and burned diesel spat out from the exhaust ports near the waterline as a wave rolled past, exposing them for a brief instant.

"I don't see how they can breathe in this," Fabriano speculated, as he heard a groan coming from the struggling engines.

"Air and water goes in the main induction. The engines take the air, and the water goes into the bilge to get pumped overboard. It's as simple as that. We'll make a bubble head out of you yet, Mikey!"

Fabriano nodded wearily at Shelby's overly enthusiastic thumbs-up sign.

"I don't know how you tin-can sailors operate," Shelby added with a backhanded jab at Fabriano's ribs, "but no self-respecting submariner worth a shit ever let a little weather stop him from catching his prey. Captain Tremain's going to get that Jap bastard, typhoon be damned!"

Fabriano returned an insincere smile beneath a brow streaming with seawater.

Whatever their prey was, wherever they were headed, Fabriano did not care. What he did care about was staying alive. Rumors had been floating around ever since the encounter with the enemy destroyer, rumors about the captain setting off and leaving the assigned patrol area to try to settle a personal vendetta against the *Shigure*. Apparently the Japanese destroyer had sunk one of his previous commands. It seemed to hang over the crew like a cloud. The last few meals in the crew's mess had seemed somewhat hushed, but that might have been because every man had lost his appetite for food, since the incessant rocking tended to bring it back up. He couldn't remember how many puddles of vomit he'd inadvertently stepped in over the past two days. If the crew was unhappy about the new direction their captain was taking them, they didn't have the strength or the will to complain. Two days of tossing seas took nearly every unruly thought out of a man.

But apparently the weather did not have the same affect on the officers. Just this morning, as Fabriano was donning his harness inside the conning tower in preparation for going on watch, Lieutenant Whately and Ensign Berkshire were conversing not two feet away from him while they hovered over the radar operator's shoulder.

"There it is again, Paul," Berkshire had said to Whately, pointing at the circular display. "A close return off our port beam, just like last night. I figured we just drove past a large rock, but the men on the bridge say they don't see anything. Maybe it's a false return."

"That's not a false return," Whately had replied with conviction. "I've seen this before. What you're seeing is the beam from another SJ radar. There's another American submarine out there somewhere, and he's painting us. He could be close; he could be miles away. There's really no way to tell."

"You mean he's stalking us?" Berkshire said, astonished.

"Possibly. We're out of our own patrol area right now, probably passing through his. For all he knows we're a Jap sub."

"But we sent a message!"

"Yes, but what our brilliant captain didn't consider was how long it takes headquarters to process and turn around those messages. If ComSubSoWesPac didn't get the notice out before this storm hit, I'd say that other subs in the vicinity have no idea about our captain's little foray." Then in a lower voice Whately added, "This whole thing is just a disaster waiting to happen. The captain should've turned the ship around the minute we ran into this damn typhoon. It makes no sense to press on. There's no way we'll catch up with this convoy now."

Whately had quickly checked his defiant talk when Monroe's face appeared at the top of the control room ladder, shooting him a scathing glance. Obviously the young lieutenant's voice had carried farther than he'd realized.

From the looks of the seas around him right now, Fabriano had to agree with Lieutenant Whately's assessment. Visibility was poor at best. He and the rest of the lookouts spent most of their time trying to hold on for dear life, bracing for the next wave, and very little time watching their sectors. They seldom had their binoculars to their faces, since they could get blindsided by a wave if they did. With these kinds of distractions, how could they be expected to sight a convoy, let alone another ship? It all seemed like a useless endeavor.

"Control Room, Bridge," Fabriano heard the officer of the deck down on the bridge shout into the intercom box. "Prepare to place a low-pressure blow on all main ballast tanks!"

The intercom box had shorted out several times in the last forty-eight hours, but it appeared to be working now, as the muffled response came from the control room.

"Prepare to place a low-pressure blow on all main ballast tanks, control room, aye."

The officer of the deck must have had the volume turned all the way up; otherwise Fabriano would not have been able to hear the acknowledgment above the wind and the crashing seas.

Fabriano glanced at his watch. It was a running policy to blow the main ballast tanks dry every half hour during rough weather, and this time the officer of the deck was right on time in giving the order. Shelby had informed him during a previous watch that air often escaped the main ballast tanks during rough seas, and recharging the tanks with the low-pressure blower was the only thing that kept the main ballast tanks relatively dry.

"Bridge, Control." The speaker squawked again. "Commencing a low-pressure blow on all main ballast tanks."

Fabriano gripped the steel rail of the lookout perch and looked over the side at the swirling water smashing against the *Whitefin*'s outer hull. He had only seven minutes of his watch left to go, and he could almost taste the acrid coffee waiting for him inside the warm control room below.

Suddenly he realized that the seas had calmed noticeably. As he watched, the waves started to subside, the shroud of dark clouds lifted higher and higher above the white-capped seascape, and the gale force winds decayed to a mere fluttering breeze. Visibility improved rapidly, and the light seemed to return to the earth. Far ahead of the *Whitefin*'s bows, he could actually see a sun-drenched patch of ocean glistening in the midst of the weakening storm. The waves no longer crashed against the conning tower, no longer threatened to pull them off it. In fact, the main deck was beginning to dry off for the first time in two days.

Fabriano exchanged astonished looks with Shelby and Heath as his drenched clothes began drying in the wind. Shelby even let go of the rail, prompting Fabriano and Heath to do the same, and, for the first time in days, Fabriano stood up tall, taking in sweet breaths of dry, fresh air.

They had survived the onslaught of nature. They had pursued their quarry into a maelstrom of wind and sea. And now, with the open sea visible all the way to the horizon, there was not a single ship in sight.

"WE'VE reached the eye of the storm, Captain." Monroe knocked on the door frame and poked his head through the curtain into Tremain's stateroom. "Weather's slacking. Visibility's improved quite a bit. I'll try to get a sun line if I can manage it, and find out where the hell we are. The DRI is showing us north of twenty-one degrees, but I don't trust it. Not with all of the head currents we've been seeing."

"Thank you, XO."

Tremain did not look up even once as he hovered over the chart laid out across the stateroom's small desk, a pair of dividers in one hand, a pencil in the other.

"I also thought you ought to know, sir," Monroe added hesitantly, when he did not get the question he was expecting. "We've got no contacts of any kind. Nothing visual. Nothing on radar. Not even that SJ contact we picked up this morning."

"What are you trying to say, XO?" Tremain asked, still poring over the chart in the scant light afforded by the desk lamp.

"Just that it looks like we've lost the convoy, sir. There's no sign of them anywhere." He paused before adding, "I'm starting to get the feeling that this was a bad decision, Captain, that we might be tilting at windmills up here."

Tremain looked up at him and stared for a long moment, long enough to lead Monroe to believe that he had just overstepped his bounds. But eventually Tremain gave him a patient smile and shook his head

"Not by a long shot, XO," Tremain said, returning his attention to the chart before adding passively, "But you're right, we'll never find them in this storm."

Monroe did his best to hold back a sigh. He'd already been approached by some of the officers. They were concerned and they had a right to be. This kind of conduct was unlike anything they had ever seen before. Tremain insisted they were going after a convoy of greater importance than the tanker fleet, but they were all college graduates, and they all knew their captain was disobeying the patrol orders. Certainly Tremain understood that, too.

But what was he, as executive officer, to do? His loyalties lay both with his captain and with his crew. He was the middle man, the man responsible for seeing that the crew carried out the captain's orders without question, but he was also the man designated to ensure that the captain didn't abuse his rank and privilege. In the last two days, every officer, even young Berkshire, had pulled him aside to personally voice a concern about what they were calling "the captain's new mission." All except for Allendale. The engineer seemed perfectly content as long as he had a technical problem to handle. And with the beating the *Whitefin* had taken from the storm over the past two days, Allendale had his hands full. He was too busy to think about where they were going and why. And maybe that was the best way to approach it. Keep the other officers busy. Make them stand their watches with greater attention, get them involved in their divisions. That might be the key to suppressing their seditious talk. That might keep them from harping on this pointless and dangerous wild-goose chase.

Monroe shot a last glance at the absorbed Tremain before he shook his head in disillusionment. The captain had seemed so reasonable, so skilled in the first weeks at sea, about the *Whitefin*, about his own career, about everything. It had been like a breath of fresh air after the dismal year under Commander Burgess. Monroe had even envisioned Tremain and him becoming an ace team like the legendary Mush Morton and Dick O'Kane, the bang-up team that made the *Wahoo* such a successful killer of the deep, sinking convoy after convoy, winning fame for the sub service and getting their picture taken in *Life* magazine. But ever since the engagement with the *Shigure*, those hopes had dissolved. Tremain had changed. He was reclusive now, isolated, and somewhat obsessive.

Monroe made to leave and had almost closed the curtain when Tremain called after him.

"You want to know how we're going to catch them, XO?" he said with a grin. "Come take a look at this."

Monroe leaned on the locker above Tremain's bunk so that he could see the chart clearly. It was a nautical chart of the South China Sea centered on Hainan, the big potato-shaped island off the southern coast of China, and roughly two hundred nautical miles west of the *Whitefin*'s present estimated position.

"Originally I thought the *Shigure*'s group was headed for Hong Kong, since their last known course checked out with that destination, but now I'm more inclined to think they'll head for Haikou."

"On Hainan?"

Tremain nodded.

"Why there, sir?"

"Those ships in the *Shigure*'s convoy are of the coastal variety, XO, and not very seaworthy. I'm willing to bet they're chugging away at no more than three or four knots, having just as much trouble as we are getting through this storm. Chances are, they've sustained some damage, and they're looking for a protective port to put in to and make repairs. Hong Kong is the last place they'll want to go, since the storm is heading in that direction." Tremain put his finger on the chart at the northern end of Hainan, where the coastal town of Haikou was annotated. "They'll head for Haikou first, and that's where we'll be waiting for them."

"Surely, the Japanese have plenty of antisubmarine defenses there," Monroe offered skeptically. "Mines, too."

"Undoubtedly." Tremain nodded. "We'll have to be on our toes, and that's why it's imperative that we arrive well ahead of the convoy, to give us plenty of time to work into a favorable position. I want you to plot a course for Hainan Strait and tell the officer of the deck to bring all main engines online. You might ask Allendale if we can get an extra knot or two if we go to reduced electrical for a while, running auxiliaries off the batteries. It's just a thought. I'll let him make the call. And we've got to take advantage of this lull while we can. We'll be heading due west, right back into the storm, but let's try to get a flank bell out of her for as long as we can."

Tremain appeared so invigorated at the prospect of ambushing the convoy, as if it were a certainty, as if he had no doubt that the officers and crew, including his executive officer, were behind him 100 percent, even eager to take part in the hunt. How could he not know the truth? That the officers were bordering on mutiny and the crew was murmuring. Perhaps he did know, and this positive, forthcoming demeanor was his way of dealing with it.

"I'll get right on it, Captain," Monroe said wearily. Despite the grumblings of the crew, and the potential dangers waiting for them at Hainan Strait, what he dreaded most at this very moment was the return to the stomach-churning, hull-battering seas. It sucked all of the fighting spirit right out of him.

As he turned to leave, Tremain called after him again.

"Thank you, XO, for holding the crew together." And then in a serious, insightful tone, he added, "I understand how difficult these storms can be on morale."

As Monroe drew the curtain shut on the stateroom and

headed down the passage, sidestepping a few sailors on their way to the forward torpedo, he suddenly realized that Tremain knew a whole lot more about the mind of the crew than he let on.

But somehow that thought did not make him feel any better.

Chapter 13

THE *Whitefin* cruised across a sun-speckled sea, making eighteen and a half knots through the choppy but manageable surf. Waves constantly broke over the main deck, dousing the wooden planks before they could dry in the sun, but few ever made it as high as the conning tower, allowing the officer of the deck and the lookouts to stand their watches in relative comfort for the first time in days.

In fact, it was so comfortable on the bridge, with a fresh, humid breeze blowing across the starboard bow and the long forgotten sun turning the hitherto ice-cold steel rails warm to the touch, that the captain had authorized topside liberty to any man who wanted it—and *every* man on board wanted it. Those who were off watch formed a line at the base of the control room ladder, where six at a time were allowed to climb up to the bridge to enjoy a fifteen-minute smoke on the cigarette deck. They seemed like kids eager to ride a roller coaster, smiling and joking about things unrelated to the boat or the war. They had all succumbed at one point or another to the nausea and queasiness born from riding out a storm while cooped up inside a cramped steel tube, and now they needed a break. Even the most hardened veterans on board needed a few moments away from the corkscrewing steel bulkheads, the putrid aroma of oil and vomit, and the almost incessant palpitations of the air-deprived diesel engines.

"Holy shit!" Chief McCune's voice resounded in the control room as he emerged from the forward watertight door, his face twisted into a disgusted scowl. The room looked like a complete disaster area, with piles of debris and puddles of various fluids strewn about, all left there during the storm, since no man had the stomach to clean house while the ship was taking such large angles. "This space is as cluttered as your sister's room, Hughes!"

"Hey, Chief, how d'you know what my sister's . . . Hey, wait a minute . . ."

Hughes was a bit slow, and he didn't catch on that he was the butt of a joke until he heard chuckling from the rest of the men in line.

"While you boys are just standing around waiting to sunbathe on deck, maybe you could put yourselves to good use and make this space look presentable again," McCune said with forced sarcasm. Though it sounded like a suggestion, every man knew better. "Davis, clean up that puke under the IC switchboard! Fisher, pick up those rags by the diving station, and while you're there, use them to wipe up that oil on the deck! Russell, you and Kiefer gather up that plotting paper and the rest of that crap! Damn quartermasters, can't keep your shit in the lockers where it belongs."

The sailors gave an audible groan, although some managed a smile as they heeded the chief's orders, moving in slow motion, their bodies sore from the ordeal of the past two days.

"Penn!" McCune shouted. "What the hell do you think you're doing standing around while everyone else has his butt in the outboards?"

"I'm waiting to go topside, Chief," Penn answered unenthusiastically. Like the others, he, too, was worn out, and just wanted a few quiet moments in the sun.

"I can see that! Why don't you make yourself useful and untangle those wet harnesses over there? Damn lookouts just toss 'em wherever they fuckin' like. Shit! You'd think I was at sea with a bunch of damn children!"

"Yes, Chief," Penn replied simply.

"And make sure you give them a good inspection, too. XC

says we're headed back into heavy weather, so the fucking lookouts are going to need those damn things again. Make sure those straps are in good shape. Got it?"

"Okay, Chief."

Penn lumbered over to the disheveled pile of harnesses and began to sort through them. The untidy heap of damp nylon straps were salt-encrusted from countless storms over the span of the *Whitefin*'s existence and stank of seawater. With the straps twisted into a myriad of dizzying knots, Penn knew that he would be busy for quite a while. Each knot would need to be untied one at a time.

He cursed McCune inwardly for the son of a bitch that he was, and for giving him such a shitty task.

Over the past weeks at sea, Penn had meandered through the motor room more than a dozen times during the midwatch, silently checking Fabriano's secret stash of cash to make sure it was still there. He never was good at keeping a poker face, and he was always fearful that one day Fabriano would see his plans in his eyes, and hide the money someplace else.

As Penn attempted several times to work his fingers into a particularly troublesome knot, the damp nylon not budging an inch, he finally resorted to giving it a try with his pocketknife. After prying the blade beneath the key piece of lanyard that would untangle the entire binding, he pulled up and accidentally sliced into the nylon a good three-quarters of an inch.

"Shit!" he muttered, holding up the piece of nylon cut halfway through. Now he had ruined a perfectly good lanyard. No lookout would want to go topside with a lanyard that probably wouldn't even hold his own weight, let alone save him from the suction forces of a strong sea wave.

As Penn pondered the tear for a moment, rubbing the nylon ends back and forth beneath his grimy fingers, an evil grin suddenly appeared on his face to match the equally evil thought forming in his head. Fabriano had been pulling lookout duty lately, assigned to Lieutenant Endicott's watch. Wouldn't it be a shame if something were to happen to him?

Penn found a piece of tape, and smiled wickedly as he discreetly wrapped it around the lanyard, hiding the tear. Of course, there were still obstacles to be overcome. Somehow, he'd have to make sure Fabriano put on this particular harness, and even then there were no guarantees that a wave strong enough to carry him off would ever swamp the lookout perch. But that could be left to chance if necessary. With a triumphant grin he finished taping the lanyard and placed the harness back in the pile with the others.

His smile quickly faded, though, and his face turned to stone, when he looked up and found himself staring straight into Shelby's dark eyes watching him from the other side of the control room.

"THE crew seems happy to see the sun again, Captain," Endicott said, trying to make small talk as the wind whipped his hair around.

Tremain simply nodded, but did not look back at the six men lounging by the twenty-millimeter gun on the cigarette deck. They needed a few moments away from their captain's all-seeing eye, and he had no desire to ruin this moment for them. Instead, he leaned on the bridge coaming with both elbows and looked out over the *Whitefin*'s bow as it drove through the blue, choppy seas.

"Looks like we've lost our fuel tail, sir," Endicott said, pointing aft at the *Whitefin*'s wake, where the ocean's surface no longer contained the shiny streak of petroleum that had been there prior to the storm. "I guess number three fuel-ballast tank must be empty now."

Of course it's empty, Tremain thought. *I get the fuel oil and water report every night, Mr. Endicott. Don't you think I know that?*

Tremain checked his frustration and began wondering why every junior officer felt that he had to fill up his captain's few precious moments topside with such meaningless banter. Such a waste.

The sun felt good on his face, hands, and neck. It felt uncommonly good, but it was not to last. Already he could see the dark wall of clouds approaching on the horizon, beyond the *Whitefin*'s plunging bow. Soon they would engulf the sun, and once again the sea would turn dark and violent. It would be tougher this time around. The seas and wind would be coming from a different direction, and the *Whitefin* would need to point her bows probably fifty or sixty degrees away from the direction she wished to go in order to keep from taking the seas on her beam. It would take some good ship driving to manage it, and he had already decided that either he or Monroe would be on the bridge at all times until the *Whitefin* had made it beyond the storm.

"Permission to come up, sir?" A head appeared at the bridge hatch by Tremain's feet.

"Come up," said Endicott.

It was Owens, the quartermaster. After gaining the top of the ladder, he approached Tremain with a smile and the all-too-familiar slip of paper.

"XO sends his respects, sir, and wishes to report the noon position."

Once again, Owens's breath reeked of the onions served with the noon meal. By now Tremain was certain that Owens did it solely for his benefit—the quartermaster's own unique way of having a little fun with the captain. Tremain pretended not to notice and took the slip of paper without flinching. It contained the *Whitefin*'s estimated position based on a sun line Monroe had taken during this precious interlude of sunlight. With the storm blotting out the sun and stars, it was the first fix he had been able to take in three days.

Tremain examined the coordinates on the small slip of paper. They indicated that the storm had set the *Whitefin* to the southwest quite significantly over the past two days, but that she was still within a hundred miles or so of where he had assumed her to be. He took comfort in the fact that the *Shigure* and her consorts had to be running into the same problems. They couldn't be too far ahead, if they were ahead at all.

"Thank you, Owens. Have we received anything yet from ComSubSoWesPac? Did headquarters get our serial about going out of area?"

"I don't right know, sir. The XO didn't tell me." The quartermaster's voice trailed off and his smile faded. Something beyond Tremain's left shoulder had suddenly seized his attention. Something off the port beam.

"What the hell?" Owens muttered, apparently unable to say any more.

Before Tremain could spin around to see what had turned the quartermaster deathly white, one of the sailors on the cigarette deck exclaimed with much desperation in his voice, "Torpedoes! Torpedoes off the port beam!"

Tremain saw them instantly: two thin, effervescent lines in the white-laced azure seas, less than five hundred yards from the *Whitefin*'s port beam and closing rapidly. Endicott was still trying to find them in his binoculars when Tremain shoved past him to get to the bridge intercom box.

"Helm, hard right rudder! Sound collision!"

The sound of a ceramic coffee cup shattering on the deck below emanated up through the open bridge hatch. Apparently, Tremain's sudden order had startled the heavy-eyed helmsman. He was certainly alert now, and despite being rattled, he executed the rudder order smartly. The *Whitefin*'s bow instantly began to swing to the right in response.

"My rudder is hard right, sir." The helmsman's voice came over the intercom and echoed through the open bridge hatch.

"Maneuvering, Bridge. Stop starboard motor, port motor ahead full!"

"Stop starboard motor, port motor ahead full, maneuvering, aye."

The torpedoes were speeding for a point ahead of the *Whitefin*'s bow, to rendezvous with the *Whitefin*'s hull at a specified time in the future. The only way to avoid them was to turn drastically off the old course, the one that the enemy submarine had used to calculate a firing solution, and head away from them. The trouble was, any submarine captain worth his salt would have made a contingency for an evasion, and would have fired his second torpedo at a point aft of the conning tower with the idea that his prey might try to evade and a lagging shot might catch him in his evasion turn. And this was certainly the case, as Tremain confirmed when he saw the two white tracks slowly diverge as they drew closer and closer to the *Whitefin*'s projected path. The torpedoes were coming on in a wide spread, but there was little he could do about it at this point. His only chance was to continue the turn and hope the *Whitefin* could get her head around fast enough to put the torpedoes astern. Like all ships, the *Whitefin* carried a certain amount of set and drift when executing turns, sometimes fifty yards or more. That small amount of set and drift could make all the difference. Only time would tell.

The men on the cigarette deck were all crowded against the port railing now, pointing with apprehension at the fast-approaching weapons. At Tremain's feet, a solitary hand emerged from the open hatch, grabbed onto the hatch wheel, and pulled the hatch down with a loud *clang*. He and Endicott exchanged momentary glances as the external hatch wheel spun around and around, squeaking loudly as someone on the other side, down inside the conning tower, dogged it tightly shut. They were locked out now. Whatever happened in the next few seconds, the men on the bridge and the men inside the hull would meet their fates separately. It was a normal part of the rig for collision, but it still sent a chill running through Tremain's spine, a chill that he tried his best to hide from the visibly shaken Endicott

The *Whitefin*'s green wake curved sharply to starboard, making a giant right angle in the water, the waves smacking against the leaning hull's starboard-side limber holes. Having turned away from the menacing white fingers, the *Whitefin* was now presenting her stern to the deadly underwater missiles, both less than a hundred yards away and closing at the rate of twenty-five yards per second.

Tremain no longer needed his binoculars to clearly distinguish the torpedoes' paths. The first would obviously miss. That much was apparent, even to an unseasoned eye. But the second torpedo was running perilously close to the *Whitefin*'s wake and was too close to call. In fact, there was a real danger that continuing the turn would swing the *Whitefin*'s stern back into the trailing torpedo's path for a hit on the starboard quarter.

Tremain knew he had to act fast.

"Helm, shift your rudder! Maneuvering, all ahead flank!"

The orders were acknowledged, but Tremain did not hear them. He was standing on the foot step beneath the bridge rail, craning his body over the side to try to find the bubbles of the oncoming torpedo which he had lost in the blinding reflection of the sun on the *Whitefin*'s boiling wake.

"You men back there," he called to the six sailors on the cigarette deck, "can you see it? Where did it go?"

He held his hand to his brow, shading his eyes from the sun, staring at the water until his eyes teared from the stiff wind. The *Whitefin* had checked her swing, and both screws now pulled together to steady her onto a straight course.

"Tell the helm, rudder amidships!" he called to Endicott, standing by the intercom box.

As Endicott relayed the order to the helm, Tremain continued to scan the sea astern, desperate to find any indication of the approaching torpedo. Suddenly, a frightful thought overtook him. Perhaps the torpedo's wake had merged with the *Whitefin*'s wake. Perhaps the torpedo was headed straight for the *Whitefin*'s stern. If that was indeed the case, he would have to turn, and right away. It didn't matter which way, it was a sixty-forty chance he'd be wrong anyway.

Just as he was about to tell Endicott to order the rudder thrown hard left, one of the sailors on the cigarette deck pointed to the water directly beneath the bridge on the port side. In the blink of an eye Tremain saw a long, green shape, just a few feet beneath the surface and less than a stone's throw away, surging along the submarine's length, like a playful dolphin sprinting to get ahead. Before the heart-stopping sight could even register in Tremain's head, the torpedo had gone by, its bubbly white wake fizzing to the surface in an arrow-straight path that stretched off into the sea beyond the *Whitefin*'s port bow.

A moment of thankful silence ensued on the bridge as every man in his own way adjusted to the realization that the ship was now out of danger. Endicott stared blankly at the sea off the port beam where the torpedo had passed only moments before.

"If you hadn't given the order when you did, sir," he mumbled, "we'd all be dead. If . . . if you hadn't pushed me aside . . ."

"Forget it, Tom. It's not worth belaboring." He half wanted to tell the young lieutenant the whole truth, that his own excessive rudder order might have sealed their fates just as easily. "Let's get away from this place as fast as we can. That sub is still out there, and is probably setting up for another shot on us right now. We'll head in the other direction at high speed for half an hour. Keep a good lookout for periscopes. I want a constant helm zigzag pattern used until further notice. Go ahead and secure the rig for collision, Tom."

"Aye, aye, Captain," Endicott replied, obviously not fully recovered from what might have been the worst mistake of his career and of his short life.

The constant helm zigzag pattern would keep him busy, since it involved shifting the rudder back and forth across a certain heading such that the ship was in a constant state of turning although generally headed in the desired direction.

As Tremain scanned the seas with his binoculars for one last look before going below, the tailwind carried the hushed conversation of the sailors far aft on the cigarette deck to his well-attuned ears.

"I can't understand why the son of a bitch didn't explode," said one who was a torpedoman. "The Japanese use magnetic exploders, don't they?"

"It didn't come from a Jap sub, shit-for-brains. It came from one of our own boats," said another. "Why else do you think the fucker didn't blow up? The Japs have good fish; it's ours that don't work worth a shit."

"If it was one of our boats, then what the hell are they shooting at us for?"

"They're shooting at us, numskull, cause they think we're a Jap. They didn't get the memo about our captain deciding to take his boat on a personal hunting expedition."

Tremain removed the binoculars from his face and glanced once at the conversing sailors. Their faces looked perfectly innocent and serene as they puffed on new cigarettes, their appearance yielding no clues of their rebellious chitchat. Obviously, they thought they were well beyond earshot, and had the wind not been blowing from the south, Tremain would never have guessed what they were discussing. Sailors were experts at keeping their true feelings hidden from their officers, but every now and then a captain came upon rare opportunities, like this one, where he got to hear what was truly going on inside the heads of his crew, in an unadulterated, uncensored fashion.

He just had to hold them together a little bit longer. They would come around. He would show them. True, for all intents and purposes, this was a personal hunting expedition. But once they had succeeded, once they could say that they were the ones who put the "Submarine Killer" on the bottom, they'd be behind him without any doubts or faltering. They were just worried right now, that's all.

Tremain considered for a moment as he stared out to sea, and then strolled aft, casually approaching the cluster of sailors on the aft gun deck. All conversation ceased as he drew closer and the group collectively stood a little straighter than they had a few moments before.

"Captain," said one, with something akin to a salute.

"Captain, sir," muttered another.

"As you were, men, please," Tremain said, raising a hand. Then turning to the sailor who only a moment before had been telling his shipmates that their captain was on a personal hunting expedition, Tremain said, "You're the hawkeye that spotted that torpedo, aren't you?"

The sailor, a machinist's mate, looked confused for a moment, but eventually nodded.

"What's your name, sailor?"

"Sullivan, sir," the sailor answered hesitantly, with slight defiance in his eyes. "Joe Sullivan, machinist's mate second-class."

Ah, yes, Tremain thought, searching the recesses of his mind. *Sullivan, from Austin. Writes religiously to his widowed mother back home. Plans to go to college and become a lawyer after the war. Knows diesel engines inside and out. Locked in the brig once in Pearl Harbor for drunk and disorderly behavior.*

"You've got good eyes, Sullivan," Tremain said with a smile. "You seem to be alert even when you're off watch."

The sailor from Texas fidgeted while shooting a slack-jawed look at the other sailors around. Tremain's compliment had obviously taken him off guard.

"I try to stay sharp, Captain," Sullivan eventually said.

"Well, that's good. You're going to have to be." Tremain paused, and waited for Sullivan's uncertain look, which came right on cue, before he extended a hand and added, "Because I'm promoting you to first class. Congratulations, young man! Anyone who can keep his head in the game like you deserves to be a supervisor. You'll be wearing three stripes before the day is out."

The whole group of sailors erupted in a collective laugh, and hands from all sides rubbed Sullivan's messy hair and violently patted him on the back. Any semblance of disobedience had gone from the young sailor's face, which now brandished a toothy grin from ear to ear.

Tremain silently faded forward, leaving the sailors to congratulate their comrade in their own way.

It was one of the oldest command tricks in the book: when morale sags, you give the men a distraction, something to think about other than their troubles. A captain's power to spot-promote came in handy in times like these. It was one of the few tools in a captain's little bag of tricks the navy gave him to hold his crew together.

That should hold them for a while, Tremain thought. *Let word of this make its way around the ship, and half of them will be bending over backward to be the next one to get spot-promoted.*

As he grasped the cold steel ladder rungs and descended into the conning tower, Tremain felt somewhat guilty about what he had just done. In a way, it seemed like a cheap way to get men to do what he wanted, and it left him feeling somewhat lesser of an officer. Where was the leadership quality in buying them off? But he had needed to buy himself some more time. He had to boost their morale long enough to find the *Shigure* and sink her.

Eventually, morale would sink to a point that even spot promotions would not work, and he could not help but wonder just how much time he had.

Chapter 14

BENEATH the mass of angry clouds hugging the ocean's surface like an inky cloak, the *Whitefin* ran once again through the raging seas spawned by the persistent typhoon. Not one beam of moon- or starlight could penetrate the thick clouds above, leaving only the frequent flashes of lightning to reveal the moving mountains of water all around her.

For the fourteenth time since the sea had returned to its angry state, Mike Fabriano made his way up the dark, slippery rails with a nimbleness that was quickly becoming second nature to him. As he gained the port-side lookout perch, latching his lanyard to the rail, he caught an acknowledging nod between the periscopes from Shelby and Heath, who had already tethered themselves to their own perches. The three comprised the fresh contingent of lookouts to replace the exhausted lookouts of the last watch. The watch turnover was now complete.

The ship still rocked with the same ferocity that it had during his previous watches, climbing up one side of the steep forty-foot waves and then crashing down into the trough on the other side. As always, he kept a vigilant eye out for any unanticipated wall of water, but not vigilant enough to keep him from casting an envious glance down at the lookouts from the last watch as they descended into the warm, red glow emanating from the open bridge hatch.

"Holding on tight up there?" A reassuring shout came from the bridge below.

All three lookouts gave a thumbs-up in unison to the upturned face of Lieutenant Commander Monroe. The XO and Lieutenant Endicott were the only ones on the bridge, and both were covered from head to foot in dark brown slickers identical to the ones that the lookouts wore.

"Look out for masts, lights, buoys, dark shapes, anything out of the ordinary!" Monroe shouted up to them, as he had at least once an hour during the last fourteen watches. "And keep your ears open for whistles and bells!"

All three lookouts exchanged grimacing glances at the absurdity of the order.

"That asshole tells me to listen for bells again, I'm gonna climb down there and throw him to the fucking sharks!" Heath said irritably from the aft perch. "You can't see a damn thing up here, much less hear anything. The bastard should keep his mind on driving the damn ship, and stop worrying about us."

"Easy, there, Heath," Shelby said. "The XO's just trying to be helpful."

Heath did not respond, but instead turned back to his sector, appearing somewhat irritated at Shelby's defense of Monroe.

Fabriano had heard about Lieutenant Commander Monroe's involvement in the *R-15* incident several times since joining the *Whitefin*. It was no small wonder that Heath was more than a little skeptical of Monroe's capabilities as a watch officer, especially since his brother perished with the ill-fated submarine. The emotional effect of losing a brother was something Fabriano could easily relate to.

"This weather reminds me of my missus," Shelby shouted over his shoulder, winking once at the rankled Heath. A wild grin then appeared across Shelby's pitted red face. "That bitch is angry all the time, angry as a muskrat sometimes. Anger to match her red hair! Did I ever tell you about my missus, Mikey?"

"You never mentioned her," Fabriano shouted back, half-heartedly. He really wasn't interested in hearing about Shelby's wife.

"I found her in a San Diego whorehouse at the beginning of the war," Shelby continued as before. "She was on hard times then, living on fifty cents a day, looking for any American sailor to marry her, anything to pull her ass out of the gutter. And I was the stupid sap that she landed, damn her! All I earn goes to that little bitch in the little house she rents by Thirty-second Street. I should've pulled the plug on her long ago. The damn thing's nothing more than a shack and I can barely pay the bills on it as it is. But, still, I've got to admit, whenever I'm in port it makes me feel like I'm a real family man for a few days. That is, until she starts nagging me. Then I'd pay the devil to get back to sea again. You ought to come over, Mikey, someday when we pull in there. She'll cook us dinner. She's not too bad at it, but, by damn, she's a slut! I don't trust her as far as I can throw her. Probably fucked every swabbie on the wharf by now, even the officers."

For a moment, Fabriano toyed at the notion that Shelby was saying all of this for his benefit, but the thought quickly vanished from his mind. No doubt Shelby was only jabbering to keep his mind off the cold wind chilling them all to the bone. Shelby had been a good shipmate to him in the past few weeks, and despite his quirky behavior, there had been moments when he almost told Shelby everything and let him in on a share of the *Chevalier*'s money.

Wiping the salty spray from his face, Fabriano strained his eyes to see his watch. Only five minutes had passed. He was only a third of the way through his rotation. And this was merely the first of many fifteen-minute rotations he would have to endure in the lookout perch over the next four hours. Just the thought of another long, miserable night of endless pummeling, of endless cold and dampness, of endless corkscrewing gyrations, filled him with utter despondency.

He glanced down at the bridge, where both watch officers were conversing, their hands waving wildly, with much animation. He could not hear a word of what they were saying. They appeared to be taking great interest in the compass binnacle and the direction of the seas. Perhaps they were discussing a change of course to improve the *Whitefin*'s attitude, which seemed to be rolling at much larger angles with each passing minute. Whatever they discussed so heatedly, Monroe seemed to be doing most of the talking and Endicott most of the nodding.

"Something's not right!" Shelby shouted.

Fabriano turned to see the sailor's weathered face staring gravely at the two officers on the bridge below.

"King Neptune is hungry tonight!" Shelby said morosely. "I can feel it!"

"That's just your head getting cold!" Fabriano chided him. "Just stick with me, you'll be all right!"

Moments later, a wave crashed against the conning tower and doused all three lookouts from head to foot.

"Listen to you, a bona fide submariner now, eh?" Shelby smirked, wiping the spray from his face. "Believe me, Mikey. When you've been in the boats as long as I have, you have a sense for such things. When I see waves like this, even I get the shakes. Better take heed, shipmate. It's a strange night up here."

A jagged branch of blue lightning streaked across the sky astern, casting an eerie shadow across Shelby's deep features. Just then the perch beneath Fabriano's feet shuddered violently, and the ship began swaying wildly from port to starboard, placing the periscopes at such an extreme angle that for an instant the lookout perches were hovering over the raging seas instead of the bridge deck. When the *Whitefin* finally righted herself, Fabriano could see Monroe on the bridge below saying something into Endicott's ear.

Endicott shouted something into the intercom moments later, apparently a rudder order. As the muffled response came over the speaker, Monroe turned to look up at them.

"Hang on up there! The seas have shifted a little to the east! We're turning to compensate! It might get a little rough until we steady on course! Just hang on!"

If the ship began turning, Fabriano never would have known it. From his perspective, he could hardly tell that the *Whitefin* was making headway, let alone what course she steered. But the course must have changed, and quickly, because he began to feel deep vibrations in the periscope shears as the *Whitefin* shifted to take the stiff seas against her starboard side. Within a few moments, the rocking seemed to subside a little, and it seemed like the worst had passed, when suddenly a boiling black mass materialized before their eyes. The surging wave had come out of nowhere, and instantly smashed into the starboard side, pressing Shelby against the shears, and yanking Fabriano from his own perch as if he were made of feathers. In an instant he was horizontal, parallel with the railing. A single hand gripping the rail and the straining lanyard attached to his harness were the only two things that kept him from going over the side. The mass of water engulfed him and tore at his feet, his legs, his torso. He felt his shoes get sucked right off his feet, but he held on, with white knuckles and an iron-fisted grip. He held on for as long as he could, but eventually his fingers began to slide on the wet railing. A massive shudder reverberated through the *Whitefin*'s steel skin as another wave hit her, and the subsequent vibration shook his hand loose.

For a moment, he thought he was going overboard for sure. For a moment, he thought it was all over. But then a sharp jolt ran simultaneously through his thighs, groin, and shoulders, as his piano-wire-tight safety lanyard yanked his body out of the wave's grasp and left him hanging above the bridge for a fraction of a second, before the lanyard snapped under his own weight and sent him plunging sideways onto the aft gun deck, his head narrowly missing a possibly fatal collision with the twenty-millimeter-gun stanchion.

As he slowly regained his senses, he realized that his shoulder had been dislocated. It had happened before, many years ago while wrestling his brother in the front parlor of their parents' home for a girl they both wanted. Now that familiar pain had returned and he was out of breath, aching from the impact and the whiplash, lying untethered on the exposed aft gun deck. It was only a matter of time before another wave came and carried him off.

He struggled through the pain, eventually mustering the energy to roll over onto his back. When he opened his eyes, he saw the dripping faces of Heath and Monroe hovering over him. Heath must have leaped from the lookout perch to have reached him so quickly, and likewise Monroe had obviously not hesitated to leave the protective cover of the bridge weather shield to come after him. While his mind was foggy at the moment, Fabriano had the wherewithal to realize that both men were putting their own lives in jeopardy in order to save his.

"Can you stand?" Monroe said hurriedly.

He struggled to answer, but he was so disoriented that he hardly knew which way was up. After several attempts to stand, he fell back to the deck, like a sailor three sheets to the wind. But he had scarcely touched the deck when Heath appeared under one arm and Monroe under the other. Together the two men lifted him bodily and began hauling him toward the protection of the bridge weather shield. Through blurry eyes, he could see Endicott standing by the bridge hatch waving his arms and cheering them on.

"Watch it!" he heard Shelby's voice bellow from the lookout perch high above. "Here comes another one!"

"Oh shit!" muttered Heath.

The wave broke over the starboard side, and the next moment Fabriano felt his body forced to the deck with Heath's and Monroe's full weight lying across him. The great force of water broke over the superstructure from the opposite side, surging through the space between the periscopes and spitting out horizontal jets of frothing seawater. The small space between the periscopes acted like a fire nozzle, and the ensuing torrent of water grabbed Heath and ripped him away toward the sea. When Fabriano managed to look up, he saw that Heath had grabbed hold of the port-side bridge railing, and was hanging on with one hand, his legs dangling over the side, his feet kicking at the churning seas below. One more such wave would surely carry him off. As the seas shifted again to batter the *Whitefin*'s broad starboard beam, the ship took on the aspect of a wild bronco attempting to shake the men off her back.

"Damn it, Endicott! Come right!" he heard Monroe call, apparently in an attempt to get the bow into the seas once again.

Fabriano now realized that Monroe was no longer lying across him, but was now inching his way toward the port-side bridge railing in an effort to reach Heath before the seas or the rolling deck shook the unfortunate sailor off.

Before the *Whitefin*'s bow could turn into the running seas, she took a much larger wave straight across the starboard beam. The massive angle brought the seas surging around the conning tower and high up on the port side, high enough to lap at the bridge railing and to completely engulf Heath's waist. The ship swayed heavily to port in an angle so steep that Fabriano had to grab hold of the radar mast housing to keep from sliding toward the rail. Just as suddenly as the wave had tilted her to port, the *Whitefin* righted herself with a jolt that knocked both Monroe and Endicott off their feet and sent Fabriano into the radar mast housing.

Heath, however, was not so lucky. As the hull snapped back to center, his solitary grip on the port-side rail had the effect of yanking his body out of the sea and sending it skyward with such velocity that he was unable to stop his upward momentum and lost his grip. His body seemed to hang in the air for the span of several seconds, spinning sickeningly, arms and legs flailing, before it made an insignificant splash into the rising slope of a black wave, where it was swallowed up entirely.

In an instant, he was gone—never to be seen again.

"Heath!" Fabriano heard Monroe wail out of apparent desperation. "Heath!"

Through dim eyes, he saw the visibly shaken XO grope farther and farther aft along the rail, seemingly oblivious to the hazard to his own safety as he searched the angry sea with eyes that appeared so full of emotion, so full of pain, that Fabriano could not be sure if it were tears or rain streaming down the XO's face.

Moments later—it seemed like moments—both Monroe and Endicott appeared above him. They were shaking him violently, telling him to wake up.

"Fabriano! Fabriano! Stay with us. We've got to get you below."

He felt himself being carried toward the open hatch in the deck. Then he felt hands, multiple hands, around his feet, his legs, his arms, even his face, as he was passed from those above to those below and all at once left the howling, violent world above for the warmth and serenity inside the conning tower. Through more hatches and doors, his body was passed until he found himself lying still on his bunk in the after torpedo room. He could still hear the waves battering the hull just on the other side of the cold steel bulkhead that lined one side of his rack.

Then the corpsman appeared, his face a mere shadow blocking the glare from a lightbulb swinging in the overhead.

"This is going to hurt a bit," the corpsman said quietly.

A sudden sharp pain shot through his shoulder, his arm, his whole body, as the corpsman set his shoulder in one swift but firm move.

"You bastard . . . ," Fabriano managed to say with a smile.

He noticed many other crewmen were in the compartment, too, curiously gawking at him as the corpsman continued to check his vitals. The lightbulb swung from side to side in the overhead, illuminating their faces at irregular intervals. In one brief flash he thought he saw Penn's face, looking gaunt and white and staring back at him from a far corner of the room. But when the light swung back again, Penn was no longer there. And soon after, he lost all consciousness.

Chapter 15

THE dark waters of Hainan Strait were calm, even restful in the predawn hours as the *Whitefin* nosed toward a position a few miles east of the narrow water passage. The strait separated the Japanese-held island of Hainan to the south from the Japanese-held Leizhou Peninsula of mainland China to the north, and measured just over ten miles across at its narrowest point. The two opposing points of land were clearly visible from the *Whitefin*'s bridge as two large, dark masses rising out of the sea to the west. The crescent moon and star-filled sky afforded just enough light to see the Chinese coast clearly, quite remarkable considering the past days of unrelenting tempest and endless churning cumulus overhead. Now only an occasional cloud wafted in from the sea, swooping low over the idle submarine and then drifting from the water to the land, casting dark shadows on the moonlit strip of beach along the peninsula's expanse before heading inland. The idyllic scene offered a brief moment of serenity to those members of the crew fortunate enough to have a battle station on the bridge this evening.

Tremain leaned on the bridge railing in a casual manner, making every attempt to display calm and confidence in the face of the nearby enemy coastline. The *Whitefin* had ventured into the strait as far as she could hope to without running into enemy minefields, and now sat no more than ten miles away from the narrowest point, close enough that Tremain could smell the aroma of land in the light breeze. Small lights along the northern coast of Hainan marked the seaport town of Haikou, occupied by the Japanese, and no doubt home to the three patrol craft now sitting at a dead stop together in a cluster ten thousand yards off the *Whitefin*'s starboard bow. For the past eight hours, ever since the *Whitefin* arrived in the strait, her periodic radar sweeps had had little trouble tracking the small enemy vessels as they completed their circuitous patrol route for the umpteenth time. In fact, the route had been so repetitive that Monroe took the liberty of marking it on the chart, complete with waypoints and estimated times of arrival at each.

Like clockwork, at the top of the even numbered hours, the patrol boats would put off from their pier at Haikou, drive into the center of the channel, then turn west, fanning out in a line-abreast formation two miles apart so that the three boats together could cover the breadth of the ten-mile-wide strait. At least one of the boats was equipped with sonar, since the *Whitefin*'s listening hydrophones had occasionally picked up distant echo-ranging reverberating off the strait's four-hundred-foot bottom. But the pressure waves were too far away to detect the keel of the surfaced American submarine that had managed to sneak up on this vital Japanese waterway connecting the South China Sea to the Gulf of Tonkin.

The circuit was precise; the schedule never deviated, and the Japanese officer assigned the ignominious task of patrolling this strait could proudly report to his superiors that his little flotilla was never late for a guard patrol. While it might have been an impressive claim in the Imperial Navy, it did not much impress Tremain. The lack of ingenuity, the lack of tactical planning, the lack of insight into the Americans' capabilities and intentions spoke volumes about the Japanese commander's quality. Obviously, he did not grasp the importance of his mission, or else he would not carry it out in such a robotic fashion. Obviously, he did not truly believe that he would ever find an American submarine on one of his patrols; otherwise he might employ his three boats in a more efficient and less predictable manner. Perhaps he even regarded his patrolling duties as foolish, dull tasks, to be carried out in form only, and without any vigor. It was a perfect example of the odd advantage American submarines often faced when attacking in these waters. More often than not, they were pitted against the Imperial Navy's unseasoned and ill-trained personnel, those officers and sailors of second-string caliber who were not cut out to man the great carriers and battleships that were no doubt at this moment far away in the South Pacific trying to coax Admiral Halsey's fleet into a decisive engagement.

"Patrol craft, dead in the water, sir, one point off the port bow," said Endicott, his binoculars pointing steadily at the dark horizon to the west.

Tremain raised his own binoculars and quickly found the three long, squatty black shapes sitting idly in the approaches to the strait. Just the sight of them, sitting there apparently doing nothing, left him feeling uneasy—because it was the first time in the past eight hours that the three enemy craft had broken their unbreakable routine, and had taken up station in the strait's eastern approaches. And there they had been waiting for the better part of the last half hour, with all lights extinguished and all engines secured. Regular sweeps of *Whitefin*'s radar served to confirm that they were not moving and remained oblivious to the American submarine's presence.

It did not take long for Tremain to come to the conclusion that the patrol boats were obviously waiting for something, most likely a ship or a convoy they had orders to escort through the strait. He held out a ray of hope that the *Shigure*'s convoy might be on the way, and he had expressed as much with forced enthusiasm to his tetchy crew, but deep inside he knew the chances were less than slim. After the slow progress the *Whitefin* had made through the storm, pushing her air-deprived diesels to their limits, changing course constantly to keep from foundering, not to mention the inherent navigation errors derived from one measly sun line in five days, Tremain fully expected the *Shigure* and her convoy to have long since reached the strait and to have either moored at Haikou harbor, or to have passed through into the Gulf of Tonkin.

Tremain glanced at the darkened patrol craft once more in

his binoculars. They looked tiny at this distance, but he thought he could make out shadows moving on their decks. Whatever ship or convoy these craft were waiting for, no matter what its size or armament, Tremain intended to sink it. It did not matter whether it was the *Shigure*'s convoy. Tremain knew his crew was at a breaking point. They needed a victory. They needed to sink something—a convoy, a ship, anything to give them that small amount of satisfaction that their struggles had not been in vain, the satisfaction that they would at least walk away from this patrol with a combat star. They had gone far enough on blind faith, and he owed them a sinking. After all, they were only human. They would only follow him so far—Monroe included.

"Bridge, XO," the executive officer's voice intoned over the muffled intercom. It bore the same heavy tone it had carried since Seaman Heath's death, three days ago. "Radar fix holds us five miles northeast of the patrol craft now, Captain. We should be in a good spot, sir."

Monroe had taken Heath's death in a hard way. That was apparent to anyone who had seen him in the past few days. Obviously, he felt somewhat responsible. Tremain couldn't help but think that his executive officer had vivid memories of the *R-15* incident running through his head. No doubt he was comparing the two events, and finding himself responsible for both. To any reasonable person, Heath's death and the *R-15* incident had no similarities, but to someone like Monroe, whose career had been filled with self-doubt and whispered rumors, it would be yet another weight upon his brooding mind. Tremain had seen it before many times in other men, even in himself. And he knew it could lead to a perpetual attitude of indifference or, worse, a run of self-destructive behavior. Like the rest of the crew, Monroe needed something to take his mind off his troubles.

Tremain drew in a deep breath. This evening, he intended to give it to him.

The *Whitefin* was setting up for a surface attack, taking up a position north of the approaches so that any convoy coming from the east would not see her low silhouette against the black backdrop of the peninsula. The move was risky, not only because the patrol boats might detect her while she was positioning, but also because the *Whitefin* carried no charts of the area bearing a date stamp beyond the year 1926. Undoubtedly the chart Monroe was using to navigate was missing dozens of shoals and other navigation hazards discovered in the last two decades. With that in mind, Tremain fully agreed with Monroe's assessment that they had gone far enough.

"XO, Captain, I concur," Tremain said into the microphone, instinctively keeping his voice low while looking out at the distant black shapes. "We hold the patrol craft visually. We'll heave to here and wait. Go ahead and secure the radar."

"Bridge, XO. Secure the radar, aye, sir."

Endicott fidgeted next to Tremain. "Won't we need it for ranging contacts, Captain?"

"The Japanese might have a couple DF stations on both sides of that strait. Maybe not, but it's possible. So far, they haven't detected us, but I don't want to take any more chances than we have to. We can see well enough up here without the radar. We'll use the old ways. Remember, Mr. Endicott, any time we transmit anything from this ship, be it radar, radio, or active sonar, we stand the chance of being detected."

"Aye, sir," answered Endicott, his grim face distorted in the red light emanating from the bridge hatch.

"Helm, Bridge, all stop," Tremain said into the intercom as he squinted one eye and lined up the binnacle sight on the enemy patrol craft up ahead. "Left full rudder. Steady on course one-nine-five."

The helmsman acknowledged the order and the *Whitefin*'s wake began to curve to the left. The large rudder angle would take the speed off her, and the new course would point her bow directly at the enemy craft, presenting the narrowest possible aspect just in case the Japanese lookouts happened to be alert this evening.

Tremain planned to use the forward tubes in the coming attack, to maximize his firepower. He also planned on conducting the attack on the surface, to afford greater visibility, greater maneuverability, and greater speed to get away, since the estimated depth beneath the keel was not more than sixty fathoms, a bit too shallow for his own comfort zone. However, submerging would always be an option, and the main deck would remain clear, the deck gun unmanned and the deck hatches shut, just in case the *Whitefin* needed to dive quickly.

As the way came off the ship and the diesels sputtered to a quiet idle, he glanced around at the men on the bridge with him—Endicott, the lookouts, the sailor manning the sound-powered phone set, the helmeted sailors huddled around the twenty-millimeter gun on the cigarette deck. If they had started out as a ragged group when this patrol began, then they had certainly devolved even further. They'd spent a week getting battered by the sea, a week in which a very few of them managed to keep a single meal in their stomachs. They'd come close to getting blown out of the water by another American submarine; they'd seen one shipmate crushed to death and another washed overboard.

They had been through a lot, but at this moment, this *precise* moment, Tremain knew that they were ready to take on anything. Call it his commander's intuition, but he had seen it before on the faces of his other crews, that one moment in time, usually just after they had reached the bottom of despair, when all of the complaining stopped, when they stopped thinking of themselves as individuals and collectively turned the corner as a crew, all mad as hell, but all hell-bent on success.

The night turned deathly quiet as they waited with Tremain's and Endicott's binoculars locked onto the distant patrol craft while the lookouts watched for any other potential dangers. The only sounds were the idling diesels, the water lapping against the limber holes near the waterline, and a few squawking seagulls who had lighted far aft on the wooden planks near the fantail and who seemed content to spend the rest of the early morning there awaiting the sunrise. Some men fidgeted for lack of a cigarette, some yawned nervously, all no doubt were preparing themselves for a long, dreary night at battle stations, half-expecting nothing to appear.

But they did not have to wait very long.

"Ships sighted, sir!" one of the lookouts called from above, his excited voice sending the seagulls on the stern into a protesting frenzy. "Three points off the port bow."

Tremain instantly whipped his binoculars over to the southeastern sector. Three new black shapes, much larger shapes, filled his field of view. This was not simply another flotilla of patrol craft. This was a darkened convoy, cautiously approaching the narrow strait from the west, undoubtedly driving toward a rendezvous with the waiting patrol boats. The convoy's path would take it directly across the *Whitefin*'s bows. It was a perfect setup, and a setup that would not have been possible had Tremain not brought the *Whitefin* to its current position well ahead of time.

Tremain allowed himself about two more seconds to relish the sight of the approaching convoy before he moved over to the portside target-bearing transmitter.

"Conning Tower, Bridge, stand by for observation," he said into the microphone.

"Bridge, Conning Tower, standing by for observation," came the reply.

Swinging the large, mounted pair of telescopic lenses toward the convoy, he centered the reticle on the largest of the three black shapes, the one in the center. When he was satisfied that the reticle was lined up on what appeared to be a mast, he pressed the button by his right thumb and the bearing to the new target was instantly transmitted to the repeater down in the conning tower. As he waited for the report, he imagined the activity in the compartment beneath his feet. Whately's hands would be mere blurs as they spun the dials to enter the new bearing into the torpedo data computer, moving naturally, methodically, as if the TDC were a fine instrument and he a devoted musician since childhood. Monroe would be hovering over the cocky lieutenant's shoulder watching him like a hawk, while the green Ensign Berkshire gazed on with wide, reverent eyes.

"Bearing one-four-five," Monroe's voice intoned over the intercom.

"Angle on the bow, thirty starboard. Use a range of ten thousand yards."

The minutes passed as Tremain sent successive bearings and ranges to the tracking party in the conning tower. With each observation, the shadowy ships grew larger in his field of view until finally they were visible to the naked eye as gray shapes far across the moonlit expanse of water. The smallest ship, a freighter, was at the head of the convoy, and Tremain judged her to be no more than three hundred feet in length. A single mast rose from her bow and appeared to sway uncertainly in the calm seas. A lone funnel stood out amidships just aft of the three-level deckhouse. But beyond those few distinguishable features, the vessel was still little more than a shadow.

It might be the small freighter from the *Shigure*'s convoy, Tremain ventured to hope, but there was no way to tell for certain.

Slowly rotating the TBT lens to the left, Tremain's heart skipped a beat as the next ship in line came into view. It was a cruiser of the Myoko class. Now his hopes rose even further. The *Shigure*'s convoy had also contained a Myoko cruiser, though there was something different about about this cruiser, something that had not been there before—something Tremain could not put his finger on. As he scanned down the big warship's length, he noted the same features he had seen over a week ago: the three eight-inch gun turrets on her bow, the two angled smokestacks amidships, the seaplane crane and catapult along with two more eight-inch gun turrets on her stern. But there was something else, something non-uniform about her main deck. An irregular dark band coated her main deck from stem to stern, and Tremain strained his eyes to figure out what it was. It took him only a few more seconds to realize that he was looking at a mass of humanity. Nearly every square foot of the cruiser's main deck was crowded with men, literally hundreds of them.

Tremain quickly deduced what had happened. The mass of men on the cruiser's deck, coupled with the absence of the transport that had been with the convoy over a week ago, led him to a single conclusion. Undoubtedly, the missing transport had foundered during the typhoon, and the cruiser, being the most seaworthy vessel in the convoy, had taken on the survivors. Now, the several hundred unlucky Japanese troops from the ill-fated transport were crowded onto the cruiser's main deck. Who knew how long they had been there. They were all probably soaking wet and cold, and more than eager to disembark once the ship put in to Haikou.

The same rain falls on us both, Tremain mused.

Both the freighter and the cruiser were traveling at a prodigiously slow speed—creeping along at what Whately's computer had calculated as barely six knots. Probably one or both of them had sustained enough damage to knock a boiler out of commission or bend a shaft. The ships were still too far away to tell for certain, but Tremain thought he could see a slight droop in the freighter's trim. Her stern sagged in the water ever so slightly, perhaps from flooded compartments.

The third ship was just coming into view now, and Tremain held his breath in anticipation, rubbing and blinking his eyes several times before allowing them to peer through the TBT lens at the new ship. It appeared to be a destroyer escort, low to the water, with sleek lines, a high bow and bridge structure forward, two short, swept stacks amidships, and a single gun turret on a tapered stern. The small warship was obviously the sole escort for the convoy, and not a Shiratsuyu-class destroyer, not the *Shigure*. Tremain's heart sank at the sight of her. That is, until he studied the new ship a bit closer. Suddenly he realized that the odd shadows along her length seemed distorted and out of proportion to her size. They especially made no sense when considering the ship's aspect to the bright moon above the eastern horizon. It took Tremain all of about two seconds to realize that this was not a small destroyer escort at all, but rather a full-sized destroyer. He had been fooled by the illusion of shadows created by the same black paint scheme he had seen from the *Chevalier*'s torpedo mount that night off Vella LaVella.

It *was* the *Shigure*.

To any unseasoned eye, she would appear to be only half of her actual size and armament, but as Tremain's eyes finally adjusted to the illusion, he made out the two additional dual-mount five-inch gun turrets on her bow and stern, both painted black to blend in with the night. He saw the familiar black bands on her smokestacks, and the black-painted deckhouse and superstructure hiding half of their height.

"The *Shigure*, gentlemen," he said loud enough for everyone on the bridge to hear.

Several of the men exchanged glances, while others raised their binoculars to see the infamous enemy destroyer. No matter how each man felt individually about his captain's week-long foray, not one of them could resist the chance to tell his mates back in port that he had seen the *Shigure* with his own two eyes.

"Bridge, XO," the intercom squawked. "We have a good solution on all three ships now. The convoy is on a steady course of two-nine-zero at six knots. Current range to track is nine thousand yards."

Tremain took in a deep breath. The convoy was to the south and would pass across the *Whitefin*'s bows port to starboard. So far, he was undetected, and now the moment of truth was fast approaching. He had stood off at this relatively safe range to prevent detection while setting up a solution, but now came the payoff. He would have to close the range, if he wanted a chance of hitting anything, and he would have to do it quickly, before the patrol boats or the *Shigure* realized they had an American submarine making an attack run from the north.

"XO, Bridge, aye," Tremain said steadily into the microphone. "We'll close the range at flank speed, fire two fish at each, and then turn around to finish them off with the stern tubes. Give me the best course to intercept their track."

After a momentary pause, the reply came. "Bridge, XO, one-nine-zero is a good course, sir."

"Very well. Maneuvering, Bridge, bring all engines on line. Helm, Bridge, all ahead flank! Steer course one-nine-zero."

The *Whitefin*'s four Fairbanks Morse diesel engines coughed to life, spitting out a black mist of choking exhaust. The noise of the engines seemed incredibly loud, and Tremain had to remind himself that the enemy was still over four miles away, and probably could not discern the *Whitefin*'s puttering diesels from their own ship's steam engines.

The submarine's bow quickly formed a creamy disturbance on the sea as she began to drive toward her prey, her three-hundred-foot hull swiftly accelerating to flank speed. Four sixteen-cylinder, opposed-piston, 1600-horsepower Fairbanks Morse diesel engines spun up to their rated speed of 750 revolutions per minute, turning the cam shafts to drive the sub's four 1,100 kilowatt, direct-current General Electric generators to produce the electrical power needed to drive the four 1,375-horsepower General Electric motors. The powerful electric motors turned at their maximum speed of thirteen hundred revolutions per minute and transmitted their rotational energy to the propeller shafts through a pinion-reduction gear arrangement, to drive both of the four-bladed, eight-foot-in-diameter screws at two hundred and eighty revolutions per minute. Within three minutes the *Whitefin* was on her stride, running slightly above twenty knots, taking the wind across her bow and into the indomitable faces of the men on her bridge. If any of them had doubts about their captain's abilities, they would be burying them at this moment, blindly succumbing to his optimism for the sake of their own nerves.

Minutes passed, and the range to the convoy's track closed rapidly, with Tremain and the others constantly scanning the sluggish convoy and the waiting patrol craft, checking for any signs of counterdetection. As if to exemplify the collective apprehension on the bridge, the men at the twenty-millimeter gun trained their weapon toward the enemy ships while the loaders checked the breech mechanism far more often than was necessary. The gunner's finger hesitated just above the trigger despite the fact that the enemy was still well out of range.

"Keep passing bearings to the conning tower," Tremain said, turning over the TBT to Endicott, mostly to give the fidgeting lieutenant something to do.

The dark shapes of the patrol craft were still sitting idly about six thousand yards off the starboard bow, while the convoy drove westward, presumably to meet them. The convoy was now roughly eight thousand yards off the port bow, and the *Whitefin* was closing the range at a rate of seven hundred yards per minute, headed for an imaginary point somewhere directly between the two enemy flotillas.

Tremain considered the tactical situation. Technically, he could unleash a salvo of torpedoes now, since the Mark 14 could travel up to nine thousand yards on the slow-speed setting. But the chances of hitting anything would be slim. It would take the torpedoes well over six minutes to make the run. Six minutes during which the convoy could change course or speed, ruining the solution entirely. Tremain wanted no errors this time, and to minimize the chances of error, he decided to close the range further to shorten the torpedo run time.

"Bridge, XO," the speaker squawked. "Range to leading freighter six thousand yards."

"XO, Bridge—" Tremain had almost finished acknowledging the report when a call came from one of the lookouts above him.

"The destroyer's picking up speed, sir!"

Tremain instantly leveled his binoculars on the *Shigure*. She was indeed gaining speed, as evident from the white foamy disturbance rising near her black bow. She quickly closed the distance to the cruiser, overtaking it on the starboard side and subsequently masking it from view, almost like a screening maneuver.

"Has she seen us?" Endicott ventured impulsively.

But Tremain did not answer. Instead he shifted his field of view to the waiting patrol craft to confirm his own suspicions. The three craft had started their engines and were now fanning out on both sides of the convoy, undoubtedly a standard protective maneuver to screen the convoy as it approached the narrow strait. The *Shigure* continued along at the same swift speed, running on a course parallel to that of the cruiser and the freighter, still heading across the *Whitefin*'s bows, but now roughly five hundred yards closer. She still showed no hostile signs, and the freighter and the cruiser continued on, one behind the other, at a stately six knots.

Tremain came to the conclusion that the *Whitefin* had not been detected, but at the same time he realized how drastically the tactical picture had changed. The enemy ships were no longer lined up for him to shoot like ducks in a row. Now he would have to make a choice between the farther off freighter and cruiser or the closer *Shigure*. Of course, it did not take him long to make up his mind. In his way of thinking, the choice could not be clearer.

"Keep the TBT centered on the *Shigure*'s main mast, Mr. Endicott. I want continuous bearings only on her until I say otherwise. Forget about the other ships."

"Aye, aye, sir." Endicott nodded, his darkened face indicating that he fully comprehended the need for the change in plan.

There was little time to waste. With the *Whitefin*'s screws rapidly closing the range, the possibility of counterdetection was ever increasing.

"XO, Bridge," Tremain said into the microphone. "Generate a new solution on the *Shigure*, and make ready tubes one through six in all respects. We'll give her a full spread."

Monroe succinctly acknowledged the order after only a slight delay, perhaps to make his way over to the microphone inside the cramped conning tower, perhaps out of concern over the decision to once again expend six torpedoes on a single destroyer.

Tremain waited with hidden anxiety while Monroe and Whately in the conning tower made the necessary computations based on the bearings Endicott was sending them over the TBT circuit. Tremain had nothing to do as he waited but watch while the enemy's bright gray hulls, clearly defined in the moonlight, steamed across the dark horizon toward the approaches to the strait. Even without binoculars he could discern the *Shigure*'s deceptive camouflage, clearly not intended for nights with a moon as bright as this one. As the swift destroyer cut along through the placid seas, Tremain noticed a great pall of black smoke suddenly belch out of her two smokestacks. The destroyer's oxygen-starved burners were obviously struggling to keep up with the heat demanded from her churning boilers, but the struggle didn't last long. Soon the black smoke was replaced by a short spit of white smoke, and then the smoking stopped altogether as the Japanese boiler technicians finally got a handle on the right fuel-air mixture.

Not bad, Tremain thought. A little sloppy, but not bad. He had seen some American ships do it faster, and he held out hope that this small slipup would only prove to the attentive men on the *Whitefin*'s bridge that the *Shigure* was not an invincible phantom after all, but merely a ship manned by fallible human beings, like every other ship on the seven seas.

"Bridge, XO, solution ready, sir!" Monroe's voice finally announced. "The *Shigure* bears one-seven-five, range four thousand yards, course two-nine-zero, speed sixteen knots. Outer doors are open on tubes one through six. All bow tubes ready for firing. All fish set to run at high speed. Depth setting eight feet."

"What's the torpedo run?"

"Three thousand six hundred yards, sir."

As much as he wished to close the range even further, Tremain knew he was pushing their luck too far. It was only a matter of time before a rogue swell slapped against the *Whitefin*'s bow, tossing a spray of very distinguishable white foam into the air for some vigilant Japanese lookout to see.

"XO, Bridge, commence firing at seven-second intervals, one degree spread!"

The ship shuddered almost before he could complete the order, as the first torpedo raced from its tube. From the open bridge hatch at his feet, Tremain could hear the sibilant sound of the venting high-pressure air as each torpedo was fired in succession. All on the bridge strained their eyes to see the razor-thin streaks of phosphorescent bubbles turn once slightly to the left and then trail off toward the southern horizon and their rendezvous with the enemy destroyer. Tremain had heard and had counted five torpedoes instead of the six he had ordered, and through the bridge hatch he could already hear Monroe's heated voice demanding an explanation. Moments later, Monroe relayed his findings over the intercom circuit.

"Bridge, XO," Monroe's voice intoned in an obviously forced flatness. "Tubes one through five fired electrically. All torpedoes running normally. Tube six failed to fire due to a jammed spindle. Probably damaged during the storm, Captain. The torpedo never started, so it should be safe inside the tube."

"XO, Bridge, aye."

It was okay. These things happened, Tremain told himself as he tried to put the faulty weapon out of his mind. The failure could be addressed later, when the attack was over. Like all captains, he had to remain flexible. At this moment, his confidence resided in the five torpedoes that were speeding toward the *Shigure*'s starboard beam. They would hit. They *had* to hit.

"Something's happening," Endicott said anxiously as he peered through the TBT. "That patrol boat, Captain—the closer one. It's approaching the *Shigure* like it's going to tie up alongside her. And I think I can see men on the *Shigure*'s deck by the starboard gangway, rigging out a ladder! It looks like they're getting ready to do a personnel transfer, sir."

Tremain found the patrol craft in his binoculars. True to Endicott's report, it was closing in on the *Shigure*'s starboard side, having swung around to travel on a parallel course with the destroyer. Next the *Shigure* cut her speed drastically, allowing the patrol craft to nestle up to her waiting starboard gangway.

Tremain felt like screaming at the top of his lungs, but he did not dare. To the men around him, he had to maintain the poise of a commander completely in control of the situation. He gripped the binoculars as tight as he could, forcing himself to remember that all was not lost. The *Whitefin*'s five torpedoes were still heading toward the *Shigure* at top speed. Despite the fact that the destroyer had slowed substantially, the torpedoes had a nice, wide one-degree spread, and there might be just enough slack in the solution for the last one to score a hit. Undoubtedly, the rest would stream harmlessly past the destroyer's bow.

"XO, Bridge. What's the count?" Tremain called into the intercom.

"Bridge, XO. Ten seconds, Captain."

"Let's bring the stern tubes to bear. Helm, left full rudder!"

The *Whitefin* needed to turn in order to shoot the stern tubes from a safe distance. She would lose her narrow, bow-on profile for just a few seconds during the one–hundred-and-eighty-degree turn, but with any luck, the enemy lookouts wouldn't see her. Not that it really mattered much at this point. The torpedoes were mere seconds away from impact. They would be aware of the *Whitefin*'s presence soon enough.

"Bridge, XO. Number one missed," Monroe reported, as the *Whitefin*'s hull listed to starboard from the hard left turn.

Tremain held his breath and tried to display no outward signs of disappointment. With his fingers crossed in the darkness, imperceptible to the men around him, he counted the seconds in his head for the last torpedo, which would be exactly twenty-eight seconds behind the first. He could see no signs that *Shigure* or the patrol craft were even aware that a torpedo with a 643-pound Torpex warhead had passed just ahead of them. There was movement on the destroyer's deck near the small gangway connecting the two craft. Obviously, someone aboard the *Shigure* was getting a personal ride into Haikou aboard the patrol craft, for some reason or another.

As Tremain watched the figures on the *Shigure*'s deck, he saw one of them begin to point wildly in the *Whitefin*'s direction. The submarine, halfway through its turn, was now presenting its full beam to the enemy and was evidently easily discernible from this range. Tremain saw some men on the destroyer's deck running forward, while more near the gangway joined their shipmate in raising awareness to the men around them that a surfaced American submarine was cruising off their starboard beam. A dull ringing resounded across the three-thousand-yard expanse of dark water as the enemy destroyer sounded general quarters.

The *Whitefin* had been spotted.

The men around Tremain began exchanging apprehensive glances, but their anxiety did not last long. It was replaced by immediate elation when the *Shigure*'s starboard side suddenly disappeared in an explosion of white water, smoke and flotsam. The fifth and last torpedo had run true.

Ka-boom!

It took several seconds for the percussion wave to travel across the mile-and-a-half range, and when it finally reached them, it sounded dull and isolated, quite out of place in the serene night.

When the smoke finally cleared, the *Shigure* was still there, sitting dead in the water. Charred metal and twisted ruins of the gangway lay across her amidships starboard side, where a moment before a dozen men had stood pointing. The patrol craft was gone, too. Undoubtedly it had taken the brunt of the Torpex detonation and had been completely vaporized.

Several of the men on the bridge, including Endicott, cheered wildly, but Tremain did not flinch. He kept the *Shigure*'s beam squarely in the field of his binoculars, uncertain of the enemy destroyer's condition.

Was she damaged? Was she sinking? There was no way to tell in this light, or from this distance. The destroyer showed no signs of taking on water, and apart from the mangled gangway, he could see little damage above the waterline. Certainly none of her armored turrets had been affected by the blast. As she drifted to a dead stop, another pall of black smoke belched from her rear smokestack. Was it a fire, was it a ruse, or was it neither? Tremain began to suspect that the *Whitefin*'s torpedo had impacted the patrol craft, and not the *Shigure*, and that the unfortunate boat had saved her consort from any substantial damage.

But an instant later, his attention was drawn away when another bright explosion suddenly appeared several hundred yards beyond the *Shigure*, where the big cruiser had been traveling on a parallel course. Undoubtedly, one of the *Whitefin*'s torpedoes, after missing the destroyer, had found the cruiser's side, the powerful detonation rattling the big ship from keel to mast, throwing dozens of bodies into the air, instantly starting fires on her decks. The flames quickly spread to the sea surrounding the big warship and soon enveloped the entire aft half of the vessel. Undoubtedly, the blast had ruptured and ignited a fuel reservoir. Moments later, another torpedo found its mark, this one striking the flaming ship a hundred feet or so aft of the first impact point. The cruiser buckled under the detonation, her seaplane crane toppled into the sea, and her stern visibly sagged before the column of water had a chance to descend back to earth. As the sea filled the ruptured aft compartments, she lost all headway. She was being dragged down by the stern.

Tremain could only imagine the carnage taking place below the waterline. He saw the figures on the cruiser's main deck and superstructure—hundreds of them—running to and fro like dark sprites in the iridescent light of the flaming oil. Some were on fire. Some appeared to be naked. More and more fell off into the burning sea as the cruiser continued taking on ever steeper angles. He thought he could hear distant screams above the *Whitefin*'s purring diesels. The doomed ship's deep draft bow now hung well clear of the water, glistening wet in the firelight. It rose higher and higher, until the straining keel finally succumbed to the enormous tensile stress, cracking just forward of her first smokestack and breaking the giant ship into two uneven sections. The gut-wrenching sound of fracturing steel reached the *Whitefin*'s bridge several seconds later, but no cheering ensued this time. Instead, each man watched in frightened awe as the fifteen-thousand-ton cruiser's forward section, with its three armored turrets, fell bow-on into the sea, like a giant ice sheet sheering off a glacier. It threw up torrents of water, displacing a massive foamy white wave in all directions. Then Tremain heard more screams, and realized that some of the Japanese sailors floating in the water were being sucked toward the massive eddy created by the cruiser's bow section as it plunged to the ocean floor. They would not be able to swim hard enough to escape the powerful swirling forces that would eventually pull them under, carrying them down hundreds of feet in a matter of seconds.

Free from the weight of the bow section, the much larger aft section now stood on its end, almost perpendicular with the ocean's surface. Tiny splashes appeared on the burning water beneath the giant structure as loose equipment, crates, and men fell at irregular intervals from hundreds of feet in the air. As the colossal tower began to descend into the fiery ocean, an explosion shook the night. One of the cruiser's boilers had ruptured, blowing a hole in her side through which a solid jet of superheated, high-pressure steam effused in a tonitruous roar, loud enough to shake the very rail beneath Tremain's fingertips. Like the dying breath of a slain dragon, the rumbling steam continued until the last contents of the ruptured boiler spat out in three final thunderous puffs. Not long after, the last visible piece of the unfortunate ship slipped beneath the burning waves.

Tremain had seen the horrors of sinking ships many times before. As he had on previous occasions, he tried his best to assume a hardened mind-set. Otherwise, the screams of the dying would surely penetrate his resolve to carry on. Deep down inside, he knew that each scream, each burning sailor, each horrific death was yet another burden he would carry with him for the rest of his life.

But there was little time to dwell on that now. The *Whitefin* had finally steadied on the opposite course, with her stern tubes and white wake pointing directly toward the idle *Shigure*. The enemy destroyer, now a dark silhouette framed by the flaming oil and wreckage beyond her, gave no signs of life. With the *Shigure*'s deck completely obscured, Tremain could not know whether her crew was abandoning ship or manning battle stations. Off to the west, the slow-moving freighter now churned out great puffs of black smoke in a desperate attempt to reach the safety of the strait, while the two remaining patrol craft sped at top speed with frothy mustaches at their bows, heading directly for the *Whitefin*. At less than two miles away, there could be no doubt that they had sighted the American submarine and were now in headlong pursuit.

Tremain realized that if he wanted to finish off the *Shigure*, he would have to do it quickly. The *Shigure* was dead in the water. He only hoped she would remain that way while he gave her a salvo from the aft torpedo tubes.

"XO, Bridge," Tremain said into the intercom, as he swung the TBT binoculars around to point aft at the destroyer. The men manning the gun on the cigarette deck instinctively stood aside, ensuring they were out of his field of view. "Stand by stern tubes. I'm passing a bearing now."

"Bridge, XO, aye," came Monroe's voice. "Ready, Captain. Bearing two-zero-eight."

"XO, Bridge. Use a zero-degree gyro angle and fire all four tubes on that bearing!"

The hull shuddered slightly, as all four aft tubes were fired in rapid succession. Tremain strained his eyes to see the torpedo wakes on the dark surface, but they were hidden by the long trail of roiling foam created by the *Whitefin*'s whirling screws.

"Bridge, XO. Tubes seven through ten fired electrically."

Tremain fostered a glimmer of hope that the *Shigure* would remain dead in the water for the entire duration of the torpedo run, but those hopes were dashed an instant later when, like a torrential cloudburst from a clear blue sky, the *Shigure* opened up with every gun she had. Flashes appeared along her four-hundred-foot length, from her dual- and single-mount gun batteries, firing fifty-pound, five-inch projectiles with a muzzle velocity of three thousand feet per second. The calm sea surrounding the small submarine suddenly came alive with white geysers reaching sixty or seventy feet into the air. Instinctively, the men on the bridge took cover behind whatever obstruction they could find, though it would do little good. Nothing on the bridge could stop even a single round from one of the destroyer's powerful five-inch guns.

A blinding searchlight mounted somewhere on the *Shigure*'s superstructure flamed to life, bathing the *Whitefin*'s bridge, deck, and the sea around her in daylight brightness and casting an eerie shadow of the conning tower onto the green water ahead of the submarine's bow.

Vibrations rang throughout the ship as one of the destroyer's machine gunners got lucky, sending a sweep of twenty-five-millimeter projectiles across the aft end of the steel conning tower, producing a shower of sparks and several hard thuds, but injuring no one. Tremain did his best to keep the destroyer in his binoculars, fighting the urge to duck behind the periscope tower like the others. The only other man not under cover was the twenty-millimeter gunner, standing with shoulders braced against the dual stocks of his weapon, firing futilely at the enemy ship, which was nearly beyond his gun's effective range.

Tremain watched as the *Shigure* thrust ahead from a dead stop, picking up speed rapidly and then making a sharp turn to starboard until its bow pointed directly at the *Whitefin*. This brought a sharp decrease in the amount of metal hailing down around the *Whitefin*, since now three of the destroyer's gun batteries were obscured by its own superstructure and no longer had a clear line of sight. Despite the fact that he had just removed three of his main guns from the fight, the *Shigure*'s captain had made a wise decision. Almost certainly, he had deduced that the submarine had fired another salvo of torpedoes, and he had turned accordingly to present the smallest aspect.

Tremain knew that his last four torpedoes had no chance of hitting at all. The *Shigure* had already maneuvered out of the salvo's path. The four ten-thousand-dollar torpedoes had been wasted, and would now streak off harmlessly into the burning sea beyond the enemy destroyer.

The destroyer was closing the distance to her fleeing prey by three hundred yards every minute, and her forward five-inch guns were growing more accurate as the water space melted away between the two ships. The *Whitefin*'s straining diesels fought to keep her at close to twenty-one knots, but they were no match for *Shigure*'s powerful steam boilers, which could push the destroyer along at thirty knots.

Tremain knew there were but two options now. Man the deck guns and try to fight it out on the surface, which would certainly lead to a one-sided slaughter, or submerge and take his chances, knowing full well that the destroyer would have the marked advantage of knowing exactly where he submerged.

Tremain rushed to the side of the lone gunner, who had just

cleared a jammed shell and was now attempting to affix another cylindrical magazine to his weapon. Tremain helped
him secure the magazine and then patted him on the shoulder,
pointing in the direction of the *Shigure*.

"Aim for that searchlight! It should be in range by now!
Fire everything you've got, but make sure you put it out. Don't
leave this gun until I tell you to! Understand?"

A sweaty blackened face nodded beneath the gray helmet,
as the young gunner pulled the slide bar on his weapon, advancing the first round into the chamber. Tremain heard the
sharp retort of the gun behind him as he ran back toward the
forward part of the bridge, motioning for the men under cover
to head for the open hatchway.

Just then two violent crashes in quick succession shook the
deck beneath his feet, followed by the close explosion of a
five-inch shell in the water not twenty yards from the
Whitefin's starboard bow. The force of the explosion knocked
him down and sent a whiplash throughout the ship. As he
picked himself up off the deck, he at first thought it was nothing more than a near miss. Then he suddenly got the chilling
feeling that it had been more than that. Those vibrations had
come from underneath, from something impacting with the
hull. Then an agonizing yell emanated from the open bridge
hatch.

"Conning Tower, Bridge." Tremain keyed the bridge microphone reluctantly. "What's happening down there?"

A long pause which seemed like minutes passed, with the
twenty-millimeter gun crashing out behind him, and he
cupped his ear near the speaker to hear the response. Finally it
came.

"Bridge, XO," came Monroe's somewhat ruffled reply.
"Took a hit in the conning tower. Passed clean through . . .
Berkshire's dead . . . Two more wounded."

Tremain cursed inwardly. The dual vibrations beneath his
feet had been caused by the Japanese five-inch shell, probably
an armor-piercing round, as it entered and exited the conning
tower's steel pressure hull. No telling what would have happened had the shell detonated inside the conning tower. It
would have killed everyone in the conning tower, and probably those in the control room and on the bridge, as well.

"XO, Bridge." Tremain shook himself to keep a clear head, putting Berkshire's death out of his mind. "Can we submerge?"

"Bridge, XO. If we seal off the conning tower, sir. Other damage reports are still coming in. We've got some small leaks up forward."

The next moment, the world grew suddenly dark once again and the men on deck cheered. The gunner had finally found his mark and had extinguished the *Shigure*'s search lamp. Certainly any Japanese sailors standing near the lamp had also been torn apart by twenty-millimeter projectiles.

Now, while the sea was still dark, while the *Shigure*'s captain was frantically ordering his gun crews to load star shells—this was his chance to dive.

AAOOOGAAAH!!! AAOOOGAAAH!!! Tremain rang the Klaxon, then immediately keyed the 1MC microphone.

"Crash dive!"

Endicott and the lookouts did not hesitate. They headed down the ladder in the blink of an eye, leaving Tremain on deck with the lone gunner, who took little more hastening than a look from Tremain before he abandoned his weapon and followed the rest below.

Great spouts of mist blew out of the *Whitefin*'s open main ballast tank vents, competing with the geysers from the enemy shells, and the big main ballast tanks began to rapidly fill with water. The submarine's bow dipped noticeably as the bow buoyancy tank filled, too, making her heavy forward, to get her cutting bow planes beneath the surface.

Tremain took one last look at the tactical picture before heading below. The *Shigure* was closing, now less than a mile away, her bow slicing through the dark sea at high speed as she charged directly toward the *Whitefin*. The two patrol craft were also closing and were about a thousand yards beyond their larger sister.

Satisfied that he knew what he was up against, Tremain dropped down the ladder, into the conning tower, and instinctively pulled the hatch shut behind him. But nothing could prepare him for the horrid sight that met him as he stepped off the ladder into a pool of dark blood covering the deck plates. Blood was everywhere—on the deck, spattered on the bulkhead, across the WCA sonar gear, and running in streaks down the shiny periscopes. A file of solemnly quiet lookouts waited their turn to drop down the hatch to the control room, each casting an inauspicious glance at a bloody canvas tarp lying in the corner of the conning tower beside the TDC. Two hands and two arms with khaki sleeves protruded at odd angles from beneath the canvas cover, giving a stark clue as to the grisly remains of Ensign Berkshire that lay beneath it.

"That Jap shell cut him in two." Monroe was suddenly standing before him, his expression unnaturally blank. "Also took a nick out the helmsman's thigh as it went out the forward bulkhead."

Tremain felt a draft on his wet leg and noticed the jagged five-inch hole in the bulkhead beside the steering stand. The helm control had already been transferred to the control room, and Tremain gathered that the injured helmsman was already in the wardroom being patched up by the corpsman.

The deck took on a sharp angle as the *Whitefin* slipped beneath the waves, and the free flood area around the pressure hull filled with water, the holes in the conning tower began spewing streams of clear seawater into the hull, splashing onto the deck and quickly dousing every man still waiting his turn to go down the control room hatch.

"We could put some pressure in here to keep this space relatively dry, Captain," suggested Monroe as he painfully watched the salty seawater drench the priceless torpedo data computer, the radar and sonar equipment sets.

"That'll waste air reserves, XO, and I have a feeling we're going to need every last pound of air we can get. No, we'll write off the conning tower to save the ship, just as long as the diving officer can handle it. Besides, we'd likely leave a trail of bubbles on the surface."

The last sailors finally dropped down the hatch just as the water in the conning tower began to lap at Tremain's and Monroe's ankles. They both made their way down the ladder and closed the hatch behind them, leaving the dead ensign as the sole inhabitant of the abandoned compartment.

Men shuffled about the crowded, muggy control room still bathed in the red night lighting. Here and there, lookouts shed binoculars and helmets and hurried off to their battle stations in other compartments. Quartermasters hovered over the chart table, cursing as they hastily wiped up puddles of seawater that had spilled on their precious charts before the hatch to the conning tower had been shut. Several men cast uncertain glances up at the closed hatch, visibly displaying the anxiety that dwelt in every man at the thought of the conning tower filling up with seawater. It would only fill to a certain point, leaving an air pocket to expand and contract with the submarine's changing depth.

Whately stood in one corner of the room, leaning against the bulkhead, his face white and hollow, his khaki uniform spattered with blood. He appeared uninjured, and Tremain suspected that the young officer had been standing next to Berkshire when the Japanese shell cut the ensign in two. Despite Whately's incessant haranguing of Berkshire, he had taken the green ensign under his wing for most of the patrol and had undoubtedly grown attached to him. Tremain reached out and patted the shaken lieutenant on the shoulder, but there was no response in Whately's eyes, or any indication that there would be for many hours to come.

Tremain forced himself to move on, making his way through the mass of men to stand beside Allendale at the diving station, drawing little acknowledgment from the slim diving officer busy scrutinizing every movement of his two planesmen. The *Whitefin* was diving much faster due to the added weight of the flooded conning tower.

"Blowing from auxiliaries to sea, ten thousand, sir," announced the chief of the watch, as he opened and shut valves, frantically responding to each one of Allendale's mumbled orders, as if he were a mere extension of the stoic lieutenant's left arm.

"You got it, Vince?" Tremain ventured to ask in a low tone.

In the past weeks at sea, Tremain had never once used Allendale's first name. It had somehow seemed out of place with the reclusive diving officer, who seemed more absorbed in the ship than anything else. But it seemed appropriate at this moment, when all of their lives relied on this man's ability to maintain the submarine on an even keel with a flooded compartment well above her center of buoyancy. It would take an exceptional level of skill to maintain the delicate balance between center of buoyancy and center of gravity while submerged, not to mention while evading depth charges and whatever else the Japanese were about to throw at them.

"Leveled off at two hundred fifty feet, sir," Allendale finally said calmly, confidently. "I have depth control. You may maneuver, Captain."

Tremain nodded. That was all he needed to hear.

"Helm, right full rudder."

The *Shigure* had to be close by now, and indeed he could already hear her screws over the open sonar speaker on the starboard bulkhead. He had to get the *Whitefin* as far as possible away from her diving point, because that was the most likely spot the *Shigure* would drop her first depth charges.

"Sonar reports *Shigure*'s rigging out her sound heads, Captain," said the phone talker standing next to Tremain. He was on the line with Doniphan, who had moved from his now inaccessible WCA console in the conning tower to the JP-1 sonar's manual training gear in the forward torpedo room. "She's making turns for an estimated twenty-five knots, closing fast. She's almost on top of us."

Tremain nodded, casting a glance at the chart sprawled out on the plot table, mentally calculating the *Whitefin*'s position relative to the shallow waters off the promontory. According to the last sounding, taken a half hour ago, there should be a good hundred feet beneath the keel, but there was no way to be sure. If he ordered the boat any deeper, it might plunge into an unmarked shoal. If he risked using the fathometer, the *Shigure*'s passive sonar would undoubtedly hear it, giving the enemy yet another data point to assist in their antisubmarine search and attack. The single-digit soundings printed in italic on the chart appeared all the more ominous in the bloodred lighting, but at this moment, with one compartment flooded, those shallows might be the *Whitefin*'s only chance of survival.

Ohwee-ohweee! . . . Ohwee-ohweee!

Echo-ranging lambasted the *Whitefin*'s hull, and the destroyer's screw noise was now audible through the steel skin.

"Helm, steady up on course one-zero-zero," Tremain ordered immediately. That would place the *Whitefin* roughly ninety degrees off her surfaced course. Hopefully, the course change would eventually shake the *Shigure* loose, but not before this particular attack ran its course. More than likely, the destroyer would drop its charges quickly, hoping for a lucky hit before the *Whitefin* could drive any substantial distance away from the diving point.

"Sonar reports the tin can's passing right over us, Captain."

It would come at any moment now. Tremain waited for the report of depth charges in the water as he half-considered the risks of taking the *Whitefin* fifty feet deeper. He waited, glancing around at the perspiring faces of the other men in the humid control room, but the report from Doniphan never came. The screw noise began to fade.

"Sonar reports the destroyer didn't drop, Captain. He drove directly over us and didn't drop a cotton-pickin' thing."

Tremain exchanged a puzzled look with Monroe, while everyone else in the room breathed easier. For the life of him, Tremain could not understand why they were not being rocked by half a dozen depth charges at this moment. It did not make any sense. Unless the *Shigure* was plum out of depth charges. It was a possibility, and the only one Tremain thought viable.

Then suddenly a loud scraping sound filled the compartment. It was an unsettling sound, the grating sound of metal on metal. It was obviously coming from outside the ship. Tremain's first instinct was a mine cable, but that thought soon evaporated when the sound persisted and it became obvious that it was not related to the *Whitefin*'s movement through the water, but rather to the *Shigure*'s. The *Shigure* was streaming some kind of weighted cable behind her, essentially trawling for the submarine. After what seemed like minutes, the cable or chain, or whatever it was, reached its end, signified by a noisy rattle as the weight or hook or whatever it was dragged along the starboard hull and up the conning tower. Tremain heard a distinct *clunk,* as if a hook had caught hold of one of the bridge rails, and then nothing. The noise was gone.

"Where's the *Shigure*?" Tremain asked the phone talker.

After a brief pause, the answer came back over the circuit. "Doniphan reports she's slowed down. Right now she's circling off the port beam."

"What the hell's he doing?" Monroe asked, stupefied.

"I don't know."

"Should we get out of here while we can, sir?" Monroe suggested, hovering over the big chart table with a pair of dividers in one hand. "We could make an eight-knot sprint for open water. If the *Shigure*'s out of depth charges, she won't be able to do much about it, except maybe call in air support, which won't do much good until after sunup. The shelf is only ten miles away; there's eight hundred feet of good water there plus a shallow thermocline at four hundred feet. By the time her help arrives, we could be in deep water with a layer over our heads. Sure, our batteries will be depleted, but that won't matter much. We can hide under the layer all day long and slip away on the surface at night."

Tremain considered the idea, casting an instinctive glance at the bathythermograph mounted above the master gyrocompass. Behind the glass window of the boxlike unit, a card of carbon paper displayed a graphical plot of depth versus seawater temperature, as measured by a temperature sensor located outside the pressure hull on the starboard side of the conning tower. The thin, black trace on the card showed a large deflection corresponding to four hundred feet. On the previous afternoon, as the *Whitefin* had approached the strait submerged, Tremain had had the foresight to order a depth excursion in order to get a good water temperature profile. To everyone's delight, a thermocline was discovered in the deeper water just outside the approaches to the strait, probably formed by the difference in temperatures between the South China Sea and the Gulf of Tonkin. The thermal layer was tempting, and Monroe's suggestion was sound, but there was still something turning on the sirens in Tremain's head.

Something was not right. The mystery of the dragging cable ate away at him. There was something in the far recesses of his brain that kept him from dismissing it as merely a frustrated destroyer, out of depth charges and trying to do anything it could to disrupt the submarine's navigation. No, there was something more to it than that, something he had read long ago, during his Academy days when he had studied the antisubmarine tactics of the Great War. The early depth charges of that war consisted of a bundle of TNT attached to an underwater kite-and-float arrangement towed astern by a destroyer. The rudimentary weapons were abandoned because they posed too much of a threat to the attacking ship, and most destroyer captains didn't like the idea of being tethered to what was essentially a mine. But Tremain also remembered reading about one particular British destroyer captain who had used the float arrangement as a means of tracking rather than destroying his prey. He would trawl over the spot where the U-boat had submerged, trying to hook a float onto the submarine's hull, or railing, or deck guns, or limber holes—anything would work. Once the hook snagged, the destroyer would release the tether and the U-boat would drag the float around everywhere it went. The destroyer captain would know exactly where to drop his depth charges. Of course, there could be a couple hundred feet of error inherent to the method, depending on the slack of the float rope. And there was no way to determine the submarine's depth. Although, Tremain remembered one of his crafty classmates at the Academy devising a way to do it. His friend had determined that if the float contained a pole, say twenty feet long, situated in such a way that it always stood vertically whenever the float was sitting still and always deflected at some angle whenever the float was being dragged, one needed only to observe the pole, measure the angle of deflection, and use simple right triangle rules to come up with a good estimate of the sub's depth. The hypotenuse—or the length of the cable—was a known constant, and the deflection angle of the pole was also known. Therefore, solving for the submarine's depth—the opposite side of the right triangle—was nothing more than simple trigonometry. Of course, there were offsets to consider due to the speed of the submarine, but four knots was usually a good assumption for a submerged submarine.

Could that be the technique the *Shigure* was using here? Was that the secret way she had destroyed so many American submarines? Tremain had never heard of any destroyer ever using the technique in this war, but who could say for sure? Sunken submariners don't make it home to tell how they were sunk. But all of the facts fit in this case. The *Shigure* was of the Shiratsuyu class. All of the intelligence on that class of Japanese destroyer indicated that it carried only a marginal set of sonar transducers, so that certainly could not be her secret weapon. Adding to that the fact that the

Shigure had just tried to hook something onto the *Whitefin*, and may have been successful at it, pointed Tremain to only one conclusion. He had to assume that the *Whitefin* was now dragging a float of some kind on the surface, marking her position within a few hundred feet. Assuming the float had a deflection pole fixed on top of it, then the *Shigure* would know the *Whitefin*'s depth. Tremain suspected the *Shigure* was not out of depth charges at all. She had sacrificed dropping charges on the first attack run so that she could drop them with pinpoint accuracy on the second run. Right now, she was simply watching and waiting for the right moment to pounce on the unwary submarine and deliver the lethal blow.

"Sir?" Monroe said hesitantly, obviously concerned that his captain was suffering from shell shock.

"All stop," Tremain ordered.

"All stop, aye, sir," replied the helmsman unbelievingly from the wheel at the forward end of the control room.

"Captain, what are we doing, sir?" Monroe asked succinctly. It was the first time he had ever questioned Tremain's orders in front of other members of the crew.

"The *Shigure*'s got us just where she wants us, XO."

"What are you talking about, sir? She's doing circles in the ocean at five knots. For all we know, she's lost us completely."

"I don't have time to explain, right now, Commander," Tremain said, in a tone that indicated his executive officer's sudden show of defiance had gone far enough. He then turned to Allendale. "Dive, come shallow. Make your depth one hundred forty feet."

The whole room gasped collectively.

"Shallower, sir?" Allendale replied. Even the unflappable diving officer appeared stunned at the order.

"Can you do it quickly, even with the conning tower flooded?"

"It'll be tough without any speed across the planes, sir. I'll probably have to blow the auxiliaries dry to stay on depth. We'll use up some of our air reserves." Allendale quickly composed himself again, and then added, "I can try, sir."

"Then do it!"

"Aye, aye, Captain."

There were no more questions. The room fell silent as the

planesmen pulled back on their controls until the *Whitefin* slowed to a point that they were useless. The low sibilation of high-pressure air filled the room as the contents of the variable ballast tanks were pushed back out into the sea, in an effort to compensate for the awkward weight of the flooded conning tower.

Then came the expected report.

"Sonar reports the destroyer's picked up speed, Captain. He's headed this way again. It looks like he's making an attack run."

Tremain nodded, trying to appear calm in front of his men. In contrast, Monroe displayed all the characteristics of a man undergoing an internal crisis. His face was distorted with a myriad of emotions. Not fear of the enemy, obviously, but more likely fear that Tremain had gone off the deep end. Tremain could only guess what hasty options were brewing in his head, and he felt the need to take a moment for explanations to ease his XO's conscience.

"They've attached a float to us, XO. That's how they know where we are. We've got only one chance now. We have to create slack in that cable. Every foot of slack is another foot of error for the *Shigure* to deal with. It's our only chance."

Monroe did not nod. He did not say anything. He simply made eye contact with Tremain, expressing in one feeble glance his reluctance to accept this one last leap of faith.

"At one-three-zero feet, sir," Allendale reported, just as the *swish-swish-swish* of the *Shigure*'s propellers became audible to every ear in the room.

This was it, Tremain thought. He was taking a calculated risk in coming shallow and going to a dead stop.

Ohwee-ohweee! . . . Ohwee-ohweee!

The *Shigure*'s probing sonar reflected off the hull as the clamor of her screws filled the control room, prompting Tremain to hope that the destroyer was too far into her attack run for the active sonar to help. A few of the veterans around him started at the piercing sound, recognizing it as the short-scale, attack frequency. They were jumpy, and who could blame them. They knew what was coming.

"Sonar reports multiple splashes, Captain. Depth charges on the way down."

"Pass the word." Tremain nodded, as he and the men around him grabbed hold of pipes, stanchions, brackets—anything to hold them down. In a matter of seconds, their undersea home was about to become their worst enemy.

As he waited for the depth charges to fall, Tremain closed his eyes, praying that he had made the right tactical judgment, and that he had not just consigned his men to their deaths. He tried to control his breathing in the last few moments of peace, trying not to dwell on the worst, but to keep his head clear.

Click-click . . .

As the first depth charge armed its firing trigger, the image of Judy appeared in his mind's eye, bringing a small smile to his face. It was the last time he would smile for a very long time.

Wham! . . . *Wham!* . . . *Wham!*

Chapter 16

TREMAIN leaned against the bridge rail casually watching the dozen or more small boats and canoes ply back and forth between the *Whitefin* and the shoreline. The battered submarine was sitting on the surface in the same small cove on the north side of Mindanao where it had deposited Major Farquhar over a month before. Then, the enemy coastline had seemed dangerous, almost foreboding. But today, it seemed perfectly tranquil. The sun had disappeared behind the steep volcanic slopes to the west, casting long shadows across the great majority of the bay, where the *Whitefin* sat tethered to her anchor, now lodged firmly in the sandy bottom. The overgrown shoreline resonated with the deafening sound of a thousand different species of bird, singing out an inharmonious melody at the setting sun.

Down on the *Whitefin*'s main deck several dark-skinned and shirtless Moros helped the *Whitefin*'s sailors swing up the last few casks of water using the torpedo-handling mast and boom. The fresh water had come from a stream farther inland; it had been carted through the jungle, rowed across the cove aboard a variety of boats, and then poured into the *Whitefin*'s thirsty potable water tanks.

Tremain smiled at the thought. The ship's distillation plant—like many other things—had been damaged beyond repair during the *Shigure*'s depth charge attack a week ago. Now the *Whitefin*'s crew would have just enough water to manage the long journey back to Australia. Only slight rationing would be necessary. It was one of the few moments of relief he had had in the week since the hellish depth charging, and he had these simple villagers to thank for it.

When the *Whitefin* had pulled into the bay earlier that morning, the locals had greeted her with cheers from the shoreline and a rather conspicuous armada of canoes that certainly could not go unnoticed by Japanese aircraft. But they seemed eager to help in any way they could, and Tremain was assured by one of the *datus*, or village chiefs, that no enemy aircraft would fly over this bay. The *datu*, an elderly Malay man of no less than sixty, wearing an exotic red head scarf, had met Tremain with a kind smile but one laced with suspicion. But that suspicion seemed to dissolve once the *datu* learned that the young wardroom steward, Miguel, was on board. After that, he seemed eager to help in any way he could. It seemed that Miguel was the chief's nephew, and had spent several years of his childhood in his uncle's village.

Miguel was now ashore, visiting old family and friends. Tremain had seen no harm in letting him go, especially since the major was running late for the rendezvous, apparently making an overland trek from some remote jungle hideout to meet the submarine. Farquhar was expected to arrive at any moment, along with two other riders that he was taking back to Fremantle with him.

"We've got close to four thousand gallons aboard, sir," Monroe called up to Tremain from the main deck. The XO was covered in sweat and wore nothing but a pair of khaki shorts.

"Not bad for a day's work, XO. Please thank our generous hosts and stow the deck for sea."

"Aye, aye, sir."

The fatigue in Monroe's voice was apparent. He had been working himself ragged over the past few days, organizing repair parties, getting the ship patched up, including the much damaged conning tower, which had to be drained and every piece of equipment torn apart and salvaged as best as possible. But Monroe was holding up better then most of the crew. They were all worn out, beaten. The lack of conversation while they worked topside on this beautiful tropical day proved it. Smiles and conversation had been scarce aboard the *Whitefin* over the past week—in the wardroom, in the crew's mess, in every compartment. That depth charging had taken everything out of them, and it showed on their detached faces. The marines had a phrase to describe it, the "thousand-yard stare." In short, they were suffering from combat fatigue.

It had been a close thing with the *Shigure* that day. Tremain did not know if his last-minute orders to come to a full stop and to go shallow had saved them from that first pattern of depth charges. But he did know that the *Shigure*'s ensuing attack had been one of the most terrifying moments of his submarine career. All told, the destroyer dropped forty-three depth charges on them over an eight-hour period. Eight hours of the most horrible conditions. Eight hours of fighting flooding and a hundred separate leaks. Eight hours of stifling heat, humidity, and darkness. Eight hours of sneaking away from the destroyer at a snail's pace only to be found again and subjected to further punishment. Toward the end, the batteries faced cell reversal, the oxygen started to dwindle, and the atmosphere carried the slight aroma of chlorine gas. Oxygen candles were lit and carbon dioxide absorbent spread on the racks to make the air breathable for just a few hours more. Some men worked hard throughout. Some suffered from heat exhaustion and dehydration. Some gave up and went to their racks. Others simply stared at the bulkhead, unfeeling and unresponsive. Eventually, around one o'clock that afternoon, the *Shigure* finally gave up, and her screws faded for good.

In the week since the attack, the crew had not been the same, and Tremain suspected they would never be the same again. Luckily, a few broken bones and some psychological scars were the worst of the lasting injuries.

Tremain stood up to take notice of a small boat shoving off from the shoreline. Leveling his binoculars on the small craft, he could see it was another long canoe and it contained Farquhar, Miguel, and several rather grim-looking Moros, much grimmer looking than the ones Tremain had been dealing with most of the day. Tremain judged that these must be the hard-core guerillas of Mindanao—the *juramentado*—vicious Muslim warriors who had put their holy war against Christians temporarily on hold while they ousted the Japanese invaders. The U.S. Army had developed a healthy respect for them forty years ago in the aftermath of the American annexation of the island, when the sword-wielding charges of the seemingly un-stoppable berserker Muslim warriors prompted the army to trade up from the .38-caliber revolver to the larger stopping power of the Colt .45. No doubt, these same warriors gave nightmares to the Japanese soldiers stationed nearby.

As the boat took something like an age to row across the half-mile stretch of water, Tremain scanned the skies above, half-wishing to call down to the SD radar operator as he had half-wished at least once every fifteen minutes for the en-tire time the *Whitefin* had been anchored here. There was a Japanese air base at Malabang, on the other side of the island, just over a hundred miles away to the southwest, and although the guerillas had assured him that any aircraft taking off and heading in this direction would be reported over the radio by the guerilla group on that side of the island, the thought of sit-ting in shallow water unable to dive still did not thrill him. He took little comfort in his gunners casually standing be-side their fifty-caliber and twenty-millimeter machine guns. The sooner they got back to the depths of the Mindanao Sea, the better.

"Permission to come aboard, sir?" a cheery Farquhar yelled up to him as the canoe pulled alongside.

"Granted. We've been waiting quite a bit longer than I'd anticipated, Major. So, I'd appreciate it if you'd get the lead out."

"Certainly, sir. Just as you say."

Tremain climbed over the rail and down the ladder to the main deck and met Farquhar just as he was stepping aboard, along with Miguel and two fatigue-clad local men.

"Captain Tremain, I'd like you to meet Jokanin and Puyo. They're both *datus*, or chiefs, in the Moro guerilla army. I'm sure you received the message that they'll be coming with us

back to Fremantle. It seems General MacArthur wants to decorate them personally for their efforts against the Japanese invaders."

"Yes, we received it. Welcome aboard. Please let me know
if there is anything I can do to make your stay on board more
comfortable."

Both men glared at him, and then began to converse in
what sounded like a form of Tagalog.

"These chaps aren't too good with English, Tremain, so
maybe I'd better relay your good intentions, or perhaps I
could . . . Cripes! That's a damn big hole in your ship, Tremain."
Farquhar had shifted his attention to the warped five-inch hole
in the conning tower. The hole contained a makeshift plug
now, but it still looked menacing.

"We had some action while you were away."

"Bloody hell, I'll say you did. Are you sure she's seaworthy, Tremain? Wouldn't want to go to test depth now with that
nasty blemish, would we?"

Several of the nearby sailors stopped working and stared
angrily at the British major, whose jovial tone seemed not to
lend enough reverence to the battle scar.

"Did I say something wrong?" he asked, after detecting the
sudden thickness in the air.

"We lost Berkshire when that shell hit, Major," Monroe offered quietly. "And we've lost two other sailors since you left
us. Heath and Collingsworth."

"Oh, dear." Farquhar seemed visibly moved. "Please for-
give me. I'm terribly sorry. I didn't mean to sound flippant.
What a bloody shame. I rather liked young Berkshire."

The major and the two guests were ushered below; good-
byes and thank-yous were said to the friendly villagers, and
the *Whitefin* weighed anchor before the last glow left the
western sky. It took the better part of an hour to navigate back
out of the narrow bay, with the aid of a local fisherman, who
knew the precise location of the various hidden shoals. The
helpful fisherman remained aboard until the *Whitefin* had
reached the open sea, and then shoved off in his small canoe
just beyond the surf. Throughout the whole excruciatingly
stealthless exercise, they never saw a single enemy ship or

aircraft, a testament to the remoteness of the place, and why ComSubSoWesPac liked to use it to deliver arms and supplies to the guerillas fighting on Mindanao. Eventually, the weary *Whitefin* reached the deep waters of Mindanao Bay, where she pointed her bows to the west to begin the first leg of her long voyage home.

AFTER two nights at sea, the major's Filipino companions seemed to gain their sea legs and emerged from their racks to become worthy opponents in the endless cribbage game that went on in the wardroom during the return leg of all patrols. The game had gone on despite the obvious strain between Tremain and the rest of the officers. They all knew what was going to happen when they made it back to Fremantle. It had been an unsuccessful patrol by the standards set for this ship by its previous captain. Indeed, it had been unsuccessful by the most common measuring sticks in the service. The *Whitefin* had been battered by enemy depth charges and gunfire until she was hardly able to withstand the sea pressure at one hundred fifty feet, leaking like a sieve all the way down. She would require many weeks in dry dock, possibly an overhaul in the States, before she ever ventured into enemy waters again. Two men were confirmed dead, another lost overboard and presumed dead. Although they had sunk a Japanese heavy cruiser, a patrol boat, and a handful of sailing yachts, their original mission called for sinking a fleet of large tankers that should have netted them well over twenty thousand tons. The admiral would not be pleased, and every man in the wardroom knew it. Upon their return, it was likely that he would enact one of his infamous "reorganizations" that left no officer's career intact except for the most junior ensign, who could not be held responsible for any harm or good done on the patrol.

"What's that letter you keep adding to, Whately?" Farquhar said after dinner one evening. "Have you a sweetheart back home in America?"

Whately appeared hesitant to share the contents at first, glancing nervously at the closed curtain leading to the passage. But eventually a void expression crossed his face when he realized that no senior officers were within earshot.

Tremain was on the bridge, and Monroe was sound asleep in his stateroom down the hall.

"This is a letter to ComSubSoWesPac," he said evenly, "to the admiral, informing him of Captain Tremain's conduct on this patrol."

"Of his conduct? What the devil are you talking about, Lieutenant?" Again, Farquhar said "Leftenant."

He noticed Whately shoot a questioning look at the faces of the other officers seated at the table, Endicott and Tutweiler. They both carried the same uneasy yet resolute expression as Whately, as if they were in uncharted waters and knew that a reef could appear at any moment to rip out their bottom.

"It's no big secret," Whately said finally, in a tone that exuded forced confidence, "Tom and Robin here are working on letters, too. Captain Tremain took this boat out of our patrol area on a wild-goose chase after a Jap destroyer he's been obsessed with for who knows how long. He had no business deviating from the patrol orders. Now we're coming back to port with our tail between our legs and little to show for it. If we had an XO with some balls, I'm sure the captain would have been relieved by now."

"Certainly, Lieutenant, your captain had a good reason for going after this particular destroyer."

"Yeah, he had a reason, all right. The worst kind of reason, a personal one—namely, revenge. He took us halfway across the South China Sea to get a shot at the destroyer that sank the *Seatrout.*"

"The *Seatrout*?"

"Our legendary captain's first command. Or didn't you know. He commanded her out of Manila when the war broke out. That's when he earned his reputation, but I'm beginning to think this so-called 'legend' is just a smoke screen to hide his incompetence."

The hitherto silent Tutweiler fidgeted in his seat and then spoke up, as if compelled to, "There we were, Major, with a whole fleet of tankers in our sights—the very fleet our orders told us to destroy—and what does our captain do? He lets them sail away. He just up and decided to ignore his orders, and risk our boat and all eighty men aboard, by tearing off after the *Shigure* on a personal mission of his own."

"Did he now?" Farquhar said thoughtfully, his eyes now staring absently at a pile of stripped chicken bones on the plate before him.

"We've had a disastrous patrol, Major," Whately continued. "A complete and utter failure. The captain's to blame for it—not us. In our minds he's unfit for command, and these letters are our case against him. We're going to recommend to the admiral that he be brought before a court-martial. The admiral can't much refuse us if he gets letters from all three of us."

"And you assume Admiral Ireland will share your views on the matter?" Farquhar said, with a barely perceptible smile.

"Listen, Major, there's no denying the captain disobeyed his patrol orders, and that he needlessly placed his men's lives in jeopardy. Hell, we were even fired on by one of our own boats, if you can believe that. Not to mention this miserable failure of a patrol . . ."

Whately's rant was interrupted by quiet laughter coming from Farquhar. The major sat with his arms crossed, shaking his head as he chortled, crow's-feet forming on the tanned skin near the corners of his eyes. But a close observer could see that the eyes themselves expressed no amusement.

The three lieutenants stared at each other, fuming and puzzled at the same time.

"Would you mind telling us what the hell is so funny, Major?" Whately finally demanded in an irate tone.

"The three of you," Farquhar said, his face instantly turning to a scowl, all the more hideous since it normally carried such a pleasant expression. "How trite you all are. That's what's so funny, or should I say *pathetic*."

Whately gasped audibly at the remark, and was about to retort, but a raised hand from the major kept him silent. The major's hand was as rigid as a board, and stretched taut, as if he might judo chop Whately if he said another word.

"What the bloody hell do you three naïve juveniles know about failure, hmmm?" Farquhar snarled. It was the first time any of them had ever heard him talk in such a vile tone. "Were you in this part of the world when the Japanese were driving us across the Pacific—killing, beheading, and bayoneting their way from the Kuriles to Burma?"

The three young officers said nothing, diverting their eyes to the table between them.

"I don't know much about Captain Tremain, mind, but I'll wager if he commanded a sub out of Manila—the *Seatrout*, I believe you called it—during those uncertain first days of the war, when the future looked so bleak, when there seemed no prospect for reinforcements or even rescue, then I know he must have developed a special bond with his men. I know I did with my men in Malaya. I've commanded many men since, but Ian Farquhar's heart will always belong to the Fifth Company, Seventh Battalion, Rajputana Rifles." Farquhar paused, his eyes drifting to the table. "Though it doesn't exist anymore—except as a handful of starving skeletons limping around Japanese labor camps in Burma.

"Those were hard days in the beginning, my young lieutenants. You have no idea what it was like. You have no idea how desperate we were. I escaped Singapore before it fell and watched my own men from the jungle as the Japs formed up the long column of prisoners and marched them off to the most wretched places in Southeast Asia. I watched them from afar, but there was nothing I could do to help. I felt so useless, so helpless. I mean, I had served with those chaps. I was their officer. They had counted on me to get them home safely, and I failed them." Farquhar's voice trailed off until it was hardly audible anymore. "Now who knows where the hell they are? Eighty thousand men surrendered in Singapore, but who's remembering their names now? I ask you, who the devil is remembering them?" Farquhar looked around the table at each one of them individually. "Who remembers the name of the Jap colonel who ordered my color sergeant punched full of holes? Only I do, it seems. And let me tell you, I'll not rest—never in my life will I rest—until Colonel Tamon Nakamoto is either hanging from a gallows or shot through the head. I owe that to my fallen comrades, and I know they would have done the same for me. Now, I ask you, gentlemen, who will remember the men who died on the *Seatrout*, if not your captain? If he doesn't avenge their deaths, then who will?"

The three officers stared across the table at Farquhar in dumbfounded silence. He could tell by the looks on their faces that they thought him quite mad. He was getting nowhere with them—if anything, he was giving them further reason to write their letters to the admiral. They had obviously made up their minds about Tremain, and no argument would sway them from their path. They were convinced that the admiral would be looking for blood upon the *Whitefin*'s return, and they were more than willing to offer up their new captain as a sacrifice.

Someday, perhaps, Farquhar thought, as he finished his coffee in silence, they would come to understand what he was talking about. Someday, perhaps, they would come to understand that there were moments when personal honor superseded official orders—moments when loyalty to fallen comrades outweighed everything else.

Chapter 17

THE *Whitefin* cut a frothy path at twelve knots on a southerly course through the placid sea as the sun descended in the western sky, bathing the ocean and the black-painted conning tower in an orange glow. Tremain stood on the gently swaying bridge listening to Allendale read the status of his department's repair efforts. The long, often tedious list covered at least three pages of the engineer's trusty notebook, an item Allendale was never seen without. Allendale quickly deciphered his own illegible scribble as the salt-encrusted yellow pages fluttered noisily in the breeze.

". . . replaced the high-pressure air compressor valve plates and springs, Captain. It seems to be functioning properly now, and sounds a lot better. The leak in the forward cooler for the number two main generator has been patched up, and the cooler recharged. It's ready for service now, as well. We're still seeing hydrogen buildup in the forward battery well, sometimes reaching three percent whenever we're at the finishing rate. Propping open the access hatch seems to dissipate it for now, but I'd really like to have the tender rework our ventilation ducting down there when we get back. Actually, I'd prefer it if they did a complete battery inspection, Captain. We've got two cells jumpered out right now, and no telling how many are about to fail." Allendale paused, raising his eyebrows, running down the list with his eyes, obviously deciding whether he needed to apprise his captain of any more issues written there. "Incidentally, Captain, the currents must have been in our favor on the way down, because we still have about twenty thousand gallons of fuel on board. We'll make it back without any problem on that score. And that's it, sir. I estimate we'll need about five weeks in port, before we can go back out on patrol."

Tremain smiled. Allendale may have been an unsociable man, but his unquestioning loyalty and certainty of the future was somewhat refreshing when compared to the junior officers, whom Tremain knew were scheming for his demise. He had seen it written all over their faces during the return voyage, and it had become more apparent, in a number of subtle ways, with each passing day. He knew from his own experiences as a junior officer that when the junior officers started eating midnight rations instead of the formal dinner with their captain, there was trouble brewing. But in Allendale there was no conniving, no hidden agenda. He obviously did not care where the *Whitefin* was going or what she was doing, as long as he could be there to see her through.

"Thank you, Vince. Type that up, will you, for our next serial to HQ."

"Aye, Captain," Allendale said expressionlessly, tucking his notepad into the back waist of his trousers and then heading down the open hatch.

"Looks like we're okay to burn some fuel, Tom," Tremain called over to Endicott, the officer of the deck, who was standing on the opposite side of the bridge, trying to appear absorbed in his binocular search. "Let's go ahead and bring another engine on line. I doubt the crew would object to pulling in a day early."

"Aye, aye, sir," Endicott replied. No smile, not even a friendly glance. Instead he simply leaned over to relay the order into the bridge microphone.

It was typical behavior of a junior officer who had lost all respect for his captain. Tremain had seen it before, in other ships, but never in those that he commanded. The thought suddenly troubled him. These were good officers, in a way, the best he had ever commanded. Had he perhaps asked too much

of them? Overstepped his bounds? Had he let himself become
so absorbed in his hunt for the *Shigure* that he had lost all con-
nection with them? The junior officers were always a good
gauge with which to measure the pulse of the ship. Monroe
and Allendale were too senior, and both were career men.
They instinctively held his rank in much higher esteem than
the junior officers did, and would follow him to crush depth,
agreeing the whole way down that he looked good in plaid.
On the other hand, most junior officers still had one foot
firmly planted in their former civilian lives, where justice and
equality prevailed above logic and reason. They were more
likely to make impulsive decisions, and with less to lose, they
were more likely to act on them.

Just then, Farquhar ascended from the hatch, nodding politely to Endicott and stretching his arms high above his head,
as if he had been confined to a small box for hours on end.
Tremain was surprised to see him wearing the same olive-
drab web belt with the holstered forty-five-caliber pistol that
Tremain had seen him wear as he stepped out of the small boat
off Mindanao.

"Planning on going ashore, Major?" Tremain asked casually. "We're still three days out of Fremantle."

"Oh, no, Tremain," Farquhar said after a sheepish pause, as
if suddenly realizing what Tremain was referring to. "I couldn't
find my other belt this morning, and my trousers are so damned
loose after gallivanting around the jungle for the past month.
My gun belt is all I could find to hold them up."

The major shifted his gaze over the rail and glanced at the
men cleaning the four-inch deck gun down on the main deck,
just forward of the conning tower. Beyond them a school of
dolphins playfully jumped in and out of the submarine's bow
wave.

"Am I to take it, Captain, that we're no longer in danger
from enemy aircraft?"

"Well, there's never a guarantee, Major, not even sitting
alongside the tender in Fremantle, but we've got six hundred
miles of open water between us and the nearest enemy airfield. Only long-range bombers could reach us out here. And
on a day like today, we'd see them on radar long before they
could get close enough."

"Jolly good," Farquhar said simply. He seemed to hesitate for a moment before adding, "Captain, would I be imposing on you too much if I and my companions took a little turn down on the main deck? Just to stretch our legs a bit. Work out the kinks, you know. Being cooped up in this pig—uh, no offense intended—is pure hell to an old infantryman like me, and it's got the two chiefs looking absolutely haggard."

"Be my guest, Major. Just be sure to keep an ear out for the diving alarm, just in case we run into anything unforeseen."

The major nodded, smiling, and then descended the ladder into the conning tower. Five minutes later, Tremain saw the major and the two guerilla leaders emerge onto the main deck from the gun-access hatch on the port side of the conning tower. Once the Moro men stepped on deck, they shaded their eyes from the blinding sun, which they had not seen for several days. The three men strolled forward together, chatting with one another, exchanging greetings with the sailors cleaning the deck gun, and glancing out at the tranquil sea. They walked all the way up to the *Whitefin*'s pointy bow, where they pointed and laughed at the dolphins leaping high out of the water only a few yards away. Then, with hands behind their backs, they all three strolled aft along the submarine's wooden deck, again past the working sailors, along the port side of the conning tower, and farther aft, stopping only when they reached the submarine's distant fantail, more than fifty yards aft of the bridge.

As Tremain watched their distant forms, he began to wonder why General MacArthur would want to bring these two men all the way from Mindanao just so he could decorate them. Surely, they were more valuable on Mindanao, harassing the Japanese occupation force. But then he remembered that Farquhar had been tight-lipped about his mission ashore, and perhaps there were other reasons that Farquhar chose to withhold.

Tremain saw a glint of shiny metal, and noticed that Farquhar had removed the silver cigarette case from his shirt pocket and was offering a smoke to his two companions. Tremain wondered if the small case still contained the little black capsule of cyanide.

"Bridge, Maneuvering," the speaker squawked loudly,

snatching Tremain's attention away from the skylarking passengers. "Three main engines on line with an eighty-ninety split."

Tremain nodded to Endicott, who casually leaned over to the microphone and replied, "Maneuvering, Bridge, aye."

Just then, Tremain heard two distinct popping sounds carried in the wind blowing past his ears. It almost sounded like distant naval guns.

"Holy shit!" he heard one of the lookouts above him exclaim. "He's just shot the bastard!"

Tremain swung around and instantly gasped at what he saw on the *Whitefin*'s fantail. One of the Moros lay crumpled on the deck, a splash of dark blood covering the wooden planks beneath him. The other stood with his hands extended, one of them still holding a cigarette, his face in abject horror as he stared at the fate that certainly awaited him. A good three or four paces away, well out of lunging range, stood Major Farquhar, his smoking forty-five-caliber pistol held at arms' length, aimed directly at the face of the terrified man. The major's face was set in stone, his back ramrod straight, as he adjusted his aim ever so slightly.

The Moro man cried out some sort of plea, clearly audible from the bridge, in a language Tremain did not understand, but his plea was cut short. In an instant, the major's pistol spat out a jet of white smoke, and the back of the guerilla leader's head simultaneously blew out in a hideous spray of blood and brain matter. His lifeless body stood there for two seconds or more before it fell headlong into the sea, with a sickening *kerplunk!*

The splash of the first body had hardly subsided when Farquhar coolly holstered his pistol, got down on his knees, and heaved the other body over the side to join it. The body slid down the hull, rolling once when it hit the curvature of the ballast tank, and then disappeared beneath the waves, leaving a streak of blood on the black steel.

The whole thing had happened so fast, and seemed so unfathomable, that everyone on the bridge, including Tremain, stood motionless for several seconds after. Eventually the two sailors who had been working on the deck gun ran aft of the conning tower to see what was going on, obviously drawn by the gunfire. They stopped in their tracks upon seeing the major all alone, a small smile on his face, as he casually walked toward them.

"Seize him!" Tremain shouted to the two dumbfounded men on deck. "That's an order!"

The two sailors appeared less than capable of carrying out the task, but Farquhar made it easy for them. Without a word, he removed the pistol from his holster, handed it over to one sailor, and then ceremoniously placed his hands in the air, all the while staring up at the bridge with that same complacent, yet unwavering, smile.

PART IV

PART IV

Chapter 18

TREMAIN and Monroe waited in the grand foyer of Admiral Ireland's country estate, Monroe seated and looking bleak, Tremain pacing up and down in a brand-new dress khaki uniform, this time one that fit him. Buying the new uniform was one of the first things he had done when the *Whitefin* returned to port two weeks ago, in expectation of an immediate summons before Ireland to receive a thorough thrashing and the long-expected dismissal from his position as the *Whitefin*'s captain. It came as somewhat of a relief when he learned that both the squadron commander and Admiral Ireland were away at a planning conference in Pearl Harbor, and would be taking a circuitous route on the return trip, making inspection stops in Brisbane, Darwin, and Exmouth.

At first he had been thankful for his short stay of execution. But after spending day upon day waiting in Lucknow's spacious lounge, waiting for the phone to ring, waiting while Monroe, himself a pale and miserable wreck, drank himself under the table night after night, Tremain wished it were already over with. Finally, after many agonizing days, the admiral returned from his trip, and the dreaded summons came. It was conveyed to Tremain and Monroe by an oddly amiable Lieutenant (j.g.) Wright. Wright's rather chipper manner seemed out of place, considering he was probably summoning the two officers to the end of their careers and perhaps arrest and courts-martial. Tremain expected at least a little intelligence from his former ensign on the *Mackerel*, but was disappointed when he got none. Wright said nothing of the admiral's reaction to the *Whitefin*'s patrol report, or of his reaction to the grievance letters undoubtedly sent by the *Whitefin*'s junior officers.

Now Tremain waited with Monroe in the foyer of the great country mansion. It was a surprisingly crowded foyer, filled with officers and enlisted of all ranks, many of whom Tremain did not recognize, and many of whom were members of the press corps, all standing around chatting, with pencils behind their ears, cameras around their necks, and notebooks under their arms. Tremain had to admit he was surprised to see the press at such a discreet location, but then reminded himself that the war was evolving every day. Often, what was one day a closely guarded secret would appear the next day on the cover of *Life* magazine.

The other submarine captains staying at the Lucknow had brought Tremain up to date on the war over several cold beers. Not much had changed in New Guinea. The Australian and American troops had made some progress toward the Japanese naval base at Rabaul, but the advance was slow going. The Central Pacific campaign, however, was a different story. In the Gilberts, the marines had landed on Tarawa and the army had landed on Makin, taking both islands in a brief, bloody fight. The Japanese defenders had fought to the last man, suffering complete annihilation in a matter of days, with only a handful of soldiers and a few hundred Korean laborers surrendering. It was a complete victory for the Americans, but it came at a dreadful price. On Tarawa alone, the marines suffered over one thousand dead and over two thousand wounded. Lying offshore, the supporting navy ships gave their share of blood, too, when Japanese submarines torpedoed the aircraft carriers *Independence* and *Liscombe Bay*. The *Liscombe Bay*, one of the newer escort carriers, sank in less than thirty minutes, taking six hundred men down with her, including the ship's captain and the admiral commanding the carrier division. Dorie Miller, the famous Pearl Harbor hero and mess attendant–turned–machine gunner—the first African-American sailor ever to be awarded the Navy Cross—also went down with the *Liscombe Bay*.

But despite the losses, the Gilberts were now firmly in Allied hands, and Tremain could almost sense the spirit of victory in the air. Everyone seemed more cheerful around the waterfront and in the towns. Everyone seemed more certain that the defeat of Japan and her allies was only a matter of time now; that they needed only to be patient, to stay the course, to pursue the strategies that were working, and the empire would eventually fall to its knees. Of course, the exuberance was somewhat premature. Tremain knew that there would have to be many more bloody Tarawas before Japan would fall.

At that moment, Tremain noticed one member of the press corps standing near him jot something down onto a notepad. Then, apparently frustrated, the reporter crossed out the words he had just written, and repeated this six or seven times before finally appearing satisfied with the wording he had chosen. Out of curiosity, Tremain inched closer and peered over the reporter's shoulder to read what had given him such angst: "AMERICAN SUB GIVES TOJO'S CHIEF THE DEEP SIX!!"

Tremain sighed. So that was the reason for the horde of reporters. One of Ireland's subs must have gotten lucky and killed someone important. Glancing around the room at the other naval officers, Tremain wondered which one of them was the fortunate commander.

A commotion suddenly stirred at the main entrance. Marine guards pushed open the double doors and courteously shuffled a few members of the press out of the way, making room for the admiral and his entourage. Moments later Ireland appeared at the door, red-faced and smiling at having just completed his customary afternoon walk around the grounds. He appeared somewhat flushed but not nearly to the degree of his staff officers, huffing away several steps behind him.

"You're all here! Splendid! Splendid!" Ireland said to the

gathering in general, while several of the photographers flashed off pictures. "Sorry to keep you all waiting. Now, where are . . . Ah, yes, Commander Tremain and Commander Monroe, there you are. Come on over here, both of you!"

Tremain and Monroe exchanged bewildered glances as they both walked slowly toward the area the marines had cordoned off around the admiral. Ireland's face was all smiles and carried none of the scowl Tremain had expected. Tremain was doubly surprised when the press photographers lined up and pointed a virtual firing squad of cameras in his and Monroe's direction, snapping away photographs, one right after the other, until he was completely blind and could see only white spots.

"How's it feel to be a hero, Commander?" one vivacious reporter asked.

"Tell us how you sank that Jap ship, sir?" asked another.

"XO, how many depth charges did they drop on you?"

It seemed unreal that they were now the center of attention in a room full of people that had hardly paid them any notice at all only a few moments before. When the two finally made it to Ireland's side, the admiral greeted them both with firm handshakes and a grin of gritted teeth.

"These are two of my finest submariners, gentlemen," Ireland said to the crowd with a forged smile that left Tremain wondering if the admiral's graciousness was real or simply a show for the sake of the press and the good people back home.

"Stand a little closer to the admiral, will you, Commander?" shouted one photographer. "XO, stand on the other side of the admiral. There, that's perfect! Just hold like that for a moment."

A dozen cameras flashed in quick succession, again blinding Tremain. When he could see again, he noticed Melinda's graceful form come up from behind and slide a blue folder into the admiral's hands. Her eyes met Tremain's for a brief, alluring moment with the same playful expression they had had when she wished him good luck from the top of the mansion's front steps over two months ago.

"I present to you, Captain, this award for the officers and crew of the *Whitefin*." Ireland spoke facing the cameras, then opened the blue folder to read the citation. "The President of the United States takes great pleasure in presenting this Presidential Unit Citation to the United States Ship *Whitefin*, for service as set forth in the following citation. For extraordinary heroism and distinct performance in execution of its duties in the South China Sea on or about 18 December, 1943, when she successfully engaged and sank a Myoko class heavy cruiser, heavily escorted by at least three destroyers and six patrol craft. The destruction of this ship resulted in the death of General Hideyoshi Shinozuka, commander of the Japanese Imperial Army's Southern Expeditionary Army Group, along with most of his staff and several hundred Japanese soldiers who were aboard the cruiser at the time of the attack. After sustaining repeated depth charge attacks by a squadron of enemy destroyers, the *Whitefin* evaded and slipped away to continue pursuing the remaining ships in the convoy, sinking many of them with gunfire. The exemplary actions of the *Whitefin*'s gallant officers and crew were found to be in keeping with the highest traditions of the United States naval service. Signed, for the President, Frank Knox, Secretary of the Navy."

Tremain was speechless as Ireland shoved the award into his hands, the cameras flashing away again, with even more fervor. It was not the gravity of the award that left him speechless, but rather the gross exaggerations and utter fantasies contained in the citation. It was a complete fabrication of the actual events. Of course, he smiled for the cameras as best he could, knowing full well that the families of the *Whitefin*'s sailors would undoubtedly see these photos someday.

"Congratulations to you both," Ireland said. "Of course, we'll do the official presentation ceremony along with all of the usual fluff when your crew gets back from shore leave, but both ComSubPac and I wanted you to have this award as soon as possible."

Tremain paused for a moment, casting one look at the mute and pale Monroe, before addressing the crowd. Tremain knew what to say. He had been in the navy long enough to know not to voice his personal opinions in front of a pack of reporters waiting to scribble down his next words.

"On behalf of the officers and crew of the *Whitefin*, Admiral, we are honored and proud to accept this." Tremain had served on a flag officer's staff before and had spoken to the press on many occasions. He knew the drill. "We accept it not just for our boat, but for every sub crew out there risking their lives to defeat our enemies and bring this war to a swift end. Thank you."

A few of the officers clapped, but none of the reporters. They were too busy writing it all down, though they had probably heard the same old patriotic drivel a hundred times before.

Half an hour later, after the press had been ushered out of the building and herded onto a truck back to Perth, Tremain and Monroe sat in the red leather chairs in Ireland's study, sipping coffee alone with the admiral.

"You two put me in somewhat of a pickle with your little foray," Ireland said grimly, his demeanor substantially different from what it had been moments before in front of the press. "I needn't remind either of you that I could, and should, end both of your careers right here and now. Lucky for you, you happened to sink something worthwhile, something that made headlines in Tokyo, and subsequently made it into the President's daily briefing. Believe you me, commanders, if the White House hadn't called for your public recognition for killing Shinozuka, you'd both be in deep shit right now. That's all there is to it." Ireland paused before adding, "And don't think you're not in deep shit with me, either. You still are. Your mission was to sink the tanker fleet, gentlemen, *not* the *Shigure*. You had no business deviating from the patrol order, no business whatsoever. Fortunately for all of us, your contact report gave us enough time to vector the *Gar* and the *Rasher* onto the Jap tankers before they could get away, and only three managed to escape."

Tremain nodded heavily, still quite a bit stupefied by the fact that he was going to get to keep his command. He had already heard the news about the tanker fleet's destruction from the skippers of the *Gar* and the *Rasher* over beers at the Warehouse. Suddenly, he wondered if Ireland had read any of the grievances lodged by the *Whitefin*'s junior officers. If he had, he gave no indication of it.

"I must admit that I was a little surprised at the citation, Admiral," Tremain ventured to say. "I'm sure Chris here will back me up when I say that it was wildly inaccurate. There was only the one escort, the *Shigure*, and the patrol craft that came along later. We certainly didn't chase down any ships with gunfire, I don't know where that came from. Besides, there was only one other ship in that convoy, sir, other than the Myoko, and we're pretty sure she made it into port, albeit in bad shape."

"Oh, Jack, you know how these things go," Ireland said dismissively. "We tell them the facts, and the politicians twist them around to suit their needs, their own propaganda. I have no doubt your photograph will end up in *Time* magazine with a printed story embellishing the attack even further. But let me reiterate to you, gentlemen," Ireland continued, taking on a more forceful tone, as if he had forgotten that he was supposed to be upset. "You're a couple of lucky sons of bitches— or should I say unlucky since you went to all that trouble and didn't even manage to sink the *Shigure*. I was ready to strangle both of you with my own two hands when I found out you had left your area—you, Jack, for thinking you could get away with it, and you, Chris, for not talking some sense into your captain. I can somewhat understand your reasoning, Jack, for going after the *Shigure*, although I vehemently disagree with your action. But you, Chris, I don't understand at all. I thought you would have learned from the other disasters in your career not to go along with a cockamamie idea like this one."

Tremain saw Monroe's face flush. Tremain had experienced this kind of treatment from Ireland before. He knew that the admiral was just posturing, while at the same time probing for weaknesses. That was his way. The way to get through it was to keep silent, let the admiral rant, and then live to fight another day. But Monroe was unused to Ireland's style, and was evidently taking every one of the admiral's words like an arrow to the heart.

"With all due respect, Admiral," Tremain interjected, hoping to head off any retort by his XO. "Leaving the area was my idea and my idea alone. I'm the captain, and I am solely responsible. Chris, here, advised me of his objections on numerous occasions, but always in private, never in front of any other officer or any member of the crew. So if you've, say, received any messages . . . or possibly letters . . . suggesting otherwise," he met Ireland's eyes and knew that the remark had hit home,"they would be inaccurate. Throughout the patrol, Commander Monroe gave me the one hundred percent support expected from any executive officer. He's a damn fine one, in my book!"

"Hrmpf!" Ireland snorted stubbornly. "I suspect we'll see about that, in due time. In any event, despite your failure to intercept the tankers, you did manage to carry out your secondary mission with satisfactory results." He hesitated, then added with a laborious sigh, "And I've received a personal thanks for your efforts from General MacArthur's chief of staff."

Tremain shifted in his chair. Just the mention of the *Whitefin*'s secondary mission, delivering and extracting Farquhar, made him feel cold inside. The iniquitous nature of the cold-blooded murders that took place on the fantail that day still weighed heavily on his mind. He was not a party to them, nor had he the chance to stop them, but he felt somewhat responsible, nonetheless. In his mind's eye, he could still see the callous British major dispensing with the body that had fallen on the deck, rolling it overboard with the nonchalance of a mess attendant discarding a weighted trash bag.

Shortly after the horrid event, after the men topside had disarmed Farquhar and taken him below to the forward torpedo room, where he was unceremoniously handcuffed to a pipe, Tremain had grilled him for answers.

"Now look here, old boy," Farquhar had said, after Tremain demanded to know the reason for his unconscionable act. "I certainly wouldn't have the impertinence to tell you how to run this ship, so please have the courtesy not to tell me how to do my job. I've got a lot of experience leading insurgencies against the Japs. I know exactly how to do it."

"We'll see what headquarters has to say about that, Major."

At that very moment, Monroe had entered the compartment with a sheet of paper in his hand. It was the printout of a decoded message.

"Captain, this message just came off the Fox broadcast. We passed it through the cipher."

"Well, what the hell is it?" he had snapped at his XO, initially irritated at the interruption.

"It's for the major, sir." Monroe paused. "It requests status of Operation Run Amok."

A snide smile formed on Farquhar's face. "With your permission, Captain, the XO may send a response. Please state simply that 'Operation Run Amok has been completed,' and add another line 'Mission accomplished.' "

"Do as he says, XO," Tremain said after a few moments of pause, and then waited for Monroe to leave the room before adding, "So this was all an elaborate ruse, to kill two Moro guerilla leaders."

"That was part of my mission, Captain. Those two chaps were causing troubles for us on Mindanao. Both wanted to be king of the guerillas, and neither wanted to heed a single word of advice. Meanwhile, they helped themselves to our weapons and supply shipments without so much as a thank-you. Both were experts at instigating sectarian strife between Christians and Muslims, and both had taken part in some rather gruesome massacres. We suspect they were even collaborating with the Japanese. Either way, they were little more than a couple of power-hungry thugs. So, you see, Tremain? You needn't shed a tear on their behalf. But now that you know everything, I must ask you to promise your silence on the matter."

"And what about the other part of your mission?"

Farquhar smiled, glancing up at his handcuffs. "That, Captain, you will have to beat out of me. I, for one, recommend the water boarding technique to achieve the quickest results."

After seeing that he would get no further with the major, Tremain had ordered Farquhar released and had hardly said two more words to him for the rest of the trip. Once they arrived in Fremantle, the major had gathered his things, obtained his confiscated pistol from the ship's master at arms, and met a waiting staff car on the pier. That was the last time Tremain had seen him.

As Tremain watched Ireland shift in the red leather chair across from him, he suddenly wondered just how much the old admiral had known about the mission to assassinate the two guerilla chiefs.

"Admiral." Monroe spoke up for the first time, and Tremain was half-afraid that it was going to be a retort to Ireland's remarks about his past, but he was relieved when it turned out to be of an official nature. "What's going to happen to the *Whitefin*, sir? She's got damage that needs a dry dock, and she's well overdue for an overhaul."

"Is she going back to Mare Island? Is that what you're asking, Commander?"

"Yes, sir."

"No," Ireland said dryly, "she isn't. She's to be repaired here to the fullest extent possible, and sent back out within the month."

"Within the month?" Tremain said, in a tone to match both his and Monroe's incredulous expressions. "Admiral, that really is quite impossible, sir. I've got several holes in my pressure hull, not to mention the fuel ballast tanks, which leave a streak of oil on the surface four miles long. My four aft tubes don't work, and won't until I get a new impulse-air flask. The evaporator's kaput. I can't make fresh water—"

"I've seen the list, Jack," Ireland said with a wave. "Don't worry, the repair shop supervisor aboard the *Pelias* tells me he can have you seaworthy within two weeks, and two weeks is all we have." Ireland paused and eyed both of them in his casual but commanding way. "You're not going on a normal patrol next time out. The *Whitefin* has been requested for another . . . special operation."

Tremain shifted in his chair. The last thing he or any other submarine captain wanted was to let his boat become the designated ferry boat for spies and commandos.

"May I ask by whom, sir?"

"Major Farquhar made the request."

"With all due respect, sir, I'd really rather not take Major Farquhar anywhere ever again."

"Well, you're going to. Those are your official orders, so there's an end to it." Ireland smiled somewhat sadistically. "Come now, Jack. We can't have the Presidential Unit Citation winner turning down a mission, now, can we?"

Tremain bit his lip. He knew any further argument would be futile.

"Of course, I can't fill you in on all the details yet," Ireland continued, "but you'll be far away from any convoy routes, so you don't have to worry about your aft tubes. In fact, you'll be stripped down, without any reloads, in order to accommodate the other equipment you'll be taking. You'll have the fish in the forward tubes, but that's it. I doubt you'll ever get the chance to use them, though. You'll get filled in on the rest soon enough when we hold the official briefing. Squadron will let you know the time and place." Ireland's tone took on a jovial but also slightly sarcastic nature. "Cheer up, Jack. At least you won't be tempted to take off after the *Shigure* again. If you do this job right, I might just let you keep your command for a few more months."

Shortly after, Wright entered the room and reminded the admiral that he had a two o'clock appointment waiting in the lobby. Tremain and Monroe rose to leave, ushered out by the proficient flag lieutenant, but just as Tremain reached the door, he turned to face the admiral still sitting in the leather chair.

"There's just one more thing I wanted to ask you about, Admiral Ireland, sir." He had to use the due courtesies afforded to the rank, especially in front of Wright, especially with what he was about to say. "Just something I found curious while catching up on the intel reports this week. One of the reports noted that the *Shigure* had been transferred to the South China Sea for convoy duty in late October, covering the central routes."

"What of it, Commander?" Ireland said in an even, yet suspicious tone that only encouraged Tremain that he was on the right track.

"The report was released to the squadron intel file back in November, only a week after the *Whitefin* put to sea, sir."

"Meaning?"

"Meaning that you had to have read it at least a week or two before that. I just found it curious that you didn't tell me about it, sir. Especially since you and I spoke at great length about the *Shigure* the day before I left on patrol."

Ireland stared directly into his eyes with a smile that exuded no joy. "Perhaps I did. Perhaps I thought it inconsequential at the time."

At that moment Tremain knew that he had been used in another of Ireland's schemes. At that moment, everything was very clear to him. Ireland had *wanted* the *Shigure*. He had said as much on numerous occasions. Who could blame him, since the infamous enemy destroyer was sinking his boats, right and left? Ireland had probably gone to ComSubPac asking permission to send a wolf pack of his submarines to hunt down and sink the *Shigure*, a mission that ComSubPac would have certainly balked at since destroyers were considered low-value targets and not crucial to the logistical support of the Japanese homeland. When he was refused, Ireland had looked for other means to enact his will. And he had found that means, purely by chance, in Tremain—a newly arrived, emotion-ridden, and politically expendable captain who also had a bone to pick with the *Shigure*. That day, before the *Whitefin* had left on patrol, Ireland had carefully and deliberately woken the fury that had slept so long within Tremain's soul. He had intentionally planted the seeds of revenge, and then had placed Tremain and the *Whitefin* in the one spot where they were most likely to encounter the dreaded enemy destroyer, leaving the rest to simple human nature. Though his official orders said otherwise, Tremain now knew that the admiral had sent him out on patrol with the specific intent of sinking the *Shigure*.

Of course, Ireland would never admit to it, but Tremain was certain that he comprehended his knowledge of the plot. It was perceptible in the way Ireland sat in his chair, with legs crossed, one foot dipping to the tune of some drum heard only inside the admiral's head. It was a simple peculiarity of Ireland's, but one that only Tremain and maybe three or four other naval officers in the entire Pacific Fleet could interpret. Ireland was nervous, but his face still wore the same fixed smug expression, and Tremain wished there was something he could do to wipe it off.

At that moment, Melinda entered the room from the side door, carrying a stack of files under one arm, undoubtedly for the admiral to hurriedly sign before his next appointment arrived.

Tremain smiled at her and she smiled back.

Then a thought suddenly entered his head. There was indeed something he could do to wipe that look off Ireland's face, something right here and now. And, if all went well, it would give him more pleasure than it gave Ireland discomfort.

Chapter 19

FABRIANO reined in the black mare as she reached the crest of the hill overlooking the pristine valley. The rugged Australian outback reminded him of the great American West, the endless wild country he had once seen from the window of a train when he had traveled from Chicago to San Diego. He was thankful for the clean outback air that seemed to have finally driven off the diesel fumes permeating every part of his being. Only now, two weeks after leaving the ship, did he not smell the *Whitefin*'s engines with every breath, and the ringing in his head had finally stopped. Even the soreness in his shoulder had subsided a great deal.

A faint howling reached his ears from across the barren valley. Tipping the brim of his fedora to shade his eyes from the sun, he saw a mother kangaroo with her pair of joeys off in the distance hopping from one patch of brush to another. The world was at war, but the wildlife out here did not care. They went on, as they always had.

He checked his watch. He had been gone for five and a half hours; hours spent riding across the plain, in the middle of nowhere, dressed in flannel shirt and jeans, like a proper cowboy. This place really was exactly as it had been advertised to him. A place for submarine sailors to get away from the stress and structure of shipboard life, a place where there were no watches to stand, no rank, no orders, and no officers. After being cooped up with eighty-five men inside a steel tube for two months, Fabriano had been thrilled to finally find a place where he could look out in all directions and not see another soul. He had, in fact, seen only a few other sailors during his daily jaunt into the wild. Some were on horseback, some on foot hiking in the hills, some fly-fishing in a nearby stream, every one of them basking in the great outdoors, taking in the fresh air, trying to forget that in two weeks, they would have to return to their iron coffins.

With his stomach grumbling after the long day of riding, Fabriano decided with some disappointment that it was time he headed back. Wheeling the mare around, he kicked her to a trot, and headed back toward the camp in a cloud of dust. An hour later, he reached it, galloping over the crest of the last hill just as the sun was setting in the red western sky. The camp was comprised of a simple array of log cabins clustered around a large clearing, complete with adjoining stables and a chow hall. From a distance, it looked like nothing more than a large dude ranch. Although Camp Kalgoorlie was a designated rest and recuperation facility for American submarine sailors, it had none of the usual appurtenances of a military installation. It was located in the outback, approximately two hundred miles from Fremantle, near the old mining town of Kalgoorlie, the last train stop heading east before entering Australia's vast and arid Nullarbor Plain.

As Fabriano approached the cluster of cabins at a gallop, he could see the long line of submarine sailors—though they all looked like cowboys—waiting in the chow hall line. The aroma of grilling steaks reached his nostrils and sent his stomach growling with a renewed intensity. Few sailors ever missed the evening meal, since it was usually comprised of an abundance of beef, bread, and fresh vegetables—much fresher than they could expect at sea.

After leaving the mare in the stables with a real Australian cowboy, Fabriano beat the dust off his clothes and walked briskly to the cabin that he shared with twelve other sailors.

Once there, he stripped down, took a two-minute shower, changed into fresh clothes, and set off for the chow hall, hoping he wasn't too late.

"Mikey!" Shelby called from the chow line as he crossed the clearing. "Thought you got eaten by a kangaroo or something! Where you been?"

"Out for a ride."

"Well, you better hurry if you want something to eat. These bastards from the *Guardfish* are gonna eat us out of house and home."

Fabriano joined Shelby in line, and the two helped themselves to generous portions of the meal of the day—twenty-ounce steaks, mashed potatoes, carrots, peas, and Swan beer. With their trays loaded down with food, they found a long bench table where several other sailors from the *Whitefin* were sitting.

"Here's to our brothers on eternal patrol," said one first-class torpedoman raising his glass, as Fabriano and Shelby were taking a seat. "To Collingsworth, Heath, and Mr. Berkshire."

Each man raised his glass and touched the glasses of the men sitting around him.

"Bless their souls," Shelby added vocally, and Fabriano noticed several other sailors instantly avert their eyes to the floor. A shadow fell across the table, and the hitherto lively conversation suddenly turned to a low murmur, with frequent inconspicuous glances cast in Shelby's direction. At first Fabriano thought nothing of it. He dismissed it as nothing more than a sober moment brought on by Shelby's sentiment for their lost shipmates.

"Funny for you to say that, Shelby," one sailor muttered, "considering you didn't lift a finger to help poor Heath."

Fabriano saw Shelby shoot him a hesitant glance before he rose from his seat and snarled back at the sailor, "If you've got something to say to me, Noah, why don't you do it in a manly voice? Stand up and say it to my face, damn you!"

Noah was close to a hundred pounds lighter than Shelby, but he must have drawn encouragement from the other sailors around him, because he stood up and squared off across the table from the big sailor.

"I said, you left Heath hanging high and dry that night when he left his perch to help Fabriano. Maybe if you'd helped him, maybe if you hadn't sat safe and sound up in your perch while he and Mr. Monroe fought to keep Fabriano here from getting swept over the side, maybe we wouldn't be toasting Heath's memory today. Maybe he'd still be here with us."

"Fuck you, Noah!" Shelby shot the smaller sailor such a fierce glare that Fabriano thought for certain he was going to jump across the table at the man. His eyes bulged, his fists clenched, and his face turned red, but he was met with a collective look of defiance from every sailor at the table—all except for Penn, sitting at the far end and chomping away openmouthed, as if his food might get away from him The prospect of facing two dozen of his shipmates in a brawl seemed to somewhat defuse Shelby. Eventually he sat back down and commenced eating his food in a huff.

The thought suddenly occurred to Fabriano that he had seen these same looks of disgust from the crew, on other occasions, whenever Shelby was near—ever since that stormy night when Heath went over the side. Fabriano had diagnosed the reaction incorrectly. He thought the crew had been grumbling about Mr. Monroe, blaming him for Heath's death, but that wasn't it at all. They had been grumbling about Shelby.

From his own relatively brief experience aboard the *Whitefin*, Fabriano thought Shelby to be one of the most goodnatured sailors aboard, especially since the big guy had gone so far in helping him to get qualified. But evidently this same man, who had been so obliging and so loyal to him throughout the patrol, was now loathed by the rest of the crew. It troubled Fabriano all through dinner, and he seldom said a word to anyone, including Shelby, throughout the entire meal.

Later that evening, Fabriano and Shelby joined some sailors from the *Triggerfish* who were on their last day of shore leave and had generously invited everyone in the camp to help them polish off several cases of beer around a large bonfire. Shelby got extremely drunk, with a perspiring red face, and began talking pure nonsense, most of which the *Triggerfish* sailors found utterly hilarious. The jokes grew coarser by the hour, and the *Triggerfish* sailors loved every minute of it. Fabriano found it quite entertaining, too, that is until one awkward moment, very late in the evening, as the campfire crackled on four-hour-old embers, when the big, inebriated sailor suddenly turned to him with a severe expression on his face.

"So where the hell do you gallop off to every day, Mikey?" he asked in an almost demanding tone, the many crevices in his large face appearing almost ghoulish in the firelight. "You got a gold mine in those hills somewhere?"

"No, no gold mine." Fabriano tried his best to sound like he had not been second-guessing his friend in his mind all evening. "Just spending some time with Mother Nature. My brother and me used to spend a lot of time outdoors. We'd stay at our uncle's country house up in northern Wisconsin. He had a nice place up there by a lake with a fishing boat, horses, the whole shebang. We stayed with him every summer when we were little."

"Ah, sounds like a nice childhood, Mikey. How fine it must be to have a family with deep pockets."

Fabriano shrugged, somewhat relieved that the conversation was heading in another direction. "My uncle had some money, but not my parents. My dad worked seventy-hour weeks in a paper mill, until '29, when he got killed in a work accident."

"So your uncle didn't take care of you?"

"He died, too, soon after my dad. Some say he drank himself to death grieving over my dad. Anyway, my uncle's widow sold the property and moved away. We never heard from her side of the family after that. All of my grandparents were dead, so my mom was left on her own to raise us."

"And now your brother's dead, too."

Fabriano shifted imperceptibly at the offhand remark. Shelby was quite drunk, and obviously his speech was somewhat marred by his condition. But still, there was some degree of heartlessness in his tone, as if the alcohol had stripped away some of the tact and good humor Fabriano had grown to expect in Shelby, and now peculiar glimmers of the real man were shining through.

"He left a wife and a little boy behind," Fabriano said, trying not to appear affected by the remark. "I know they're struggling right now, but I'm going to take care of them when all this is over."

"And just how do you suppose you're going to do that?" Shelby asked in a gruff, almost accusatory tone. It was as if the big sailor were suddenly furious with him over something he had said.

Fabriano looked over to see that Shelby had sat up on the log and was now staring directly at him, his normally pleasant features gone, replaced by the same fierce glare he had worn when facing down Noah in the chow hall. It was even more menacing in the flickering firelight. Fabriano had experienced more than a dozen hellish naval battles in his career, but the look on Shelby's face sent chills running up and down his spine. In the two months he had known him, he had never seen him act this way before. But what was even more shocking was that it all seemed so frighteningly natural.

"I have my own plans, Clem," Fabriano finally answered, taking a swig from the bottle and trying to appear unruffled. "Which I think I'll keep to myself."

He decided to leave out the part about the *Chevalier*'s $47,000, but he wondered just how safe his secret was since Shelby was acting like he already knew about it.

At least a half hour of uncomfortable silence passed between them, before Shelby returned to his usual merry self, telling the amenable men from the *Triggerfish* lurid tales of the depraved sexual acts he had performed with his wife and countless other women. When Shelby finally spoke to Fabriano again, his voice was strangely docile, even consoling, but Fabriano detected a trace of artificiality in it all.

"Talking about living hand to mouth, Mikey, take me and my missus, for example. She's a good egg, bless her heart, waiting for me all these years in that shack in San Diego. After the war, I'd like to buy her a house, some nice place on a hill overlooking the ocean. Maybe raise a few kids and settle down, maybe live the good life, for a change. But who am I kidding, right? I'll never make enough money to support a family. I'll never live proper like that. Three squares a day and a roof over my head's all I can hope for, whether it's on land or afloat."

Fabriano found it odd that Shelby was speaking so fondly of his wife, especially since only a few moments ago, he had been bragging about fairly recent exploits with other women in a dozen different ports. Shelby had often commented on patrol about how he couldn't stand to be around his wife for very long.

"But, then again, who knows?" Shelby continued, swallowing a mouthful of beer. "Maybe good fortune will come my way. Maybe it'll land in my lap. I can only hope."

Fabriano instantly shot a suspicious glance at Shelby, but the big sailor was looking elsewhere. By all outward indications he had made the remark innocently, in an offhanded fashion, but the conversation had suddenly come far too close to the mark for Fabriano's comfort.

"Well, it's late," he announced, rising from the log. "I've been riding all day, and I think I'm beat. I'm gonna hit the rack. See you later, Clem."

"You'd help me, wouldn't you, Mikey?" Shelby said in a suddenly serious tone that didn't match the smile on his face. "If you ever was to find that gold mine, you'd give your old shipmate a cut, wouldn't you? You wouldn't forget about your old shipmate, after all the times he stuck his neck out for you."

"I think you're drunk, Clem," Fabriano said, forcing his face into a casual smile. "And I don't know what the hell you're talking about. See you later."

PORT Beach was not far from Perth, and just up the coast road from Fremantle harbor. A sunbather lying on the beach could clearly see the spirelike masts and cranes belonging to the ships in the harbor, poking above the tank farms and low sand dunes to the south. With its close proximity to the harbor, the beach was a popular escape for the sailors of the various navies, and this clear Saturday afternoon was no exception. The summer sun shone down on a throng of bare-skinned men and women, some frolicking in the surf, some sunbathing, some strolling along the beach. A flock of seagulls squawked noisily overhead, riding the brisk offshore breeze that kept the powdery sand cool to the touch.

"The water is absolutely frigid!" Melinda exclaimed as she bounded up the beach and ran into the towel a tanned and shirtless Jack Tremain held waiting for her. She was wearing a bright yellow two-piece bathing suit that did little to hide her womanly curves, and Tremain could not help but gawk from behind his sunglasses as she took the towel and began patting herself dry.

As she leaned over to squeeze the water from her long dark hair, she eyed him with a suspicious smile.

"You really ought to go for a swim, Jack Tremain."

"No, thanks. I drank enough seawater on that last patrol to last me for a while."

She shot him a pouty look, then began toweling herself off rather seductively, moving her hips back and forth until she erupted in a roar of laughter at the wide grin growing on his face.

Tremain suddenly wondered what Melinda thought of him, or rather what a prude she must think he was. After spending sixteen years with Judy, he hardly knew how to act around another woman. Judy knew his ins and outs, and he knew hers. Now he had to keep the sailor in him at bay, and stay on his guard against doing or saying something that Melinda might take as offensive. But he had to admit, Melinda's carefree manner had a way of making him feel relaxed, as if they had known each other longer than the few brief meetings at Ireland's mansion. Her mere presence had a therapeutic affect on him that took him away from the boats, away from the war, for just a few treasured moments.

So far, the day had been perfect, and he could say that he felt genuinely happy—if he didn't count the frequent intervals of guilt that mired his conscience every time Melinda said or did something remotely similar to Judy's habits.

She finished drying off, and they both plopped down on an oversized towel. Tremain reached into the small picnic basket and produced two sandwiches and two ice cold bottles of beer with shards of ice sliding down the dark curved glass. He had procured the beer from the Lucknow, since there was always an ample supply available for submariners. The sandwiches he had purchased at his favorite deli in Perth before picking her up.

"Wow! This really is first class!" She smiled with delight, snatching one sandwich from his hand, tearing open the paper wrapper, and taking an enormous bite, all in one swift motion. "Swimming always makes me hungry." He sat in silence watching her, alone with his thoughts.

"You know, Jack Tremain . . . ," she said, cutting her eyes at him after swallowing a mouthful of turkey and ham.

"Call me Jack, please."

"It doesn't seem right, somehow. You being a superior officer and all. But, as I was saying, *Jack*, the thought just occurred to me that I might have seen you naked before."

"I beg your pardon?"

She laughed teasingly, with her mouth full and her sandwich held delicately in both hands. "When I was a teenage girl, back in the early thirties, I lived with my father in Manila. He was an accountant for the Negros Navigation Company and worked in their offices there. We had a house in Cavite, overlooking the bay, with an excellent view of the American navy yard across the water. My father, being an old navy man, picked the house just for that reason, and he used to point out the different ships and try to get me to remember their names. Of course, that's the last thing on a nineteen-year-old girl's mind, right? But anyway, one Sunday afternoon, I was in my room, staring out the window through my father's binoculars, when I came across three submarines all bunched up together by a pier. The little boats looked funny to me, but what really caught my eye was the crowd of stark naked sailors milling about on deck. At first I couldn't imagine what in the world they were doing, but then I saw some buckets and sponges and figured out that this was how submarine sailors took their baths. I could hardly believe it. All those pale white fannies and . . . other parts . . . dangling around for all the world to see. Oh my!" She fanned her face jokingly. "You weren't stationed there around that time, were you, Jack?"

"Maybe I was," Tremain said, smiling, "but I remember we used to rig canvas sheets along both sides of the deck, so as not to frighten the public—or any teenage girls who might happen to be looking."

"Ah," she giggled with one finger raised. "I remember those things. I'm sure they were put up with good intentions, but they didn't stop *this* teenage girl from looking. The balcony of my room just happened to be at the perfect angle. I could look between the sheets, so to speak, and see what was going on in there—with the help of my father's binoculars, of course. It really was quite an enlightening experience. I saw some of the oddest tattoos, in some of the oddest places."

Tremain chuckled, tilting his head back to take a drink. As he brought the bottle back down, her face was suddenly there, and in the blink of an eye she had kissed him on the cheek. Instinctively, he pulled away, but immediately regretted it when he saw the puzzled and somewhat hurt look on her face.

"Sorry," he said lamely, hoping he had not hurt her feelings. "I'm a little rusty at this."

"So I gathered," she said with a wink and a smile.

"So what was that for?"

"For asking me out on a date. I haven't had this much fun in ages."

"I meant to ask you out earlier, but you were away with the admiral, and then yesterday he was commandeering practically all of your time."

"He has a way of doing that." She averted her eyes momentarily, and then her face broke out into a big grin. "But did you see the look on his face when you asked me right there in front of him?"

They both broke out in a roar of laughter to the point of tears.

"Do you mind if I ask you something?" Tremain said, after they had both wiped the streaks from their eyes.

"Yes. Because you're going to ask me if there's ever been anything between Steven and me. I suppose that question's been gnawing at you for some time now."

Tremain dithered, somewhat embarrassed.

"The answer is," she continued, apparently amused by his visible discomfort, "*yes*, there was, and *no*, there isn't. Is that good enough for you?"

Tremain nodded uncertainly.

"Don't worry about any reprisals from him, Jack. He's not *that* much of a tyrant. Besides, he's the one that broke things off with me. He still cares about me, just not in that way. He would never try to interfere in my personal life, especially since he and my father go way back."

"That's comforting," Tremain said sarcastically.

"Actually, Steven should be quite pleased, you being his favorite and all."

"His favorite?"

"You are, you know. I know he can be downright unbearable in person sometimes, but you'd be surprised at some of the things he says in private. He thinks very highly of you. The whole time you were out on patrol, he practically lived in the communications center, on tenterhooks for any news about the *Whitefin*."

"Really? Were you around when he got word that we were leaving our area, going after the *Shigure*?"

"I think so. He seemed to be all for it, from what I remember. He was always asking for updates on your pursuit, but they were few and far between."

"That's what I thought. The bastard!"

"Go easy on him, Jack," she said, caressing his brow and inching minutely closer to him. "After all, you're the one who ended up with the girl."

Melinda's eyes sparkled with life, like two great searchlights that could not help but brighten up all that they beheld. Her eyes were much like Judy's. There was a reflective, charitable soul behind them, and Tremain could tell that, despite her outward cheerfulness, she was someone who was fully aware of the pain and suffering in the world. She merely accepted it and continued on. The dozen or so barely perceptible freckles across her nose and cheeks accentuated her natural beauty, and suited her playful nature.

"It doesn't get any easier," she said suddenly, looking into his eyes.

"Excuse me?"

"In case you were wondering. It doesn't get any easier. You spend your time putting things off, thinking that someday the hurt will go away, that someday it will subside enough so that you can pick up the pieces and get on with your life. But it will never happen. Your wife will always be there, Jack. She has a right to be. She's earned a place in your heart for all time, and don't you ever let any woman tell you different." She paused. "But every now and then, it's okay to let someone else in, too."

Tremain felt suddenly naked and exposed. Of course, sh

knew that he had lost his wife. Ireland had probably mentioned it in passing on some occasion. She had intruded into his protective sphere, and now he instinctively wanted to tell her to mind her own business, but he did not. How could he when she looked at him in that vibrant but caring way, like a beacon calling him back to the land of the living. He did not lash out at her. Instead, he gently and briefly kissed her waiting lips. With her hand in his, he pulled her closer, and she came willingly, leaning into his shoulder until they were wrapped in each other's arms. They sat there for a very long time, embracing, watching the sun set, staring into the stiff breeze blowing in from the sea.

After the sun went down, they went for a walk along the white-laced strand, their bare feet buried in the cold, frothy surf. Above the din of the crashing waves, they chatted about anything and everything, joked around, played in the water, held hands. Then, during a flirtatious moment, when she mischievously and unsuccessfully tried to push him into a bubbling wave, he wrapped her up in his arms, lifting her high into the air. She laughed out loud, wrenching at his tight clasp in a mock effort to get away. When he finally set her down again, he did not let go, but instead looked directly into her eyes. The moon caressed her perfect face in a bluish glow. The smile on her face had vanished. It had been replaced with a look of ravenous desire, which seemed to pull him closer and closer like a magnet. Their lips touched once ever so slightly. Then her hand was behind his neck, pulling him to her. This time their kiss lasted much longer, with no regard for the sea crashing at their ankles, or the stiffening breeze, or any aspect of the world around them.

Chapter 20

THE conference room on the old *Pelias* was spacious when compared to the wardroom of a submarine, but it still had that oddly cramped feeling to it, as if its narrow, rectangular shape had been more of an afterthought to the ship's designers than a necessity. A long table sat in the center of the room, conveniently bolted to the floor to accommodate the tender's infrequent moments at sea. A dozen chairs surrounded the table, with hardly enough room to pull them out on one side without hitting the two short canvas-covered sofas against one long bulkhead. Along the opposite bulkhead sat a low row of small round portholes casting conical beams of sunlight across the smoke-filled room. One of the portholes had been left open to vent off the toxic pall circulating in the room from a dozen cigarettes, but after receiving a nod from Admiral Ireland sitting at the head of the table, Lieutenant (j.g) Wright reached up and shut the open porthole in the flash of a gold-laced epaulette. Everyone else took notice and quickly found their seats.

"Good morning, gentlemen," Ireland said, bringing the meeting to order. "I'm sure every one of you is eager to know why we've assembled such an interesting gathering . . ."

It was an interesting gathering indeed, and one in which Tremain felt out of place as one of the few naval officers in the room. Most of the men present belonged to the United States Army. Along one side of the table sat two army lieutenants, a captain, a major, and one lieutenant colonel, the last of these sitting on the admiral's right. They all looked remarkably similar, and could pass for the age progression of a single man, or the line of succession of a single family, with the substantially older colonel playing the part of the patriarch. Each had extremely short hair and a perfectly cut uniform hanging on a chiseled body that had not known fat for many years, if ever. They all sat up straight in their chairs, practically at attention, and practically unmoving except to crane their heads to give the admiral their fullest interest. The lieutenants did not speak unless spoken to by the captain, who didn't speak unless spoken to by the major, who said very little. Occasionally, the major would lean over to receive a whispered message from the colonel, after which he would write a careful note onto a small notepad and then set it back down on the table directly in front of him with the cover closed. Behind the army officers, on and around the two sofas, sat and stood a handful of sergeants of various rank who appeared as fearsome as their officers did immaculate.

Tremain sat on the other side of the table along with Marty Pancheri of the *Triggerfish*. Both men could have been the antithesis of their army counterparts. Their wrinkled khaki uniforms indicated that they had already spent many hours of this day negotiating the narrow passages and bilges of their repair-laden submarines, for a submarine captain's work never ended, and often intensified whenever his ship was in port, regardless of the relief the repair crew afforded.

Tremain had been surprised to see Marty here, but he was glad to have such a close comrade with him. It gave him some comfort to know that his wasn't the only submarine being converted into a passenger ferry. Earlier, when he entered the room, Marty had met him with a grin and a hearty handshake.

"Jack!" he exclaimed, laughing out loud, seemingly oblivious to Admiral Ireland's glare from the head of the table. "Don't tell me you're assigned to this mission, too. Now I *know* it's a milk run. Just make sure you stay in your own area this time. And please have the decency to stay the hell out of the way of my torpedoes."

The army officers showed signs of confusion at the mention of the incident, but Marty offered no explanation. Shortly after returning from the last patrol Tremain had discovered that the *Triggerfish* had fired the torpedoes that came close to sinking the *Whitefin* that day in the eye of the typhoon. Over the past few days, both he and Marty had learned to laugh about the near disaster, but Tremain knew the near brush would stay with him for a long time, and he suspected the same was true for the outwardly imperturbable Marty.

Then Marty had said, "Damn, Jack, you got a smile on your face like a man who's spent the last twenty-four hours in a Bangkok whorehouse."

Tremain instantly blushed, slightly embarrassed over the remark. His new army acquaintances appeared to take little notice, but out of the corner of his eye he saw Ireland shift uncomfortably in his chair. Last night was one that Tremain would treasure forever. He had already caught himself earlier that morning daydreaming about Melinda while Allendale gave him an update on the *Whitefin*'s repairs. He could tell it was going to be difficult to remain focused during this briefing.

Directly to the admiral's left sat Major Farquhar, looking prim and proper as ever, wearing the same smirk on his face that Tremain had come to loathe. So far, Farquhar had hardly cast a glance in his direction, and that suited Tremain just fine. If he could somehow ferry the major to his next destination without seeing or speaking to him for the entire trip, he would be content.

"I'd like to start off by introducing Lieutenant Colonel Joseph Buckles, commander of Force X, an experimental unit of U.S. Army commandos. His unit specializes in lightning-quick, hit-and-run raids. Their activity has been very low profile thus far, but they've already participated in several key operations in the New Guinea campaign. They will be your passengers on this trip, gentlemen." Ireland looked directly at Tremain and Pancheri. "Of course, Major Farquhar will be along for the ride, as well. This mission is his baby, so I'll let him take it from here."

"Thank you, Admiral," Farquhar said, rising. He moved to an easel in the corner of the room and threw back a sheet of green canvas covering the stack of charts. The first chart showed a map of an area Tremain recognized as the northern coast of Mindanao. The map was highlighted with two big red circles, one on either side of a large promontory, approximately ten miles wide and extending northward into the sea.

"This briefing is primarily for the benefit of you navy chaps," Farquhar began. "The colonel and his men are already quite familiar with the mission and have been training extensively for it for the past two months. I wanted them to be here since we'll all be working closely together during the final phase of the training, which will involve you naval chaps to some extent."

A nod from the colonel and the admiral was the only response.

"This is our destination, gentlemen," Farquhar said, pointing to the area on the chart bounded by the red circles. "No doubt, you recognize it. I know Commander Tremain does. This is the northeastern coast of Mindanao, in the Philippine Islands. It has been occupied by the Japanese for going on two years, with an active insurgency leaving most of the countryside in contention. This particular area on the coast is sparsely defended, since there's nothing here but a few small villages connected across the jungle by dirt roads and trails. There are no harbors here, no airfields, nothing strategic, and it's more than fifty miles from the large Japanese garrison at Cagayan de Misamis. It's just a rugged, volcanic, jungle-covered piece of terrain, and as you might expect, the Japanese have chosen to garrison it with a very minimal force. The only presence there is a single company of Kempeitai operating from a makeshift fortification near a small Moro village, about two miles inland and south of the promontory." Farquhar pointed to a red X on the chart marking the spot. "It's a relatively quiet sector of the war, save for a few operations carried out by our guerilla allies, which have been more of a nuisance than anything else. They've not caused the Japanese any real angst so far." Farquhar paused as he heard footsteps in the passage beyond the closed door. He waited for the footsteps to fade into the myriad of dull noises emanating from the floating repair shop, before continuing. "I'm sure you both are wondering why this particular spot in the jungle interests us, especially after the utterly worthless value I've just ascribed to it."

"What are those two red circles on the chart, Major?" Marty asked eagerly.

"I'm just getting to that, Commander Pancheri. This first area," Farquhar pointed to the circle to the northeast, "is where you and your submarine will land Colonel Buckles and his three platoons. One hundred and eighteen men in all, along with their weapons and equipment. I've been told by the admiral that you'll have to strip down your submarine and leave most of your torpedomen behind in order to accommodate them, and I believe at this very moment your main deck is being fitted with two watertight compartments to add some additional stowage space."

The admiral, sitting with his arms crossed, nodded from his chair.

"You won't have any torpedoes aboard, Marty," Ireland said, with an encouraging glance. "The army needs every square foot in your torpedo rooms to hold their rafts and equipment, and that includes the tubes. Your torpedomen won't be needed."

"Son of a bitch!" Marty muttered under his breath, loud enough for only Tremain to hear.

Farquhar continued. "The other area shown here, closer to the mouth of the river, is where Commander Tremain will land me and my team of Filipino scouts. The *Whitefin* will be in the same boat—if you'll pardon the pun. She won't be near as crowded as the *Triggerfish*, but she'll be weighed down by close to a million rounds of thirty-caliber ammunition, five hundred mortar rounds, along with a plethora of other supplies for the guerilla units ashore. Everything from army boots to 'I shall return' cigarettes. The water's close to seventy-five feet deep there, so that should be plenty of depth for you, Commander, since the draft of your vessel is only sixteen feet, if my memory serves. Am I correct, Commander?"

Tremain exchanged skeptical glances with Pancheri, and drew an instant scowl from the admiral. Obviously Ireland would have been much happier if his submariners put on a show of shallow-water bravado in front of the army officers.

But a submarine captain always thought in terms of stealth and submergibility, and Tremain knew that seventy-five feet of water would barely cover up the periscopes, nor would it allow for any depth protection from a strafing aircraft loaded with depth bombs. And then there was the possibility of running aground, and the fact that the latest sounding chart of the area was probably surveyed when the U.S. took over the Philippines at the turn of the century.

"So what's the objective?" Tremain asked, adding with slight sarcasm, "Or are we not allowed to know that?"

Farquhar seemed unfazed by the remark and flipped to the next chart with one quick sweep of his arm. The new chart was a black-and-white photograph of a bald Japanese man wearing glasses and sitting on a hidden chair for what was undoubtedly a posed portrait. Tremain assumed the picture had been taken before the war, since a note in the corner, undoubtedly scrawled there by some intelligence analyst, read "1936." The man appeared small in stature, which was of no surprise given his race, and he had a pleasant smile on his face, indicating that the photo was probably taken for his family and friends. He bore no signs of the fanatic banzai warrior character which the American propaganda machine liked to ascribe to all Japanese people.

"This man is our objective. Our mission is to capture him. His name is Dr. Raizo Shokei, and he's one of Japan's leading physicians. Indeed, he was renowned worldwide before the war, even in the United States and Great Britain. In his particular field—which happens to be neurosurgery—he's been responsible for several notable breakthroughs, all appearing in prominent publications such as *The New England Journal of Medicine*. When the war began, Dr. Shokei, like any good doctor, volunteered his services to his country, and was given the rank of colonel as a physician in the Imperial Army. No doubt, he had every intention of putting his talents to use saving the lives of his fellow countrymen wounded on the battle-field. But, alas, the warlords in Tokyo had other plans for him. They shipped the good doctor off to Manchuria, where he was assigned to a little camp known to Allied intelligence as Unit ", which the two of you—and the rest of the world, for that ter—have probably never heard of until this moment."

Tremain and Pancheri shook their heads.

"That's part of the problem. Unit 731 goes under the guise of a regular army medical ward, healing those poor Chinese civilians suffering from the disease and hunger brought on by this war. But in reality, it's an experimental medical detachment—one of several across Japanese-occupied China—where Chinese prisoners are shipped by the hundreds to be the human guinea pigs in some of the most reprehensible experiments ever known to man. I can hardly convey to you two gentlemen the atrocities that we suspect are committed in these camps. Suffice it to say, they are abhorrent. Experiments with frostbite and hunger, experimental amputations, organ removal to see how long the body can last without a liver or a kidney or intestines, pregnant women ripped open at various stages of pregnancy and the fetus removed to see how long it can survive, experiments with new biological weapons—I'm talking the whole cup of fish, here.

"I see by your faces that you get the picture. It's a form of barbarism beyond belief, and that's the problem. It's so unbelievable and kept so tightly under wraps by the Imperial Army that we literally have no proof that these experiments are taking place. All we have are rumors from escaped prisoners, along with a handful of intercepted radio messages." Farquhar paused and placed his pointer on the photo of Dr. Shokei. "And along comes the doctor, just the man the army needs to dissect a few poor Chinese brains. But the problem is, the doctor's got a code of honor. He's got a passion for his profession that's akin to the bushido spirit. He's a firm believer in the Hippocratic Oath, as his journals well indicate. We know he was assigned to Unit 731, and we know that in less than a year, he was stripped of his rank and reassigned to Mindanao as a mere lieutenant. We suspect the reassignment was punishment for refusing to participate in the experiments, and meant to place him as far away as possible from his family, and from the Japanese populace, since the knowledge he carried in his head could send shock waves throughout the empire, perhaps leading some in the Japanese military to doubt the honor of their own leaders and turn on them.

"One of the secondary purposes of my last mission to Mindanao was to find out if the doctor was indeed there, and to

termine what kind of a force it would take to capture him."
Farquhar flipped back to the map and placed his pointer on a
small X next to a town a few miles inland from the coast.
"This is where the good doctor is now stationed, with a small,
lightly armed company of *Kempeitai* wash-ups. The garrison
consists of no more than a hundred men, living in a fenced
compound surrounded by a couple of loops of barbed wire.
They don't expect to be attacked by anything heavier than a
small guerilla force, and the guerillas have never tried it before, so they've got no reason to be anxious. The doctor
spends most of his time inside the compound, and though he
does lend his medical skills to the local villagers, he doesn't
do house calls. He never ventures out with the troops, even
when they go off for several days to hunt for guerillas in the
jungle.

"So, here's the plan. The *Triggerfish* will land the commandos at night on the east side of the promontory, approximately five miles to the north of the compound. My scouts
and I, aboard the *Whitefin*, will land on the other side of the
promontory, where we'll make contact with the local guerillas
and set up a series of diversionary explosions and ambushes
to draw a good portion of the garrison off into the jungle away
from home base. Meanwhile, Colonel Buckles and his men
will march inland, killing every Japanese soldier left behind,
capturing the good doctor, then making a beeline back to the
beach to escape aboard the *Triggerfish*. Likewise, I and my
scouts will return to the *Whitefin* and make our escape, and
then both submarines will join up in wolf pack for the return
trip. All of this must happen before dawn."

"What about Japanese air assets, Major?" the admiral asked
with his hand on his chin, as if he, too, had suddenly become
concerned about the safety of his submarines.

"The only Japanese airfield that might present a problem is
at Malabang, one hundred miles away, on the extreme western
side of the island. There's usually a couple of squadrons of
Zekes stationed there, and if alerted, they could reach our
subs in under forty-five minutes. To prevent this from happening, we've coordinated with Colonel Fertig's rebels in that
area to conduct a harassment attack on the airstrip on the
same night we plan to conduct our raid. If there are any last-

minute changes to our plans, we'll send a message to head-quarters to be relayed back to Colonel Fertig notifying him of the change. All he has to do is lob a few well-aimed mortars onto the runway and the Japs won't try to take off for several hours."

"I estimate I'll have my men back aboard in less than four hours, Admiral," Colonel Buckles said assuredly. "We'll be well clear of that place by sunup. Don't you worry, sir."

Ireland nodded with an appreciative smile.

"Are there any questions?" Farquhar asked.

"Just one." Tremain spoke up. "It seems that this plan is predicated on the idea that the Japanese aren't going to throw us a curveball. Where are the contingencies? I mean, what if Colonel Fertig's men don't ground the Jap air force? What if one of the subs runs aground? What if the guerillas decide not to help us?"

"I think I can ensure the support of the locals, Commander," Farquhar said airily. "As for the rest, let's just say, I trust our people, including you. To loosely quote Lord Wellington, we will endeavor to find out what we don't know, by what we do. We have eliminated our chief obstacles. The rest must be left to the fortunes of war."

"That's what bothers me, Major. You eliminated those two guerilla leaders and now you expect to go back and muster the support of their followers?"

"There you go again, Tremain, trying to tell me how to do my job," Farquhar snapped. "I think I have a better grip on the situation on the ground than you do, old boy, so why don't you confine your questions to matters involving transportation. That's all you need concern yourself with."

Tremain gripped the arms of his chair, but another scowl from Ireland made him bite back a response. The mission seemed so far-fetched and fantastical, as if someone wanted to do something creative so they thought up this crazy thing. Did Farquhar dream this one up one night and approach General MacArthur's staff with his wild idea? Could it really be worth two fleet-class submarines and over a hundred elite soldiers to capture this doctor whose worth as an eyewitness to Japanese death camps was dubious at best?

Once again, Tremain was beginning to suspect that something vital was being withheld, that this wild mission must have some ulterior purpose. Maybe the admiral was in on it, maybe the colonel, too. Who could tell? Either way, there was no sense in arguing the point. The mission was set; the submarines had been assigned. The *Whitefin* and her crew would be going. The only thing he could do now was follow orders and do everything in his power to protect his men.

This time, he would not let them down. This time, he would put the past behind him and be the captain they needed—*the captain they deserved.*

Chapter 21

THE northern coast of Mindanao looked much the same as it had when Tremain had seen it two months before. The night-shrouded shoreline appeared as nothing more than a great dark void stretching across the periscope's field of view. There were no lights, no ships in the world above, only blackness.

He pulled his face away from the eyepiece, taking a moment to give his eyes a break. Even with the conning tower and control room bathed in the red night lighting, he still had to strain to see anything at all in the dark world above. But that was a good thing, he kept telling himself. The Japanese could see no better, and it had not been by accident that the army chose a moonless night for this operation. It was one of the few elements of this plan Tremain had agreed with.

Tremain turned the periscope slowly through another complete revolution, focusing on the barren world above, but also mindful of the goings-on around him. The watch had just been relieved; new faces had replaced the men at the various stations with few words exchanged between them. They all knew the situation. After the mind-numbing two weeks of endless briefings and practice exercises, they all knew their part in the mission.

"Course zero-nine-zero, making turns for five knots," Tremain heard the new helmsman repeat to his predecessor before the latter followed the rest of the off-going watch down the hatch to the control room. The old faces had been replaced with new ones, but they were all familiar to Tremain, and they could have been clones of the men he'd served with in previous commands.

Brooks, the helmsman from Marvell, Arkansas, who had pushed mule-driven plows across his family's cotton fields prior to making his living at the controls of a multimillion-dollar submarine. Schroeder, the assistant quartermaster and first-generation American, whose grandparents still lived in Nazi Germany, and whose cousin now fought in the Wehrmacht. Valasquez, the periscope assistant and son of a copper miner, who had spent his youth catching sunbaked scorpions in the remote desert town of Ajo, Arizona. And fourscore others in the compartments below, each one an unwitting representative of a different piece of America. They were from a myriad of different backgrounds, different paths, all coming together at this one place and time, here and now, aboard the *Whitefin*, sitting off the coast of Japanese-held Mindanao Island, clear on the other side of the world.

"Sounding, eight fathoms." The report floated up the hatch from the control room.

"Very well." Tremain glanced at the clock on the bulkhead before returning his face to the periscope lens.

The seascape ahead was dark and barren, with a dazzling star-filled sky rising beyond the black horizon. Somewhere, in the darkness up ahead, no more than a thousand yards away, the *Triggerfish* was also prowling beneath the surface. According to the little wolf pack's agreed plan, the *Triggerfish* would be traveling on a matching course and speed, running parallel to the coastline in the same fashion as the *Whitefin*. No doubt, Marty Pancheri was peering through his own periscope at this very moment, searching the coastline for the little bay marking the spot where the wolf pack would part company.

Monroe cleared his throat and reported from the chart desk, "By dead reckoning, I hold us less than a mile away from the bay now, Captain."

"I concur, XO. I hold it visually," Tremain said, focusing the lens on a barely discernible outcropping of land to the southeast. "We should be hearing from our consort soon enough."

As if on cue, Doniphan announced, "Picking up transients, Captain."

"Put it on speaker."

At the flick of a switch the sonar set crackled to life. A series of irregular metallic taps was audible just above the background noise. The sharp staccato had an eerily lonely nature to it as it traversed the dark depths separating the two submarines, echoing off the sandy bottom only fifty feet below.

Tremain shot a glance at Monroe, who had already broken out the codebook.

"That's it, sir," Monroe said, holding his finger on the open page. "That's the signal to surface."

"Very well. Diving officer, surface the boat!"

Aaaooooggaaa! Aaaooooggaaa! Aaaooooggaaa!

The diving alarm sounded, followed immediately by Allendale's "Surface! Surface! Surface!"

High-pressure air sibilated into the main ballast tanks, shooting the *Whitefin*'s black hull to the surface in a flurry of bubbles, the only disturbance on an otherwise placid sea. Moments later, another rush of bubbles a quarter mile off the port bow proclaimed the *Triggerfish*'s rise from the depths. Men sprang from the hatches of both submarines and quickly manned the sparse surface weaponry, a precautionary measure against unexpected enemy patrol craft or barges. Then the diesel engines of both submarines came to life with a pulsating clamor that seemed out of place on such a quiet night.

Now standing on the wet planks of the *Whitefin*'s bridge, with the suction from the low-pressure blower whipping air past his ankles into the open hatch, Tremain turned to receive a report from Whately, the officer of the deck.

"Two engines on line, *sir*. The ship is manned for battle stations surface. Low pressure blow on all main ballast tanks in progress. Safety and negative tanks are flooded. Conning tower hatch, mess room access hatch and main induction are open. Depth eighteen feet."

Though his report was professional, the young officer's manner and his unnecessary emphasis on the word *sir* bordered on insolence. For the past two weeks Whately had made it clear that he still harbored a grudge from the last patrol. Most of the *Whitefin*'s junior officers had more or less accepted the fact that Tremain was to remain in command—two weeks of shore leave had a tendency to soften even the most mutinous of sailors. But with Whately it was a different story.

"Very well," Tremain answered, ignoring the attitude he'd been unable to curb during the weeks of training and the long northbound voyage from Fremantle. "Helm, Bridge. All ahead one-third. Left standard rudder. Steer course zero-seven-five."

The helmsman's acknowledgment floated up through the open hatch, and moments later the *Whitefin* began creeping forward, slowly closing the distance to the idling *Triggerfish*. Through his binoculars Tremain could see the other submarine's main deck, already alive with black-clad figures passing equipment and ammunition crates up from belowdecks and breaking out a dozen rafts and machine guns from the two awkward storage cylinders mounted just aft of the sub's conning tower.

"Halloo, Jack!" Marty Pancheri's voice resounded through a huge megaphone as the two submarines came alongside each other, separated by no more than fifty yards. "What are you fellas doing out here in the middle of nowhere!"

"Just following you, Marty!" Tremain called back, cupping his hands. "That rattletrap of yours makes so much noise, an LST could track it."

Several of the black-faced men on the *Whitefin*'s gun decks and lookout perches chuckled nervously at the remark.

"Haw, haw, haw! Verrrry funny!" Marty's amplified voice returned.

The main deck of the *Triggerfish* was now teeming with small clusters of army commandos checking packs, checking weapons, and inflating rafts. It was an impressive sight to see, 18 black gun barrels and black-greased faces glimmering faintly in the scant starlight.

"Well, this is where we leave you, Jack. We'll meet you back here tomorrow morning at oh-five-thirty!"

"Right, Marty!"

Tremain was suddenly aware of Major Farquhar standing silently beside him in black commando attire, flanked by his four grim-looking Filipino scouts, all armed to the teeth with Thompson machine guns, forty-five-caliber pistols, and grenades.

"Anything you'd like to add, Major?"

Farquhar shook his head, his face stoic as he stared across the water at the other submarine. He and Tremain had made it a point to avoid each other for most of the voyage. Every time they had a chance meeting, the major's face had worn that same carefree smile Tremain had grown to loathe. That is, every time until this moment. Now Farquhar appeared anything but carefree. In fact, he appeared quite distressed, as if he had suddenly come to the realization that the success of the entire mission rested solely on his shoulders.

"Hang on a second, Jack!" Marty called. Tremain saw a dark figure standing next to Marty on the *Triggerfish*'s bridge lean over and say something into his ear. Then Marty's face broke into a big grin as he lifted the megaphone again. "Colonel Buckles sends his Godspeed, Jack!"

Tremain smiled and waved. Marty and the colonel turned their attention back to their own ship. The *Triggerfish* picked up speed and pulled away, heading for its landing zone farther up the coast, its deck covered with the colonel's company of heavily armed soldiers.

"Mark the turn to the inlet, Captain." Monroe's voice came over the intercom. "New course one-seven-three."

The *Whitefin* had reached the spot where she would turn into the inlet and head up the small bay toward her own shallow landing zone.

"XO, Bridge, aye. Helm, right fifteen degrees rudder. Steady on course one-seven-three, all ahead one-third."

As the *Whitefin* came over to her new course, leaving a small wake behind her, Tremain noticed that Farquhar was still staring at the distant *Triggerfish*, now little more than a black patch in the dark night.

"He who desires, but does not act . . ." Farquhar quoted

a low murmur, his voice almost inaudible, with his eyes fixed in a dreamlike gaze.

"Are you all right, Major?"

At first, Farquhar did not answer. In fact, he appeared not to have heard Tremain at all. But after a few moments, he snapped out of his trance and turned to face Tremain, reverting to some semblance of his usual countenance.

"Of course, I'm all right," he said airily, but then paused for a moment, his face drawing suddenly sincere. "Listen, Tremain. Whatever happens ashore, in case something goes wrong, I want you to know that I'm deeply sorry for the unqualified pain in the arse I've been to you these past weeks. I want you to know that if I ever offended you with anything I've said or done, there was nothing personal in it. I really do appreciate your being a good sport on this trip."

"Maybe you could show your appreciation by telling me why you wanted my boat for this mission."

Farquhar smiled. "Let's just say that, despite all of our professional differences, I feel that I can relate to you on a personal level. We are not as different as you might think, Tremain. You and I share a unique brand of loyalty to the men who have fought under our commands. Neither of us would ever forget those who gave up their young lives, nor would we forget the enemy who snuffed them out. We both believe that the score must be settled, no matter what the cost, if we ever hope to remunerate the tormented souls that haunt our dreams at night."

Tremain suddenly realized that Farquhar was referring to his short-lived obsession with the *Shigure*. Farquhar had probably learned about the whole thing from the junior officers over cribbage, and, for some reason, that annoyed Tremain extremely. The smug look on Farquhar's face bothered him, too. The English major appeared to be completely content, and Tremain could not tell if it was from satisfaction at having guessed the inner workings of his soul, or if it was for some other reason. Whatever the reason, the simple fact that Farquhar knew about the *Shigure* incident made Tremain uneasy. For Farquhar to bring it up now, in such a blatant yet underhanded way, with H-hour fast approaching, could only mean that he wished to deliver one last parting stroke before he disembarked. The final blow in the battle of wits they had been engaged in since day one.

"I'm afraid I don't know what the hell you're talking about, Major," Tremain said, intent on depriving him of the satisfaction.

"Oh, I think you do, Tremain. I think you do."

Chapter 22

"**FABRIANO!** Shelby! Penn!" Whately called from the dark brush above the beach. "Get those rafts off the beach and hide them up here. This is where we'll wait."

Fabriano ran down the beach with both Penn and Shelby and dragged the two heavy rubber rafts up the steep sandy slope to the patch of bushes where Whately sat with the signal lamp. Fabriano's arms were exhausted, and his bad shoulder was sore from rowing back and forth to the *Whitefin* for the past two hours. The submarine was now idling three hundred yards from the shore, in the center of the little bay. He had made eight round trips, rowing boxes of ammunition and other supplies to the eagerly waiting Moros lining the starlit shoreline. Only minutes before, this beach had been a silent frenzy of three or four dozen dark figures, carting supplies off into the jungle, but now it was barren. Fresh footprints in the sand were the only indication the Moro guerillas had ever been there. They had vanished into the jungle along with all of the supplies, and the British major and his four scouts had gone with them.

Now, out of breath and thankful for a few moments rest, Fabriano plopped down on the soft sand in the concealed spot

Whately had chosen. According to plan, they were to wait here until the major and his men returned, and then ferry the weary commandos back to the submarine.

"Here, take a drink."

Whately held out a canteen, which Fabriano gladly accepted. The water had the distinct metallic taste of the ship's potable water tanks. On top of that, it was lukewarm, but it tasted good all the same. When he had finished drinking, Fabriano somewhat reluctantly tossed the canteen over to Penn, who was lying on the ground next to him, and saw his slightly, shadowy form take a long drink as well, passing it in turn to Shelby.

"Aye, that's fine submarine water, isn't it?" Shelby said.

"Damn shit tastes fishy to me," Penn commented.

"Penn, you asshole, you've never been thankful a day in your life for what the Good Lord's dropped in your lap."

"Would you two shut up?" Whately scolded. "There might be Jap patrols out there. Just keep quiet and wait! That's all you have to do!"

"What are we waitin' for, anyway, Lieutenant?"

"For the major and his men to get back, Shelby. If you'd listened to the fucking briefing, you'd know that. Now just sit there and keep quiet!"

Fabriano tried not to look at the two sailors next to him, but he could feel their eyes on him, and it left him wondering when they would finally make their move. Their sudden, last-minute inclusion on this mission certainly could not have been by chance.

In the two weeks of training leading up to it, the *Whitefin* had spent several days sitting in a small bay south of Fremantle practicing ferrying supplies ashore using the two ungainly rubber rafts Fabriano had become so familiar with. Naturally, Fabriano had been chosen as one of the coxswains, since he had more experience with small boats than nearly everyone else aboard. The plan was for Lieutenant Whately to serve double duty as a rower in Fabriano's boat and as the officer in charge of the operation, while two other strong-backed sailors, Davison and Morely, handled the other craft. The four had practiced and practiced until they could row the ten tons of equipment ashore in less than an hour and fifty-five minutes. But shortly before the *Whitefin* arrived in the small Mindanao inlet for the real thing, Davison and Morely had both come down with sudden chills and high fever, and subsequently both were confined to their racks. The pharmacist's mate had hardly made his diagnosis before two new volunteers stepped forward to take their place—Shelby and Penn.

Of course, Fabriano knew something was up. Ever since Shelby's strange comments in Camp Kalgoorlie, things had not been the same between them.

From the moment Penn and Shelby volunteered for this mission, Fabriano knew that they were in cahoots. Undoubtedly, Penn had told Shelby about the money, and now the two were out to split a small fortune between them—that is, if they could get their hands on it. The only person Fabriano was uncertain about was Whately. True, the lieutenant had eagerly accepted them as the new volunteers, but Fabriano could not tell whether he was involved. It was a distinct possibility, and one that he could not rule out.

Fabriano suddenly considered his present situation. All three sailors were unarmed, their three M1A1 carbine rifles leaning against a nearby tree. Only Whately carried a forty-five-caliber pistol, holstered on his belt. Fabriano suddenly wondered what would happen if he were to make a move toward the rifles. If Whately was in on it, then he would undoubtedly try to stop him.

He had made up his mind to do it, when a low rumble that sounded like thunder rolled across the jungle. It seemed to come from the east, far inland, on the other side of the mountainous promontory. It could not have been thunder, since the starry night sky was perfectly clear.

The rumble sounded again, and was soon accentuated by short staccato reports, undoubtedly the sound of distant automatic weapons fire. Fabriano naturally assumed it to be the army elite troops carrying out their own mission, but Whately did not seem as dismissive. The lieutenant sat up straight and glanced at his watch several times.

"What the hell?" he muttered.

"Isn't that just our army buddies making noise, Lieutenant?"

"If it is, then they're a bit early. They're supposed to wait for the major's diversion, and according to plan that's not supposed to happen for another ninety minutes."

The distant weapons fire continued, increasing in intensity with each passing minute. The *Thump!* and *Kaboom!* of distant mortars thundered across the miles of jungle. Whately appeared somewhat flustered as he tried to understand what was going on. He cast a glance down at the lamp by his feet and was obviously considering signaling the *Whitefin*. The submarine's black hull was completely invisible from the shoreline, but they knew it was there, sitting in the bay, only a few hundred yards away. Surely, the men on the *Whitefin*'s bridge could hear it, too.

"Lieutenant," Shelby's deep voice intoned from a dark shadow that hid his face, "don't you think you ought to go try to find the major? Maybe he knows what's going on."

It was at that moment that Fabriano knew Whately was not involved in Shelby and Penn's little conspiracy. Shelby never would have made such a suggestion unless he was trying to get Whately out of the way. Now Fabriano knew that the two cohorts were acting by themselves—and that they would make a move the instant they got him alone.

"No, Shelby!" Whately retorted, completely oblivious to the small drama being played out within his little squad. "Our orders are to stay right here. If those army assholes want to act like a bunch of cowboys, they can. But we're sticking to the plan."

Fabriano thought he heard a muffled curse come from Penn's direction, but he pretended not to notice. Better that they not know he was on to them.

"SIR, it sounds like more gunfire. Lots of it," one of the lookouts called from his perch.

Tremain and every other man on the bridge scanned the dark mass of land to the east. For the better part of an hour they had heard distant gunfire from both large- and small-caliber weapons, the sounds of a great land battle emanating across the land- and seascape. Far inland they could detect faint flashes against the night sky. The flashes seemed to accompany the larger, more thunderous reports, and Tremain concluded that they had to be mortars going off.

"Bridge, XO," the intercom intoned. "I've taken a line of bearing on those flashes, Captain, and plotted it on the chart. Assuming the *Triggerfish* landed the troops two hours ago on the other side of the promontory, those flashes correspond perfectly with Colonel Buckles's estimated position."

"XO, Bridge, aye."

Tremain looked at his watch. H-hour was still thirty minutes away. Something was wrong—terribly wrong.

According to the plan, Farquhar and his Moro guerillas were to launch a diversionary raid against a small Japanese refueling station along the coast road a few miles inland and to the south, mustering out the Japanese garrison and drawing them away from their compound so that Buckles and his men could make a lightning assault and steal away with the doctor. H-hour was set for the moment Farquhar and his men commenced their attack on the refueling station. That was the instance that was supposed to set the whole ball in motion. But that was not supposed to happen for another half hour. Right now, this mass of gunfire was not coming from the south, but from the east, somewhere along Buckles's line of advance. The seemingly incessant fusillade of distant machine gun and mortar fire certainly did not have the characteristics of a lightning-fast, hit-and-run raid. Tremain could only conclude that Buckles and his men had run headfirst into enemy troops during their march across the jungle, and were now engaged in a major firefight.

"Bridge, Radio. *Triggerfish* has broken radio silence, sir. I've got Commander Pancheri on the RBH-2 radio."

In less than ten seconds, Tremain had dropped down both ladders to the control room, shoving his way aft past the curious onlookers until he reached the radio room, where the radioman of the watch sat adjusting the fine-tuning knob on the AM set.

"Able Dog Mike, this is Romeo Easy Baker, over," Marty's garbled and staticy voice intoned over the small speaker.

Tremain snatched up the handset. "Romeo Easy Baker, this is Able Dog Mike, go ahead, over."

"Able Dog Mike, we've encountered heavy resistance." Distress was apparent in Marty's voice, not to mention the fact that he had abandoned the codebook to speak in plain English. "Buckles's men were ambushed . . . walked into a trap . . . heavy resistance encountered . . . regimental strength, at least . . . Buckles dead . . . many casualties . . . evacuating survivors . . . abort mission, repeat, abort mission."

Tremain took a few moments to digest the information.

So that was it. The mission was a scrub, a total disaster. Undoubtedly, they had been betrayed by someone, probably one of the guerillas who had been trusted with prior knowledge of the plan. How many brave American soldiers had lost their lives, how many of the men who had been in *Pelias*'s briefing room that day? And all for nothing.

"Romeo Easy Baker, this is Able Dog Mike," Tremain spoke as evenly as he could. "Understood. Godspeed. Out!"

Tremain gave the handset back to the radioman, and then took a moment to consider the situation. He took no notice of the gaggle of onlookers filling the doorway of the cramped room, their faces red in the night lighting.

He was left in a precarious position. If the Japanese had enough prior knowledge about the operation that they were able to move an entire regiment into the area, who knew what else the Japanese had in store for them? His ship and crew were in danger. The mission, the Japanese doctor, the Moro guerillas—none of that mattered now. The only thing that mattered was getting his men back aboard, and back home again safely.

He looked at his watch. It read 0034. Farquhar and his scouts were not due back for another several hours. The smart thing to do, the easiest thing to do, would be to get Whately and his men back aboard and head for open water immediately. It would be dawn in five hours, and he had to assume that enemy planes would appear overhead with the rising of the sun— that is, assuming the plan to disable the enemy airfield at Malabang had also been compromised. If that were indeed the case, then the *Whitefin* would need time to get out to deep water before the enemy aircraft arrived. This shallow bay hardly afforded enough room to submerge the *Whitefin*'s masts, let alone hide her three-hundred-foot-long hull, below a few feet of its calm, crystal-clear water. An enemy pilot flying overhead would need only to look down to spot the American submarine lying just beneath the surface.

That was the smart thing to do. Get Whately and his men aboard, clear the area, live to fight another day. No doubt, the major and his scouts had heard the battle, too, and would realize the plan had gone awry. Hopefully they would have the wherewithal to head deeper into the jungle to seek refuge among the guerillas rather than attempt to make it back to the submarine. They could be extracted some other time, perhaps in a few weeks, after things had quieted down again.

Still, there was always the chance that Farquhar was counting on the *Whitefin* to be there to extract him, and was hustling back to the bay at this very minute.

"Try making contact with the major. One of his scouts had a handy-talkie. See if you can reach them."

"They might be able to hear us, Captain," the radioman said with uncertainty, "but I doubt we'll be able to hear them. Those little SCR-536s only have a range of about a mile. But I'll give it a try, sir."

As the radioman lined up his equipment to transmit, a thought suddenly occurred to Tremain. He had already broken radio silence once, responding to the *Triggerfish*. Perhaps that transmission, though lasting only a few brief seconds, had raised the attention of a Japanese EMF listening station. It would be odd for the Japanese to have such a station in such a remote area, but it was not unheard of. And although the pre-mission intelligence briefing had not mentioned the presence of any, Tremain concluded that it was better to play it safe. If the Japanese did have listening stations somewhere nearby, any further emission from the *Whitefin*'s powerful radio transmitter would only help them to lock down the submarine's position.

"On second thought, belay that. Don't transmit." Tremain glanced up at the shelf holding the radioman's manuals and books. "Hand me that pad of paper. I have an idea."

"Aye, Captain," the radioman answered, looking somewhat puzzled.

Tremain scribbled a few lines down and then ripped off the sheet, parting the crowd of onlooking sailors as he groped his way back up the ladders to the darkened bridge.

"Flash this to the men ashore," Tremain ordered, handing the paper to the sailor holding the signal lamp.

"Aye, aye, sir," the sailor answered, holding the paper in the red glow emanating from the open bridge hatch, and raising his eyebrows as he read it.

As the signal lamp's noisy shutter clattered open and shut, Tremain glanced at the dark promontory, its far side still alive with faint flashes and the muffled rattle of gunfire. He could only imagine what Marty was going through right now. Somewhere over there in the bay beyond the dark land mass, the fleeing commandos would be piling into their rafts in decimated squads, with pursuing Japanese troops hot on their heels. Some would be left to fight a rear-guard action attempting to buy their brethren precious time to escape. Or perhaps the Japanese had had the foresight to set up secondary ambush points along the commandos' line of retreat. Perhaps they had hidden machine gun nests along the shoreline to rake the flimsy rubber rafts as the commandos frantically rowed them across the several hundred yards of open water to the *Triggerfish*. Of course, Marty would wait for them as long as he possibly could, giving them whatever covering fire the *Triggerfish* could afford. Perhaps he'd even move in closer to the shore, risking a lucky shot from an enemy mortar. But at some point, he would have to get out of there. The *Triggerfish* would have to break off and head for the open sea, undoubtedly leaving some of Buckles's men to the mercy of the Japanese.

It was a tough call to make, and one that Tremain hoped he himself would not have to make in the next few hours. Then he suddenly wondered if the disgruntled Whately was cursing his name up and down at this very moment for assigning him to lead the shore party. Of course, he had had good intentions, with the thought that something different, a little excitement, a little time ashore on an enemy-held island might be just the thing to quell the young officer's bitterness. As the situation stood now, Whately was probably not very happy about the assignment.

"They're acknowledging, sir," the sailor with the signal lamp reported.

Tremain nodded, and then looked out at the dark shoreline, three hundred yards away. A dull solitary light flashed back at them from the blackness. Whately and his men had received the message.

Chapter 23

"**WHAT'S** it say, Lieutenant?" Penn asked anxiously as the four men crouched in the cover of the brush watching the flashes from the *Whitefin*'s signal lamp.

"It seems we're to abort the mission," Whately said with incredulity. "They want us to try to reach the major on our walkie-talkie. They want us to find out what his status is. If he's close, we're to wait for him. If not, we're to leave one raft behind and return to the ship immediately."

"You mean all that gunfire out there is from the Japs?" Penn asked in disbelief.

"What do I look like, Information? All I know is what I just told you."

Fabriano instinctively crouched down, glancing at the dark jungle all around them. Up until now, this had been nothing more than a simple supply drop. Now he was faced with the thought that the entire area might be alive with enemy troops. From all that Fabriano had heard about Japanese soldiers, he assumed they were good jungle fighters. According to a marine he had shared a smoke with on Tulagi, the Japanese had a way of moving noiselessly through the dense brush. The marine thought they had better night vision, too. That fact left

Fabriano feeling quite uncomfortable, even diverting his thoughts temporarily from Shelby and Penn's looming plot.

Whately groped around in the darkness, rustling with the pack at his feet until he came up with the bread loaf–sized SCR-536 handheld radio. A muffled tone of static emanated from the small speaker as he extended the forty-inch whip antenna and turned up the volume.

"Well, here goes nothing," Whately said hesitantly, holding the radio to his face like a telephone and depressing the talk key. He was obviously uncomfortable with the idea of transmitting in enemy-held country. "Able Dog Fox, Able Dog Fox, this is Stingray, over . . . Able Dog Fox, Able Dog Fox, this is Stingray, over."

All four men waited intently, as he repeated the same call three or four times.

"I think I hear them," Whately said finally, pressing the speaker against his ear. "I can hear something. It's sporadic."

"Could be the Japs, sir," mumbled Shelby.

"Not unless they're speaking English." Whately then stood up and walked into a nearby clearing, evidently in an attempt to improve the reception. "Able Dog Fox, this is Stingray. Abort. Repeat, abort, over . . . Able Dog Fox, did you copy my last, over? . . . Able Dog Fox, say again . . . Able Dog Fox, come in."

Obviously, Whately was having difficulty hearing the person on the other end.

"I think it's the major," he said, adjusting the frequency knob, "but I'm not sure he heard me. I'm only picking up bits and pieces."

"It's this damn jungle, Lieutenant," Shelby intoned. "I bet if you walked a hundred steps in that direction, you'd find the major and his men sitting behind a tree, talking on their radio wondering where the hell we are. They might be only a couple hundred yards away, and you'd never know it."

"Or they could be miles away, sir," Fabriano said, instantly picking up on Shelby's strategy and trying to head it off before Whately got any wild ideas into his head. "There's no way to tell."

"What do you want me to do, Fabriano, just abandon them here?" Whately snapped with an admonishing tone.

Fabriano said nothing. He said nothing because Whately was absolutely correct. He did want to abandon them. He cared little for the British major or his scouts. Their well-being was no concern of his. At this point, his own personal safety depended only on returning to the ship, where Shelby and Penn would be hard-pressed to corner him. It was the surest way to avert whatever the two had in store for him.

"No, sir," Fabriano said blankly. "I was just thinking we could take one of those rafts and leave the other one behind for the major. Isn't that what the *Whitefin* ordered us to do, anyway?"

"Use your head, Fabriano," Whately said, the strain of indecision apparent in his voice. "What if some of the major's men are wounded? Then what? We can't just leave them here."

"An excellent point, sir," Shelby said from the shadows. "I'm surprised at you, Mikey, wanting to turn tail and run. You ought to be ashamed of yourself. Remind me never to trust you to watch my back."

Fabriano could not see Shelby's features in the darkness, but he was certain the sailor's big round face was set in an evil glare.

"I have a better idea, Lieutenant," Shelby continued. "Didn't I hear the major say there was a dirt road just a few hundred yards yonder?"

Whately nodded impatiently. "Yes, the coast road. Go on, get to your point."

"Well, sir, the way I see it, one or two of us could take the radio and start walking toward that road. If we can't raise the major by the time we reach it, we come on back to the beach and do what Mikey here wants to do. We head back to the ship."

Fabriano easily detected the playacting in Shelby's voice, the sinister civility, but Whately seemed too overcome with anxiety to notice.

"At least that way, sir, we'll be able to say we did all we could before we left them here." Shelby added, "I for one know it'd clear my conscience."

"All right," Whately said finally. "Who'll go then?"

"I'd be happy to do it, sir," Shelby said innocently, motioning to the radio in Whately's hand. "Except that I don't know how to use one of those things, and I know Mikey and Penn don't know how to either."

"So, I'll have to go." Whately concluded.

"I'll go with you, Lieutenant." Fabriano spoke up eagerly, suddenly realizing that Shelby's so-called plan would leave him alone with Shelby and Penn, while the lieutenant—his one and only prospect for assistance—went gallivanting across the jungle on what might be a fool's errand. His best hope was to stay with Whately.

"Begging your pardon, sir," Shelby said before the lieutenant could answer. "But Penn here's a much better choice for that. He used to be a logger up in Alaska before the war. Used to spend days out in the woods with no one around. He's got a keener sense of direction than anyone you've ever met, sir. Isn't that so, Penn?"

There was a pause as Penn was evidently slow to pick up on his cohort's cue. "Err-uh, yeah . . . that's right, sir. Spent years in the woods."

"Really? All right, Penn, you're with me. Get your rifle. Shelby and Fabriano, you two stay put and watch for any signals from the ship."

"He's full of shit, sir!" Fabriano said abruptly. "I doubt Penn's spent a day in the woods in his life. I'm the one who volunteered. Let me go."

"Damn it, Fabriano," Whately fumed. "Keep your voice low! Not two minutes ago you wanted to leave the major and his men to fend for themselves, and now you want to help me go find them. I don't fucking buy it. You're staying here, and that's final. Come on, Penn."

Penn smiled smugly at Fabriano as he shouldered his weapon. While Whately was checking the magazine on his own forty-five-caliber pistol, Shelby strolled over to Penn and whispered something into his ear, prompting Fabriano to wonder if the two also had ill plans in store for the lieutenant. For a moment, he considered blurting out all of his suspicions to Whately before the officer disappeared into the jungle, leaving him alone with Shelby. But what could he say? That Shelby and Penn were after him to extort the nearly fifty thousand dollars he had stolen from the *Chevalier*? That Shelby and Penn might go to any lengths to get their hands on it? Whately would either think he was off his rocker or have him arrested once they returned to the ship.

"Good luck to you, sir," Shelby called out, as the shadowy forms of Penn and Whately moved swiftly across the clearing and plunged into the brush, parting fronds out of their way as they made for the coastal road. Soon they disappeared from view, with only an occasional rustling piece of foliage to mark their progress. Within minutes the jungle had swallowed them up entirely, and the night fell deathly silent once again, except for the gunfire of the distant battle.

Now Fabriano was all alone with Shelby.

Out of the corner of his eye, Fabriano noticed that Shelby had moved over to stand beside the rifles leaning against the tree. His face was hidden by shadow, but Fabriano could tell that Shelby was looking at him. The hooligan was undoubtedly pleased with himself for achieving the upper hand. Outwardly, Fabriano pretended not to notice. Inwardly, he was cursing himself for not paying closer attention. Now that Shelby had control of the weapons, he was faced with only two options. The first was to approach Shelby in a friendly manner, acting as if there was no tension between them, coming straight out with a proposal to give him and Penn even thirds of the money as long as they kept silent about it. Of course, that option assumed they were willing to share the money and did not want all of it for themselves. $23,890 each certainly sounded a lot better than $15,926 each.

The other option was to run and hide, to get away from Shelby, and to lay low in the brush until Whately and Penn returned. But how long would that take? Suddenly, Fabriano realized the grievous error he had made in letting Whately get out of his sight. He should have demanded to go with him, not taking no for an answer.

Now, with the possibility of enemy foot patrols in the area, calling out for the officer would be too risky. He would have to go after Whately, catch up with him, give some lame explanation for his actions, and then make sure that he stayed arm and arm with the lieutenant for the rest of the time ashore—until the moment they set foot back on board the *Whitefin*.

"Where the fuck do you think you're going?" She

called to him. Evidently the big sailor was watching his every move, and had noticed that he was inching closer to the bank of foliage on the other side of the clearing.

"I got to take a leak," Fabriano replied with forced calmness, then turned abruptly and began to walk toward the dense underbrush, now less than fifteen yards away.

Behind him, Fabriano heard the buckle from one of the rifle straps clinking against a gun barrel and immediately assumed that Shelby had grabbed one of the guns. Fabriano needed no further prompting to make a break for it. He sprinted forward, darting for the relative safety of the brush. Once there, he was certain he could lose Shelby, since the brawny thug would have a much harder time navigating through the dense foliage. Running as fast as his sea legs would take him across the soft sand, he had almost reached the first layer of trees when he heard a strange sound behind him. It sounded like the whirring rotor of a fan blade. An instant too late, he realized that it was one of the carbine rifles, flying through the air, spinning end over end with a velocity that only Shelby's powerful arms could have produced. The flying rifle had been thrown with incredible accuracy, the butt end striking Fabriano squarely in the center of the back, knocking him off balance, and sending him face-first into the sand.

As Fabriano rose up, struggling to breathe through a nose and mouth caked with the powdery sand, he turned around to find Shelby's dark form already standing behind him, his large hands clutching the recently thrown rifle.

"Thought you could get away from me, did you, Mikey?" His voice sounded sadistic, almost vengeful. "You should know better than that."

"What the hell did you do that for, asshole?" Fabriano tried his best to play dumb.

But that did not go over very well with Shelby, who instantly swiped the butt of the rifle across Fabriano's jaw, knocking him senseless and once again facedown in the sand. When Fabriano collected his bearings this time, he realized that blood was pouring from his mouth, and that two of his teeth were missing. Reeling from the pain in his jaw, he rolled onto his back and was met once again by the butt of the rifle as Shelby brought it down with great force onto his unprotected stomach. His lungs exhausted every last cubic inch of air, and his face turned blue in the long minute that passed before he could take in another breath.

"I thought we were shipmates, Mikey," Shelby said to the crumpled, wheezing figure at his feet, as he fingered the bloody butt end of the rifle with his free hand. "I thought you might come around, so I told Penn to wait. I told him to hold off. That's right, I did. I told him, 'Mikey's my shipmate, and Mikey's going to share that money with me, don't you worry none.' But that never happened. That never fucking happened, Mikey! You were going to walk off this ship someday and never even let your old pal Shelby know about the loot. I gave you ample opportunity. Yes, I did. You had plenty of chances to let me in on it, but you didn't."

"I don't know what the fuck you're talking about," Fabriano mumbled through swollen lips.

"That's not the attitude I'm looking for, Mikey!"

An instant later Fabriano's face met one of Shelby's size thirteen steel-toed boots. His head recoiled from the impact in a splash of blood and saliva. A sharp, biting pain covered his entire face as his nose shattered from the blow. In a foggy daze, Fabriano struggled onto his hands and knees and made a desperate attempt to get away from his antagonist, but the butt of the rifle stopped him dead in his tracks again, coming down hard onto his back with such force that he felt his back might break. He was having trouble seeing straight, and his body ached all over from the pummeling. There was no way he could fight back. Shelby was employing very little restraint, meting out the beating with a much greater degree of enthusiasm than Fabriano had expected.

After a few more minutes of the same, Shelby finally let up and allowed him to take in a breath of air and collect his senses. He was completely at Shelby's mercy. Any moment now, he fully expected Shelby to make him a simple offer. Agree to share the *Chevalier*'s money, or the beating would continue—how much longer, Fabriano could only guess. Shelby certainly did not intend to kill him, since he was the only one who knew the location of the money, and killing him would defeat the whole purpose of Shelby and Penn's plan. But Fabriano did not intend to find out how far Shelby would go. He had put up enough resistance for believability, and now it was time to capitulate. He would agree to share the wealth to save his skin. Of course, when the time came, he fully intended to lie about the money's location.

"Well, Mikey," Shelby said, his voice showing a trace of its previous compassion for the first time, "I don't right know what to say before I finish this thing."

"Wait, Clem," Fabriano said between breaths, raising a bloody hand in the air and trying to sound as convincing as possible. "You don't have to. You're right. I should have told you about the money. I wanted to lots of times, but didn't. Look, you and Penn have won. Okay? I'll split the loot with you. I'll even give each of you guys a third."

Shelby peered down at him, and in the darkness Fabriano could not tell if he was scowling or smiling, or both. After a few moments, Shelby began to chuckle coolly.

"That's mighty big of you, Mikey. Thanks, but I think we'll take it all, just the same."

"Don't push me, Clem. We're splitting it into thirds, or the deal's off."

"And just what deal are you referring to, Mikey?"

Fabriano looked at Shelby. Though his face was still fixed in a wide grin, Shelby's eyes looked nothing less than evil.

"Look, Clem. You and Penn both know you need me if you ever hope to lay your hands on that money. It's not on the ship anymore. I've hidden it in Fremantle, and I've hidden it well, believe me. You could spend every last hour of every liberty call for the next year searching the town and I guarantee you'll never find it. So you either agree to splitting it into thirds, or the two of you can go to hell, and you'll never get your slimy hands on it."

Shelby broke out in laughter, obviously unmoved by the threat. Fabriano certainly did not expect this kind of response, and was considering changing his offer to a forty-forty-twenty split, when Shelby finally stopped laughing and looked at him with a contemptuous expression.

"You did hide it well, Mikey, that's for sure." Shelby said then smiled diabolically before adding, "It took Penn an hour to find it, and another half hour to dig it up."

Fabriano instantly felt his face turn white and his fingers go numb, half-disbelieving what he had just heard.

"You really ought to watch your back out there in that Australian countryside, Mikey. Hell, I'm just an old submariner, but even I know horses leave tracks that are easy to follow."

For several seconds Fabriano sat dumbfounded, suddenly insensible to every one of his many wounds. All this time, throughout the entire patrol, ever since Camp Kalgoorlie, Shelby and Penn had had the money. Penn must have followed him that day when he rode out into the country and buried it three feet down on the small hill overlooking the creek a few miles outside the camp. And just like that, all of his efforts to get the money back home, all of the deceit, all of the close calls he'd had since becoming a submariner, had amounted to nothing. But even that dismal thought did not compare to the cold realization that suddenly came over him as he saw Shelby squeeze the rifle in both of his hands, holding it like a baseball bat.

If Shelby and Penn already had the money, then his whole hypothesis about their plot had to be wrong. They had not planned on blackmailing him at all. *They planned to murder him.* He was now the only variable that stood in the way of their plans.

Fabriano met Shelby's cold, unfeeling gaze. The big sailor was winding up for the final blow, eyeing Fabriano's head as if it were a ball sitting atop a baseball tee.

"Wait, Clem. Don't do it."

"Sorry, Mikey. It's nothing personal, you know, just business between sailors."

Fabriano tried to scurry away, but Shelby came after him.

"Hold still, you asshole. This'll all be over in a jiffy." Shelby said it almost laughing, apparently amused by the chase.

The butt of the rifle swung once, and caught only air. Fabriano had ducked in the nick of time. But he did not adjust in time for Shelby's counterswing, which made contact with the side of his head, pitching his body into the sand once again was a hard blow, and he could see nothing but stars for next several seconds, even with his eyes wide open. blinking several times and regaining his vision, he disco that Shelby was hovering over him again. Apparently, lous brute was waiting for him to come to before dealing him the final blow.

"I might think twice about this, if I weren't having so much fun," Shelby said in a devilish manner as he lifted the gun above his head, preparing to bring the rifle butt down in a vertical, spiking jab, a blow that would certainly split Fabriano's head like a coconut.

Fabriano closed his eyes and waited for the crushing blow, somewhat resigned to his fate. He had no choice. He could not get away.

Then suddenly he heard a crack, like the sound of a rifle butt coming in contact with a human skull, but it was not his skull, so it had to be Shelby's. Then he heard Shelby moan, and felt the dull thud as the two-hundred-twenty-five-pound sailor fell to the ground.

When Fabriano finally opened his eyes, he was not surprised to see Shelby's bulk lying motionless in the sand beside him. However, he was surprised to see Whately and Penn kneeling side by side only a few paces away, both looking quite frightened, both with their hands behind their heads, and both bleeding from several contusions on their swollen faces. Behind them and all around the small clearing stood more than a dozen dark figures, holding rifles tipped with shiny foot-long bayonets. Fabriano assumed that one of these must have knocked Shelby unconscious. At first he thought these were the guerillas that had off-loaded the supplies from the rafts earlier that evening. But then his heart nearly seized when he discerned that these men were wearing uniforms. In the faint starlight, he could make out the distinctive puttees covering the lower legs from the ankle to the knees.

The triumphant moment of surviving Shelby's attack dissolved instantly and was replaced by stark terror as Fabriano realized he was completely surrounded by Japanese soldiers.

Chapter 24

THE two figures in the rubber raft pulled up their oars just in time to let the low surf carry their tiny craft the rest of the way in to the shore. The raft skidded to a stop on the steep, sandy beach, and each man stuck a leg over the side to anchor the craft until the foamy surge ebbed back into the bay. Within seconds they had pulled the raft up to the concealment of the brush, and they sat there for a moment making sure the situation around them was safe.

Jack Tremain tugged at the black sweater and cap as he held the M1A1 Thompson submachine gun at the ready, waiting for any sign of trouble to emerge from the jungle around him. When he was satisfied that there was no one around, he made a hand signal to his companion that they could continue hiding the raft. Miguel gave him an acknowledging nod from underneath a similar black ski cap and began covering the small craft with the fallen fronds strewn on the sandy ground around them.

Tremain took his eyes off the surrounding jungle for a brief moment to observe his steward turned commando. He could hardly believe that he had asked Miguel to come with him on such a crazy and potentially hazardous foray ashore. But he needed someone who knew the country and spoke the language in case he ran into the guerillas, and Miguel had seemed eager to go. The trusty steward was certainly no combat soldier, and certainly had never in his life fired a weapon like the M1 carbine now hanging loosely by its shoulder strap low across his back.

Tremain considered that he himself was one to talk. He was no soldier either. Who was he kidding? He hardly belonged here on this dark enemy shoreline, armed to the teeth and dressed more like a fisherman than a commando.

The last few hours seemed like a blur to him, almost like a dream now that he was no longer in the controlled habitat of his submarine. The long hour on the bridge spent waiting for any indication at all from Whately and his men. The hour of contemplation after that, weighing his options and finally coming to the conclusion that he would go ashore to find the misplaced lieutenant and his team and get them back aboard the ship. The time spent breaking out the *Whitefin*'s own rubber raft—a raft much smaller and much more ungainly than the ones used by Whately and the commandos. The time spent searching for a suitable pair of blue dungarees to replace his khaki pants, which would have stuck out in the night like a white flag. And finally, the long row across a half mile of water to reach the ominous but beckoning shoreline. It all seemed to run together.

The decision seemed crazy now, looking back on it. What could he hope to accomplish here? He was well outside of his domain. He belonged on the bridge of his ship, a fact that Monroe had reminded him of at least half a dozen times during the last-minute preparations before disembarking, as Monroe followed him around the ship.

"They could've run into trouble, Captain," Monroe had said on one of the many occasions. "They could be dead. Who knows what you'll be walking into."

"That's a chance I have to take." Tremain had turned on his second-in-command to say with finality, "We're not leaving until those men are back aboard."

"You're place is here, sir," Monroe said, pausing and then adding feebly, "Please, Captain. Let me go instead."

Monroe's tone had sounded pleading, almost desperate in nature, and Tremain had begun to wonder whether his executive officer was more worried about being left in command of the ship than he was about his captain's safety.

"I have to go, Chris. Those are my men. I sent them there. It's my responsibility to make sure they get back home. And, besides, I owe it to them after that last patrol."

Though Monroe still appeared on the verge of panic, he had made no further attempt to stop Tremain and Miguel as they stepped into the fragile raft from a rope ladder draped over the *Whitefin*'s port side. Tremain could still see Monroe's sullen face as his executive officer waved forlornly from the submarine's main deck. It resembled that of a child watching his mother's car drive away after being dropped off for his first day at school, and it almost made Tremain reconsider his decision to go ashore. But he had to do it. It was partly a matter of principal and partly a matter of personal honor. Whatley was over there, and probably in trouble. Despite Whately's arrogance, and his sometimes selfish behavior, Tremain saw something of himself in the young lieutenant. For his own conscience's sake, he could not simply abandon Whately, or the three crewmen with him. For some reason he felt the pressing need to prove that he was not the captain portrayed in Whately's letter to the admiral.

"Do you know this area?" Tremain asked in a whisper as Miguel finished covering up the raft. There was no one in the immediate vicinity, and no sign of the *Whitefin*'s missing officer or the three sailors.

"I know it well, sir," Miguel said with a grin. "I used to play on this beach as a boy."

"The major had planned to use an abandoned sugar mill as his jumping off point. I'm guessing our guys ran off in that direction to try to find him."

"I know exactly the place, sir."

"Then let's go. You lead the way, and I'll cover you."

The two headed inland, with Tremain following only a few paces behind Miguel, both men holding their weapons at the ready. Tremain was amazed at how quickly the jungle swallowed up the available starlight, leaving them to walk in pitch blackness. Somehow, Miguel could feel his way through and moved at a much swifter pace than Tremain had anticipated. Tremain's initial impulse was to ask Miguel if he was su where he was going, but then he noticed that the ground they were walking on consisted of solid dirt, well trodden and packed firmly by decades of repeated use. They were following a trail. That was Miguel's secret. Miguel certainly did not know every tree in this jungle, but he did know where all of the trails were and probably knew where they all led, too. Even on a night as dark as this one, he had needed only a few minutes to find one of the footpaths in the area.

They quickly crossed the rugged countryside, warily stopping at every suspicious noise. Eventually, they reached a spot where the jungle abruptly parted, allowing the light of the stars through once more and revealing a dirt road running off to the left and right, disappearing into the dark in both directions. Tremain's shoe hit a dry, crusty ridge of earth, and he almost tripped as his next step dropped into a deep tread mark on the road, undoubtedly left by a heavily laden vehicle during a recent rain when the firm dirt had turned into slushy mud.

"This is the coastal road," Miguel whispered. Then he pointed down the road to the west. "There is a side road a few hundred yards that way that leads to the sugar mill."

"What's down that way?" Tremain asked, pointing in the opposite direction.

"My uncle's village. About two miles away."

Tremain maintained a blank expression at the steward's remark. Like most of the *Whitefin*'s crew, Miguel had not been briefed fully on the mission; otherwise he would have mentioned two other critical landmarks near the village. Miguel would not be wise to them since he had left Mindanao years before the Japanese ever arrived. Tremain remembered from the briefing map that the Japanese refueling station Farquhar and his men were supposed to have attacked to kick off the operation was a half mile on this side of the village. The compound for the local Japanese garrison was located just a quarter mile beyond the village. Both enemy installations were a little too close for comfort, in Tremain's opinion, especially with the Japanese already alerted and turned out to repulse the army's raid. He could still hear the distant fighting resonating through the jungle, although its original vitality had diminished to sin- gle, distinctive shots separated by long intervals and interlaced with occasional bursts from a machine gun. It was a mopping-up operation now, and Tremain felt a notion of guilt when he selfishly hoped that any Japanese in the area would stay over there, pursuing the commandos on the other side of the promontory, well over five miles away. There was little he could do to help his beleaguered army comrades, but they *could* help him. Their sacrifice might make all the difference, distracting the enemy long enough for him to find his own men and get them the hell out of here.

"Lead on, Miguel."

The Filipino sailor nodded and started down the road leading to the west, with Tremain following him only a few paces behind. The two moved along the side of the road near the thick brush, staying well clear of the open center of the road. They had walked on for perhaps a hundred yards before Tremain discerned a small clearing in the darkness up ahead. It was the turn leading to the sugar mill, a fact confirmed by Miguel's quickening pace. They had almost reached the fork in the road when the hairs suddenly stood up on the back of Tremain's neck.

Something was wrong. The incessant chorus produced by the jungle's millions of critters and insects had fallen silent all at once, and Tremain could sense that he and Miguel were not alone on that dark road.

Suddenly, several clicking noises resonated from the brush lining the left side of the road only a few feet away. Instinctively, Tremain spun around and dropped to a knee, bringing the machine gun up to his hip in one swift motion. When his eyes adjusted, he found that he was facing the muzzle ends of a dozen rifles extending from the foliage, their barrels casting a dull bluish hue in the faint starlight. The rifles' owners were completely obscured by the darkened jungle beyond, but Tremain could see enough to know that half of the rifles were pointing at him, and the other half were pointing at Miguel.

Tremain half-wanted to spray the side of the road with his Tommy gun, forcing his assailants to take cover while he rolled into the foliage on the other side of the road. But he hesitated when he saw that Miguel still stood upright, presenting himself as the perfect target. The wardroom steward had little propensity for land combat, and obviously no instinct for tak ing cover. Tremain was considering his options when the dark hands holding the rifles suddenly emerged from the shadows, followed shortly by their owners. As they stepped into the starlight, Tremain could see clearly that they were not Japanese soldiers at all. The dozen men wore a variety of loose-fitting trousers and button-down shirts in various states of cleanliness and wear, or no shirts at all. A few wore wide-brimmed hats. A few wore head scarves. It was the same hodgepodge of local civilian attire that he had seen on the Moro villagers that day when they had helped the *Whitefin* load water. Undoubtedly, these were the guerillas.

Miguel greeted them in Cebuano and they immediately took notice of him, running over with wide smiles to greet their old friend from days past. These men all looked roughly the same age as Miguel, and Tremain imagined that at least some of them had been Miguel's playmates when they were boys.

With faces beaming, the cluster of Filipinos continued chatting far longer than their situation afforded, long enough that Tremain began to think that both Miguel and the so-called guerilla fighters had entirely forgotten where they were.

"Any luck, Miguel?" Tremain interjected, finally drawing the group's attention.

"Err-uh, yes, Captain," Miguel said, appearing somewhat embarrassed for getting too absorbed in the reunion. "The major and his men are at the mill. My friend here, Torivio, will take us to them."

"I haven't seen them, Tremain," Farquhar responded dispassionately. The major appeared to be only half-paying attention to him as he peered out of the open window at the dark jungle surrounding the dilapidated building.

The sugarcane mill sat on one of the few flat acres of land in this part of the island, and probably dated back to the days of Spanish rule. Quite possibly, its Spanish owners had abandoned it at the turn of the century, when the United States purchased the Philippines at the Treaty of Paris, officially ending Spanish-American War and marking the end of the United s' last great land grab. The relatively level area had once

been cleared to accommodate the four small buildings surrounding the horse-drawn mill, but the jungle was in the process of reclaiming the clearing, while time and weather were
claiming the buildings. The soundest of the three—a rectangular, caved-in, rotting wooden structure that had once served
as the mill's washhouse—now served as the guerilla's headquarters, and it was here that Miguel's friend Torivio had
brought Tremain to meet an anxious-looking Farquhar.

Farquhar had greeted him cordially, but did not look happy
to see him. The smile that was normally a permanent fixture
on the British officer's face had been replaced by a look of an-
tagonism and worry. Farquhar seemed somewhat preoccupied, as if he still had pressing business to take care of despite
the evident failure of the mission. It only added more weight
to the theory that had been playing out in Tremain's head
since that day in the *Pelias*'s briefing room: the theory that
there was more to this mission than Farquhar was sharing
with him.

"Did you attack the fuel depot?" Tremain asked curtly.

"No."

"Too bad. It might have taken some of the heat off our
army boys. Maybe a few more of them would have made it to
the *Triggerfish* if some of the Japs had been pulled in this direction."

"The thought occurred to me, Tremain."

"Then may I ask why you didn't do it?"

"Because of them," Farquhar said, thumbing over his
shoulder. He was motioning toward a handful of Filipinos
clustered in a corner near a burning candle, one of the few
sources of light in the dimly lit room. Earlier Tremain had
been introduced to these men, a grim-looking lot who he
learned were the guerilla leaders. They included, not surprisingly, Miguel's uncle—the elderly chief that Tremain had met
during the *Whitefin*'s water stop two months ago. Tremain
imagined the group could instill fear in the hearts of the Japanese, but right now they appeared anything but fearsome as
they lounged casually on the floor, their rifles propped betwee
their legs, their faces wreathed in awe as Miguel told th
about one of his many adventures aboard the *Whitefin*.

"What do you mean, because of them?" Tremain asked.

"I needed their help, and they refused to give it. In fact, they carted off the weapons and ammunition we delivered to them faster than you can say skulduggery, and now they won't tell me where the bloody hell they hid them." Farquhar anticipated Tremain's confused expression and added, "The satchel charges, Tremain. I needed them to blow up the fuel depot, and the bastards took them, too."

"Why did they do that?"

"Well, actually, it seems you were right, old boy." Farquhar paused for a moment, shooting Tremain a brief conciliatory glance, before continuing in a much lower tone. "They want to know what happened to poor old Jokanin and Puyo. Of course, I could never tell them the truth, so I gave them some story I'd been rehearsing the whole trip up here. But they didn't buy it. They won't budge from this spot unless I fess up." Farquhar cast a glance over his shoulder at the group of guerilla leaders listening to Miguel. "And I'm sure your man there is filling them in on the real scoop, right this very moment."

"No he's not," Tremain muttered. "As much as I despise what you did, Major, I made Miguel promise not to talk about it. He's a submariner; he knows how to keep quiet about things."

"Well, I suppose we'll see, won't we, Tremain? If they come at us with swishing kris blades in the next few minutes."

"Getting back to Whately," Tremain said, not to be diverted from his sole purpose in coming ashore. "Did he contact you at all?"

Farquhar kept looking out the window, but averted his eyes for a brief moment. "We heard something on the radio about two hours back, but couldn't make it out. I rather assume it was Whately."

"Two hours ago? Then why didn't you head for the shore, Major? That was the contingency plan we agreed on."

"I made the decision to remain here."

"So let me get this straight." Tremain paused, simmering. e was growing more than a little perturbed by the major's parent lack of interest in the matter. "You knew the mission a failure. You knew Whately was trying to contact you.

You knew you had no way to blow up the fuel depot. And yet you just sat here? And did absolutely nothing?"

"I didn't say I did nothing, Tremain. I said I decided to stay here." Farquhar continued to watch the jungle, evidently unfazed by Tremain's mounting indignation.

"You could have had the damn decency to send a runner to tell Whately not to wait for you, so he wouldn't be sitting there on the beach wondering what the hell to do! Did you ever think of that, Major?" Tremain paused again, checking his tone after some of the Filipinos on the other side of the room glanced in his direction. He had reached his fill of the arrogant British officer, and it took every bit of self-control to keep from striking him.

"I've sent my scouts off with a couple of the loyal locals to reconnoiter the situation, and see what we might salvage out of the mission. I expect them to return at any moment."

Tremain shook his head in incredulity. "I've got news for you, Major. This mission's over! There's nothing to salvage! My men are missing now because of you, you son of a bitch! They probably went looking for your sorry ass, and got lost in the jungle!"

"Ah! Here they are!" Farquhar announced with enthusiasm, completely ignoring Tremain.

Tremain looked out the window to see a group of dark figures dart into the clearing and trot toward the washhouse. For a moment, he had hopes that it might be Whately and his men, but a few moments later, the door opened and two Filipinos entered the room. One was wearing black fatigues with a Thompson slung under one arm, and Tremain instantly recognized him as Farquhar's lead scout, Sergeant Lopez. The other was a local boy of probably no more than sixteen. They were both met at the door collectively by Farquhar and the guerilla leaders.

"Report, Sergeant," Farquhar said.

"We have trouble, Major," Sergeant Lopez answered grimly. "The Japanese captured the four American sailors who wer watching the boats, and now they are holding them in the vi lage. They've commandeered the *datu*'s house and are usin as an interrogation facility."

"Never mind that," Farquhar said flatly, "I sent you to check on the Jap garrison—the Kempeitai."

"That is what I am trying to tell you, sir. The enemy garrison troops have moved out of their compound and into the village. They're going house to house, searching for more Americans. Enemy foot patrols are everywhere. We came very close to getting caught ourselves on the way back here."

"But what of the Japanese commander, Sergeant? What of him?" Farquhar asked with what seemed like frantic impatience, as if everything Lopez had reported thus far was insignificant.

Before the Filipino sergeant had a chance to respond, the boy guerilla spoke up in agitated broken English. "Colonel Nakamoto question the Americans in *datu*'s house! He threaten village for supporting them! What we do?"

Tremain's heart sank at the news. He felt like a sledgehammer had hit him in the gut. His men were prisoners now. They were being interrogated and might, under torture, reveal the *Whitefin*'s location. The Japanese colonel would only need to call in aircraft from Malabang to catch her in the shallow bay as she tried to slip away before dawn. Tremain knew what he should do. He should collect Miguel, the major, and his scouts and head back to the ship without delay. Once there, he would bring on all engines and drive the *Whitefin* at flank speed away from the coast, placing as many miles of deep ocean between her and the island of Mindanao as her twin screws could manage before dawn. Whately and his men would have to fend for themselves as prisoners of war.

But Tremain could not bring himself to do it. He could not bring himself to abandon them. He had heard the rumors about the abysmal treatment of allied prisoners at the hands of the Japanese. After weeks of torture and interrogation, Whately and his men would be shipped to one of the infamous work camps, where they would be subjected to back-breaking labor, starvation, and long-term exposure to the elements. The labor camps were bad enough, but getting to one would be an ordeal in itself. They would spend weeks aboard some ancient, slow-moving freighter, stuffed into a dank, dark hold along with hundreds of other prisoners. They would have very little food or water and certainly no facilities. They would be sealed up belowdecks in tossing seas, sealed up for weeks on end with their own urine and feces, sealed up inside a miserable compartment that would certainly become their tomb should the ship get sunk by an American submarine. If they survived the voyage in the hell ship, they would then suffer the terrible plight of all prisoners of war of any nation. They would be stigmatized, written off, and forgotten by their own nation until the war's end.

Tremain felt utterly powerless to help them, but in his heart he knew that he could never leave this place without at least trying.

He shuffled his way to the front of the now murmuring crowd of guerillas, until he was standing before Lopez.

"Sergeant, my men, have they been harmed in any way?"

For a brief moment Lopez looked somewhat surprised to see Tremain here. Eventually he shook his head. "I cannot say for certain, Commander. But they've been cooped up inside the *datu*'s house along with the Japanese colonel and several other officers for more than an hour."

"Guarded?"

Lopez nodded. "Heavily, sir. There are at least two platoons in the village, along with a few machine-gun positions."

As the insane idea started to formulate in Tremain's head, he considered what he was up against. Two platoons of Kempeitai, roughly thirty to forty men, not quite the caliber of regular infantry, but well armed nonetheless, and situated in good defensive positions. Add to that the foot patrols roaming throughout the jungle, and the fact that these Japanese had been living here for close to two years and would have a much better feel for the country. And then there was the Japanese infantry regiment, pursuing what was left of Buckles's men, not more than five miles from the village. They were all formidable obstacles, and Tremain knew that he and Farquhar and the Filipino scouts could not surmount them. They would need help if they stood any chance at all to save Whately and his men. They would need to enlist the help of the guerillas. It was the only option. To do that, he would have to convince Farquhar to come clean to the guerillas about the fates of Jokanin and Puyo, and Miguel would have to convince them that the *Whitefin*'s sailors had played no part in the executions.

Tremain looked at his watch. It read 0315. Dawn was only three hours away. He would have to act quickly.

"Major," Tremain said as he quickly crafted in his mind how he was going to persuade the aloof British officer to tell the truth. "Major?"

Tremain looked around the room, but Farquhar was nowhere to be seen.

"Sergeant, where did the major go?"

"I . . . I don't know, Commander. The last time I looked he was standing over there by the window. His pack is still here, and there's his weapon." Lopez pointed to the short submachine gun leaning against the far wall by the major's black knapsack.

Tremain asked around, but no one in the room had seen the major leave. A quick check with the scouts and guerillas outside revealed that they had indeed seen the major, only a few minutes before. He had emerged from a door at the back of the building and sprinted off into the jungle without even the slightest pause. That in itself was perplexing enough, but what was even more puzzling was that the major did not appear to be carrying any weapons with him. Apparently, he had gone into the jungle alone and unarmed. A most odd thing to do, considering the enemy patrols about.

At first Tremain suspected the major had fled to get away from the guerilla leaders who would no doubt eventually come to the conclusion that Jokanin and Puyo had been killed. But when Tremain went back inside the building, Miguel pulled him off into a corner and provided him with the one crucial clue that lit up the whole murky mystery. Like a dozen star shells shining over a convoy on a placid sea, what Miguel had to say revealed to Tremain every aspect of Farquhar's twisted reasoning.

"Captain," Miguel said, "I don't know if this is important, sir, but that Japanese colonel's name, Nakamoto, it sounded familiar to me. I couldn't place it at first, sir, but now I remember exactly where I heard it before. Major Farquhar used to mention that name all the time on the last patrol while playing cribbage with the junior officers."

Suddenly, the pieces clicked into place in Tremain's mind. "Nakamoto. Was that the Japanese colonel that massacred his men in Malaya?" Tremain asked.

"That's right, sir! That's it. He used to always say he was going to kill Nakamoto before the war ended. He was worried that if the colonel survived the war, he might escape punishment." Miguel paused, and then asked, "Do you suppose that's where he's gone, sir? To kill the colonel?"

Tremain did not say anything, but he knew the answer in his heart. He now knew that he and many others had been mere scenery on a stage Farquhar had been setting for months, if not years. Undoubtedly, while still in Malaya, the major had learned through some intercepted communiqué that Nakamoto had been assigned to northern Mindanao. That would explain the major's odd request for transfer into an American-controlled sector of the war. No doubt all of the major's missions to Mindanao, while outwardly in pursuit of legitimate Allied objectives, were meant to ascertain Nakamoto's exact station on the island. Once Farquhar had determined that Nakamoto was in charge of the garrison in northern Mindanao, he needed only to come up with a viable reason for a raid. The reason had to be a good one; it had to be slightly out of the ordinary, something just interesting enough to guarantee endorsement by the romantics on General MacArthur's staff. The plot to capture the Japanese doctor had fit the bill perfectly. In the end, the entire mission had been a ruse, a scheme carefully orchestrated by one man to exact revenge on one Japanese officer who had committed atrocities against his prisoners. Despite the risks imposed on the crews of the *Whitefin* and the *Triggerfish*, despite the now deadly outcome for Colonel Buckles and his commandos, despite the risks to the local villagers and the guerilla movement on this island, the British major had formulated his plan with only one objective in mind—to kill Colonel Nakamoto.

Now, with his long-awaited plan on the verge of collapse, Farquhar had set off on his own in an attempt to personally fulfill the one and only reason he had come here.

But Farquhar was no concern to Tremain anymore, and he quickly put the major out of his thoughts. His only concern now was to free Whately and the others from the Japanese.

"Sergeant Lopez," Tremain said as he approached the Filipino scout. "I'm afraid the major won't be coming back. That means you and your men are under my command from here on out."

Lopez appeared somewhat puzzled, but eventually nodded.

"Our first order of business is to rescue my men." Tremain raised a hand when Lopez started to interject. "If you're going to say it's a crazy idea and we don't stand much of a chance, then don't bother. I already know that. Right now, what I need from you is your expertise. Land warfare is not my specialty."

Tremain paused, waiting for the conciliatory nod from Lopez that finally came.

"Yes, Commander. What can I do?"

"Assuming you had to rescue four sailors being held in a village teeming with Japanese soldiers, sometime in the next two hours, how would you go about doing it?"

Lopez crossed his arms and considered for a moment before answering.

"I don't think it's possible, Commander, without the help of the guerillas and access to our satchel charges. I mean, we're so greatly outnumbered—"

"How would you do it?" Tremain demanded.

Lopez cast a skeptical glance at Tremain. The sergeant appeared to be somewhat shocked at the fierceness in his commander's voice. "Well, I guess I'd probably stage two of my men with me south of the village. We should be able to get there without being detected, since the enemy patrols are more concentrated near the shoreline. Then I'd have my remaining scout set up some sort of diversion, probably take a snipe at a patrol in the jungle and set off a few grenades. Hopefully the Japanese commander will send some of his troops away from the village to investigate, depleting their forces in and around the house where the prisoners are being held. Then we assault the house and take away the prisoners." Lopez gazed at the dirt floor for a few moments with a fire in his eyes, as if he were suddenly optimistic that the plan might work. But then, just as suddenly, the fire faded and he shook his head. "But I doubt the diversion will work, sir. It'll be hard for any one man to make enough noise to draw out a platoon or two, especially since we've only got Thompsons and grenades. We need something much more enticing if we want to get the Japs' attention. We need something that puts the fear of God into them. Something that will cause confusion on the battle-field, and make their officers and sergeants indecisive."

Out of the blue, a wild thought entered Tremain's head. They had no mortars. They had no satchel charges. But they did have one final piece of heavy artillery, one that would certainly get the enemy's attention.

"I'll take care of the diversion, Sergeant. Get your men ready. Take all three of them with you. Take up position south of the village, just as you said." Tremain looked at his watch. "Be ready to move in at oh-four-fifteen. Get my men out of there and then meet me at the extraction point."

Lopez nodded uncertainly and then left the room to gather his scouts.

"Miguel." Tremain called the wardroom steward over.

"Yes, Captain."

"Do you think you can find your way back to the raft with-out any problem?"

"Oh, yes, sir!"

"I need you to do something for me. This is very impor-tant. I need you to get back to the ship and tell the XO to pre-pare the deck gun for ranged fire against the Japanese fuel depot just outside the village. He'll know what I'm talking about. He can use the chart to estimate bearing and elevation. Tell him I know he probably won't hit anything, but that's not important. What is important—what is crucial—is that he must start the barrage at precisely oh-four-ten. Is that clear?"

Miguel nodded.

"Tell him to use high explosive ordnance and to keep up a steady fire for ten minutes. Then he's to secure the gun and make ready for getting under way." Tremain glanced at his watch again. "You don't have much time, so you better get going."

Without delay, the trusty Miguel hurried out of the room, not even stopping to bid farewell to his uncle.

Tremain saw the old *datu* watch him go, much like a fat watching his son march off to war. The chief was prob wondering why his nephew had left in such haste. Event the old man's eyes settled on Tremain in a suspicious and dis-approving stare.

Tremain knew that the Moro leader had a thousand reasons to distrust Americans. The chief was certainly old enough to remember the contentious early years of American rule, when Filipinos had as much reason to fear American troops as they did the Japanese occupiers of today. No doubt, he remembered the massacres at Bud Dajo, Bud Bagsak, and Samar, among others—names indelibly etched in the minds of most Filipinos but virtually forgotten by the people in the United States.

Tremain took in a deep breath as he strolled over to the cluster of guerilla leaders. Although the wheels had already been set in motion, Tremain knew that his impromptu plan had a much better chance for success if he could get the guerillas to help. He knew what he had to do. He had to treat these people with the forthright honesty and respect they had been denied in the past.

He had to tell them what happened to Jokanin and Puyo and hope they did not respond with a wavy kris blade through his throat.

Chapter 25

MICHAEL Fabriano realized that the pain in his arms and shoulders had surpassed that of his throbbing face. Of course, the tightly wound and fraying coils of hemp rope, along with the bamboo pole braced behind his back, played a big part in that. For nearly an hour, he had been sitting naked inside the crude but spacious hut, with his arms bound behind him, sneaking glances through swollen eyes at the Japanese officers sitting around a small table on the opposite side of the room. The four enemy officers were engaged in a hot debate, and Fabriano guessed it had something to do with the recent interrogation.

Whately had put up a good fight, by Fabriano's judgment, especially for an officer. Even when they pried off the lieutenant's fingernails, he revealed nothing more than name, rank, and service number. Then, after repeated kicks to his genitals, they managed to get out of him that there were two submarines instead of just the one that the Japanese were evidently already aware of. They appeared very interested in this, and one of the officers hurriedly scribbled a message onto a piece of paper and sent it off with one of the soldiers, presumably to find a radio and notify the local Japanese airfields about the *Whitefin*'s location. The brutal questioning

then continued, but Whately held his ground and divulged no
more. Eventually, the senior Japanese officer present—a short,
pudgy, round-faced colonel with beady eyes and a mouth per-
manently fixed in a superior smile—got frustrated with
Whately's continued reticence and ordered him beaten senseless. They had stopped just short of killing him, no doubt to
preserve him for future interrogations, and Whately now lay
naked on the floor in a pool of his own vomit and blood with
a Japanese doctor hovering over him.

The doctor had been called in after the beating, presumably to verify that Whately would eventually recover to be of
further use to them. Considering the cruel treatment Fabriano
had just witnessed, he was shocked when he saw this Japanese
doctor—a small, intelligent-looking man, bald and wearing
glasses—gingerly roll Whately onto his back and hold his
hand while he checked his pulse and breathing. With his face
locked in an expression of grave concern, the doctor muttered
a few consoling words to the American officer in English,
words inaudible to the Japanese officers on the other side of
the room, but quite clear to Fabriano, who was much closer.

"You are going to be all right, young man," the doctor said
to the unconscious Whately, in a refined accent that indicated
he had spent many years before the war living in English-
speaking parts of the world. Whatever his background was,
the doctor obviously made no distinction between friend and
foe when it came to his profession, and he appeared very
much disturbed over Whately's condition. Twice during the
examination, Fabriano caught him shooting poisonous glances
at the other four Japanese officers, who were too absorbed in
their argument to take any notice. Obviously, the doctor did
not approve of the treatment of the prisoners, but he was powerless to do anything about it. The beady-eyed colonel was the
one calling the shots.

Fabriano glanced over at Shelby and Penn. Like him, both
them were naked and both bore cuts and bruises from the
ltiple blows inflicted by the Japanese soldiers during the
mile march along the dirt road to the village. Both men
d at the floor now, having learned earlier that they were
make eye contact with their Japanese captors. Fabriano,
r, was a little more brazen, and had often in the last

hour sneaked a peek at his surroundings, whenever the situation allowed.

At the moment, the situation allowed him another look. None of the Japanese were looking in his direction. The four officers were absorbed in their discussion and the doctor was absorbed in his patient. The two sentries stood just outside the doorway, facing out into the dark night holding their rifles and bayonets at the ready. From time to time Japanese soldiers passed by outside, probably canvassing the village for other spies. Periodically, muffled screams rang out in the night, and Fabriano could only guess that the bored Japanese soldiers were amusing themselves with the local female villagers. It certainly would not surprise him, since this particular bunch of enemy soldiers had proved to be an exceptionally wicked lot. They had beaten him and kicked him repeatedly during the grueling march from the beach. One of the soldiers even kicked him in the genitals, and Fabriano still wanted to wince whenever he closed his eyes and saw the strange boot with the two toes flash to his groin. It was the strangest sort of boot Fabriano had ever seen—soft, like rubber, with two distinct compartments for the toes, presumably to better accommodate the shape of the foot and to minimize noise when marching through dead leaves or rocks. As Fabriano had writhed in agony from the blow to his groin, he remembered experiencing an odd moment of elation. For he had discovered how the Japanese were able to sneak through the jungle unnoticed. It was a strange thing to think about at the time, but he had to divert his thoughts to something in order to deal with the excruciating pain.

Again, Fabriano risked a look in the direction of the Japanese officers on the other side of the room. He had learned over the past hour that these four men were an extremely sadistic group, and that the brutality the Japanese soldiers had exhibited during the long march from the beach did not compare with the cruelty these four officers were capable of.

Just then, one of the officers looked up from the tab prompting Fabriano to quickly avert his eyes to the floor. officers stopped talking, and Fabriano could hear slow falls on the wooden floor, as one of them rose from the and approached him. Soon, Fabriano was looking at a pair of muddy but otherwise resplendent jackboots on the floor in front of him.

Fabriano did not have to look up to know that they belonged to the wiry Japanese captain with the mustache—the officer who had administered Whately's beating so thoroughly. He was distinctive among the rest of the officers in that the heat and humidity of the jungle appeared not to affect him. While the other officers were covered in perspiration and stripped to white shirtsleeves, the Japanese captain wore his full field uniform with green button-down wool jacket.

"Your officer has not been very cooperative," the Japanese captain said in his hideous high-pitched voice. He was the only one of the Japanese officers present, besides the doctor, who spoke fluent English. "You can see here the price of his defiance."

One of the jackboots planted a solid kick in Whately's white ribs, yielding no response from the unconscious lieutenant, but prompting an immediate verbal protest from the doctor. A few heated words in Japanese were exchanged between the captain and the doctor before the Japanese colonel, still sitting at the table, snarled an order that sent the doctor off brooding in a corner.

"We will use a different tactic for our next interrogation session, gentlemen," the Japanese captain said in a poisonously polite tone. "Perhaps the three of you have more information to give us? Perhaps something that your officer forgot to tell us? We would be most interested in anything you have to say. And please keep in mind that you are enlisted men. You are not worth as much to us as your officer. He will live, but we have no reason to keep the rest of you alive. It is simply something to keep in mind."

At that, the Japanese captain shouted something in Japanese, and Fabriano heard the two sentries enter through the open doorway. Out of the corner of his eye he saw them wrestling Penn to his feet and forcing him to the center of the room.

"No. no. Please don't. Please don't," the fearful Penn rted to protest in a low murmur, but was instantly silenced a loud slap across the face administered by the Japanese ain.

Fabriano snuck a quick peek to see Penn's thin, pale form being drawn up in the same bloody spot where Whately had received his beating. Penn's hands were tied to a rope looped over one of the rafters and pulled so tight that his arms stretched out high above his head and his toes barely touched the floor. There was nothing but abject fear in Penn's eyes, and Fabriano found himself feeling somewhat sorry for him, despite the fact that Penn had conspired with Shelby to murder him.

One of the other Japanese officers gave an order, and one of the sentries approached the bench. A gleaming bayonet appeared under Fabriano's chin, prompting him to look up. Then the sentry did the same to Shelby. Just as during Whately's beating, the averted eyes rule was temporarily rescinded so that they could watch what was happening to their comrade. And now Fabriano could see the other sentry standing directly in front of the outstretched Penn, holding his rifle with affixed bayonet at the ready.

"Wait a minute!" Penn called out, fervently. "Wait, I'll tell you everything you want to know. I know where the other sub is. I can tell you!"

The Japanese captain smiled and cast an inquisitive glance at the colonel, who remained by the table with arms crossed, casually puffing on a pipe, his face still set in a smug sneer. The colonel simply shook his head, as if unsatisfied with Penn's offer.

At this, the captain nodded, and a moment later the sentry let out a battle cry that split the air in the muggy room. His face transformed into a beastlike stare as he lunged forward with his bayonet, puncturing Penn's raised left arm just above the armpit, releasing a stream of dark blood that ran down the sailor's outstretched pale body. Penn instantly cried out in pain, and continued to wail as the Japanese soldier kept the blade lodged in his arm and slowly twisted it through three hundred and sixty degrees.

"What the hell?" Penn eventually managed to mutter through gritted teeth. "I told you I'd—"

The captain stepped forward and struck him across the face. "You will keep silent! You are only a third-class petty ficer. You are nothing!"

The captain then turned to face Fabriano and Shelby.

"You both outrank this man. I am only interested in what you have to tell me. This man means nothing to me. If you do not tell us the exact location of the other spies that have landed, along with the names of the locals who have helped you, I will kill this man!"

All three sailors had freely given their name, rank, and service number at the moment of capture, and now Fabriano was wondering if that had been a mistake. Obviously, the Japanese officers had some misguided understanding of the narrow gap between second- and third-class petty officers in the U.S. Navy. Evidently they believed that a lower rank sailor like Penn could know nothing of importance.

With no answer from either Fabriano or Shelby, the captain said something over his shoulder, and the sentry responded by yanking the bloody blade out of Penn's arm, then immediately thrusting it into Penn's left thigh. Fabriano could hear the blade grate across the femur as it passed clean through Penn's skinny leg and out the other side. Instantly, rivulets of blood streamed from the wound, joining the other stream trickling from his arm wound. The soldier had been careful not to hit any arteries, and Fabriano guessed that he had done this many times before.

Penn yelled out in agony. "Stop. Oh, please stop. Oh, please . . ."

"Quit your whining, you pussy!" Shelby suddenly shouted. "Have some fucking balls!"

Penn fell silent all at once, staring back at Shelby with confused, hurt, and angry eyes. He looked almost as shocked as Fabriano was that Shelby would ridicule him while he was being handled so cruelly.

"Do you care nothing for this man's life?" the Japanese captain asked with a slight smile on his face.

"No," Shelby answered solidly and without hesitation. "Serves him right for getting us into this mess." Then he paused before adding in a lower voice, "But I'll tell you whatever you want to know, to save his sorry ass."

The Japanese captain appeared pleased and motioned for one of the lieutenants to stand ready with a pencil and a pad of

"We are, as you say in America, 'all ears,'" the captain said.

Instinctively, Fabriano wanted to stop Shelby, but there was nothing he could do as the big sailor began telling everything he knew. Shelby was not privy to all aspects of the *Whitefin*'s mission, or its ultimate goal, but he certainly had gleaned enough information, during the two weeks of training and the wolf pack's long journey to Mindanao, to keep the Japanese officers on edge. While Penn hung in the middle of the room bleeding from the two terrible wounds, the long bayonet still lancing his thigh, Shelby proceeded to describe the whole operation in detail. Through all of this, the taciturn Japanese colonel, with his face wreathed in pipe smoke, hardly moved a muscle. He simply sat at the table, observing the interrogation with a casual stare. Only the corners of his mouth gave any indication that he was listening. Fabriano noticed that they turned up slightly at every new piece of information about the guerilla forces in the area, and it was quite obvious that this was the information he primarily wanted.

When all was done, and Shelby had nothing more to tell, the Japanese captain approached Fabriano.

"Do you wish to add anything to his statement?"

Fabriano shook his head and said nothing.

"Surely there is something your friend left out," the captain added with the same sadistic smile.

"I really wasn't listening," Fabriano said sarcastically, then winced as the Japanese captain slapped him hard across the face.

"You will give me one new piece of information," the captain said in an enraged tone, "or your friend dies."

Fabriano simply looked up at the enemy officer, meeting his gaze. He hated this bastard, and he was not about to give him any more information. He didn't want to give this Japanese asshole the satisfaction. Fabriano liked to think that he had some notion of personal pride, and he made a resolution right then and there that he would endure whatever treatmen these assholes decided to mete out and never utter a word.

Evidently realizing Fabriano's determination to ke silent, the Japanese captain turned to look at the colonel guidance. The colonel simply sat indifferently as he to few more puffs on his pipe. After a few long momen gave a simple nod. Without a moment's hesitation, the captain shouted a succinct order to the poised sentry.

In a flash of bloody steel, the soldier withdrew the bayonet from Penn's thigh, triggering a thrash of agony. For a moment, the sentry held the dripping blade horizontal before Penn's bruised face. Then Penn realized what was about to happen and shot a feverish look at Fabriano.

"Fabriano! Tell them *something*! Holy shit! Tell them something, *please*!"

Fabriano did not look at him. He was determined not to break eye contact with the Japanese captain.

A moment later, the sentry let out a war cry, then reared back and plunged the bayonet into Penn's chest with enough force to bury it to the hilt. The foot-long blade made a sickening crunch as it hit Penn's spine, then passed clean through his back, protruding as a slick red point on the other side. Penn's body thrashed repeatedly, his open mouth gurgling until it exuded a surge of blood. From the other side of the room, the Japanese doctor shouted a pleading protest but was quickly silenced by a reprimand from the colonel. After close to a minute, Penn's body finally went limp and the gurgling sound stopped. Like a machine, the sentry unceremoniously removed the blade from the bloody body, yanking on the rifle several times to work the bayonet free, completely insensitive to the staring eyes of his dead victim.

It was over. Penn was dead.

Throughout the entire grueling moment, Fabriano had kept constant eye contact with the Japanese captain, not blinking even once.

A deathlike silence descended on the room as the two sentries cut down Penn's body and then dragged it from the room with little more reverence than if it were a bag of rice. A long, bloody streak on the wooden floor marked their path.

"You will be next," the captain said, still looking into Fabriano's eyes. "Let us see if you will respond to the bayonet like your friend did."

Fabriano thought about spitting in the bastard's face, but a sudden commotion outside got the Japanese captain's attention. Through the open doorway, Fabriano saw a flurry of dust and heard Japanese soldiers shouting what he assumed to be

Japanese obscenities while they roughed up someone, presumably a new prisoner. He heard fabric tear as the soldiers took the standard security precaution of stripping their prisoner naked, ensuring that he carried no concealed weapons.

Eventually, two soldiers picked the prisoner up out of the dust and dragged him inside the house, into the light, where Fabriano got his first good look at the man. He appeared to be in very bad shape, practically unable to walk. His arms were bound behind his back with a pole, just like Fabriano's and Shelby's, and his face was swollen from repeated jabs with rifle butts, especially on one cheek, where the skin was coated with a dried mixture of blood and mud. But Fabriano instantly recognized the man, despite his deplorable condition. If the few remaining identifiable features of his face did not give it away, then surely the shiny blond hair did.

It was Farquhar, the British major.

Chapter 26

LIEUTENANT Commander Chris Monroe could feel more than a dozen pairs of skeptical eyes on his back as he scanned the dark shoreline through his binoculars. The lookouts in the perches above, the men manning the twenty-millimeter guns, and even Endicott standing next to him were all watching him and wondering what he was going to do about the event they had just witnessed. Silently, he cursed Tremain for leaving him in charge of a boatload of sailors who trusted him no more than they did a navy recruiter.

Since Heath's death, the entire crew had treated him with a noticeable degree of reservation. Up until now Monroe had been able to ignore it. But now he was in command, and he found himself unable to ignore it. Every time a watchstander came to him with a standard report, he sensed the man's hesitation, his anxiety about Monroe's ability to do anything with the information. Even the normally indiscriminate Chief LaGrange had shown a measured amount of apprehension. Two hours ago, when Tremain and Miguel shoved off in the rubber dinghy, LaGrange had sought Monroe out with a big smile, congratulating him on his first command at sea. Initially, the silent cob's words had been heartening to Monroe's doubting mind, but their effect soon melted away when he later noticed LaGrange following him from compartment to compartment. Whether he ventured onto the bridge, down inside the conning tower, or into the control room, LaGrange seemed to always find a reason to be only a few steps away. The idea that the *Whitefin*'s chief of the boat, the senior enlisted man on board, thought him incapable of handling the ship on his own, without a chaperone, both angered and dispirited Monroe immensely. But he really could not blame LaGrange, or any of them, for their doubts. Heath's death, coupled with the *R-15* incident, had awoken the superstitious mind in each of them. Monroe was certain that they no longer perceived him as simply the ship's second in command, but rather as a walking, talking portent of some impending disaster.

Perhaps the men around him on the bridge were thinking that at this very moment, especially after what they had just seen. Everyone on the *Whitefin*'s blacked-out bridge had been watching the shoreline, minutes ago, waiting for any signs of the captain's return. As they watched, a dark figure suddenly emerged from the brush and began running across the starlit sandy beach. The figure was only a shadow among shadows, but Monroe's trained eye could tell that the man was toting something bulky from the tree line down to the beach. He instantly concluded that it was the *Whitefin*'s rubber raft, and that the dark figure had to be either Tremain or Miguel preparing to return to the ship. Monroe was hardly prepared for the overwhelming sense of relief that came over him at the mere prospect of Tremain's return. He no more wanted to command this crew than they wanted to be commanded by him, and he was more than ready to be relieved of the burden. As the solitary figure in the raft crested the first bubbling wave and started rowing at a brisk pace toward the *Whitefin*, still more than three hundred yards away, Monroe even took back some of the derogatory terms he had inwardly applied to Tremain over the past two hours.

Then, as every man on the *Whitefin*'s bridge watched, flashes suddenly appeared in the dark tree line beyond the man in the raft. They were followed one and a half second later by the reports of multiple rifles. A dozen fountains white spray shot into the air all around the little raft, completely obscuring it from view. By the time the firing stop there was nothing left of the raft or its occupant except for a dark lump on the surface, indistinguishable from this distance. Monroe could not tell whether it was the remains of the raft, or the rower's floating body.

"Holy shit, sir!" LaGrange exclaimed next to him. "I sure hope that wasn't one of our guys."

Monroe did not answer but instead kept his binoculars to his face, intently examining the piece of black flotsam now drifting inshore with the current. He was slightly annoyed at the Cob's presence on the bridge, and was not in the mood for his almost certainly forthcoming words of advice.

"Maybe we should open up with the twenty mike-mikes, XO, to help him out?" LaGrange suggested somewhat condescendingly. "If he's still alive, he could probably use some covering fire."

"I'll make that decision if and when the need arises, Cob," Monroe replied, fighting to hold back the perturbation in his tone. "Now, you could be a much greater help to me if you would go below and make sure the men are ready for anything the Japs might throw at us. Let's make sure we're stowed for sea. I want a full sweep of each and every compartment."

Monroe felt LaGrange at his elbow, hesitating for a moment before he headed below to carry out the order.

That would keep him busy for a while, thought Monroe, as he continued to scan the shoreline, looking for any signs of life. He had considered ordering the twenty-millimeter guns to open up on the beach just as LaGrange had suggested, but then quickly decided against it. Tremain's orders had been clear: Wait here and avoid detection. So far, Monroe had no indication that the *Whitefin* had been detected, and he was not about to sacrifice the stealth of the ship. For all he knew, the shooters on the beach were still unaware of the *Whitefin*'s black hull sitting in the middle of the dark cove. As if to confirm his conclusions, Monroe noticed that the jungle had already returned to its formerly peaceful state, with no trace of those who had destroyed the raft with the fusillade of gunfire.

"Bridge, Sonar," Doniphan's voice intoned over the bridge speaker. "Picking up distant explosions on a bearing of zero-two-five."

Monroe and Endicott whirled around to the seaward side of the ship, and aimed their binoculars down the northeasterly bearing, anticipating trouble. Monroe saw nothing, except the shadowy flat sea and the black, rocky spit of land that formed the *Whitefin*'s shallow cove, jutting out from the western side of the promontory. The explosions were nowhere to be seen or heard topside, but Monroe did not doubt that they were there. The *Whitefin*'s QB sonar hydrophone was far superior to human ears, and if the water temperature conditions were just right, they could hear noises that were sometimes more than two dozen miles away. The basketball-sized hydrophone extending beneath the ship was covered with sensitive Rochelle salt crystals, which compressed and contracted at the touch of even the slightest pressure wave, creating a piezoelectric effect that converted any sound energy received into an electric current. That electrical current was then mixed, amplified, and filtered to reproduce the sound in Doniphan's headphones.

"Sonar, Bridge, we don't see anything."

"Sir." Doniphan's voice sounded much more frantic this time. "I think those explosions are depth charges!"

With his curiosity and his fears both piqued, Monroe removed his binoculars, looped them around the gyrocompass repeater, and dropped down the ladder into the conning tower. Inside the cramped room illuminated by the red night-lights, Doniphan faced the *Whitefin*'s new WCA sonar console and gingerly turned the dial that controlled the direction of the hydrophone beneath the ship. The console was a shiny replacement for the one that had been flooded during the last patrol, and now its myriad of dials and switches appeared blood red in the night lighting.

"What do you have?" he asked the absorbed sonar operator.

"Definitely depth charges, XO," Doniphan said, holding up the extra set of headphones for Monroe.

Monroe put them on and began listening to the same thing Doniphan was hearing. It wasn't long before he heard a series of muffled explosions, followed by a long interval of silence, and then another series of explosions. Monroe could not decipher them from any other explosions he had heard in his career, so he had to accept Doniphan's expert conclusion that they were indeed depth charges. And if that were the case, then it could only mean one thing. The *Triggerfish* was under attack.

"The interval of silence happens when the enemy destroyer goes around to get set up for another run," Doniphan offered helpfully.

But Monroe did not need any help to imagine what was going on out there, miles away in the open sea. Undoubtedly, the *Triggerfish* had completed taking on the surviving commandos and was heading for the relative safety of deep water when she came upon some kind of enemy vessel, and now she was taking one hell of a beating. Monroe counted sometimes eight separate explosions in a single pass, meaning eight depth charges dropped. It gave him chills to think about Captain Pancheri and the men of the *Triggerfish* riding out that persistent storm of underwater TNT detonations. It was hard enough to withstand a depth charging while sealed up inside a humid submarine with its normal crew complement breathing up all of the oxygen, but it had to be utterly intolerable inside a submarine packed to the gills with the cries and moans of wounded, exhausted, and beaten soldiers. That was the stuff of physical and mental breakdown.

The distant barrage rumbled on for at least ten more minutes while Monroe half-wondered if he should abandon the men ashore and make some attempt to help the beleaguered *Triggerfish*. It would be light out soon, and then he would have no choice but to abandon the men ashore and head for deep water. Maybe he should go ahead and do it now, since the *Whitefin*'s wolf-pack mate was in trouble. But that thought evaporated after one particularly heavy barrage reverberated across the deep—a barrage that made Doniphan's face turn even more grim.

"What is it?" Monroe asked.

Doniphan tapped a finger to his headphones, indicating that Monroe should listen closer. Monroe pressed the headphones to his ears. After a few seconds, he could just make out a faint, intermittent sound that resembled that of a series of doors being slammed shut in quick succession.

Kalump-kalump . . . Kalump-kalump . . .

"What's that?" Monroe asked hesitantly, but he already knew what it was. He had heard the same noises many times before, coming from enemy ships in their final death throes.

"That's the sound of multiple compartments imploding, sir," Doniphan said dismally. "The *Triggerfish* . . ." Doniphan's voice faded off as he and Monroe listened to the last of the *Triggerfish*'s nine watertight compartments implode in a sickening crunch. Any further reports were unnecessary. Monroe removed his headset and stared blankly at the blood red bulkhead as a hush descended on the conning tower. The other sailors in the room seemed to sense his despair, and a whole career's worth of leadership training could not wipe the funereal look off his face.

Marty Pancheri, the officers, the crew, and an untold number of army commandos aboard the *Triggerfish* were gone—crushed by the sea in those last horrifying moments.

TREMAIN was frustrated as he stared down Miguel's uncle. He had spent the better part of the last hour trying, pleading, practically begging the Moro chief and his fellow guerilla leaders to put aside their differences with the Allies and join in the attack on the Japanese garrison. He had talked until he was blue in the face, but had come up with the same answer every time. Luckily, Miguel's uncle spoke a workable amount of English, since he had interacted often with the Philippine constabulary and its American advisors through most of his young adult life.

"We will not attack Japanese tonight," the Moro chief repeated for the seventh time. "It is too dangerous. You Americans will sail away and leave us here alone to face Japanese punishment."

"My men and I might sail away, but the Allies will be back. Remember, you have General MacArthur's word on that."

"Yes." The chief nodded skeptically, removing a pack of cigarettes from his pocket adorned with the "I shall return" logo, one of the many pieces of Allied propaganda distributed to the various Filipino rebel groups whenever American submarines made supply drops. "I remember it whenever smoke. But we are not happy for MacArthur to return.

want the Japanese to go, yes, but we do not want MacArthur to return."

Although General Douglas MacArthur's father, Arthur MacArthur, had commanded U.S. infantry divisions in the American invasion of the Philippines and had become military governor shortly thereafter, General Douglas MacArthur had enjoyed only a measured amount of popularity among the Philippine populace while serving as a field marshal in the Philippine Army prior to the war. Obviously there were still some, like the old chief, who viewed him as nothing more than another American imperialist general bent on securing the islands as a United States territory once again. Tremain thought this was an odd stance for the *datu* to take since his own nephew was a member of the United States Navy, but then political, religious, and bloodlines did not always intersect.

Tremain hesitated to press the issue any further. He had already pushed the limits of the rebels' patience by telling them about the deaths of Jokanin and Puyo. Understandably, the news had upset them considerably, and Tremain gathered from their heated conversation afterward that they planned to tear the British officer apart, limb from limb, the next time they saw him. But from all appearances, they had believed Tremain when he told them that he and the crew of the *Whitefin* were unwitting accomplices. But if he persisted in trying to persuade them to join the attack, they might get annoyed with him and decide that an American commander would serve as a compensatory sacrifice just as well as a British major.

Tremain checked his watch. It was 0406. The issue was academic now, for he had run out of time. He had to abandon all hopes of enlisting assistance from the guerillas now. In less than four minutes, the *Whitefin* would begin her naval bombardment. Like a battleship softening up a beachhead, she would shell the fuel depot with round after round of indirect fire from her four-inch deck gun, hoping that one of the high explosive shells hit a fuel dump and initiated secondary explosions. If all went well, the sight of the fuel depot going up flames would cause confusion among the Japanese military ce troops in the village and perhaps draw off enough of to allow Lopez and his men to storm the house where the ers were being held, and steal away before the enemy knew what happened. Of course, the percussion of the deck gun would also alert every Japanese soldier with a radio inside a ten-mile radius that an American submarine was riding at anchor in the bay west of the promontory, and they would most certainly summon planes or patrol boats to descend upon the isolated cove. But Tremain tried not to think too far ahead of himself. He had to trust that Monroe would handle the ship appropriately until he retuned. There would be time enough to worry about planes and patrol boats after Whately and his men were safely aboard the ship.

Right now, he had to concentrate on getting back to the beach, finding Whately's two rafts, and getting them ready to go before Lopez and his scouts arrived there toting the rescued prisoners. Presumably the two craft were hidden somewhere in the brush just above the beach, and hopefully no Japanese patrols had stumbled across them.

"I'm sorry," Tremain said to the chief as he shouldered his Thompson and checked the forty-five-caliber pistol holstered on his belt. "But the fireworks are about to begin, and I have to go now."

Tremain was extending his hand to the chief when he heard a sudden commotion among the guerilla fighters outside. The muffled voices sounded disconcerted and frantic. Something was wrong.

Moments later the front door flew open and a procession of four rebel fighters, soaking wet from head to foot, entered the room carrying a litter which contained a prostrate and shirtless man. In the dim candlelight, Tremain could see at least five dark red holes in the man's bare chest and lower abdomen, obviously a mixture of entry and exit wounds from a hail of bullets. One of the man's arms, apparently broken, was folded underneath his back at a sickening angle. Tremain concluded that the man was dead before the four rebels had even set the litter down on the floor. All four men were out of breath and appeared to be exhausted, probably from carrying the litter a great distance. Tremain noticed that the pants and hair of the dead man were also quite damp.

One of the guerilla leaders said something in Cebuano the four men, apparently demanding an explanation, which prompted all four men to simultaneously blurt out the de as if in a race to see who could get the whole story out first. The guerilla leaders listened intently—all except for the old Moro chief. Tremain suddenly realized that the old chief had fallen to his knees and was leaning over the body, sobbing quietly and mumbling something in Cebuano. At first Tremain did not understand any of it, but then he finally heard a single word that gave him chills beneath his skin on this hot and humid Mindanao morning.

Miguel.

In an instant Tremain was beside the chief, poring over the body, looking into the hollow, half-open eyes of his dead wardroom steward. He had not recognized Miguel before in the poor lighting, or perhaps the chest wounds had distracted him, or perhaps it had been the salt-encrusted, bloody mat of hair, or the missing ear. Miguel was dead, and now Tremain cursed his own stupidity for sending his steward on the ill-fated errand all alone. What was he thinking? Miguel was no commando. Neither was he.

"What happened?" he finally asked the chief in a solemn tone.

"The Japanese shot him as he was trying to return to your ship," the chief said quietly, not taking his eyes from his dead nephew, but apparently still cognizant enough to listen to the young rebels who were providing the guerilla leaders with the details. "These men were nearby when it happened, but too far to help. They witnessed everything. After the Japanese left, they pulled Miguel from the water, already dead."

The distress of losing one of his sailors was bad enough, but now the full impact of Miguel's death suddenly hit Tremain. Miguel did not make it back to the ship. That meant the *Whitefin* had not received the orders to shell the fuel depot. That meant that there was no forthcoming diversionary attack, and that his whole plan to rescue Whately and the others had just fallen apart. Tremain had no contingency plan to fall back on. Now his men were doomed to endure a pitiable existence as Japanese prisoners of war, not to mention the perils facing Sergeant Lopez and his men now hiding in the jungle south of the enemy-held village, waiting for a diversion that would never come.

Tremain darted outside, suddenly in dire need of fresh air.

With the glow of the new day now just beginning to tint the eastern sky, Sergeant Lopez and his men would soon lose the cover of darkness, as would the *Whitefin*. Though he had not asked to come here, and though he had played no part in the planning of this operation, Tremain could not get the thought out of his head that he was responsible for this military disaster. The familiar headache from his old wound now throbbed with every beat of his heart. He felt exhausted, both physically and mentally drained, and the words Ireland had uttered all those months ago now haunted his crowded mind.

I don't think you're fit to command anymore, Jack. Hell, I don't even think you're fit to be my valet.

Harsh words for an admiral to apply to one of his captains. But now, as he stood there in the clearing beside the sugar mill's washhouse, out of options and out of ideas, with dawn fast approaching, some of his men now prisoners, some about to be, and his submarine sitting in a shallow bay that might very well become her death trap, Tremain was beginning to believe them.

Then a great shouting emanated from the washhouse, first one voice and then many, all yelling at the top of their lungs. Tremain turned to see the guerilla leaders emerge from the front door, where they were met by an equally fervent group of guerilla fighters outside. Some of the younger Moros among the group held their foot-long, wavy, two-edged kris blades high above their heads and began shouting, *"La ilaha il-la'l-lahu! La ilaha il-la'l-lahu!"* while rapidly working themselves into a frenzy. Tremain recognized some of these as the young men Miguel had introduced him to earlier, the young men who had been his childhood playmates. Some of the non-Muslim fighters also joined in the ruckus, firing their M1 rifles into the air, their faces twisted in rage. Then more fighters appeared from out of the shadows, apparently the ones who had been on guard duty, and they, too, joined in the uproar. Within a matter of minutes, Tremain saw the small handful of guerillas grow to upward of a hundred men, most brandishing U.S.-supplied M1 carbine rifles, but a great many, perhaps thirty, carrying nothing more than their shiny kris blades. All of the kris-wielders were now shirtless, and their chant seemed to intensify with each passing second, as if they were under the influence of some secret island herb.

It was complete madness, Tremain thought, to raise such a clamor with Japanese patrols combing the jungle, but the guerillas did not seem to care.

Suddenly he noticed the old chief standing next to him.

"What's going on?" Tremain asked.

"My nephew was loved by all here. The young Muslim men now vow revenge on the infidels who killed him. The rest are simply young and foolish."

"What are they going to do?"

"They will attack the Japanese at the village, and they will be slaughtered. They no longer listen to me, or the other leaders. They wish to die like the *Juramentados* of old. To find *parang-sabil* on the white horse. To recline on couches lined with brocade. To eat the fruit of the two gardens and to know the damsels no man has touched." The Moro chief paused, his eyes displaying the silent wisdom of one all too familiar with the fantasies of young men. "You have the attack you wanted, Commander."

Tremain grimaced. This was not what he wanted at all. He had envisioned using the guerillas as part of a harassing force to cover Lopez and his men as they freed the prisoners, and that whole idea was predicated on the *Whitefin*'s diversion— the diversion that would now never come—drawing off some of the Japanese troops. He certainly had never wished for the rebels to make a frontal assault on a fixed Japanese position. The chief was right. Such an attack would be suicidal.

But suicidal or not, Tremain could see that most of the amateur fighters gathered in that dark clearing seemed intent on making the Japanese at the village pay for the killing of Miguel. As if of a single mind, the clamor died down, and the blade-wielding Moro men rushed off into the jungle, no doubt following old footpaths unfamiliar to the Japanese occupiers and well separated from the main coast road. Moments later, the non-Muslim guerillas shouldered their weapons and did the same, the entire contingent disappearing into the dark brush in a matter of seconds. They were headed east, toward the village, and their certain fates.

As Tremain stared after them, he knew what he had to do. He should return to the ship immediately and head the *Whitefin* for deep water before the sun came up. But who was he kidding? As long as there was a chance to save Whately and his men, or to save Lopez and his men, he had to take it. Tremain cast one look at the Moro chief, whose eyes were still filled with emotion over the loss of his nephew. He and only three of the other leaders remained behind.

Tremain gave a heartwarming nod to the chief. Then, without a word, Tremain shouldered his Thompson submachine gun and trotted off in the direction of the guerilla fighters.

Chapter 27

"**BRIDGE,** Sonar, echo-ranging and high-speed screws to the northeast! Constant bearing, getting louder, sir!"

The report somewhat shocked Monroe, enough so that he motioned for Endicott, who was standing by the bridge speaker, to acknowledge the report while he focused his binoculars on the sea near the rocky spit of land to the northeast. As before, there were no ships in sight all the way to the flat horizon, even with the grayish glow of the coming dawn. It led Monroe to conclude that the enemy ship was hidden from view by the outcropping of land, and that Doniphan's sonar was picking up refracted sound pressure waves bending around the rocky mole. That would explain the constant bearing. The enemy ship was approaching the point of land from the seaward side.

Undoubtedly, this was the same destroyer that had sunk the *Triggerfish*, and it was now searching for another victim. The fact that it had chosen to head directly for this particular cove left Monroe wondering if the whole plan had been compromised, right up to ship movements and positions. Of course, one of the army commandos or even some of the *Whitefin*'s people could have been captured and forced to talk. One or another, Monroe did not doubt that the approaching enemy destroyer knew the *Whitefin*'s exact location and was now heading this way at high speed to trap the American submarine inside the shallow cove.

Once again, Monroe felt every eye on the bridge watching him. As if to emphasize the gravity of the moment, Chief La-Grange climbed up the bridge ladder and approached him.

"I hear we've got a destroyer approaching, XO," LaGrange said briskly. "Don't you think we ought to do something about it?"

Monroe ignored him, doing his best to put all of their distrustful stares out of his mind while he collected his thoughts. He did not need the chief of the boat doubting his every move, or even his indecision, especially not now. There were, after all, very few options on the table. The *Whitefin* had only six torpedoes aboard, all loaded in the forward tubes. The torpedo data computer and the torpedo firing panel were still out of commission from the flood damage on the last patrol—the tender had not been able to repair them during the *Whitefin*'s short interval in port. At that moment, Monroe wished he had made more of a protest over going to sea in such a state. Now he was going to have to take on an enemy destroyer using the antiquated and error-prone angle-solver to come up with a firing solution. The torpedo gyros would have to be set manually, which in itself produced another factor of error. Finally, the tubes would have to be fired from the torpedo room, adding yet another two or three seconds of error.

"Bridge, Sonar," Doniphan's voice intoned over the speaker again. "High-speed screws holding steady on a bearing of zero-two-five. Still getting louder. Ship is definitely approaching, sir."

Monroe brushed past the simmering LaGrange and crossed to the pelorus mounted on top of the bridge gyrocompass repeater. The pelorus was simply a sight glass that allowed the officer of the deck to quickly look down any bearing, using the compass indicator as a guide. Right now, as Monroe used it to look directly down the bearing of zero-two-five, he found that his suspicions were confirmed. The bearing corresponded perfectly with the extreme western tip of the rocky outcropping lying three thousand yards to the northeast of

Whitefin's anchored position. The sound was indeed being refracted around the point of land. Therefore, in all probability the enemy destroyer would not come into view until it rounded the point, and then it would be only three thousand yards away—less than two miles—a distance that could be covered by a high-speed destroyer in less than four minutes.

"Control Room, Bridge." Monroe reached over and keyed the speaker, "Quartermaster, how much water do we have under the keel?"

After a slight delay, Owens's deep voice responded. "Bridge, Control. Seventy-four feet under the keel, at the last sounding."

Monroe mulled over the seventy-four feet. It was not much, but it was just enough room for the *Whitefin* to submerge. At periscope depth, the *Whitefin* would draw sixty feet of water. So she would have a comfort zone, if it could be called that, of about fourteen feet. Monroe knew there were shoals scattered throughout the area, since he had marked them on the chart himself during the *Whitefin*'s last patrol, when the local fisherman helped him update the ship's charts of the area. But he knew there were no shoals anywhere in the *Whitefin*'s immediate vicinity.

He *could* submerge the *Whitefin*, and feel confident that she would not run aground, but then what? The destroyer obviously knew the *Whitefin* was somewhere in the small cove, otherwise it would not be approaching at such a fast speed. Once it was around the point of land, the destroyer's sonar would find the submerged submarine in a matter of minutes. With the *Whitefin* sitting at periscope depth and unable to go any deeper, the destroyer would not even need its depth charges. It could simply ram the submarine at thirty knots, using its knife-edged bow to cut a mortal gash in the *Whitefin*'s pressure hull.

Monroe once again scanned the long, rocky point of land stretching several hundred yards into the bay. The dull glow in the morning sky allowed him for the first time to see the sheets of white foam thrown into the air by the crashing waves on the far side of the jagged rocks. It was essentially a fingerlike formation of volcanic rocks completely devoid of vegetation from the continuous pounding of the sea. No doubt the natural barrier had been thrown there thousands of years ago by an ancient volcano, perhaps from an eruption of the nearby Mount Balatukan. The sleeping volcano's eight-thousand-foot peak was also just becoming visible in the growing light, as an onminous triangular mass in the distance, rising up above the mist hanging over the jungle along the western side of the bay.

As Monroe kept his binoculars focused on the low point of land, a thought suddenly occurred to him.

"XO, what are you going to do, sir?" LaGrange said in a demanding tone.

Again Monroe ignored him. He had an idea. The captain of this enemy destroyer was in a hurry, and Monroe thought he just might be able to turn his enemy's haste against him.

"Control Room, Bridge," he said evenly into the intercom. "Does our chart show elevation data for that point of land to the northeast of us?"

Owens's voice responded again. "Bridge, Control. It sure does, sir. The whole thing's no more than twenty feet above sea level."

Monroe quickly calculated the right triangles in his head, and came up with the answer he was looking for. Without another moment's hesitation, he swung around to face the questioning glances of the men around him, most noticeably LaGrange, who looked certain that Monroe was about to make another blunder, and one that would mean all of their deaths.

"With all due respect, XO, that destroyer's coming on fast," the chief said abruptly. "Too fast. The way I see it, we've got no business just sitting here, sir. We ought to hightail it out of here on the surface, before we get caught in this cove."

"We're not going to hightail it, Cob. Now I want you to go forward and supervise the anchor handling party."

Then, before LaGrange could respond, Monroe barked out a flurry of orders in such a suddenly authoritative tone that some of the men nearby jolted beneath their gray helmets.

"Secure the guns! Clear the bridge!" Then Monroe keyed the microphone. "Maneuvering, Bridge, start two engines! Prepare to retrieve the anchor!"

The gunners secured their guns and headed below, followed by the lookouts, and finally by Endicott and the uncertain LaGrange, leaving Monroe alone on the darkened bridge. Monroe took the conn and ordered up astern propulsion to unseat the 2,200-pound anchor from the sandy bottom. LaGrange appeared down on the forward main deck, along with three other sailors who quickly manned the forward capstan controls and reeled in the eighty fathoms of anchor chain, until the anchor was secured within its hawse pipe inside the *Whitefin*'s bow superstructure. Monroe heard LaGrange order the men to stow the capstan head, and then all four of them descended into the ship through the gun access hatch on the port side of the conning tower.

"Prepare to dive!" Monroe called over the intercom. Instantly, he heard the rustle of feet through the open bridge hatch as the crew took up their diving stations belowdecks. "Helm, Bridge, all ahead two-thirds."

He was just about to pull the Klaxon when a sudden outbreak of far-off gunfire erupted from the hills of the steamy jungle. This time it did not come from the other side of the promontory where the commandos had landed but rather emanated from inland, roughly in the same direction as the local village he had marked off on the chart earlier. Evidently, somewhere near the village, a major firefight had just begun. But Monroe tried to stay focused on his more immediate concerns as he leaned over to key the microphone.

"Dive! Dive!"

Aaaaooooogaaaahh! . . . Aaaaooooogaaaahh!

As the main ballast tank vents opened, blasting a spray of misty air into the main deck superstructure, allowing the *Whitefin*'s seven main ballast tanks to fill with 358 tons of seawater, Monroe quickly descended through the bridge hatch, wondering if the captain was anywhere near that gunfire, or if he was even still alive.

FABRIANO tried not to wince as he felt the warm blood from the bayonet wound in his left thigh trickle down the length of his leg. The pain was excruciating both from his punctured leg and from his contorted shoulders as he hung by his arms in the middle of the foul-smelling hut. He had fully expected to receive the next blow to the other thigh, but the sudden clamor of gunfire outside, along with several agitated Japanese voices, had for the moment captured the Japanese captain's attention. The soldier who had been acting as the instrument of torture was now at the door along with the other soldier, looking outside with curiosity. The Japanese officers—all except for the doctor, who had taken cover behind the hut's wood-burning stove at the first sound of gunfire—now had their backs to the prisoners as they peered out the long, open window on the other side of the room.

The roar of machine guns filled the air, growing more intense with each passing second. Obviously the Japanese troops outside were engaged in some sort of firefight, and Fabriano could only hope that it was the army commandos, regrouped and re-formed and coming to rescue them.

"Pssst! Hey, Yank!"

Fabriano heard someone calling him, but couldn't place the source until he looked in the direction of Major Farquhar sitting on the bench next to Shelby. The major's arms were bound behind his back as before, but instead of appearing on the verge of unconsciousness, as he had from the moment he had been brought into the room, the major now appeared to be fully alert. He stared back at Fabriano through swollen but blazing eyes.

"You two!" he whispered harshly, glancing at both the hanging Fabriano and the sitting Shelby. "Be ready to back me up!"

"What?" Shelby said stupidly in a normal voice, drawing the notice of one of the Japanese lieutenants by the window. But then another explosion rang out outside and quickly turned the enemy officer's attention back to the window.

"Keep quiet, you bloody fool!" Farquhar scolded Shelby in a hoarse whisper, with a venomous glance. Then to both of them he added, "Just be ready, both of you. And watch for my signal!"

Fabriano suddenly realized that the major's beating had not worn him down nearly as much as he had led his Japanese captors to believe. In fact, he appeared fully vibrant, anxiously studying the Japanese officers on the other side of th room like a lion stalking a herd of wildebeest. Fabriano cou not guess what the major hoped to accomplish, and for the life of him, he could not imagine what kind of backup the major expected him to provide, while hanging from the rafters with a bayonet wound in his thigh. Shelby appeared equally confused with his arms firmly bound behind his back.

But neither one of them had a chance to ask the major any questions. Moments later, the Japanese colonel mumbled a few heated words to the Japanese captain, and the latter quickly buckled his gun belt around the slim waist of his green field tunic, pulled out his sheathed samurai sword, and motioned for the two lieutenants to follow him. The three officers then left the hut, presumably to investigate the source of the weapons fire, leaving only the colonel, the doctor, and the two distracted sentries alone in the room with the prisoners.

The captain and the two lieutenants had hardly left when Fabriano saw the British major, with his arms still bound behind his back, rise from the bench and start approaching the Japanese colonel, who was still staring out the window, completely oblivious to what was going on behind him. Fabriano noticed that somehow the major's cheek was no longer swollen, and that his lower jaw was moving up and down as if he were chewing on a large piece of gum. Silent as a shadow, his slim, naked, and barefoot body moved nimbly across the floor, covering half the distance to the colonel before the Japanese doctor looked up from his hiding place behind the stove and shouted out a feeble alarm.

Then everything seemed to happen in slow motion. The major abandoned his catlike approach and chose to bound the rest of the way across the room, reaching the Japanese colonel just as the enemy officer was turning in reaction to the doctor's cry. With his arms still held by the bamboo pole, the British officer leaped into the air in the last few feet, driving a full-bodied double-kick directly into the colonel's chest, knocking the colonel flat on his back. Before the colonel could get up, Farquhar was on top of him, straddling the colonel's chest and one of his arms with both legs. The Japanese officer's face contorted into an expression of abject terror as Farquhar lunged downward with his face. With his free hand, he colonel reached up and grabbed Farquhar by the throat to try to stop him. But the pudgy Japanese officer had obviously not spent much time on the front line. He was a rear-echelon soldier who had grown soft and was not well-suited for hand-to-hand combat. Farquhar, on the other hand, was like a stalwart piece of hardened steel, and despite the veins bulging on his temples and the hand crushing his throat, he steadily pressed forward until his face was inches away from the Japanese officer's.

The two preoccupied sentries suddenly realized what was happening and cried out as they dashed to help their fallen colonel. In order to reach him, they had to brush by the hanging Fabriano, and when they did, Fabriano took all of his weight onto his bound wrists and kicked at the closest soldier as hard as he could with his good leg. The soldier was unprepared for the side blow. It knocked him off balance and sent him falling into his comrade, who also stumbled and fell to the floor. The two soldiers were down for only two or three seconds, but it was long enough to seal the fate of their commander. As the colonel opened his mouth to let out a futile cry for help, Farquhar made a final thrust forward with his face and pressed his mouth hard against the colonel's. The colonel tried to wrest his mouth free, but Farquhar had firmly bitten down on his lower lip and any movement to either side drew a fresh dribble of the colonel's blood. Even when the two Japanese soldiers thrust their foot-long bayonets deep into his back, Farquhar kept the colonel's lip firmly clenched in his teeth. Then the colonel began to cough violently. His body went into convulsions and a foamy mixture began to exude from the small space between the two men's mouths.

An acidic odor filled the air, awaking Fabriano's nostrils and leading him to conclude that the major had poisoned the colonel, and that he had carried the poison inside his feigned swollen jaw. Finally, one of the Japanese soldiers put the muzzle of his rifle to the side of the major's head and fired a round into the major's skull, blowing his brains onto the nearby wooden wall. But Fabriano figured that the major was dead already, killed by the same poison that the Japanese colonel now choked on as he gurgled up a sickening mixture of blood and foam.

Then, as the soldiers knelt over their wide-eyed and ve

much dead colonel, Fabriano heard voices shouting outside. They did not sound Japanese, but they did not sound American either. It was some other language, spoken in such a frenzied yell that it sounded almost inhuman.

Suddenly, two heavily perspiring, bare-chested local men—madmen, for that was the only way Fabriano could describe the expressions on their faces—burst into the room holding short, gleaming blades above their heads. When they caught sight of the two Japanese soldiers, they let out a blood-curdling cry of *"La ilaha il-la'l-lahu!"* and charged them. The Japanese soldiers had only a fraction of a second to prepare to meet their attackers. One dropped to a knee and fired his rifle into the chest of one onrushing Moro. Fabriano saw an exit wound appear on the man's back, but the Moro kept charging, impaling himself on the Japanese soldier's extended bayonet, while at the same time slashing his wavy short sword in a long sweep that made contact with the soldier's throat. Fabriano guessed that the blade was razor-sharp, because the slice nearly decapitated the Japanese soldier and sent a pulsating geyser of blood into the air as the soldier's head shifted grotesquely to one side.

The other Japanese soldier, the one who had killed Penn, fared only slightly better. He was much better with the bayonet than his comrade, and he chose to remain upright and meet the other charging Moro head-on. He easily parried away a jab from the Moro's sword, and when the Moro man tried to recover by delivering a cutting blow to the soldier's midsection, the soldier thrust his bayonet directly into the Moro's face, piercing straight through his left eye and into his brain. The Moro went into convulsions and fell dead to the floor, with the bayonet and rifle still firmly lodged in his skull. The Japanese soldier smiled in a brief moment of elation, until he realized that the Moro's swipe had actually connected with his lower abdomen. He looked down with horror at the ten-inch gash in his belly, through which some of his intestines were oozing out. With his gut bleeding, the soldier dropped to the floor, his face contorted in agony. But the look of agony was soon replaced by sheer terror as the soldier suddenly realized that Shelby was standing over him wearing a killer's glower.

Though Shelby's arms were still bound to the bamboo pole behind his back, and though he was still naked, the big sailor found no difficulty in delivering a powerful kick to the Japanese soldier's throat, a blow that undoubtedly crushed the soldier's larynx and sent his body whirling back onto the floor. The soldier writhed with one hand on his throat as the other tried in vain to keep in his intestines. Shelby smiled balefully, his face wild with rage, as he shot a lightning-quick kick to the soldier's genitals.

"That's for Penn, you asshole!"

The soldier squirmed from the pain and tried to go into a fetal position, but Shelby quickly came down with another violent stomping blow to the man's throat. And he repeated this over and over again, driving his heel into the man's throat at least a dozen times, until the Japanese soldier no longer moved and the bones in his neck would have been little more than shattered bits and pieces.

Red-faced and worn out from the earlier beating, Shelby sat back down on the bench and took a moment to catch his breath before glancing around at the abundance of dead bodies strewn across the floor. The gunfire continued to intensify outside, and periodically a spray of bullets would slice through the thin walls of the hut, making Fabriano quite anxious about his exposed position.

"Well, Mikey," Shelby finally said between breaths. "I guess that leaves just you and me—and him." Shelby nodded in the direction of the still prostrate and insensible Whately. "Only, he's knocked out, you're all drawn up, and I'm tied to this damn pole. Wouldn't last long out there in that firefight."

Fabriano glanced at one of the kris blades still held firmly in the hand of its dead owner. It was positioned at just enough of an angle that Shelby could probably move his bindings up against it and cut them loose. Fabriano was about to suggest the idea when the thought suddenly occurred to him that if Shelby got free, he would probably go ahead and finish the job he had started on the beach. With that in mind, Fabriano quickly averted his gaze away from the exposed kris blade, so as not to give Shelby any ideas. But it was too late. Shelby h followed his stare, and his swollen face now smiled smugly

"Thanks for the idea, Mikey!" he said, casually. He

trudged over to the dead Moro warrior, got down on the floor, and backed up against the exposed blade. Fabriano began to wonder what was going to kill him first, his bleeding leg, the bullets interlacing the hut, or Shelby as soon as he got free.

Chapter 28

THE Moro village consisted of nothing more than a collection of two dozen dilapidated raised wooden huts, straddling both sides of a narrow dirt road. Some had slanted corrugated tin roofs, and some had thatched roofs, but all were built along the same haphazard principals. They were constructed using wood from the pine trees abundant to the higher elevations. Each structure was rectangular and quite plain, with little to set it apart from the others. Most appeared to consist of a single large room with open windows on each wall. Little thought had been given to aesthetics, and one would be hard-pressed to find two planks cut to the same length.

In the early light of dawn, from his position hiding behind the cluster of rattan trees in the brush to the west of the village, Tremain could see the situation clearly. The village was separated from the dense forest on all sides by a large clearing extending at least fifty yards out. No doubt this space of jungle had been hewn down over the years by the locals for firewood. On the west side of the village, the Japanese had placed two Japanese machine-gun nests, one on each side of the road, but far enough apart, approximately twenty-five yards, to give them good fields of fire and complete command of the approaches to the western side of the village. From what Tremain could make from his position in the tree line directly opposite to the south-side machine-gun nest, both positions contained a standard Japanese Type 1 tripod-mounted 7.7-millimeter heavy machine gun, with three Japanese soldiers, protected by a circular arrangement of crates stacked waist-high.

Tremain could see the two dozen shirtless and motionless bodies scattered throughout the clearing, the aftermath of the Moros' attack. The Moro Juramentados had arrived about two minutes before the main body of guerilla fighters, and no doubt their howling war cries had awoken the Japanese gunners, who greeted the charging kris-wielding warriors with a hail of deadly 7.7-millimeter projectiles. Tremain had heard the machine guns come to life as he trudged through the forest footpaths attempting to stay on the heels of the main body of guerillas, and although he had arrived on the scene several minutes after the Moro attack, he could clearly see what had happened. The Moros had rushed the machine-gun positions, as indicated by the placement of the bodies, some of which lay only a few feet away from the machine guns that had killed them. Tremain thought it possible that some of the Moros had broken through to the village beyond, and perhaps that explained the sporadic firing coming from that direction. But judging from the number of bodies in the clearing, only a handful could have made it through. Perhaps some of them had broken off from their jihad frenzy long enough to warn the village's women and children to take cover.

The non-Muslim guerillas had chosen a much more cautious approach. They had moved through the forest to the north side of the road and were now engaged in a heavy firefight with both Japanese machine-gun positions, concentrating their fire on the north-side gun. Tremain had lost them just as he approached the village, and now found himself all alone crouching in the tree line southwest of the village, with the south-side machine gun nest less than fifty yards away.

The Japanese gunners in the south-side gun emplacement had not seen him yet, but he could clearly see them, as their helmeted heads peeked over the stacks of crates to cover their brethren to the north. Periodically, Tremain would see a guerilla fighter break from the tree line and try to rush the left of the north-side machine gun nest, only to be cut down by flanking fire from the south-side machine gun. Clearly, these guerillas were amateur fighters and had little direction. They had no leadership to organize them, and no one to arrange a flank attack on the unapproachable machine guns. Tremain saw at least two of the Japanese loaders get hit by lucky shots from the guerillas, but they were quickly replaced by two more soldiers who sprinted out to the nests from the cover of the village. Whenever the Japanese gunners did not have any targets in the open to shoot at, they spent their time raking the tree line, where the guerillas were taking cover, with a devastating fire that turned the densely packed trees to mulch. The guerillas were doing their best to keep up a steady return fire, but it was becoming less and less vigorous with each sweep of the Japanese guns. It was only a matter of time before the guerillas broke and ran.

Tremain thought that maybe he should open up with his Thompson. His weapon was made for close combat, and his unskilled marksmanship could never hope to hit anything at this range. But he might draw off some of the Japanese fire, perhaps just long enough for the guerillas to organize a flanking assault.

Since it was the guerillas' only chance for success, Tremain quickly resolved to do it. He seated the wooden stock firmly in his shoulder, using the side of a tree to steady his weapon, and took aim on the pale green helmets poking above the crates surrounding the south-side machine gun. He was about to squeeze the trigger, when he noticed four figures dressed completely in black rise up suddenly from the tall grass only a few yards away from the Japanese machine-gun nest. It was Sergeant Lopez and his three Filipino scouts. Undoubtedly they had been lying on their bellies in the tall grass south of the village waiting for the *Whitefin*'s diversionary attack. When it never came, and the guerilla attack did, they must have slithered their way through the tall grass to a spot close enough to the south-side machine gun emplacement to take the Japanese there completely by surprise.

Now all four dark-clad figures rushed the nest, raised their Thompsons over the stack of crates, and fired their full magazines into the Japanese gunners and loaders. Tremain wanted to let out a cheer as he watched Lopez and his men climb the crates and man the Japanese Type 1 machine gun, instantly turning it on the north-side machine-gun emplacement. The Japanese at the other machine gun suddenly found themselves under fire from two sides. They ducked down behind the protection of the crates, and only managed a few sporadic bursts in return. Evidently, the guerillas realized what had happened, that the north-side Japanese emplacement was now suppressed by Lopez's steady fire, and they began advancing cautiously across the clearing. Seeing that one of their emplacements was taken, the Japanese that were concealed in the village fired their single-shot rifles at Lopez and his men, but the Filipino scouts had already reinforced the crate wall on the village side of the machine-gun nest, rendering any fire received from that quarter useless.

For the first time, Tremain began to think that the attack was headed for success, as the guerillas crept forward, closing in on the suppressed Japanese machine gun. But then Tremain noticed a group of five Japanese soldiers break from cover in the village beyond Lopez's machine-gun nest. All of the Japanese soldiers Tremain had seen so far were wearing loose-fitting, short-sleeved white shirts, no doubt to deal with the heat and humidity of the jungle, but the officer leading these soldiers wore an olive green, long-sleeved field tunic, buttoned all the way up to the neck. As if that were not odd enough, the Japanese officer carried a samurai sword in one hand and a pistol in the other as he spurred his men to hurry into one of the raised huts on the extreme western edge of the village.

Tremain thought little of it at first, but upon closer examination of the hut, he realized that it was lifted up on stilts just high enough to give anyone in the window a clear line of fire over the crates protecting Lopez's machine-gun nest. With only seconds to act, Tremain broke into the clearing and began sprinting toward Lopez's position, shouting, yelling, shooting his gun in the air, waving his arms, trying everything he could think of to get their attention. But the Filipino scouts could not hear him over the clamor of the heavy machine gun. Their concentration was fixed on the other Japanese machine-gun nest.

Tremain watched helplessly as the Japanese officer appeared

in the open window of the raised hut, along with one of his soldiers, who carried a Type 100 submachine gun, with its telltale curved magazine extending from one side. With one point of the samurai sword, the Japanese officer directed the soldier to shoot down onto Lopez and his men, and he did so with terrible results. The soldier took aim and sprayed an entire magazine of eight-millimeter projectiles into the machine-gun nest. Two of the Filipino scouts' heads exploded instantly in a cloud of red mist. Another scout managed to raise his Thompson to return fire but took two rounds in the neck and fell over clutching a throat spurting streams of blood. Lopez had absorbed several of the eight-millimeter bullets across his back and would have been further riddled had he not leaped from the nest at the last minute and rolled into the cover behind the crates on the clearing side of the nest. Lopez lay there prostrate on his back, and Tremain assumed that the bullets had damaged his spine, because the sergeant appeared to have limited movement in his arms, and none at all in his legs. As the Japanese soldier changed out his magazine, Tremain suddenly realized that he himself was still out in the open, and that the Japanese officer and soldier in the window were looking directly at him. The soldier appeared to be having trouble advancing the first round from his new magazine, and it was a good thing, too; otherwise Tremain would have been under fire at that very moment.

Then Tremain saw Lopez pull a black cylindrical object from his ammunition belt and toss it over the crates in the direction of the raised hut. The can rolled a few yards and then popped with a flash, instantly exuding an immense cloud of white smoke. Before the Japanese soldier could clear the chamber of his weapon and advance a new round, a blanket of smoke had enveloped the hut and the machine-gun nest, completely obscuring his field of view.

Lopez's smoke grenade had bought Tremain some time, and he did not intend to squander it. Sprinting the last few yards, Tremain reached the relative safety of Lopez's position and quickly knelt beside the wounded Filipino sergeant. Bleeding exit wounds covered the sergeant's chest and stomach, and he coughed up blood with nearly every breath. But his eyes still managed to meet Tremain's with a determined stare.

"Take them out, Commander," Lopez grunted, using all the strength he could muster to thrust a grenade into Tremain's hand. "Take them out before the smoke clears."

With that, Lopez's eyes lost their entire cognizance, and his body went limp. As if to ensure that his dying wish was fulfilled, Lopez's right hand flopped lifelessly into the dirt, and Tremain noticed that the free pin of the grenade was wrapped around the index finger. Tremain had little choice now. Luckily he still had a firm hold on the safety lever, so he was not in a race against the grenade's fuse, but he was in a race against the rapidly clearing smoke screen.

As the Japanese soldier's submachine gun once again rang out overhead, Tremain used the muzzle flashes in the white smoke to judge the distance to the hut's window. It was approximately fifteen yards away, and though he may have played football at the academy, his athletic days were long past, and he stood a very slim chance of making the throw from here. He had only one other alternative. Taking the calculated risk that the Japanese soldier was firing blind and could not see anything, Tremain used his free hand to sling the Thompson behind his back, then rose from the cover of the crates and made a mad dash through the drifting smoke, reaching the stilts of the hut in a matter of seconds. Looking up at the open window, he could see the smoking barrel of the Japanese submachine gun protruding over his head, still firing off into the clearing where he had been when the Japanese first laid eyes on him. Apparently the Japanese soldier did not know he was now only inches away. With careful aim and a steady hand, he hooked the grenade through the window and then raced back to the cover of the crates. Once there, he heard a brief exclamation in Japanese and then a loud explosion that shook the ground beneath his feet.

When Tremain finally dared to lift his head above the cover of the crates, the hut had collapsed on one side, and dark smoke drifted out of the open window. Initially, he assumed that everyone in the structure had been killed, but then he saw movement in the wreckage. Moments later the Japanese officer emerged, bleeding from the nose and ears, his green tunic now covered in white dust. He no longer had the pistol, but remarkably he still carried the samurai sword. He used it as a cane as he stumbled away from the ruined hut and headed back into the village.

Tremain raised his Thompson and fired off several quick bursts at the fleeing Japanese officer, but he only managed to pepper the nearby buildings with forty-five-caliber ammunition. The officer soon ducked out of sight. Then Tremain was forced to take cover, as the morning breeze carried away the last remnants of the smoke grenade and the Japanese soldiers concealed in the village took him under fire.

As he hid behind the crates, out of breath, with Lopez's dead body sprawled out beside him, he noticed that a small handful of guerillas had managed to overrun the other machine-gun nest and were now turning the gun around to aim it at the village. It appeared that the tide of the battle had finally turned, as the Type 1 heavy machine gun opened up and began pecking away like a woodpecker at the thin-walled huts hiding the enemy troops. Tremain peeked over the crates to watch the carnage as the 7.7-millimeter projectiles turned the flimsy huts into splinters. He could only pray that the women and children of the village—as well as his own men, wherever they were—had the wherewithal to take cover.

THE firefight outside had intensified, as Fabriano hung in the middle of the room with his arms completely numb and his left thigh throbbing with pain. With stray bullets whipping through the hut much more often now and his exposed position becoming more and more precarious, he gave up any hope that Shelby would ever cut him loose.

It had taken Shelby about ten minutes to cut himself free using the razor-sharp kris blade, and after taking several long minutes to stretch his arms and shoulders, the big sailor removed the pants from the largest of the dead Moros, cut them into shorts, and put them on over his naked body. Then he rifled the bodies for weapons and ammunition and other items of value, even the bodies of the dead Moros. Through a quick but methodical examination of the contents of their wallets, their fingers, and their wrists, he came up with a small collection of valuable trinkets and shoved them into the front pocket of the cut-off shorts. Shelby did it in such a systematic manner and with such nonchalance that Fabriano concluded the big sailor had been a thief long before he ever laid his hands on the *Chevalier*'s money.

"Well, Mikey," Shelby finally said with a smile. "I guess this is it."

"Look, asshole, you need me. How long do you think you'll last out in the jungle with Jap patrols everywhere?"

"Well, that's where you're wrong, Mikey. I did my homework, see. I looked over the chart on the quartermaster's table before we came ashore." He paused and winked. "I was looking for a good spot to put your body. But while I was looking, I happened to see this here village on the chart, as well. And now I got it all in here. I know exactly which direction I have to go to find the *Whitefin*."

"What if she's not there? What if she's left or been destroyed?"

"Oh, Mikey," Shelby said with a hand on his chest. "I'm so flattered that you care about my personal well-being. But it doesn't matter if the *Whitefin*'s gone or not. I'll just hook up with those guerillas and hop aboard the next sub that comes in for a supply drop. You see, Mikey. You can't stop me. That money of yours is all mine. Penn might have been a useful shipmate if we ever made it to a POW camp, but now that I know I'm going to get out of here, I'm glad the Japs got rid of him for me."

Somehow Fabriano was not surprised at Shelby's callousness, even regarding his now-dead partner in crime.

"Cut me down, you son of a bitch," Fabriano muttered, knowing the demand would fall on deaf ears.

"I can't do that, Mikey. But I'll tell you what I will do. I'm not going to kill your sorry ass. How about that? And I'm not going to kill that asshole either." Shelby pointed to the unconscious Whately. "I'm going to let the Japs have that privilege. I sure wouldn't want to be the two of you guys when those Japs get back and find their colonel deader than a can of tuna. I bet they'll be mad as hell, and I'm sure they'll take real good are of you and the lieutenant, Mikey. Oh well, I'll be seeing ou."

With that, Shelby picked up one of the Japanese rifles, slid of the kris knives into the waist of his makeshift shorts, and headed for the door. As his big frame crowded out the doorway, he looked over his shoulder to cast one last smug glance in Fabriano's direction. But then he suddenly winced, and his smile transformed into a look of shock and agony. As Shelby dropped the rifle and stumbled back into the room, Fabriano could see that a samurai sword was firmly lodged in his bare belly. It had run him through completely and was protruding from his back. As the big sailor's wide eyes stared in horror at the blade buried deep within his abdomen, the Japanese captain groped his way into the room. He looked nothing like the pristine officer who had left the hut only a few minutes before. Now he looked more like something raised from the grave, with his face and hair covered in dust, his uniform torn in several places, and his wool tunic stained by the streams of blood oozing from his nose and ears. But despite his pitiful appearance, the Japanese captain still seemed to have some fight left in him. He took two steps toward the staggering Shelby and, in one swift motion, yanked the blade from the sailor's abdomen. Shelby let out a cry of pain, which was quickly silenced when the captain swung his sword with two hands in a high sweeping arc that ended with the blade lodged three-quarters of the way through Shelby's neck, nearly decapitating him. Shelby's big lifeless frame stood upright for several seconds before it collapsed to the deck in a clump of twitching limbs.

Fabriano felt the bastard had gotten what he deserved, but he was still sickened by the sight. Shelby would never get the chance to spend the *Chevalier*'s money now.

Then Fabriano noticed that the captain had retrieved his sword and was approaching him using the sword as a cane. The Japanese officer was surveying the ghastly display of death in the room, and his eyes blazed with rage when he finally noticed the colonel lying dead in a puddle of foamy blood. At that moment, Fabriano knew that his own fate was sealed.

"You American dog!" the Japanese officer snarled as he positioned himself in front of Fabriano and brought the sword up in both hands. Fabriano was determined not to give the bastard the satisfaction of letting him know he was afraid, and he stared directly into the Japanese officer's eyes all through out his windup to deliver the lethal slash.

Then a shot rang out inside the room. First one, then three more in quick succession.

The Japanese officer dropped the sword, and his face distorted into a deathlike stare. When he finally fell to the ground at Fabriano's feet, Fabriano saw that the Japanese doctor was standing by the colonel's dead body, holding the colonel's smoking pistol in his hand. He must have been hiding behind the big iron stove for the last half hour, and only now left his hiding place in order to save Fabriano's life. The small man had tears streaking beneath his glasses, and Fabriano could see that the revolver shook in his trembling hand. The doctor remained in that same rigid stance for almost a full minute before he finally dropped the revolver to the floor and somewhat composed himself.

For a moment, Fabriano wondered what his intentions were, as the doctor approached him and took up the captain's bloody sword. But when the doctor used the sword to cut his bindings loose, Fabriano knew that he intended no harm. Fabriano fell to the deck, welcoming the rush of blood back into his arms, and the relief to his aching legs. He lay there for several minutes, allowing himself a few moments of recuperation from nearly an hour in that terrible outstretched position. At one point he realized that the doctor was kneeling beside him dressing his bayonet wound. When the doctor finished, he helped him onto the bench then dug around in a nearby basket until he came up with two pairs of rather wretched-looking pants, giving one to Fabriano. The pants belonged to one of the local villagers, whoever owned this hut, and consequently they were extremely tight and uncomfortable. But they would do. Whately had started coming to, but he was still too weak to stand, so both Fabriano and the Japanese doctor together put the other pair of pants on him.

Then the doctor helped both men get onto their feet. Fabriano threw one of Whately's arms around his shoulders, taking most of his weight.

"Why are you helping us?" Fabriano finally ventured to ask as the Japanese doctor handed him one of the rifles to use as a crutch. "Why did you kill one of your own officers to save me?"

The doctor did not look into his eyes, but kept his head low, as if he were now living in shame.

"He was not one of my own," he said simply, then ushered Fabriano to the door. "Now you must go, before someone else returns."

"But what about yo—" Fabriano did not press the issue any further, as the doctor brushed past him, descended the wooden steps of the hut, and walked briskly in the opposite direction of the gunfire, joining a throng of Japanese soldiers fleeing the village. The panic-stricken mob was in such a mad rush to get away that none appeared to take notice of the two white-skinned Americans standing on the porch of the hut.

"W-What's going on, Fabriano?" Whately mumbled in his semiconscious state. "Where are we? And what are all those Japs doing here?"

"Don't you worry none, Lieutenant. Just hang on to me, sir. We're gonna make it back home."

Chapter 29

"**ARE** all torpedo tubes ready for firing?" Monroe demanded as he kept the periscope firmly locked on the rocky stretch of land. He could feel his heart pounding inside his chest as he waited for the first glimpse of the enemy destroyer. Judging from the volume of the screw noise in Doniphan's headset, it would not be long now.

"Forward torpedo room reports tubes one through six ready for manual firing in all respects with the exception of opening the outer doors," the phone talker at Monroe's elbow reported.

"Very well. Open outer doors on tubes one through six, stand by for gyro angle settings."

As the phone talker relayed the order to the torpedo room, Monroe removed his face from the eyepiece long enough to shout down the ladder to the control room. "Owens! What's going on down there? Where the hell are my gyro settings?"

Before Monroe returned his face to the eyepiece, he caught a doubtful glance from LaGrange standing at the base of the control room ladder. The chief of the boat still did not trust him, and he wondered how much that sentiment pervaded the rest of the crew.

"Got it, sir!" Owens finally proclaimed, calling up the

open hatch. "Set gyros to starboard four-point-five degrees, Captain. Err-uh, I mean XO, sir."

Monroe was too busy looking through the periscope to notice the several raised eyebrows at Owens's slight slip of the tongue. If he had noticed it, he would not have cared. At this point, for all intents and purposes, he was their captain. Whether they liked it or not, they had no choice now but to follow him into harm's way and hope for the best.

"Pass the word to the torpedo room," Monroe said to the phone talker. "Set all torpedoes to high speed, set depth to five feet, and set gyros to starboard four-point-five."

"XO," Endicott said, standing at the angle-solver, next to the broken and useless TDC. "Could you tell us what we're shooting at, sir? You haven't even taken an observation yet."

"We're shooting at the enemy destroyer, Tom, and believe me, I'll be giving you plenty of observations any minute now."

"But how can we set the gyros when we don't even have a solution on the target, sir?"

"I don't have time to explain, Tom. What I need you to do right now is to get on the banjo and calculate a reverse solution using a gyro setting of starboard four-point-five degrees. Assume a target speed of ten knots, a course of two-six-zero, and a range of three thousand yards. Work that out for me and let me know the firing bearing. Understood?"

"Aye, sir," Endicott mumbled.

From Endicott's tone, Monroe could tell that he was still confused, but he had every bit of confidence that the capable junior officer would carry out the order in exemplary fashion. Ever since Berkshire's death on the last patrol, Endicott had been brushing up on the use of the handheld Mark 8 angle-solver, also known as the banjo.

In all reality, Monroe probably could have afforded a few moments to explain his strategy to the young officer and all of those around him, but he did not want to. He was tired of the suspicious stares and the second-guessing, and he wanted no more of it. Not from Endicott, not from LaGrange, and not from any other member of the crew. He knew they would think his plan was crazy.

Half an hour ago, he had submerged the ship under the a sumption that even at periscope depth he would be able to the masts of the Japanese ship poking above the low point of land just before the warship made its turn into the cove. He had based this assumption solely on his own memory of the chart.

Monroe may not have been the best of leaders. The men under him might doubt his ability to command a ship. But the one thing he had always prided himself on was his astute abilities as a ship's navigator. He took pride in the flawless accuracy of his fixes, and he took pride in committing entire charts to memory. He remembered vividly the various shoals he had marked on the chart while consulting the local fisherman who had helped pilot them back to deep waters during the first patrol. From the information gleaned from the fisherman, Monroe knew that the waters just beyond the cove's entrance were much more dangerous than the smooth surface led one to believe. The entire bay was cluttered with dangerous shoals, some lurking less than a foot beneath the surface, just waiting to grab the keel of the next hapless vessel. Monroe also knew that the intricate maze of submerged sandbars prevented any ship from approaching the cove except by two natural, unmarked channels. One was the passage on the west side of the bay, which the *Whitefin* had used the night before to creep into the little cove. The other was on the east side of the bay, undoubtedly the same passage now being used by the approaching Japanese destroyer. Monroe remembered that the eastern passage was particularly winding and narrow, which would explain why it was taking so long for the destroyer to reach the cove. The next-to-last leg of the passage ran westward, horizontal to the seaward side of the rocky mole and just one thousand yards away beyond it. Then, after clearing the mole, the unseen channel made a sharp ninety-degree turn to the south, onto its final leg, which ran in a straight line for a mile and a half, straight into the relatively safe waters of the cove. That was the way Monroe remembered it. After the *Whitefin* submerged, a quick jaunt down to the chart table in the control room had confirmed this. Thanks to the information imparted the local fisherman, the entire channel was clearly marked the *Whitefin*'s chart. So theoretically, without even a single scope observation, Monroe knew the exact path the Japanese destroyer would have to take.

Of course, there was always the chance that the fast-moving

enemy warship would run aground, but Monroe certainly held out no hopes for that. The Japanese had owned these waters for more than two years and had undoubtedly charted every shoal and reef in the area. But one thing that he could count on was that the enemy destroyer would follow the invisible channel all the way into the cove, since any deviation from it meant certain grounding. With that in mind, Monroe had taken a series of fixes on the local landmarks and had conned the *Whitefin* to the extreme end of the channel's final leg, where she now sat at periscope depth with her bow tubes pointed directly up the narrow passage, like a hungry mongoose waiting for a snake to emerge from its hole. The gyro setting Owens had just passed him would drive the *Whitefin*'s torpedoes directly up the center of the channel to an imaginary spot where the destroyer would at some time in the future turn onto the final leg.

But here was the catch. The optimum time to attack the destroyer was not when it was driving down the channel toward them and presenting a narrow bow-on aspect. The optimum time to attack was when the destroyer was making the sharp ninety-degree turn onto the final leg. In those brief moments, while the enemy ship was turning to the south, her broad beam would be exposed to the *Whitefin*'s torpedo tubes for just a few precious seconds. The trouble was, that turning point was over three thousand yards away from the *Whitefin*'s current position, which meant that the *Whitefin*'s torpedoes would have to be perfectly timed to cruise up the mile-and-a-half leg of the channel and reach the turning point at the precise moment the enemy destroyer did. Also, a torpedo run of three thousand yards meant that the Mark 14 steam-driven torpedoes would have to be fired from a distance that was very close to their maximum high-speed range, increasing the probability that an enemy lookout might sight their wakes and alert the destroyer in time to avoid them. If all of that were not enough rain on Monroe's parade, there was the fact that the markings on the *Whitefin*'s chart were not official. They were based on the memory of a local Filipino fisherman who Monroe had spent several hours struggling to communicate with—one of the reasons he did not want to take the *Whitefin* any farther up the channel to close the range.

He did not share his plan with the others, because he

it was far-fetched and he knew it had holes in it. But he also knew that it was their best chance of coming out of this mission alive.

Just then, Monroe saw the masts of the enemy ship finally come into the periscope's field of view, sticking up over the promontory and rapidly moving to the left. They were unmistakably the swept masts of an enemy destroyer, and judging from their bearing rate they were traveling at close to twenty knots. Now Monroe's adrenaline took over, and any pessimistic thoughts about the plan were instantly purged from his mind.

"Enemy destroyer in sight!" he announced to the men in the conning tower.

As he felt his men brushing past him on the way to their designated battle stations, Monroe tried his best to line up the reticle on the destroyer's leading mast, but it was moving so quickly to the left that he could hardly keep the periscope centered on it.

"Bearing, mark!"

"Zero-two-seven."

"Range, mark! Use a ninety-foot mast head height!"

"Three thousand four hundred yards."

"Angle on the bow, port ninety."

Endicott entered the data into the angle-solver and did the required calculations in his head. One minute later, Monroe took another observation, allowing Endicott to come up with a rough solution.

"You were right about the course and range, XO, but wrong about the speed. I've got him on a course of two-six-zero, at twenty-four knots, at a range of three thousand two hundred yards."

"Very well," Monroe answered, somewhat startled that the enemy destroyer had not yet slowed down to a safe speed to negotiate the upcoming turn. His whole plan was dependent on destroyer slowing to a constant speed so that Endicott could rmine the exact moment to launch the *Whitefin*'s torpedoes. oe heard Endicott behind him using a grease pencil to le a shorthand equation on the TDC's glass cover.

that speed, XO, he'll reach our aiming point in two and inutes. We don't have much time."

Monroe knew Endicott was correct. It would take a full two minutes for the *Whitefin*'s Mark 14 torpedoes, traveling at forty-six knots, to cover the three-thousand-yard distance. But Monroe also knew that the enemy destroyer would have to slow down prior to the turn. Perhaps this destroyer captain was crafty and had counted on the American submarine to do exactly what Monroe was attempting. If so, the destroyer captain certainly knew what he was doing. Waiting for the last possible moment to change speed was an excellent tactic to throw off a torpedo-firing solution.

"Stand by to fire tubes one through six!" Monroe barked out of frustration, now concluding that he simply had to start shooting and hope for the best.

"Tubes one through six, ready," the phone talker reported.

"Fire one!"

The deck beneath his feet rumbled as the first Mark 14 torpedo left its tube, fired up its internal combustion engine, took a slight turn to the right, and drove off at forty-six knots under steam power.

"Number one torpedo fired manually, sir."

Since there was little chance now in calculating the precise time the destroyer would reach the turn, Monroe counted down ten seconds before firing the next one, to give the torpedoes a good spacing and maximize the chances of scoring at least one hit.

"Fire two!"

Torpedo two left its tube, followed at ten-second intervals by all of the others.

Now, with the *Whitefin*'s six torpedoes in the water traveling up the channel, the first one already halfway to its aim point, Monroe finally saw the masts of the enemy destroyer slow down. After two more quick observations, Endicott revised his calculations.

"Enemy destroyer is at eight knots. Range, three thousar yards."

Monroe nodded but said nothing as he watched the stroyer's mast reach the end of the mole. He was eager t the enemy's hull at last, but there was little left to do nc watch as all six torpedoes sped toward an uncertain rend with the enemy ship. He already knew that the first tw miss, since they would reach the bend in the channel several seconds before the destroyer got there, but torpedoes three and four had an excellent chance of hitting the destroyer while it was in the middle of the turn.

But as Monroe saw the first glimpse of the enemy destroyer's bow emerge from behind the rocky mole, he felt his face lose all of its color, and his temples immediately break out into a cold sweat.

The black bow of the enemy destroyer was unmistakable in the gray light of dawn, and soon the forward dual-gun turret was visible, too, along with the squat superstructure and the familiar black-ringed smokestacks.

It was the *Shigure.*

For a moment, Monroe forgot where he was or what he was doing. Just the sight of the destroyer that had inflicted so much damage during that dreadful depth charging on the last patrol sent his head spinning.

"I've got a bearing rate on the target now, sir," Doniphan reported as he steered his hydrophone. Now that the *Shigure* was no longer being masked by land, the *Whitefin*'s sonar was picking up direct sound waves, allowing Doniphan to track the enemy ship.

"You should be able to see it now, XO," Endicott said with curiosity in his voice. "Can you see it? Can you identify it?"

This was it, Monroe thought. This was the moment when his luck ran out, when he sealed the fates of the men aboard the *Whitefin*, like he had on the *R-15*, and that night when Heath was swept away. He suddenly believed the superstitions, that he was plagued with bad luck, a Jonah of submariners. As he watched the sleek profile of the veteran destroyer *Shigure* slowly cruise toward the turning point, he was convinced that er lookouts would sight the torpedo wakes. He was con- nced that she would avert the torpedoes, then steam angrily wn the channel and smash the trapped *Whitefin* with her ging bow.

XO?" Endicott said again, with slight impatience in his "Request you identify the target, *sir.*"

uld he tell them? Monroe wondered. Was it really im- for them to know they were facing the *Shigure*?

"Shiratsuyu class," Monroe said evenly, and resolved to say no more.

"Ten seconds to impact on number one."

In high-power magnification, Monroe placed the reticle directly on the bubbling mass of torpedo wakes driving up the center of the channel. The *Shigure* was still far to the right, and she appeared to have slowed even further. Perhaps she had finally seen the wakes.

Then Monroe saw a dirty brown geyser of mud and water shoot into the air. The first torpedo had reached the end of the channel and had continued on into the shoal waters beyond, detonating on a sandbar. Now there could be no question that the *Shigure* was alerted to the incoming torpedoes. Her screws must have switched from ahead slow to all back emergency, because she suddenly slowed to little more than a snail's pace. Monroe watched helplessly as the next torpedo also detonated on a sandbar.

"XO?" Monroe heard Owens's voice call up the hatch from the control room. "Request a land fix, sir."

"Damn it, Owens!" Monroe shouted at the top of his lungs. "We're in the middle of a fucking attack! We can take a land fix later!"

"Yes, sir. Sorry, sir. It's just that the tide table shows we should be feeling a pretty good ebb flow right about now. I wouldn't have bothered with it, sir, but seeing as how we're near them shoals and the current's probably carrying us toward them, I thought you might want to take another fix to check out our position. That's all, sir."

Of course! Monroe thought. The blessed current! He remembered the tide tables as if he had just read them. How could he have been so stupid to forget?

"Right you are, Owens," he said, now suddenly energized. "I'll ring up a backing bell, to compensate."

"Aye, Captain," came Owens's jolly reply.

"Helm, all back one-third."

As the helmsman rang up the astern propulsion, Mor swung the periscope back over to the *Shigure*, compl ignoring the detonation of the *Whitefin*'s third torpedo a the sandbar. He no longer cared about the torpedoes, a sudden excitement had nothing to do with the ebb tide's impact on the *Whitefin*. But it had everything to do with the tide's impact on the *Shigure*. The enemy destroyer was just a thousand yards off the tip of the rocky mole, and he suspected the current would be much stronger there. And his suspicions were confirmed when he saw the *Shigure* execute an awkward turn to port while she was still in the westbound portion of the channel. By slowing to avoid the torpedoes, she had lost the counteracting effect of her rudder, and now the outbound current was setting her toward the shoal waters on her starboard side. Obviously, her sudden turn to port was meant to keep her from running aground. But Monroe was delighted to see that the maneuver had been ordered a few seconds too late, when the *Shigure* suddenly shuddered and came to a complete stop with her starboard quarter buried in the sand.

"She's run aground!" Monroe exclaimed, and heard a few cheers in the compartment around him.

Then, as the *Whitefin*'s fourth torpedo exploded harmlessly on a shoal, Monroe watched the *Shigure* do the unthinkable. Rather than waiting several hours for the next flood tide, when she could have floated off with hardly a scratch, she made an attempt to drive off right now, against a strong current and inside a narrow channel. Her captain must be bloodthirsty, and yearning for yet another submarine trophy to add to his war chest. Great plumes of black smoke belched from her stacks as he ordered up more steam. Then, with an all-or-nothing spirit, the inevitable flank bell was ordered and the ship lurched. In high-power magnification, Monroe could see the *Shigure*'s masts shudder from the immense vibration as the giant screws fought to pull her free. Then, suddenly, she was free—free from the sandbar and surging forward. The Japanese captain had the foresight to order an immediate starboard turn to keep his bow from being driven into the other side of the channel. But what he had not anticipated was his ship's forward momentum, which was now carrying her directly toward the channel's turning point, and directly into the path of the *Whitefin*'s remaining two torpedoes.

A great flurry of foam bubbled near the *Shigure*'s stern as she put on emergency astern propulsion. Her advance started to slow, but she was still drifting forward as the *Whitefin*'s fifth torpedo exploded on the sand just two hundred yards off her starboard bow.

Monroe held his breath and squeezed the periscope handles as he waited for the *Whitefin*'s sixth and final torpedo to run its course. He had the reticle lined up on its wake, and the *Shigure*'s black bow was just a hair's breadth to the right of it. It was going to be close.

TREMAIN sat on the damp earth beneath the jungle canopy, smelling the salty air of the nearby shoreline as he cradled Whately's head in his hands. The lieutenant was unconscious, as he had been during their brief trudge through the jungle when Tremain and Fabriano had carried him from the coast road to the spot where he now lay, a mere stone's throw from the beach.

Tremain had been exceedingly happy to find his two surviving crewmen when the guerillas finally finished wresting the village from the Japanese, but he had been shocked and angered by their condition. Despite Fabriano's wretched state, the ex–destroyer sailor had managed to greet Tremain with a smile and had assured him that he was fully capable of carrying the lieutenant all the way back to the beach by himself if necessary. Fortunately, that had not been the case, since the Japanese had left two of their trucks behind, and Fabriano used his skills as an electrician's mate to hot-wire one. As they had loaded Whately onto the flatbed truck, Tremain had thanked their guerilla comrades and wished them good luck and Godspeed. Their small victory would be short-lived, and they knew it, but as Tremain drove the truck off in the direction of the bay, he could see them in the rearview mirror waving good-bye and beaming with pride.

It would not be long before the regiment of Japanese regular troops that had spent the morning hunting down and killing the last of Buckles's men arrived in the area and retook the village. Even now, as Tremain sat in the brush tending to Whately, he could hear the thumping of mortars in the distance. If the Japanese were bombarding the village with hopes of killing rebels, then they were engaged in a futile effort, for the village would almost certainly be deserted by now. One of fighters had told Tremain that they planned to cut across country with their families and join up with Colonel Fertig's several-thousand-strong rebel army, on the other side of the island.

Tremain sincerely hoped that they made it.

Whately suddenly moaned in his semiconscious state and coughed up some blood, prompting Tremain to turn his head to make sure that he did not choke on his own saliva. The young lieutenant was lucky to be alive, especially after the brutal torture he had been subjected to. Fabriano had described the whole ordeal during the bumpy two-mile drive along the coast road, including Major Farquhar's fate. The British officer had certainly accomplished what he set out to do, but how many lives had been altered, scarred, or ended during his obsessive pursuit was anyone's guess. Was the death of one Japanese colonel worth the lives of the *Whitefin*'s fallen sailors, or the three dozen guerilla dead, or an unknown number of Buckles's commandos? Despite Tremain's personality and moral differences with the British officer, as he looked at Whately's beaten and bruised body, he began to think maybe so. In any event, Farquhar had deprived the gallows of yet another war criminal when this whole thing was over.

There was a rustling in the brush nearby. Tremain fingered his Thompson cautiously until he discovered that it was only Fabriano limping back through the jungle. Undoubtedly, there were still Japanese patrols scattered throughout the jungle, and he could never be too careful. Tremain had sent Fabriano off to find the rubber rafts and to determine whether they were still seaworthy. Despite his leg wound, Fabriano had to go since he was the only one who knew where the rafts were hidden. As Tremain watched Fabriano approach, he certainly did not expect to see the sailor's bruised face consumed with the wide grin.

"Well, did you find them?"

"Yes, sir, I sure did!" Fabriano said excitedly as he lifted his bandaged leg over a fallen log. "The Japs never found them, Captain. Both boats are there, all ready to go, just like we left them. And I found this signal lamp, too. And the *Whitefin*'s out here, too, sir, sitting just a couple hundred yards offshore. I aved to them and I think they saw me."

"And what else? What is it that you're beaming about, Fabriano? You look like the cat that swallowed the canary."

"Well, sir . . ." Fabriano hesitated. "Maybe you ought to go see for yourself."

Tremain sighed, and then nodded. He handed Whately over to Fabriano, picked up the signal lamp, and headed off toward the beach, partly to find out what Fabriano had found so interesting and partly to give the injured sailor's leg a few moments' rest before they both had to carry Whately down to the beach.

Beams of sunlight now streaked through the jungle canopy as Tremain stepped through the dense foliage, and he found himself wondering just how long they had before enemy aircraft appeared overhead. He could only assume from the absence of planes in the sky that Colonel Fertig's men had successfully disabled the airfield at Malabang. But the Japanese certainly had float planes at least in one of Mindanao's many harbors, and it was only a matter of time before one of them showed up.

Reaching the edge of the jungle, Tremain parted the last fronds and emerged onto the sloping beach that allowed for a clear view of the cove. Just as Fabriano had said, there was the *Whitefin* a few hundred yards offshore. Tremain could see figures standing on her bridge and in the lookout perches. Her condition had not changed since he left her, except that her anchor appeared to have slipped a great deal. Tremain then noticed a billowing cloud of black smoke rising up beyond her, and he quickly moved up to a nearby hill to get a better view.

When he reached the top of the rise, all questions were put to rest about what Fabriano had found so interesting. There, at the edge of the point of land marking the entrance to the cove, lay a Japanese destroyer heeled over on its side and burning ferociously. It was missing its bow section, and the rest of the hulk was resting on one of the shoals, preventing it from sinking, and allowing the intense fires to consume everything above the waterline. Across the water he could hear the sound of a general alarm, leading him to conclude that some of the crew were still alive and trying to fight the fire. As Tremain watched, an enormous secondary explosio probably the detonation of the forward magazine, blasted the bridge and superstructure apart. Three giant hulks of steel soared away from the explosion and fell into the bay, trailing three individual parabolic arcs of black smoke behind them.

As the remnants of the destroyer shifted in the sand, allowing Tremain to see her stern, the only part of the ship that was not covered in flame, he recognized the familiar camouflage pattern that had been seared into his soul.

It was the *Shigure*. And she was no more.

Epilogue

"**HERE'S** the sailing list, XO," Chief LaGrange shouted cheerfully from the main deck, waving a sheet of paper in his hand after crossing the brows of the five submarines moored inboard of the *Whitefin*.

Up until that moment, Monroe had been daydreaming on the *Whitefin*'s bridge, staring out at the mass of merchant shipping moored around Fremantle harbor. He found it odd that every time he got under way from this place, there were more and more ships in the harbor. Surely, the Allies' progress in the war was to blame. Some of the freighters were nested four, even five deep, with hardly any room between them, and the harbor was alive with puttering tugboats that never seemed to rest as they roamed to and fro, herding the big ships like busy little bees. Certainly, Fremantle harbor contained more ships now than it ever had in its entire history, but bigger and grander offensives required bigger and grander supplies.

As LaGrange finally reached the top of the conning tower ladder and stepped onto the bridge, Monroe could see that the older chief was slightly out of breath. LaGrange had just returned from a quick dash across the brows of the six nested submarines in order to deliver a copy of the *Whitefin*'s sailin list to the squadron offices on the tender. The sheet he now held in his hand was the original, and it contained the names and service numbers of every man that would be getting under way aboard the *Whitefin* this morning. It was a precautionary ritual performed before every cruise. In the event she was never heard from again, the squadron would know exactly who had been aboard the *Whitefin*. But Monroe did not expect any trouble on this trip.

"Is everyone aboard, Cob?"

"Yes, sir," LaGrange replied. "Even Fabriano's made it aboard, sir. He got medical clearance just this morning."

"Good."

"I sure am going to miss this place, sir," LaGrange said as he looked around the harbor, removing his hat to wipe the sweat off his brow. "It's a lot colder in Mare Island. And those San Francisco lassies aren't anything like these good Australian girls. They're liable to get our boys into all kinds of trouble."

Monroe simply smiled and nodded. Like LaGrange, he did not want to leave Fremantle. It had been his homeport, and the *Whitefin*'s, for more than a year now. But the *Whitefin* had been pushed to her absolute limit, and she was long overdue for an overhaul and retrofit. This time she would not be going into Japanese waters, but rather to the Mare Island naval shipyard in San Francisco Bay. The ten-thousand-nautical-mile voyage would take at least a month, and Monroe was not looking forward to it. Only one consolation of the trip appealed to the navigator in him. The beginning of the *Whitefin*'s journey would take her around the south side of Australia, in the lower latitudes, where he might just get a glimpse of the Aurora Australis—the southern lights.

"There's the captain," one of the lookouts announced.

Monroe glanced at the pier and saw Tremain step out of a staff car wearing dress khakis. Monroe could see that the car was driven by a woman, and he immediately recognized her as Admiral Ireland's personal secretary. At first, he thought it odd that Tremain had stepped out of the front seat of the car rather than the backseat, but then he was doubly shocked when his captain leaned over to the car's open window and kissed the beaming woman on the lips. This, of course, drew several catcalls from the *Whitefin*'s lookouts, which, luckily, Tremain was too far away to hear.

Monroe watched as Tremain bid good-bye to the woman, picked up his bag, and disappeared behind the hulk of the *Pelias*. A few minutes later, he emerged at the tender's starboard gangway and descended the long ladder to the nest of submarines. As Tremain briskly crossed the brows of the inboard submarines, each one rendering him the honors due to a submarine captain, Monroe noticed that he held a large manila envelope in one hand. But before Monroe could guess what it contained, Tremain had already reached the *Whitefin* and the boatswain was piping him aboard.

Endicott, the officer of the deck, dutifully leaned over to the bridge microphone and keyed the 1MC circuit to make the obligatory announcement: "*Whitefin*, arriving."

Tremain did not bother to go inside the pressure hull, but instead used the exterior ladder to climb up to the bridge, just as LaGrange had done.

"Good morning, Captain," several voices said at once as every man on the bridge brought up a salute.

"Good morning, gentlemen," Tremain said, eagerly returning the salutes. "Are we all ready to go?"

"Yes, sir," Endicott reported. "The maneuvering watch is set, all engines are warmed, and we're ready to cast off lines, sir."

"All departments report ready for sea, Captain," Monroe added.

"Very good, Tom. Thank you, Chris," Tremain said jovially, rubbing his hands together and then glancing somewhat mischievously at LaGrange. "Is *everyone* aboard, Cob?"

"Everyone who's supposed to be, Captain, *plus one*," LaGrange answered with a strange grin as he held up the folded piece of paper. "I've got the sailing list right here, sir."

"You *do* mean the modified sailing list, I assume. You *did* get my phone message, didn't you?"

"Yes, I do, sir. And, yes, I did."

Now LaGrange was smiling as well, prompting Monroe to wonder what they were conspiring between them. Tremain and LaGrange obviously had plotted some sort of prank, but Monroe could not guess who the unlucky subject was.

"Well then, Cob," Tremain continued, with the worst play-acting Monroe had ever seen in his life. "If what you say is true, and we've got one extra man on board, then I think we better kick the bastard off before we get under way."

"I heartily agree, sir," answered LaGrange with a toothy grin.

"Captain," Monroe finally interjected, "this really is ridiculous, sir, I—"

"Let me be the first to congratulate you, Commander," Tremain interrupted him, extending both hands—one for him to shake, and the other to give him the envelope—"This letter just arrived at the admiral's headquarters this morning, and just in the nick of time, too. It's from the command board. They met in Washington two weeks ago. You've been selected for command."

Monroe's mouth went dry, as Tremain shook his hand and he tried to digest what he had just heard. He was simply speechless, while he stood there gaping at the envelope, and everyone else on the bridge broke out in a roar of laughter. Apparently, the Cob had let them all in on it beforehand.

"It seems Admiral Ireland put in a good word for you," Tremain added with a smile. "It looks like you're his favorite captain now."

In spite of all his efforts to resist it, Monroe's face could not help but break out in an uncontrollable grin, and it remained fixed that way as he tore open the envelope and read the letter that only confirmed everything Tremain had just told him.

"I . . . I don't know what to say, Captain."

"Well, you better say good-bye. You've got orders to report to PCO School in New London in ten days!" Tremain looked at his watch. "The next gooney bird to Brisbane takes off in just under an hour, so you better get going. There's a car on the pier to take you to the airfield, compliments of the admiral." Tremain pointed to the same car he had arrived in, and then added in a questioning tone, "I believe the Cob saw to it that your bags were packed?"

"I did, sir," LaGrange reported merrily. "It wasn't easy, either, sir. But they're all packed and waiting for you down there by the gangway. I even made sure those stewards folded your clothes all nice and neat, sir."

Monroe could not believe it. "But, sir, how—I mean what about the *Whitefin*?"

"Don't worry about it," Tremain said, placing an assuring hand on his shoulder. "Allendale is fully capable of assuming the XO duties, and this is the perfect cruise for him to get his feet wet." Then in a much more sincere tone he added, "Just go, Chris. You don't need to look back anymore."

"DID all the *Whitefin* sailors check out, Miss Olivia?" the master chief petty officer asked as he leaned over the reception desk at the Wentworth Hotel in downtown Fremantle.

"Oh, yes, Ernie," the pleasant middle-aged woman behind the desk replied. "They all checked out this morning."

"They didn't give you any trouble, did they? No lights broken? No beds caved in?"

"Oh, no, Ernie. Not at all. They were the sweetest boys."

"Okay, ma'am. Just checking."

Master Chief Petty Officer Ernie Quinn was the squadron master chief, and he always liked to make sure that his submariners were not abusing the hospitality of the local establishments. The Wentworth Hotel had catered to the public prior to the war, but after the war broke out, its generous owners had leased it to the U.S. Navy as a barracks for submariners. The hotel was still manned by its original civilian staff, but now instead of catering to Australian tourists on holiday, their clientele consisted entirely of sex-starved, alcohol-seeking American submariners on liberty. Quinn found that most of the owners of the local establishments appreciated it if he was forthcoming in addressing their complaints. It made for good community relations, which reaped its own rewards.

Unfortunately, that was not his reason for visiting the Wentworth this afternoon.

"I'm here to pick up the personal effects of three of the *Whitefin*'s sailors, Miss Olivia," he said. "Did the squadron yeoman call you this morning to tell you I was coming?"

"Oh, I was afraid you were going to say that," Miss Olivia said, her face suddenly turning sad as she pointed at three large laundry bags along the wall behind the desk. "Yes, he did, Ernie. They're over there."

"Penn, Shelby, and Aguinaldo?" Quinn asked as he read from his notepad.

"Those are the ones. It's such a shame, those poor young boys. Isn't it a shame, Ernie?"

Quinn did not answer. He did not want to tell her that, earlier in the day, he had visited the Ocean Beach Hotel, where he had collected the personal belongings of fifty-eight sailors lost aboard the *Triggerfish*.

"I'll just take them off your hands if you don't mind, ma'am?"

"Help yourself."

As Quinn checked the tag on each bag, he noticed something very odd about Penn's and Shelby's bags.

"The seals are cut," he said curiously. "These bags have been opened, ma'am."

"Oh-uh, yes," Miss Olivia said, stammering, appearing quite embarrassed. "I'm so sorry, Ernie."

"What happened?" Quinn eyed her suspiciously. "Go ahead, ma'am, you can tell me."

"Well, you see, a friend of those two dead boys came to me asking to look inside their bags. He said he knew they had some . . . well, *things* . . . that neither of the boys' mothers would appreciate knowing about."

Quinn sighed heavily. "Miss Olivia, how many times do I have to tell you, our sailors know they're not supposed to do that. You have every right to refuse them. As a matter of fact, you're supposed to refuse them. You know we go through all that stuff up at the squadron office. We'd never ship a nudie magazine home to some dead sailor's folks."

"I know I'm not supposed to let them do it, Ernie, but it's so hard not to. I mean, I keep thinking about how I would feel if I were one of those poor mothers."

Quinn finally smiled, understanding that he would have to give this same speech to her again someday. "Well, did he find anything?"

"Who?"

"This friend of Penn's and Shelby's. Did he find anything obscene in their bags?"

"Oh, I don't know. I never like to see those things, Ernie." She paused for a moment, and then appeared to remember something. "Come to think of it, he did find something in Penn's bag. I just caught a glimpse of it as he was taking it out. It looked like a simple tin can, but I didn't even want to guess what it might contain."

"Did you ever think it might have contained Penn's spending money?"

"I guess it never occurred to me."

Quinn sighed once again. He could see that he was getting nowhere. "Did this 'friend' have a name, Miss Olivia?"

"I won't be getting him in trouble, will I?"

"Probably not."

"It was Michael Fabriano, one of my best tenants. He's such a sweet boy, that one."

Quinn rubbed his chin. There were a thousand sailors in the squadron, and he could not place the name with a face. Either way, the *Whitefin* had gotten under way that morning and would not be back in this part of the world for a very long time. Maybe he would pass the name on to the squadron legal office, and then they could have this Fabriano fellow arrested and searched when his sub reached Mare Island. Then again, maybe he wouldn't, since he hardly had the time to bother with the matter, and he hardly wanted to subject a fellow submariner to such an ordeal. No, he would give this Fabriano the benefit of the doubt, and assume that the tin can had contained something lewd or offensive.

Quinn quickly replaced the seals on the bags containing Penn's and Shelby's gear, then grabbed all three bags by the neck and swung them over his shoulder.

"Thanks again, Miss Olivia. I'll be seeing you."

"Good-bye, Ernie."

Historical Note

THE naval battle of Vella LaVella, portrayed at the beginning of this novel, actually happened. I have taken some dramatic liberties with the chronology of events and the ship locations, but the ships engaged, the damage sustained, and the outcome of the battle are all historically accurate. The action off Vella LaVella was to be the last surface victory for the Japanese, and it exemplified the terror of the night-surface engagement that became a trademark of the Solomons campaign.

Whether a U.S. Navy sailor was engaged in a horrific night-surface battle, or found himself squarely in the sights of an approaching kamikaze, his life during World War Two was in no way a pleasure cruise. In four years of warfare, 36,488 U.S. Navy sailors lost their lives due to enemy action and another 26,000 lost their lives due to non-battle causes, like plane crashes, ship collisions, et cetera. To give these numbers some perspective, the U.S. Marines' losses numbered 19,568 killed due to enemy action and 5,000 due to non-battle causes. Of course, the percent lost versus percent engaged was higher for the marines, but this daunting figure of navy casualties still paints an adequate picture of the risks run by those who fought on the sea.

The typhoon that the *Whitefin* encounters in the South

China Sea was by no means an unusual occurrence. Though World War Two was a modern war and the ships were made of steel, submariners and surface sailors alike often found that the cyclones of the western Pacific Ocean could be more deadly than the enemy. A clear example of this occurred on December 18, 1944, when Admiral Halsey's fleet, cruising in the Philippine Sea, was struck by a typhoon, resulting in three U.S. destroyers capsizing and sinking, taking 790 sailors down with them.

The fate of Monroe's former submarine, the *R-15*, is a product of fiction; however, a similar event did occur on June 12, 1943, involving the U.S. submarine *R-12*. While cruising on the surface off Key West, Florida, the *R-12* sank suddenly and mysteriously in six hundred feet of water, leaving her captain and four other members of the crew floating on the surface. They were the only survivors. Forty-two sailors, including two officers of the Brazilian Navy, went down with the *R-12*. The cause of the accident was unknown, but a court of inquiry suspected that she suffered catastrophic flooding after a torpedo tube was opened to the sea.

Lastly, the Imperial Japanese Navy destroyer *Shigure* did exist. It was indeed at the Battle of Vella LaVella, but the similarities between the real *Shigure* and the one portrayed in this novel stop there. Though a highly effective surface combatant, the real *Shigure* was not the submarine killer I have made her out to be. She was considered to be somewhat of an unsinkable ship, however, since she participated in nearly every major naval engagement of the war and survived them all. During the American invasion of Leyte in October of 1944, she was the only Japanese ship to survive the Battle of Surigao Strait, where two Japanese battleships, one cruiser, and three destroyers were sunk by the American covering force. She finally met her end in January of 1945, when the U.S. submarine *Blackfin* sank her in the Gulf of Thailand.

As always in war, atrocities were committed by both sides, and each rival in the heat of combat employed ethnic slurs to objectify and vilify the enemy. The ethnic slurs that appear in this novel are there solely for the sake of realism, and by no means do they reflect the opinion of the author.

Don't miss the page-turning suspense, intriguing characters, and unstoppable action that keep readers coming back for more from these bestselling authors...

Tom Clancy

Robin Cook

Patricia Cornwell

Clive Cussler

Dean Koontz

J.D. Robb

John Sandford

Your favorite thrillers and suspense novels come from Berkley.